STAGED

Additional Rock Star
Erotic Romances
by Olivia Cunning

Exodus End World Tour Series

Insider
Outsider

Sinner on Tour Series

Backstage Pass
Rock Hard
Hot Ticket
Wicked Beat
Double Time
Sinners at the Altar

One Night with Sole Regret

Try Me, Tempt Me, Take Me
Share Me, Touch Me, Tie Me
Tease Me, Tell Me
Treat Me, Thrill Me
Treasure Me, Trust Me

STAGED

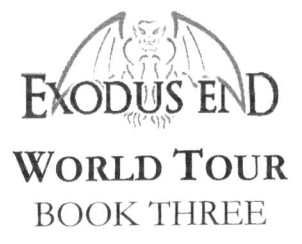

EXODUS END
WORLD TOUR
BOOK THREE

OLIVIA CUNNING

Copyright © 2018 Olivia Cunning

Published by Vulpine Press

Sinners logo by Olivia Cunning
Sole Regret logo by Pamela Sinclair
Exodus End logo by Charity Hendry
Rights to Cover Images obtained from Depositphotos
Cover design by Charity Hendry
Interior design by Olivia Cunning

All rights reserved. No part of this book may be reproduced in any form—with the exception of short segments for reviews—without the written consent of the author.

The characters and events in this work are fictitious. Any similarities to persons or events are coincidental and not intended by the author

ISBN-10: 1-939276-34-9
ISBN-13: 978-1-939276-34-6

CHAPTER 1

ROUX SUCKED IN her stomach while Raven tugged both ends of the ribbon at her back and cinched the black lace corset as tight as it would go.

"I guess I won't be sitting down anytime soon," Roux said, rubbing her hands over the red velvet stays along her sides as if the action would make it easier to breathe.

"Does that mean you're going to lie down in the limo?" Raven asked.

Glancing over her shoulder, Roux rolled her eyes at her best friend and the band's stylist. Raven also happened to be her foster sister. "I'll be standing with my head out the sunroof. Obviously."

Raven chuckled. "I'd better add a few more bobby pins to your wig, then. You wouldn't want to surprise some unlucky driver behind us by shooting this black and red hairy beast into their windshield."

Roux laughed, feeling a slight bit of ease for the first time that night, until she remembered why she would be riding in a limo in the first place. *Breathe, Roux. Breathe.*

Raven wrapped several strands of the underlayer of the wig around her fingers and arranged the long curls against Roux's bare shoulders. Roux's real hair was naturally red, but her trademark color in the band was a vibrant crimson. Each of the five women of Baroquen had a particular color for her costume and hair to offset the black goth dresses and makeup they wore in public. And with her name, she'd had to choose red as her color.

"You're as gorgeous as you're going to get," Raven said, taking a step back to admire her work.

Roux struck a pose and then stuck out her tongue at her reflection in the full-length mirror. She scarcely recognized herself when she was in costume. Which meant when she was out of her dark and heavy makeup, no one would realize she was the keyboardist for an up-and-coming band that would soon go on tour with the most highly regarded metal band in existence. They were supposed to meet the members of Exodus End that evening and attend a party as their special guests, which was why all the women in her band were in full costume tonight even though they didn't have a gig.

"Go put on your boots and practice breathing," Raven advised. The petite black-haired goth/punk/emo designer genius gave Roux a little shove and then turned to Lily, who had her sleek black and white wig on backwards. Again.

"It's shorter in the back than the front," Raven explained to the frustrated drummer. Again.

"Not sure why I voted in favor of this stupid idea," Lily complained as Raven removed the wig and spun it around before slipping it back down over Lily's naturally pale blond hair. "No one can see me behind the drums anyway. I could wear jeans and a T-shirt."

"You don't like the costume I designed for you?" Raven asked, her lashes fluttering as she fought fake tears.

Roux smirked. She'd been Raven's roommate since they'd been preteens, so Roux knew when Raven was laying on the bullshit. There was currently enough in the room to load a wagon.

Lily, on the other hand, had roomed with their lead singer, Iona, so the band's little drumming sweetheart was susceptible to Raven's ploys. Lily laid a hand on Raven's slight shoulder and squeezed.

"Oh, Raven, your costumes are gorgeous. We're so lucky to have you."

"And don't you forget it," Raven said through a mouthful of bobby pins. She jabbed a few into Lily's head to hold her wig in place.

Roux chuckled and slipped her foot into one of her lace-up, knee-high leather boots. The tongue was the same shade of red as her jagged-edged petticoat, her corset stays and the ribbon that laced it up her back, as well as the underlayer of her wig. Every other inch of her outfit was black lace except for the giant garnet stone at the center of her choker necklace.

"You don't get to be comfortable if the rest of us have to suffer, Lil," Roux said. "Besides, the fans will want to see those huge knockers of yours."

"Bite me," Lily said.

Roux chomped her teeth at the woman who would always be her big sister, even if they weren't related by blood.

Lily adjusted said knockers inside her white corset. She had to tape those puppies in there when she played live to avoid jiggling out of her top, but her boobs should survive a party with Exodus End unseen unless she got drunk enough to dance and started air drumming. Then costume malfunctions were all but guaranteed.

"Are you guys ready?" Azura called from the adjoining hotel room. The door between the two suites was open, so it was almost like their overcrowded studio in the East Village where the six of them lived on top of each other.

"Lil put her wig on backwards," Raven said.

Lily extended a hand toward the other suite and stomped her foot. "Azura is the one who helped me put the damned thing on in the first place."

"You need a longer wig," Azura said, coming into their suite. She was already dressed in her blue and black stage-persona gear, and her wig was waist length, so there was no chance she'd put it on backwards unless she were attempting a Cousin It look. "I can't tell the front of yours from its back."

"You and me both," Lily muttered under her breath.

"You said the long one was too hot when you play," Raven reminded her. "That's why we switched to the short one."

"The long one was a living hell, but this one isn't much better. It's like wearing an oven on my head." Lily shook her head back and forth to send the longish white ends on either side of her face swaying.

"The black goes in back, white in front," Raven said.

"Sounds like my kind of threesome," Azura said, throwing up a peace sign.

Roux flushed at the very idea of a threesome. Her boots now laced up and tied in neat bows, she stood straight and tugged down the back of her skirt. The top lacy layers were fluffy, but short as hell. If she hadn't been wearing a red silk petticoat under the skirt, her panties would have shown with every step, and her thong didn't match her outfit. Raven would have been mortified to know Roux was going out in public in pink underwear. Raven abhorred pink. She also abhorred underwear unless they were her boyfriend's boxers.

Perhaps Roux knew a little *too* much about her foster sister.

The landline rang in the adjoining suite. "The limo is downstairs!" Iona yelled a moment later. "Now is not the time to be fashionably late. Let's move."

"They're not going to leave without us," Sage said in the other room, her calm voice as serene as ever.

"A thousand bands would slit our throats to take our spot on this tour," Iona said.

Roux covered her neck with one hand and grimaced. "I'm going to need a new necklace. One with steel reinforcements," she whispered to Raven, who winked at her.

"I'll get right on that. The keyboardist always dies first in these situations."

Somehow Iona got them all headed in the right direction—ultimately for the limo, where they'd meet their tour mates for the first time. Heads turned as the ladies of Baroquen walked through the posh lobby of the hotel. The five of them looked like rock stars, even if none of them *felt* like rock stars. The band did have a large local following of dedicated fans, but this tour—to Europe and then around the world—would make or break them.

Roux's stomach was already churning with nerves, but when her gaze landed on Sam Baily—Exodus End's amazing manager, who had taken it upon himself to make stars out of the members of Baroquen—it took a dive for the floor. She instinctively reached for the bullet that dangled from a bracelet she always wore, drawing strength from the small chunk of metal.

Holy shit! This was really happening. They were going to meet the living legends that made up Exodus End. They were going on tour with them. To fucking Europe. Holy shit!

"Breathe, Roux," Sage said, placing a calming hand on the center of Roux's back.

Sage could tell that she was hyperventilating? Not good. Roux didn't want to come across as an unprofessional idiot in front of the guys. Yet she wasn't exactly a seasoned professional.

"It's this damned corset." Roux tugged at the bottom edge of the stiff garment, needing something on which to blame her sudden breathlessness.

"At least yours doesn't have all these buckles," Sage said,

running her fingers over the row of buckles running down the center of her belly. "When I sit, they try to eviscerate me."

"You'll have to stand next to me in the limo with your head out the sunroof," Roux said. And the driver behind them could deal with a black and green wig as well as her red one attacking their windshield. "I can't sit worth a damn in this contraption." Fortunately, she stood to play her keyboard. If she sat, as she did when playing piano, the corset would be a definite no-go.

"You all look gorgeous," Sam said with a pleased smile, and Roux vowed to stop her complaining.

They were truly blessed by the opportunity Sam had given them by signing them to a new record deal and as an opening act for the *real* stars he represented. He looked every inch the high-profile band manager, from his highly polished alligator shoes to his immaculately styled dark hair graying at the temples. Even his smile was polished.

"The guys can't wait to meet you."

Yeah, right. Roux was certain the members of Exodus End had far better things to do than hang around with five nobodies all evening.

"Are they in the limo?" Sage asked, standing on tiptoe to peer out at the long, sleek car parked in front of the hotel none of them could afford. Sam was footing the bill for their extravagant accommodations.

"We're picking them up from Madison Square Garden," Sam said. "They should be offstage by the time we get there."

Madison Square Garden. Roux's fingers began to twitch with nervous energy. She couldn't even fathom how amazing it would be to perform on that stage.

Iona climbed into the limo first. Being the lead singer gave her first dibs on everything. Or maybe she always went first because her color was purple and that made her think she was royalty. Yet if not for Iona and her unique way of getting noticed, none of them would be on tour with a retired bridge club from Hoboken much less on a world tour with Exodus End, so Roux didn't cause a stink about not getting the window seat and settled in the middle between Lily and Azura, sitting so straight in her corset that she felt a foot taller than usual. Roux licked her lips, the taste of her black lipstick a foreign reminder that she was playing rock star for the rest of the night, and tried tromping down the nervous flutters churning in her belly. This was all moving so fast. Her life had gone from subdued to overwhelming within a month. She loved every damned minute of it.

Sam was talking to Iona about the after-party they were attending. Apparently, no expense had been spared. The tour had rented two floors of some artsy high-rise so that the co-headlining band, Sinners, could have an after-party of their own in the same building. Roux planned to attend both events, but she couldn't focus on Sam's words. She was too busy trying to sit still so her corset stays didn't break a rib.

Outside the arena, Sam left them to wait in the car while he collected the members of Exodus End.

"While we wait, we should play fuck, marry, kill," Iona said.

"For Exodus End?" Lily gasped.

That got Roux's attention.

Iona chuckled and nodded, her dark eyebrows moving up and down. "You go first, Lil."

"Um, okay." Lily sat for a full minute wringing her hands. "I can't. I can't kill any of them."

"But you'd fuck them all," Roux said.

Lily slapped her. "I'm married!" And very happily so, but that didn't mean she couldn't play their little game.

"Let's switch this up," Azura said. "There are four of them, so let's play suck, fuck, kiss, slap instead. Then no one has to die."

"An angry slap or a playful one?" Sage asked, taking the game far too seriously.

"Whatever turns you on, Sage," Roux said.

"So . . . angry then." Azura elbowed Sage, her best friend and roomie, in the ribs.

"I'd slap Steve," Lily said. "He's so full of himself."

"As are all drummers," Iona said, teasing their drummer, Lily, who poked her in the belly.

"Jack isn't full of himself," Lily said.

Roux smiled at Lily's defense of her husband, who also happened to be a drummer.

"I'm sorry, but no. Steve's the hottest one," Roux said, hoping to turn their attention back to the game. "I'd fuck him until I couldn't move and save my slap for Max's ass just so he'd slap mine back."

Iona snorted and shook her head. "Steve, the hottest? Puh-lease. Max is the hottest. I'd kiss, suck, fuck, and slap him. Then fuck him again."

"This game isn't going as planned," Sage said, worrying her

bottom lip with her teeth, which, if they hadn't left Raven behind, would have made her freak out over Sage's makeup.

"Yeah? Which one would *you* fuck?" Roux asked Sage.

Sage licked the lip she'd just nibbled. "Dare. Definitely Dare."

"She's always liked her men dark and quiet," Azura said.

"I think I'd suck Dare," Roux said. "Love to see that man come undone."

"Love to see that man come *period*," Sage said.

They all laughed, and Roux shuddered at the spectacular mental image.

"No takers on Logan?" Azura asked.

"He's so damned cute," Iona said. "I'd have to kiss him. Everywhere."

"I don't think anyone would angry-slap him," Sage said. "Not with a smile like his."

They were still hashing out their fantasies when the limo door opened.

"A good surprise?" Maximillian Richardson's unmistakably deep and sexy voice asked from nearby. Even when he wasn't singing, his voice messed with a woman's ability to think rationally. Roux's breath stalled in her throat. Max was just outside the door, she realized. And this wasn't the wettest dream she'd ever had. It was really happening.

"The best I've found in over ten years," Sam said.

Every woman in the car went instantly stiff. Their little game had been great for passing the time, but now they'd have to look the men in the eye and try not to think about the naughty things they wanted to do to each and every one of them.

Max poked his head into the car, his eyes scanning the interior. Exodus End's lead singer was far more gorgeous in person than in any video or photo Roux had seen. He had dark hair cut in a short, trendy style, a strong jaw, and a mouth made for kissing. He was also built. And tall and gorgeous and . . . Roux wasn't sure if he'd actually said anything before he disappeared from the open door.

"Maybe this isn't such a good idea," Max said to someone outside.

"Nonsense," Sam said.

Roux exchanged a worried glance with Lily. Exodus End didn't want them there? It seemed the only explanation for Max's words.

"Iona?" Sage leaned forward to send their fearless leader a questioning look.

Iona's eyes were closed, so she didn't see Sage's concerned face, but she took a deep breath and plastered on a confident smile before sitting up straighter. "No one guaranteed this would be easy," she said.

"Yeah," Roux said, "but Sam didn't mention we weren't wanted."

"I'm sure that's not—"

Iona's words were cut off when someone ducked their head into the car.

Roux was surprised it was a woman. Reagan Elliot—the amazing though temporary rhythm guitarist for Exodus End—looked them over carefully and offered a friendly smile. The brilliant guitarist had won some sort of talent contest to take over Max's guitar playing while his wrist healed after surgery. Or something like that. Roux had read about her. A lot about her, actually. The cute rocker chick's complicated love life was currently smeared all over the tabloids. Reagan nodded at them and pulled out of the car.

"Why do I feel like they're trying to decide if we're too gross to ride with?" Lily whispered.

Roux chuckled. "I don't think it's that. Seems they don't like surprises."

"We're excellent surprises," Iona said. "Fabulous. We're the best surprises that ever waited in a stuffy limo outside Madison Square Garden."

"Maybe you should take a cab." Max again.

"You take a cab," a man answered in a deep voice.

Roux almost swallowed her tongue when the sexiest man on legs—or off them—slid into the limo. Exodus End's drummer had a reputation, but nothing had prepared Roux for meeting the man. He was tall and lean with muscles and bulges in all the right places and gorgeous chestnut brown hair that fell past his shoulders. There was something exotic about his heavy-lidded brown eyes as they scanned the interior of the limo.

Steve Aimes settled into the leather upholstery and grinned at the five of them as if he'd just opened the best birthday gift of his life.

"Right on," he said, his deep voice sending shivers down Roux's spine. "The hookers are already here."

Hookers?

CHAPTER 2

STEVE HAD BEEN CHASING pussy since he could walk. The family cat had been terrified of his grabby toddler self and had run for her life, but he now appreciated the practice. Since puberty, he'd been chasing pussy of a different sort. And the five sexy goth ladies who were currently directing eye daggers in his direction—apparently they hadn't appreciated being called hookers—might be running now, but he was sure it wouldn't take much effort to catch his pick. And he already knew which one he wanted.

"I call dibs on Red," he said when his bandmates shuffled into the car. Red was a mix of fire and ice he couldn't resist.

"Excuse me?" she said, blinking a pair of stabby green-gold eyes.

He wondered what she looked like without the dark and heavy makeup, without the fancy clothes, with all her barriers down. He guaranteed he'd know before the night was over.

Dare, who was sitting to Steve's right—apparently the entire band seemed keen on squashing Steve against the far wall—elbowed him in the ribs.

"You fucking moron," Dare said close to his ear. "Those women aren't your entertainment for the evening."

Steve begged to differ.

Dare whispered, "They're the members of the band joining us on the next leg of the tour."

The ones that had ousted Zach's band, Twisted Element, from their tour lineup? Well, fuck them and their fantastic tits. Zach was his best friend. That made these chicks his enemies.

"Is it too late to take that cab?" Steve asked, eyes narrowing at the newly recognized threat in goth clothing.

"Stop being a drama queen," Sam said, his boner for the new talent he'd scouted obvious. "This is the band I was telling you about. Baroquen."

Steve forced himself not to roll his eyes. What a stupid name. They didn't look broken to him.

"Nice to meet you," Reagan said to the enemy. "I haven't gotten a chance to listen to your music yet, but Sam says you guys rock."

Why was Reagan kissing their asses?

"You'll get to hear them tomorrow during your satellite radio performance," Sam said. "It's all been arranged."

Steve went entirely still. So not only was Sam giving these newbs a spot on the tour, but also one on Exodus End's satellite radio segment. What the fuck?

"You gave them our airtime?" Max asked, his voice hard and lethal.

Steve knew from experience that one did not stand in the way of Max's success.

Sam—who Steve had long since dubbed his number one enemy—shook his head and extended a placating hand in Max's direction. "Not all of it. They're just playing one song."

"If it's a problem—" The woman with blue hair tried to get in a word.

"It's not," Sam said. "Let me introduce you all."

Steve pretended not to care, but he was listening because he still wanted under Red's skirt. Maybe to get back at her for being part of Sam's big plan to destroy his best friend's band. Maybe because her black-painted lips would look spectacular wrapped around his cock. Or maybe because the instant his eyes had met hers, he'd wanted her.

Sam nodded toward the green-and-black-haired woman on the far end. Was that a wig? Were they all wearing wigs? Did none of the carpets match the drapes? Or had the carpets been removed? Another important fact Steve vowed to know the answer to by the end of the night.

"Sage plays guitar."

Sage lifted a hand in greeting. She looked . . . nice. Too nice for Steve. Her type always got quickly attached on an emotional level.

Steve didn't do emotional attachment. Not since Bianca had destroyed his naturally romantic nature and replaced it with the cynical man left standing. The romantic part of him was curled up in a corner somewhere, sucking its thumb.

"Lily plays drums."

The woman with short black hair, with longer white strips framing her lovely face, nodded. Happily taken. Steve could always tell when a woman was off limits, and he never fiddled with another man's diddle.

Sam's attention shifted to Red, and Steve couldn't help but stare. God, she was beautiful. And from the icy glare she directed at him, she apparently hated his fucking guts. He'd have fun turning her ice to fire.

"This is Roux," Sam said.

Roux. Her name whispered through his subconscious, making his belly tighten and his balls ache. What a sexy name. He couldn't wait to whisper it to her while he filled her with his cock.

"She plays keyboard and sings harmony," Sam added.

Steve's illusion of perfection completely shattered.

"Keyboard?" he snorted. "What kind of metal band has a keyboard?"

"We're more a mix of punk, goth, progressive, and hard rock than true metal," the purple-haired woman said. She was the band's leader. Probably the vocalist. Male or female, they were all alike: bossy and self-important.

Roux extended a finger in Steve's direction. The middle one on her right hand. He was going to show her where to stick that finger later. And watch, his mouth watering, as she obeyed.

Steve was so lost in his fantasies that he didn't catch the rest of the conversation. A couple of the chicks were blabbing about guitars or something with Dare, which didn't interest him in the least.

What interested him most wasn't even how snug and warm Roux's pussy would feel when he fucked her later that night. Zach had been devastated when Steve had told him that Sam was replacing his band on the tour, though he'd laughed it off. Zach laughed off everything that hurt him deeply. But the two of them had made plans to take Europe by storm. The idea that Twisted Element had been replaced by this vat of estrogen in black lace and excessive eyeliner had Steve seething.

"How can you possibly think our fans will like this group of goth girls better than Twisted Element?" Steve asked Sam, giving zero fucks that the goth girls in question were listening.

"I don't think that," Sam said. "I think the opposite of that. Baroquen appeals to a younger fan base. A fan base Exodus End currently lacks."

Steve snorted and shook his head. All their greedy manager cared about was dollar signs.

"So you think teenage goth kids will flock to see these wannabes and when we play them some real music, they'll become our instafans?"

Roux snorted. "Already living up to that asshole reputation of yours, eh, Aimes?"

Steve smirked. She was all talk now, but soon she'd be all moans and begging followed by crying and whining when he kicked her out of his bed before morning.

"His best friend is in Twisted Element," Reagan said. "How do you expect him to feel about them getting fired so you can take their place on the tour?"

It was nice that someone in the band understood where he was coming from, even if his bros never backed him up when he went toe to toe with Sam.

"We didn't ask for Twisted Element to be fired," Roux said. "But we'd be fools to turn down this gig."

The blue-and-black-haired chick squeezed Roux's leg. Lesbian leanings? God, he hoped so. But maybe just friendship. He wasn't sure.

Blue turned her attention to Steve and his bandmates. She even looked sincere when she said, "We are incredibly lucky to have been given this opportunity. We won't let you down."

Steve was trying not to like these women. Trying to hold a grudge. It was useless. Sam was the asshole here. Especially since he sprang this surprise on the band when they couldn't freely speak their minds. Roux might be thinking that Steve was being an asshole, but in truth he was reeling himself in far more than he'd like.

"Twisted Element was allowed to finish out this leg of the tour," Sam said. "They should be glad their mediocrity was allowed on your stage in the first place."

Steve's jaw hardened. Old guy was apparently looking for a fat lip. His hand clenched into a fist. "Mediocrity?"

"Really, Sam?" Dare shook his head and pressed his knee hard into Steve's thigh to give him the grounding he needed to maintain his cool. "Must you always push his buttons?"

Sam smirked. Steve's fist tightened.

"Did you really give up some of our unplugged satellite radio segment?" Max asked. "You know how important it is. The reach is nationwide. Hell, it's global. This isn't some local radio station you're talking about here. It's *satellite* radio, Sam."

And maybe that action would be what finally shifted Max to Steve's side. He'd been trying to get the band to dump their manager for years. Logan had seen Steve's logic from the beginning, but Dare and Max had always sided with Sam, thinking Sam, rather than their talent, was responsible for their enormous royalty checks.

Sam lifted both hands and shrugged. "We'll discuss this later," he said. "Tonight I want you all to have a good time. Get to know each other. Stir up some interest."

Oh, Steve would be getting to know these ladies, all right. And he'd do it by stirring up something far more pleasurable than interest.

The limo pulled to a halt, and the door on Steve's side of the car opened. Their chief of security, Butch, popped his head into the car, his wide face friendly and his large mustache quivering slightly with each breath.

"You all ready? There's a line about a block long of people wanting autographs. You can bypass it and go straight upstairs to the party if you're not in the mood."

"Always in the mood for adulation," Steve said, exiting the car.

The crowd started screaming excitedly the moment he came into view.

"Did he say adultery?" he heard Roux ask.

He grinned, wishing that had been what he'd said. They were going to have a great time together after he got his ego stroked by some fans. Roux would just have to be satisfied with stroking the rest of him.

Steve headed for the crowd, taking any piece of paper shoved in his direction and scrawling his signature on it, stopping to be photographed with and often groped by numerous female fans as well as to take photos—sans groping—with a few dudes. Steve had the adulation thing down pat. A band's drummer was usually one of the lesser known members of the band, but not in Exodus End. He was as well-known as Max and Dare—at least—and far more recognized than Logan, who was usually left with scraps. Luckily, Logan was too good-natured to care that at least twice as many fans vied for Steve's attention. And Steve found it easy to ignore the fact that their male fans flocked around Dare like he was their personal guitar god while the ladies tried to get a hand on Max. Steve was satisfied having an equal parts "rock god" and "sex symbol" status. He could just as easily shoot the breeze with wannabe drummers as flirt with the ladies. Normally he'd take a few hotties upstairs to the after-party with him, but tonight he decided for once to do what Sam suggested. He wanted to get to know the ladies of Baroquen, one lovely red-haired vixen in particular.

When he decided the crowd was never going to thin out—for every fan that left happy, two or three more arrived to seek attention—he signaled Butch that he was ready to call it quits, said his goodbyes to nearby fans, and headed inside. With a relieved expression, Dare followed him.

"I didn't think we'd ever get away," Dare said once several members of their security team had ushered them safely inside the building.

Steve snorted at Dare's predictability. As an unapologetic introvert, the guy wasn't exactly the life of any party. Funny how no one seemed to notice that.

"Is Zach going to be here?" Dare asked.

Steve shook his head. "I didn't ask him. I figured he wouldn't want to celebrate the end of his career."

Dare took his eyes off the closed elevator door to give him an odd look. "You didn't say that to him, did you?"

"Of course not. I'm not that much of an insensitive asshole."

Dare looked unconvinced.

"He's going out with his band tonight," Steve said. "He told me that before I got the chance to invite him, okay? Plus, if he sees Sam, it isn't going to end pretty." And Steve would be more likely to join the fray than to try to stop it.

The elevator dinged as the doors slid open. They stepped inside, two members of their security team joining them. Steve was so used to the presence of tough dudes in bright orange T-shirts that he didn't bother censoring conversations.

"Sam is trying to do what's best for us," Dare said. "Why don't you get that?"

"Sam is doing what's best for himself."

"I don't think the young women of Baroquen feel that way about him."

"Because they think he's going to make them stars."

"He *will* make them stars."

That was probably true. "But he won't care who gets hurt along the way."

"And that's perfectly normal in this business."

"Yeah," Steve said, widening his stance and crossing his arms over his chest. "Well, maybe it shouldn't be."

The doors slid open, and a rush of adrenaline surged through Steve's body as loud music poured out of the enormous ballroom. His gaze landed on Roux at once. Not that she was hard to spot; dozens of party attendees surrounded the members of Baroquen, all wanting to hear the story of how they'd gotten a gig as an opening band on Exodus End's world tour. When she didn't return his heavy stare, he went to the bar and ordered a whiskey on the rocks. A moment later Logan arrived. By himself. Which was odd because he'd been surgically attached to the nerdy reporter chick who'd been following them on tour for the past few weeks.

"You didn't bring Toni?"

Logan smiled. "She's in the bathroom."

"Ah."

"You haven't picked up a woman yet?" Logan slapped him on the back. "Isn't like you to have an empty arm."

Steve glanced to the open spot at his left. Logan was right; it wasn't like him. As if conjured by magic, a stunningly gorgeous woman filled the spot and smiled up at him, her dark eyes and the top three buttons of her blouse open in invitation.

"Buy me a drink?"

"Open bar tonight," he said before turning back to Logan, who jerked away slightly and eyed him as if Steve had been replaced with an imposter. "Do you think I need to apologize?"

"For telling her it's an open bar?"

Logan peered around Steve's back and grimaced slightly. The drink woman must still be standing there. Not that Steve cared.

Steve ran a hand over his face. "Not for that. For calling our new opening band hookers."

Logan turned to where a twittering crowd still surrounded the members of Baroquen. Steve had to admit he loved their sexy image, and apparently he wasn't the only one.

"I doubt they took you seriously."

"I called dibs on Red, for fuck's sake." And he felt bad. Steve did have a conscience. He just liked to keep that little secret under wraps. Made it easier to check his emotions and make people think he was too cool to give a shit. Plus, when he acted like he gave zero fucks, pussy magically fell into his lap. No-strings-attached pussy. The easiest kind to get over.

"It was a pretty shitty way to introduce myself to them," Steve added. And maybe he wanted an excuse to talk to them. Well, one of them. "What kind of drink do you think Roux would like?"

"Roux?" Logan's blue eyes lowered as he puzzled over the name. "Like rue the day or a baby marsupial from Australia roo, or the gravy mix kind?"

"I think it's the French word for red." Steve snorted. "But I'd love to mix her with some of my creamy sauce."

Logan shook his head. "You see? That's why you offend women."

He would never say that to a woman. Probably. "Roux is the one in red." And even though he wasn't currently looking at her, he was very aware of her.

"Oh, so that's why you think her name is French for red."

Actually, it was because that was the sexiest option. His mind couldn't comprehend anyone naming her after a marsupial. But he nodded.

"Probably not a good idea to fuck around with any of those women, man," Logan said. "We have to be on tour with them for months, and if one of them grows attached to you . . ."

Steve would normally consider Logan's advice spot-on, but he wasn't feeling very normal at the moment. He was feeling—like every other person in the room, apparently—compelled, intrigued, interested. In Roux's tits. Yeah, that was all it was. Attraction. Desire. Longing. She had a fantastic rack. That was all he cared about.

He turned toward the woman beside him. His brush-off hadn't sent her packing. "What are you having?" he asked.

"Appletini."

She sipped the pale green cocktail through a tiny straw, her eyes giving him hints about what she'd be willing to suck on if he presented it to her.

"Wanna taste?"

She held her glass out to him, but he lifted a hand and shook his head. He didn't want to lead her on. It wasn't his style. She was hot, and normally he'd have loved to have a great time with her, but he wasn't interested. Not tonight. Having always been driven by feelings and needs, Steve wasn't one to overthink why he didn't want her. He just didn't.

"Do most chicks like those drinks?" he asked the bartender,

who shrugged. Steve sighed. "Give me an appletini."

While he waited for the bartender to mix the vile-looking concoction, he glanced over his shoulder and saw that the crowd had finally thinned around Baroquen; Max had entered the room, and crowds naturally gravitated toward him. Even five hot chicks in corsets and short skirts were less of a draw than Exodus End's exasperating lead singer.

Steve scraped his drink and the newly mixed appletini from the surface of the bar, gave Logan a nod—though he was deeply immersed in conversation with Toni now and didn't notice—and crossed the room, unable to take his eyes off a certain keyboardist. Perhaps she sensed the weight of his interest because when he was about ten feet away, she sent a few exceedingly sharp eye daggers in his direction and turned her back on him.

Steve stopped walking and gawked at her very cold shoulder. It had been a while since a woman had rebuffed him. Been even longer since one had posed any challenge. The corner of his mouth curved upward as he resumed his current trajectory. He stopped about two feet from her.

She tried so hard to ignore him that her body went stiff. If he shifted into her peripheral vision, she turned away slightly, until they were practically twirling in circles.

"The asshole brought you a drink," he said.

"No, thank you."

"He also wanted to apologize for calling you a hooker." Surely that would make her at least glance at him, maybe even smile. But no. "I didn't really think you were a hooker. It was a joke."

"Not a very funny one."

"Yeah, well, I am sorry. I didn't mean to offend you."

She angled toward him—finally—and their eyes met. Hers were a deep green with a beguiling rim of gold around the iris—undoubtedly the most beautiful eyes he'd ever stared into. His heart skipped a beat and began to pound as familiar lust scorched his veins. She licked her lips and turned again. "Apology accepted. Excuse me."

She walked away. From Steve Aimes. Like he was just some random douchebag on the dance floor hitting on her. What the fuck? He trailed after her and tapped the edge of her drink glass against her shoulder.

She stopped and turned slowly.

"Your drink."

"I don't drink," she said, her eyes cold as she stared up at him. "And in case I wasn't clear, I'm not interested, so go bother someone else."

He actually felt a stab of hurt with the added knife twist of insecurity. He hadn't been rejected in a great long while, and he wasn't sure why instead of turning him off—he could have his choice of easy pussy in the room—it made him ache for her.

"I think you've misjudged me," he said.

"Do you?"

"Yeah."

"I seriously doubt that."

At least he had her talking. "I wanted to welcome you to the tour and ask if there was anything I could do to make this transition easier, but I guess you're perfectly capable of taking care of yourself."

She stiffened slightly.

"So I'll be on my way." He tossed back her drink, forcing himself not to wince at the sweet and tart flavor of it. "Thanks for the drink." He tilted the empty glass in her direction and nodded.

When he turned to walk away, she touched his arm. Her fingertips seemed to burn into his flesh.

"Wait," she said, shouting over the loud Pantera song blaring in the background. "You probably think I'm some ball-busting megabitch." He liked that about her. "If you want to talk business, I'd love to hang out with you, but if you're just trying to get in my pants . . ." The fire was back in her sensational eyes as she quirked an eyebrow. ". . . still not interested."

"I assure you," he said, "I only want to talk business." When had he become such an accomplished liar? He almost had himself believing his words.

"Do you want to go out on the balcony?" she yelled. "It's a little quieter out there, and I could use some fresh air."

And privacy? Was she looking for privacy? Hell yeah, he wanted to go out on the balcony and be alone with her.

"Do you want to grab a drink first?" He jerked a thumb toward the open bar.

"Just water for me, but you go ahead."

He didn't want to drink if she wasn't drinking. "I could use some water myself. I get dehydrated onstage, and we played three encores tonight." That statement usually made a woman gush her appreciation of his skill on the skins—he knew for a fact that he was the most imitated drummer in all of metal music—but Roux merely nodded.

"I know exactly what you mean," she said.

He wasn't sure how much sweat could pour off a keyboard player, but the stage lighting was brutal regardless of the amount of energy one expended onstage. She followed him to the bar, and Steve got more than one odd look when he ordered two waters. He handed her a little plastic cup brimming with ice water, took his own, and followed her toward the balcony. He tried not to stare at her ass and legs too much as they crossed the now-crowded dance floor. Max, who loved to dance, was surrounded by two-thirds of the women in the room as his dance partners. The charismatic lead singer even managed to give each one of them a bit of personal attention. Steve concentrated on following Roux as she navigated the edge of the undulating crowd, pulling his eyes off her ass every few seconds to make sure she didn't catch him checking her out. But who could blame him? The woman was fucking exquisite.

A cool breeze stirred against his heated skin when she pushed the balcony door open. Dare was standing alone, staring out into the lights of the city. He turned toward them and nodded, a greeting that Steve returned. Steve wasn't sure how Dare managed to be a loner no matter the size of the crowd around him. Was even less sure how he could like being alone, but there was no denying he did.

"Hello, Dare," Roux said. "Is it okay if I call you Dare? Or should I call you Mr. Mills?"

Dare chuckled, his good-natured smile turning up the corners of his mouth. "Dare is fine. You're Rrr-raww-*roxie*?" He squinted, as if that would make him recall her name.

"Roux," Steve said. "She's the one who plays keyboard."

Roux slapped his forearm playfully. "*An instrument Steve does not approve of in a metal band.*"

Fuck. So she remembered *all* the stupid shit that had spewed from his mouth in the limo? Sam had been there. Steve could not be expected to maintain good manners with that greedy son of a bitch in close quarters. Regardless, Steve shouldn't have insulted her. He was sure Roux was an excellent musician. Because greedy sons of bitches like Sam wouldn't waste time on a band that wasn't phenomenal, no matter how sexy they looked. Unless Sam planned to market their look rather than their sound. Steve wouldn't put it past the guy. He kept trying that stupid shit with Reagan, and Reagan wouldn't have it, but these young women seemed a bit more accommodating to Sam's bullshit. Steve wondered if he could protect them from the wolves. Or at least one wolf.

"I'm sure you could prove me wrong," Steve said, tossing back his water and wishing it was whiskey. "Maybe a keyboard isn't completely stupid. Progressive rock bands seem to like them okay."

She stuck her tongue out at him, and he couldn't help but smile. He'd known at first glance that she was beautiful and sexy, but it seemed she was playful and fun too. He did love a good time.

"A lot of metal bands are introducing new elements to their music," Dare said. "Keeps things interesting."

"I prefer the standard bass, rhythm and lead guitars, and most importantly, drums, but I'm old school," Steve said.

"Are you sure you're not just old?" Roux smirked as she sipped water through a tiny red straw.

Was that why she wasn't interested in him, because he was *old*? Since when was thirty-four old? Since she was probably twenty. He tried not to think about the logistics of the age difference too much. She was definitely a fully grown woman.

"You're not even old enough to drink, are you?" he asked. "That's why you refused that apple shit I tried to give you."

"What?" She shook her head. "I'm plenty old enough to drink and have been for several years. I just don't."

"And why not? Afraid you'll fall for my charm if you're drunk?"

"That's the only way I'd fall for a guy like you."

A guy like him? What kind of guy did she think he was?

"He's actually pretty cool when he doesn't drink," Dare said. "But judging by the size of the party in there, that condition's not going to last long."

"I don't have to drink to have a good time," Steve said.

"But it helps." Dare shifted away from the railing and turned to the glass doors that led back to the good time inside. "It was nice talking with you, Roux. If you or any of your bandmates need to vent, I'm told I'm a pretty good listener."

She beamed. "You're a real class act, Dare Mills," she said, toasting him with her half-finished glass of water.

Unlike your friend here remained unspoken, but Steve felt the insinuation clear to his bones.

Dare opened the patio door, and the blare of an old Aerosmith song punctuated his return to the party. Steve would have bet his favorite drum set that the guitarist would seek out his little brother, Trey, within the next few minutes and then leave the party early.

Dare was predictable that way. It was not a trait Steve shared with him.

He turned to Roux, who was admiring the city lights of the New York City skyline. "I'll miss this while we're in Europe," she said.

"Not if you're doing it right," he said with a laugh. He'd made so many plans with Zach regarding what they'd do at each stop along the tour—hadn't been much sightseeing in those plans. Steve stared down into his glass of water—was he seriously drinking water just to get in this chick's pants—his mouth set in a hard line. Technically, it wasn't her fault that Zach's band had been kicked off the tour prematurely. That was all on Sam.

"I'm sorry I called you an asshole," she said.

He shrugged. "I've been called a lot worse."

"I'm the only one of my friends who doesn't drink, so I'm always the designated driver, and drunks are really fucking annoying when you're sober."

"Never noticed that."

"You're probably one of the drunks, then."

He chuckled. "True. Is there a reason you don't drink? Or do you just not like it?"

She stared at him for a moment, as if trying to decide if he was worthy of knowing her secrets. "My father was an alcoholic."

"I see." He felt there was a lot more to the story than that, but he didn't press her. "How did you get into music?"

Her body relaxed slightly. "My foster mother was a music teacher."

Foster mother? There was definitely more to the alcoholic father story, then.

"So she introduced you to music?" He moved closer to Roux at the railing until their arms touched—a little test of her receptiveness to him—and she produced a little shudder. When she didn't move away, he knew he wasn't the only one feeling the attraction between them.

"Not just me," Roux said. "All of us."

"All of who?"

"My bandmates. Mama Ramona raised us all. Gave the gift of music to as many of us that would take it."

"You grew up with your bandmates?"

"For the most part. We're foster sisters. I didn't start living with them until I was twelve. Lily—she's our drummer—was Mama's first foster daughter. Mama's had twelve of us in her care at one time or another. I guess that would be thirteen now. I think a new little one moved in a few weeks ago. I've lost track now that we moved from Boston."

Boston? She didn't have an accent that he could detect.

"You don't seem bitter about your family situation at all," he said, watching her face and the genuine love that shone in her eyes as she spoke of Mama Ramona.

"Why would I be bitter? That woman took me in, showed me love, taught me how to believe in my dreams, how to make a future for myself, gave me the gift—and curse . . ." She laughed, the soft sound making him want her even more. ". . . of a dozen sisters. On top of it all, she taught me how to play the piano."

"So what happened to your real parents?" he asked, genuinely interested.

"It's not a fun story," she said, her hand fiddling with something dangling from her bracelet. After a moment, she released what he assumed was a charm of some sort and pressed her wrist out of view behind her back. "Aren't we supposed to be celebrating tonight?"

"If you don't want to talk about it—"

She shrugged. "Telling the story doesn't bother me. It bothers the people I tell."

"I think I can handle it." He leaned against the railing, expecting to hear a story of abandonment. As her focus shifted inward, the flash of pain that crossed her face and the unexpected tug at his heart made him wonder if he could handle seeing her hurt.

CHAPTER 3

ROUX DIDN'T WANT to like Steve. Lust him? She was okay with that. She could appreciate his gorgeous face, the deep and expressive brown eyes, and the lean, muscular body without taking their attraction any farther. But liking him as a person made him all that much harder for her to resist. And she absolutely refused to sleep around with anyone on this tour. This was her job—unbelievable as that still was to her—and business and pleasure should never mix. So maybe she shouldn't let him see her heart, because if he saw it—damaged as it was—and he accepted it, she knew she wouldn't be able to walk away from the lust between them. So she'd be perfectly okay with him deciding her past was too fucked up for him to handle. Maybe that was why she was so willing to share the details she usually kept to herself.

Without speaking, Roux tugged the bodice of her dress down to expose the inner curve of her breast. His eyes widened, and he licked his lips, taking an eyeful without apology. She knew the exact moment his gaze found the puckered round scar just to the right of her breastbone, because he stiffened, and his eyes lifted to meet hers.

"Is that . . . ?"

"My father gave me that the night he shot my entire family and then turned the gun on himself."

"Your father? Your father shot you?"

He lifted his finger toward the scar, the only external reminder of all her other scars. Ones that ran so deep, she'd never forget. But she didn't want to forget what had happened that night, and she would never forgive the drunk who'd taken everything from her.

Steve's finger hovered an inch from her skin, but he didn't touch her, not with his flesh. She could feel his soul reaching out to hers, however, as they stared into each other's eyes.

"He shot my mother first. He always got paranoid when he was drunk, thought she was fooling around on him. I was upstairs in my room, but I could hear her down in the kitchen screaming that she was leaving for real this time and that she was taking the kids with her. He told her that she'd never leave him. He wouldn't allow her to take his kids from him. When she tried to run upstairs, he shot her in the back."

"God."

"I heard his footsteps on the stairs. Panicked, I hid in my closet. Instead of trying to stop him, I hid. My little sister was running down the hall to my room for protection when he shot her in the face. She was eight." Roux could have provided more details, but the cruelty of her father's actions was gruesome enough without sharing the full reality of his crimes.

"Roux, I don't know what to say."

She could feel him pulling away from her, shielding himself from the dark corners of her past, but she didn't stop. She couldn't stop herself from telling him the rest.

"My baby brother was in his crib. Not quite two years old. He was screaming in terror; the sound of gunfire had woken him. My father silenced him next, and then he came for me. He was as angry as he was insane by the time he grabbed my ankle and dragged me out of the closet. Maybe that's why he shot me in the chest instead of in the head. I was still conscious when he put the gun in his mouth and finished what he started." Lost in memories, she could feel the rain of his hot blood over her face followed by the heaviness of his arm across her hips. She didn't remember what had happened next or how she'd survived. She'd been unconscious when the police arrived.

Steve covered his mouth with one hand and swallowed. Did her story make him sick? Good. Let it fester in him the way it had festered in her until she'd found an outlet for her anguish. She wasn't sure she would have ever moved on without music in her life. The classical piano she'd been introduced to first had soothed her aching soul. The angry rock she'd later discovered had become an outlet for her rage. The closeness of her bandmates and the pasts that tried to destroy each of them in a different way had finally given her the ability to look to her future instead of being crippled by her past.

Words tumbled from her lips, each delivered to push the rock god before her farther away.

"The bullet meant to end me grazed my heart and lodged in a rib in my back. I still don't know why I'm alive. The doctors said it was a miracle. The bullet missed the major blood vessels behind my heart by a fraction of an inch." She showed him her bracelet that had a bullet dangling from it like a charm. The only thing lucky about it was that it hadn't killed her, but it had given her strength for years. If she could survive being shot point blank in the chest by her own father, she could survive anything. "A truly amazing surgeon took this out. They were afraid the bullet would work free and end me long after the bastard who put it there was cold in his grave, so they risked the surgery."

"Roux."

She dropped her gaze, the empathy in Steve's eyes more than she could stand. "I was in the hospital for months. Having no family willing to take me, I was released into foster care. My grandparents were too old to take care of themselves, much less me. They're gone now. My aunts thought I'd be too much trouble, with the mental problems I was sure to have. So Mama Ramona took me in. CPS sends her the girls they can't place anywhere else."

"I can't imagine. I'm sorry."

"For what?" She shook her head, sparing him a glance. "There's nothing anyone could have done to prevent what happened. *Except* get my alcoholic father treatment before he snapped." And she wasn't sure that would have made much of a difference. "So to answer your question, *that's* why I don't drink. Alcoholism runs in families, and I refuse to follow in that man's footsteps."

Steve upended his half-empty glass over the balcony railing. She appreciated the symbolism, but remembered he'd been drinking water. She waited for him to find an excuse to leave. Few could stomach looking at her once they knew what she'd been through, Mama Ramona and her foster sisters—who'd survived childhood tragedies of their own—being the exceptions.

"You'll have to excuse me," he said, proving her right. He couldn't handle her tragic past. "But I can't just stand here and not hold you right now."

Huh?

When his arms went around her, she stiffened, but when his embrace remained merely comforting and not the sexual come-on she expected—perhaps wanted—she began to relax.

"I can't fathom what that must have been like for you," he whispered.

"You survive," she said. "If you don't . . . well, you don't get to tour the globe with Exodus End, now do you?" She lifted one corner of her mouth.

His huff of a laugh was breathless with emotion, and his arms tightened around her. "So your bandmates are all foster kids?"

"All survivors," she said. "Mama Ramona's girls."

The balcony door opened, and Sage—one of those survivors she'd mentioned—poked her head outside. "Been looking for you everywhere," she said to Roux. "Should have known you'd be macking with Steve Aimes on the balcony."

Steve's hold on Roux loosened. She pressed her face against his chest and breathed in his scent, hoping to use it to recall this tender moment later.

"We weren't making out," Steve said. "I was behaving like a perfect gentleman."

Roux leaned away and gazed up into his deep brown eyes. He averted his gaze, a smirk on his lips.

"For the first time in my hedonistic life."

"That's not what I saw, but who am I to call Steve Aimes a liar?" Sage teased. "Sam wants a group photo of Baroquen at our first world-tour party. We need you for just a minute, Roux, then you can get back to *not* standing tits to chest with a living legend."

And what a nice, hard, well-defined chest her tits had been pressed against. Funny how she hadn't been fixated on that when she'd had the opportunity. Roux had been too enraptured by the feeling of security and reliable strength Steve provided. She was pretty sure a quintessential rock star wasn't supposed to make a woman feel safe. He was supposed to make her feel reckless, dirty, a bit dangerous. Not wanting to miss the opportunity to show him she wasn't a tragic snowflake due to her dark past, she rose on tiptoe and kissed the corner of his mouth. It was meant to be a tender thank-you for listening to her tale. She didn't anticipate him cupping the back of her head and turning his mouth to her chaste kiss, or him taking charge of her innocent smooch to make it something that burned through her body like a fuel-ignited inferno. Her arms fell limp at her sides as she opened her mouth to his gently stroking tongue, not wanting anything—not even the feel of his flesh beneath her palms—to interfere with her enjoyment of his claim on her mouth.

"Ha!" Sage clapped her hands. "I knew it."

Steve released Roux's mouth with a slow, tingling suction, and said in a deep voice that shredded her already frayed nerves, "Maybe I'll see you later."

"Maybe," she said calmly, though inside she was screaming: *Maybe? What the fuck do you mean, maybe?*

"Come on, Roux," Sage said. "They're waiting for us."

Roux forced herself to follow Sage back to the party, though every atom in her body was inexplicably drawn to the man she left on the balcony. She and the rest of her band posed through dozens of pictures with various party attendees—it seemed everyone wanted to be recognized as being present for Baroquen's debut, though the *new* band had already released two albums and had been playing locally for years. She tried not to be too obvious about noticing when Steve returned to the party or when Steve greeted acquaintances or when Steve laughed at something some woman said. She had no claim over the man or anything he did. Hell, she didn't even like the guy. More accurately, she didn't like the guy she'd thought he was before she actually spent a few minutes alone with him.

Eventually, everyone who wanted a picture with Baroquen had taken the opportunity. Roux sighed in relief that she was free to move around the room again. Or better yet, now that several people were deep in drink and acting obnoxious, to return to the balcony.

"I'm going back outside for some fresh air," she told Sage. "Just wanted to let you know in case I'm needed again."

"I think Sam wants us to network," Sage said.

"I'll network outside."

"Steve isn't out there," she said, as if she knew Roux was hoping he'd follow her. "I think he's found someone else to mack with."

Roux spotted him standing against the bar, a drink in one hand, a woman's ass in the other. So much for him proving that she was wrong about him. He really was an asshole. And rather than look ashamed or uncomfortable, he seemed completely in his element.

"Yeah, well, whatever," Roux said. "I need some air."

Sage didn't press her further. Sage and the rest of her bandmates knew Roux wasn't big on parties involving alcohol. It wasn't that she was afraid that some drunk might try to kill her. She was afraid that she might see everyone having a good time, decide she might as well get drunk herself, and then wind up an alcoholic like her father had been. Alcoholism started with one drink, and she refused to risk it.

She pushed open the balcony door, leaving it cracked a bit because she enjoyed listening to the music. She gripped the cool metal railing and swayed to the beat, her eyes closed, heart wide open to the music. Perhaps the dance floor was where she belonged tonight.

"Were you hoping I'd join you?"

Steve's deep voice made her pause for several beats, but then the music found her again, and she continued letting the heavy bass line live through her body's motions.

"I'm not sure what to think of you," he said. "You look like a party girl. Right now you're acting like a party girl. But when you speak?"

She turned to find him shaking his head in bewilderment.

His eyes lifted, and he met her gaze. "You speak from the heart, Roux."

"Party girls don't have hearts? Is that what you're getting at?"

"I'm sure they do," he said. "I've just not been allowed to glimpse any."

"They're probably afraid you'll ditch them if they show the slightest substance." That was initially why she'd opened up to him. She'd assumed the honesty would send him packing. She'd wanted him to ditch her. And then he had to go and surprise her by being kind and empathetic. At least that bit of deception hadn't lasted long. There'd been no sympathy in that kiss.

"I'm not that callous," he said.

She lifted an eyebrow.

He laughed, muscles tightening in all the right places, and pulled a hand through his shoulder-length brown hair, gathering it into a fist at the back of his head. "Okay, you got me. I can be that callous, but only because I don't want to get hurt."

She rolled her eyes. "Right. Like any woman could hurt you."

She turned back to the cityscape to enjoy the view and barely heard him whisper, "It's been known to happen."

Her heart twisting with unexpected remorse, she whirled around to apologize, but he was gone. She caught sight of him through the glass, walking away. Before she could take three steps to follow him, the woman from the bar moved up beside him, cupped her hand around his ear, and stood on tiptoe to whisper something. Through the glass door, Steve caught Roux's gaze. Never breaking eye contact, he listened to the woman's whispers, nodded tersely, and then allowed the now-widely-smiling woman to lead him away.

Every time Roux started to think Aimes wasn't the biggest asshole she'd ever met, he immediately proved her wrong. Well, screw him. She wasn't going to let thoughts of him fucking that woman ruin her evening. She left the sanctuary of the balcony and rejoined the party, dancing until she was so amped on adrenaline that she didn't give a second thought to Steve Aimes for the rest of the night.

Nope, she gave *every* thought to him.

CHAPTER 4

STEVE WASN'T sure why he'd brought the woman into the private conference room at the end of the hall. She'd made it clear that he could do anything he wanted to her body. Touch her anywhere in any way he liked. Fuck any hole he felt like fucking. Strange and sad thing was, he didn't want to do anything of a sexual nature. He wanted to talk to Roux. See more of her heart so that maybe, just maybe, he could trust her with some of his. But now that this other woman was here, and shedding her clothes in a rather seductive tease, he couldn't tell her to get lost. The manliness authorities would run his man-card through a shredder. And a rejection would make this very attractive woman feel unwanted, unbeautiful. And he'd never met a woman he didn't find beautiful in some way. Well, one. But he didn't have to see Tamara much now that he'd divorced her sister. Luckily, his phone rang just as his stripteasing companion straddled his lap and buried her hands in his hair to draw his mouth to the tip of her lush breast.

"Sorry," he said, just before her nipple brushed his lips. "I need to take this." He didn't. And when he saw that the caller was unknown, he really knew he didn't need to take the call.

That didn't stop him from answering. "Hello?"

"Are you satisfied with your current cellular service?"

"What?" He allowed shock to register on his face, hoping his lap lounger couldn't hear what the caller was saying. "Are you sure?"

"Um," the telemarketer murmured, and then continued to read his script. "We have a plan with unlimited—"

"I can be there in about ten minutes." He hung up on the

telemarketer and lifted the woman's hands to his lips. He kissed her knuckles. "I'm going to have to take a raincheck on the rest of this sexy dance, sugar," he said, gently pushing her off his lap. "Something suddenly came up."

And for once it wasn't his dick.

"Is there anything I can do?"

She looked up at him with genuine concern, and he hated to lie, but he wasn't interested in anyone but Roux tonight, even if she didn't want him. Admittedly atypical for him, he had no plans to settle for some random chick just because she was easy.

"Are you going back to the party?" He didn't want to go back himself, but he did want to see Roux, even if just to watch her from afar and imagine the feminine ass in his hand belonged to her.

"Unless you want me to wait here until you get back," she said. "Did something terrible happen?"

"A friend is in trouble," he said, which probably wasn't a lie. Zach was out there partying somewhere without Steve, which was bound to be trouble. But not as much trouble as he'd have been in if Steve had been with him. "I need to help him out. I doubt I'll be back tonight."

Her face fell. "Oh, well, maybe some other time."

"Yeah. Sure," he said. "I'm going to have such a case of blue balls from this. My friend better appreciate the sacrifice I'm making." Lies. All lies. Sure, they were offered to protect the woman's feelings, but that didn't make his words any truer. "If you need a ride home . . ."

She shook her head. "Nah, I'm going to stick around. How often does a music blogger get to hang around with rock gods? Not often enough."

So that was why she was at the party. And that meant Steve couldn't return to the festivities for a long while or he'd be caught in his stupid lies. He should have just been blunt with Hot Blogger. *Look, I saw this special woman watching us when you propositioned me, and she looked a little jealous, so I thought, hey, maybe she won't be able to stop thinking about me if she realizes I'm irresistible to a hot chick like you, but I don't actually want you. I want her.*

Nope, he couldn't say that.

"Enjoy your evening," Steve said as he hurried from the conference room.

Free of his unwanted guest, Steve passed right by the open doors of the ballroom and hunted down the man who fixed all his minor problems and many of his major ones. He found Butch in the meal prep area, taking a break with several other members of Exodus End's security team.

"Shouldn't you be next door keeping the rock stars alive while they get wasted and high?" Steve asked as he slid into the empty chair to Butch's left.

"Seems the biggest troublemaker I'm responsible for is right here beside me," Butch said, his eyes on some boxing match airing on the television on the wall.

"I was wondering if you could do me a favor."

"Anything," Butch said, still not looking away from the television screen.

"Can you get Roux to my hotel room? I need to speak to her alone."

Butch turned his attention from the TV to stare at him with his mouth slightly open beneath his bushy mustache. "I must have heard you wrong. Did you just ask me to kidnap a woman?"

"What?" Steve jerked his head to one side. "No. I want you to convince her to go to my room. Don't tell her it's my room, or she probably won't come. But I really want to see her. Alone."

"Why don't you go ask her?" Butch asked. "It's not like any woman can resist your . . ." He spread his hands wide as he struggled to find the right words. ". . . whatever it is about you they like so much."

"His general badassedness," one of the security team supplied.

True, that was what drew most women to him like bears to honey, but that wasn't what he wanted Roux to see in him.

"You said you'd do any favor for me," Steve reminded Butch. And Butch had never let him down in the past. Steve had faith that the band's personal miracle worker could pull off his simple request.

"Roux is the red one of those Baroquen ladies, right?" Butch said, sliding from his chair.

Steve couldn't help but smile. Butch was his ace in the hole, and he played the card whenever necessary. "Yes, the red one."

"And you want her in your hotel room. Alone." Steve was a bit surprised Butch wasn't writing this all down on his trusty clipboard.

"That's right."

"I'll see what I can do. You should probably be there when she arrives," Butch said.

"Right," Steve said. He slid off the barstool.

Butch left his side immediately, sporting his getting-down-to-serious-business look. Steve smiled. What could possibly go wrong when he played his trump card?

Chapter 5

ROUX HAD ALL BUT FORGOTTEN about Steve—*sure*—and scarcely noticed when that blogger chick returned to the party without him—*obviously*—so she was more than a little surprised when Exodus End's head security guy tapped her on the shoulder.

"Sorry to bother you, Miss Roux," he said, "but can I speak to you for a moment?"

"Uh, okay," she said, shrugging. "What is it?"

"Perhaps in a place a bit less loud," he shouted over the Sinners song blaring over the dance floor.

She followed him out to a hallway that was only slightly quieter since the ballroom doors remained open. She guessed there weren't any other events on this floor tonight and wondered if the Sinners party on the next floor up was as crazy as this one was turning out to be. Maybe she'd head up there next and check it out.

"Is something wrong?" she asked the guy. She was pretty sure his name was Butch, and a quick glance at the name on the all-access pass around his neck proved her memory sound.

"I've dedicated my life to these boys." Butch clutched the back of his neck. "Well, I suppose they're men now, though sometimes it's hard to tell. One of them has a request for you, which I will make as promised, and then I'm going to offer you some advice. You can do with both as you see fit."

Roux had no idea what he was talking about. "A request?"

"Aimes would like you to meet him in his hotel room, alone, at your earliest convenience."

Her ears burned with unexpected heat before the sensation moved to her cheeks and then her chest. She didn't know whether she should be pissed, embarrassed, or aroused. She settled on the first option. "Is that so?" She crossed her arms over her chest and glared at a guy who probably didn't deserve her wrath. "Does he often send you to make such requests?"

"Actually, no," Butch said, his mustache twitching. "He doesn't have to. Women typically fall into his lap with their pants down."

Roux snorted on a laugh, wishing this guy was less likable so she could maintain her anger. Maybe she'd take Aimes up on his ridiculous offer in order to direct her rage at the proper person.

Butch smoothed his mustache down with one hand. "I can only guess he sent me on this ridiculous errand because he's afraid you'll reject him."

Well, duh. Who wouldn't reject such a pompous, arrogant ass who had only one thing on his mind? She bit her lip. If she were honest, she knew that most women—even her—would have a hard time turning Steve down. He was famous, gorgeous, rich, successful, talented, built like a fitness model, and knew how to have a good time. She'd guess he was a pro between the sheets as well, but that was one skill she'd have to keep guessing at, because there was no way she was stupid enough to fall into bed with the guy.

"I'm afraid he's right," she said, glad her head was in control of her mouth rather than her foolish heart leading her words, or worse, being at the whim of her burning desire. "I'm not interested."

Butch smiled, the tension leaving his shoulders. "I guess you don't need my advice, then."

"I'd like to hear it anyway."

Butch lifted a hand in greeting to someone leaving the party. Over her shoulder she caught sight of Dare pushing the elevator button. Why couldn't a nice guy like Dare be interested in her? And why didn't her belly quiver at the mere sight of him the way it did when Steve was near? Stupid abdominal muscles had it all wrong.

"I was going to advise you to take him up on his offer if you wanted him to leave you alone," Butch said.

Roux crinkled up her face.

"And reject him if you want him to pursue you relentlessly." Butch grinned. "I guess you already figured that out about him, though." He patted her arm. "Good luck. He's a prize if you manage to capture his heart. And I'm not saying that just because he pays me." He offered her a wink and left her staring after him.

She was still puzzling out Butch's bizarre advice when Sage came out into the hall. "There you are! I thought maybe you took off with Steve since you both turned up missing all of a sudden."

"No, I didn't take off with Steve." Why did everyone think she wanted him?

"Can you take Azura back to the hotel? She's feeling a little sick. I warned her to stay away from the tequila."

"Why should I be the one to take her back to the hotel?" Roux was usually the designated driver, but they didn't need one tonight with a limo at their disposal.

"Everyone is getting pretty drunk," Sage said, squeezing Roux's arm. "I figured it was getting to be around the time you start feeling uncomfortable."

If Roux paid attention to those around her, she did feel uncomfortable, but she'd been dancing in the middle of a crowd when Butch had interrupted her good time and hadn't noticed if guests were shouting in slurred voices and swaying drunkenly rather than actually dancing. She recognized the behavior now, though, thanks to Sage's pointing it out. A familiar feeling of panic made her heart pound, and she clutched the bullet dangling from her bracelet to steady her sudden nerves.

"I guess it is time for me to bail," Roux said. "Where's Azura? I'll take her home."

"She's in the bathroom, wishing she could puke."

So Azura had drunk a *lot* of tequila. Roux honestly didn't understand how anyone would willingly poison themselves with alcohol to the point that they *wished* they could puke. She just prayed Azura's wish didn't come true in the limo.

"That Butch guy is supposed to call for the limo when we need it," Sage said. "Any idea where he is?"

"I was just talking to him." Having one of the strangest conversations of her life. Steve's heart a prize? Hardly. His body? Yeah, she could see that being a prize, but his heart? Did he even have one? Out on the balcony when he'd held her, she thought she'd glimpsed it, but she was sure she was mistaken. Less than five minutes later, he'd had his hand on some other woman's ass.

"Go have him call the limo. I'll haul Azura away from the toilet she's hugging and help you get her to the car."

"Maybe you should call it a night too," Roux suggested. "Help me get her all the way back to the hotel."

"And miss out on my first official after-party?"

"Newsflash," Roux said. "It's *my* first after-party too."

Sage flipped a hand toward the chaos inside the ballroom. "Well, if you really want to spend your night in there—"

At that moment, some guy Roux didn't recognize emerged from the ballroom, opened his pants, and began to take a piss in the garbage can next to the door.

"What are you ladies doing in the men's room?" he asked Roux and Sage, who exchanged looks and laughed.

"This isn't the men's room," Sage said. "You're in the hallway."

"I was sure this was the men's room," he said, turning away from the garbage can. He missed pissing on Roux's boots by inches. Not cool.

"Go get Azura," Roux said. "I'll have Butch call the limo, and I'll meet you both downstairs."

"Thank you." Sage kissed Roux's cheek. "I knew I could count on you." To the drunk, she said, "Are you going to clean that up?" and nodded toward the pale yellow puddle on the floor.

He emitted a rather wet-sounding belch and wiped a hand across his mouth. "Is your hair green, or am I hallucinating?"

Sage flipped the green strands of her hair behind her shoulder. "You're obviously hallucinating. Someone needed to cut you off about five drinks ago."

"Wanna dance, greenie?"

He followed Sage back into the ballroom, and Roux blew an amused breath out her nose when he continued to follow her straight into the ladies' room.

It didn't occur to Roux, until she was standing face-to-mustached-face with Butch, how her sudden request to go to the hotel would sound. She asked him anyway, despite her embarrassment. No doubt he thought she was a lust-crazed groupie who'd decided to take Steve up on his offer after all.

"My friend isn't feeling well, so we need the limo to take us back to the hotel."

Butch lifted his eyebrows. "Your friend?"

"Yes, my friend. Azura. She drank too much tequila."

"And you need to accompany this friend?"

"If you think I'm going to see Aimes—"

Butch lifted a hand and pulled out a cellphone. "I didn't say that." He called the driver and assured Roux that the car would be waiting for them outside the building.

"Thank you," Roux said.

"When you see Steve," Butch said, "tell him I sent you."

He laughed, and she resisted the urge to flip him off as she stomped out of the room. She was not going to the hotel to see Steve. She was going to tuck Azura into bed and sit up gossiping with Raven until the rest of the band crawled back to the hotel, probably near dawn.

Azura was leaning heavily on Sage as they exited the elevator in the lobby almost twenty minutes later. Roux had been waiting for them for quite a while, but no matter. The limo had just pulled up outside, and a crowd of interested onlookers surrounded the car, trying to see through the tinted windows.

"You aren't going to get sick in the limo, are you?" Roux asked.

Azura lifted the empty white plastic bucket dangling from her free hand. "Just in case."

"Why do you do this to yourself?" Roux didn't get the appeal of alcohol and not only because her father had been a substance abuser. Was the head-buzz worth the poor decision-making, the potential nausea, and the really bad breath? Roux turned her head to the side to avoid Azura's undoubtedly flammable breath as she shouldered her weight to help her inebriated sister out to the car.

Exodus End's well-trained security team led the way, keeping the onlookers at a safe distance, though camera flashes were going off everywhere. Roux was certain few of the gawkers even knew who she and Azura were, but if the two of them were getting into a limo and had security, then they must be important. A tall, well-built security guy with dark skin and a knockout smile opened the limo door.

"Ladies," he said with a polite nod.

"Thank you." Roux practically dumped Azura into the car. The seats formed a U-shape with the door at the opening, so it wasn't exactly easy to get Azura to a more comfortable place than the floor.

"I was expecting your friend," a deep voice said from inside the car.

Roux recognized the voice at once, and for a moment considered backing away and allowing Azura to fend for herself, but she took a deep, calming breath and scrambled over her sister, who was currently on her hands and knees with her face planted in the nearest unoccupied leather seat.

"Ah, there's the one," Steve said in what Roux considered a rather smug tone.

"Make yourself useful," Roux snapped. "Can't you see she

needs help?"

"Is she drunk?" Steve asked, shifting out of his relaxed pose against the far window, but not before Roux noticed what she could only describe as his "I'm a male model waiting for you with one foot on the seat and my arm resting seductively on my knee" pose. Who sat in cars in that position? Steve Aimes, that was who.

"Jusssssst a little tipsy," Azura said, her words muffled by the seat against her mouth.

Roux massaged her brow, trying not to laugh at the ridiculous and exasperating situation she found herself in. Steve managed to get Azura into a slumped seated position before returning to his original semi-reclined position. The car started forward, and Roux, who'd been crouching, trying to figure out where she should sit, tumbled back onto Azura's lap with the momentum.

"Maybe you should try his lap instead," Azura said in what she probably thought was a whisper. Steve's smirk made it clear that he'd heard her.

Roux adjusted herself so she was sitting next to Azura instead of on top of her. But that put her closer to Steve's foot, which was resting on the seat. Again, who the hell sat like that in a limo? Was he anticipating a photographer would show up with a camera and do a fashion shoot?

"I wasn't expecting you to bring a friend, but I'm game," Steve said.

Roux's face went hot. She hoped he took her heightened color for the anger she felt, not the added arousal his innuendo had flushed through her.

"I didn't know you'd be in here," she said "I figured you'd already be at the hotel. Waiting." She lifted her gaze to meet his. "Alone. As I'd planned to leave you."

"Roux!" Azura snorted. "You're joking, I hope. You don't leave Steve Aimes alone. You just don't."

Steve offered Azura a sensual smile that made Roux's toes curl inside her boots. Now why couldn't he smile at her like that? Maybe because she was so contrary in his presence. But she couldn't help it. He pissed her off! No one should be as full of himself as he was. Not even a living legend.

But she had glimpsed a different side of him. A side she was pretty sure he kept hidden from most people. His tender side. There were no signs of it now, however.

"So what do you say?" Steve's gaze moved from Azura to

Roux. There was a question in his exotic brown eyes. "Two's company, three's a ménage."

Before Roux could tell him to fuck off, Azura's scrambling hands reached for her bucket and she heaved the contents of her stomach, accompanied by a forceful splash, into the plastic container.

Roux cringed, fighting her own waves of nausea, but dutifully held back the hair of Azura's waist-length blue and black wig as the poor thing found more to throw up. Thank God she'd thought to bring a bucket.

"I'll take that as a no," Steve said. "Some other time maybe."

"Sorry," Azura said between pants for air. "I thought I could make it home before . . . Before—"

She puked again, and Roux was pretty sure she'd join her if she didn't soon get away from the stench wafting from the rapidly filling bucket.

The limo pulled to a stop, and a different security guard opened the door. Without so much as a blink, the poor guy accepted the bucket of puke Steve took from Azura and handed to him. Steve exited the car and then reached inside to scoop Azura into his arms.

"I've got you," he said, cradling her against his chest. "Where to?"

As Roux watched him hold her friend in his strong arms, she suddenly understood one reason it might be beneficial to get falling-down, throwing-up drunk. She hurried ahead of them, glancing back every few seconds to make sure Steve was behaving himself around her judgment-impaired sister. Roux probably should have been more worried about Azura making moves on Steve since she breathed him in and murmured, "You smell nice."

"Better than you do at the moment," he replied, the corners of his eyes crinkling in amusement.

Azura was too wasted to be insulted. If she remembered his words in the morning, though, she'd likely be mortified. She had puked her guts out in front of the iconic drummer of Exodus End.

"Tequila is not your friend, Azura," Roux muttered as she followed security into a waiting elevator car in the hotel lobby.

"But you are, Roooo-zey," she slurred. "You always take care of us." She blinked up at Steve. "Who are you?"

"I'm Steve, but some call me Trouble."

Azura laughed as if he'd said the most hilarious thing she'd ever heard. "Trouble. That's a funny name."

And fitting, Roux wagered. Azura went a bit green as the elevator began its climb to their floor. Roux tried to focus on her sister's well-being instead of the distracting bulging biceps in her peripheral vision, but damn if the man didn't have the most amazing body she'd ever seen.

"Thanks for helping us get to our room," Roux said.

"I might have a few ulterior motives."

"Yeah, Butch told me about those."

"And?"

She licked her lips and met his gaze steadily, Butch's advice playing through her ears. "It's not happening, Aimes. You might as well get the idea out of your head." She wondered if she meant that, or if she was actually hoping that Butch's warning about Steve pursuing her relentlessly became her reality. She just wasn't sure how long she'd keep running.

Was ten minutes long enough?

CHAPTER 6

STEVE SHIFTED the drunk girl in his arms and watched Roux fiddle with the velvet stays of her corset. He had a hunch that dear old Butch had told her to play hard to get, the bastard. What neither of them knew was that while that ploy used to work on him, he was wiser and more mature than he'd been when he'd fallen head over ass in love with Bianca. He knew what that level of passion and obsession brought—utter misery and irreparable heartache. He was not looking for a repeat of the anguish his ex-wife had pressed upon him.

The elevator dinged, and he followed Roux down the hall, hoping Miss Too-Much-Tequila didn't puke all over him before he dropped her off. As far as he could tell, the woman was unconscious. She'd become a complete deadweight in his now-straining arms, but hell if he'd drop her and show an ounce of weakness in front of Roux. Roux used a keycard that had been hiding in her bra—lucky card—to unlock a door and pushed it open. A pretty, dark-haired girl—wearing only a pair of men's boxers and a black bra—whirled around at their intrusion.

"For fuck's sake, Roux. What the hell are you doing back so early? Are you ever going to learn to party? It's not even midnight!"

"Azura hit the tequila a bit too hard," Roux said. "Is the connecting door unlocked?"

That was when the yet-to-be-introduced woman noticed Steve leaning against the wall to help support Azura's ever-increasing weight. Miss Wears-Men's-Underwear gaped at him, her mouth and eyes wide with disbelief.

"Steve Aimes," he introduced himself. "And you would be?"

"Oh my God, what is he doing here?" the woman shrieked.

He couldn't tell if hers was a positive or negative reaction. Roux had ventured toward door along one wall, and he shifted Azura more securely in his arms to follow her.

"Her name is Raven," Roux said.

"Hello, Raven," he said as he passed her.

"Oh my God, he's even sexier in person!"

He was glad someone noticed since Roux seemed impervious to his obvious appeal. He placed Azura on one of the beds in the adjoining room, and before Roux could loosen her clothing to make her more comfortable, Raven rushed over and pushed Roux aside.

"Don't mess up her costume," Raven said, leaning over Azura with splayed hands, as if protecting a golden shroud. "I've got this. And take him with you. You know how Azura is about being naked in front of ridiculously hot guys."

Based on the confused look on Roux's face, she had no idea what Raven was talking about. Either that or Roux didn't think the ridiculously hot description fit him. Steve took Raven's words as his cue to exit the room, and he tried not to overhear Raven whisper to Roux, "Now's a good time to loosen up. Here, you might need this."

"Why would I need a condom?" Roux's voice got closer as Raven started shoving her from the room.

"Just a hunch," Raven said.

Raven shut the connecting door in Roux's face, leaving her alone with Steve. He wasn't ready to leave—not unless she was coming with him. She glanced at him, her cheeks pink, and tucked the condom into her corset. He hoped that meant she trusted Raven's hunches.

"Have you had second dinner yet?" he asked.

"Second dinner?"

"I'm starved. After a show I always need second dinner. Usually it consists mostly of alcohol, but—"

"You can drink," she said. "I never suggested you couldn't drink."

He didn't want a drink. "I think I need to be in full command of my senses when I'm around you."

Her amazing gold-rimmed green eyes narrowed. "Why?"

He didn't honestly know, but said, "You're beguiling enough without the thought-scrambling detriment of whiskey."

She smiled, and color rose up her throat. His heart skipped a beat. Fuck, she was beautiful when she smiled. And when she didn't smile. Or when she scowled or produced any expression or none at all. She was beautiful.

"It's the costume." She ran a hand down the velvet stays of her black lace corset. "The makeup." She drew a fingertip along her fair cheek. "The wig." She tugged at a strand of crimson hair. "If you met the real me, you wouldn't be beguiled in the least. You probably wouldn't even notice I exist."

"Only one way to find out," he said, wanting, needing, to see her without the makeup and costume. There was absolutely no fucking way he wouldn't notice she existed. He was uncomfortably aware of her every expression, every move, every breath.

Roux straightened, which made her tits look fantastic in that corset, but for once he wasn't stupid enough to let the compliment fly.

The fire in her gaze as she narrowed her eyes lit a corresponding one in him.

"Mr. Aimes, if you're suggesting I strip—"

"You can change in the bathroom. I won't peek. Lose the wig. The makeup. You can throw on some street clothes if you like or wear nothing at all. I would like to see you naked. Can't deny that fact."

Her jaw hardened, but it was because she was trying to suppress a smile, not because she looked angry. "All right, but only to prove you wrong."

"Then we're having second dinner," he said. In his hotel suite. But he'd give her that detail after he proved her wrong. "What do you like to eat?"

"I'm a vegetarian," she said. "So no meat."

He had some meat she was sure to enjoy, but again, he withheld his inappropriate comment. "Strict vegan or lacto-ovo?" he asked, but not because he wanted to impress her with his SoCal knowledge of the different forms of vegetarianism. Unless it worked. Then that was totally what he was doing.

"I eat the occasional egg, and I love cheese and yogurt. I just avoid meat. All meat."

Well, that didn't bode well for the meat in his pants.

"Will you hurl if I eat a steak in front of you?" He'd once gone to dinner with a staunch vegan who'd done exactly that. She also tried to change him to her ways with drawn-out speeches about ethics, and yeah, that never worked with him.

"No, it's fine. Just like with drinking alcohol, it's your body—put whatever you want into it."

He simply could not ignore that opening. "And if all I can think about is putting something in *your* body?" His tongue, fingers . . . dick.

"You should probably keep those thoughts to yourself."

She went to a suitcase that was lying open across one of the two double beds and scooped clothes into her arms before hurrying to the bathroom. She met his eyes just before she closed the door, and he held her gaze and his breath until she was no longer in sight.

He blew out that breath, staring at the ceiling for a moment to center himself, and then sat on the bed. He grabbed a menu from near the phone and called for room service. The kitchen was happy to accommodate his every request, which was what he was used to. They had no problem agreeing to deliver the food to his room down the hall.

The connecting door opened, and Raven peeked into the room. "I knew I didn't hear enough moaning and rhythmic thumping from in here. Did she bail on you?"

"She's changing into something a bit more comfortable."

Raven grinned. "According to her, a suit of armor is more comfortable than that corset."

He smirked. "I personally prefer the corset."

"Roux's a bit of a stiff until you get to know her."

"I hadn't noticed."

"Liar." At a thud from the bathroom, Raven stepped back into the adjoining suite. "Be good to her, even if it's just for tonight. Be good to her."

Before he could respond, the bathroom door opened, and the connecting door shut behind Raven. Steve was almost afraid to look at Roux. Makeup could completely transform a woman's looks. What if Roux was a warty green toad under that makeup? What if that corset had been responsible for her amazing figure? He decided it didn't matter. He wasn't always attracted first by a woman's looks; sometimes he was turned on by something else about her. Her smile, her voice, a nervous habit, her personality. That sexy dip above a collarbone. A scar, a stray freckle. Hell, there were thousands of things that made a woman beautiful to him. If Roux didn't look as gorgeous as he expected, he'd just focus on the parts of her he was attracted to. Which was pretty much every part.

He turned to face her, and the earth stopped spinning as he

held himself suspended in that first glimpse. Her natural hair was shoulder-length and a burnished coppery red. Light danced upon the strands in shimmers. Her pale skin wasn't flawless—no warts, thank God—but pale freckles spotted the bridge of her nose and smooth cheeks. Her lips, now a light, natural pink instead of jet black, parted slightly as she licked them. His searching gaze hadn't even made it as far as her eyes, but he knew he was a goner.

Her pretty lips twisted into a wry smile. "Why do you make me feel naked no matter what I'm wearing?"

His quick downward glance took in a baggy gray sweatshirt that did her figure no favors and the delicious curve of her hip undisguised by a pair of distressed skinny jeans. Her bare toes with black-painted nails wiggled under his scrutiny. And then he forced his gaze to meet hers. Those eyes of hers were the same—rock star disguise or no—and he felt dizzy as the earth whirled back into motion beneath him.

"Because I see you," he said. "I don't just notice or look. I *see*."

Her slightly trembling hand tucked a lock of her hair behind one ear. "So that's why I'm so nervous all of a sudden," she said a bit breathlessly, not realizing her admission allowed him to see even deeper. And as much as he wanted to taste her lips, her skin, and the heat between her legs, he didn't want to give her any excuse to put up barriers.

"I ordered room service. It should be delivered in a few minutes."

She smiled. "Good. I'm actually starving now that I'm thinking about food."

"We'd better go, then."

Her smooth brow crinkled as she drew her eyebrows together. "Go? We'll need to be here when the food arrives."

"It's being delivered to my room down the hall."

"Ah, so there's your move. I was wondering when you'd make it."

He lifted both hands, pleading his not-so-innocence. "We won't do anything you don't want to do. I'm not that kind of guy."

She grinned. "You just plan to be so charming, I can't resist you, is that it?"

"Something like that."

"Good luck, Aimes."

She headed for the door in self-assured strides, and if her gentle beauty hadn't already completely undone him, that confident walk of hers would have.

"Just so you know," she said as she opened the door and waited for him to pass her and go into the hall, "I am the epitome of self-control."

"Is that so?" He stopped beside her and placed a hand on her lower back.

At his touch, her breath came out in a trembling rush, but she nodded.

"We'll just have to see about that," he said close to her ear, coaxing her bare feet—which seemed to have rooted themselves to the carpet—forward.

She stood straighter as she moved into the corridor, but without those killer boots of hers, she barely reached his shoulder. He promised himself he wouldn't make a move on her. He would not be to blame when she tossed self-control out the window and embraced the complete lack of control that Steve typically preferred.

"Which way?" she asked, peering down the empty hall in both directions.

Glad he'd looked up his room number when he'd ordered room service so he could lead the way rather than have to scramble for the information, he showed her to his door. He half expected her to turn away and run to safety—not that he was a threat—but she entered his room and switched on the light. He spent the next several minutes tossing dirty clothes into the closet and empty beer bottles into the trash. There was half a pizza lying in an open box on the middle of his bed that had seen better days, and his entire room smelled like greasy cheese and pepperoni. Every time he came to New York, he had to have a pizza, because even though he was from Illinois, he much preferred a good New York pie to a Chicago one. He was especially interested in the New York pie watching him trying to make the place presentable. Perhaps they should have stayed in her room after all. She seemed far less at ease here.

A knock drew him to the door.

"Room service!" the visitor announced.

Steve exchanged the pizza remains and a decent tip for his freshly seared steak and Roux's eggplant lasagna. Roux was staring out the window when he set their second dinner on the table in the corner of the large room.

"At least we didn't have to wait long," he said.

She glanced at the food, his king-size bed, him, his bed again. He could only guess the train of her thoughts, but they seemed to involve the bed.

"Would you rather eat in bed?" he asked, nodding toward the wide expanse of mattress that he would love to decorate with her nude body.

She hurriedly sat at the table and folded her hands in her lap. To keep her from seeing his smirk, he walked around the table and behind her, leaned over her narrow back, and lifted the cover from her plate. He blew a breath over the side of her neck, and she squirmed, tilting her head into the sensation. Okay, so he couldn't resist making a few moves on her. He wanted her, after all. He refused to be overly aggressive, but it didn't hurt to prod her in the right direction.

"I hope the eggplant lasagna is to your liking," he said. Her food actually looked better than he'd anticipated when he'd ordered it for her. The dish had come highly recommended by the guy who'd taken his order.

"It smells delicious."

She turned her head to offer him an appreciative smile, and her mouth was so close to his, he could feel her breath against his lips. He waited, hoping she'd take the kiss he so desperately craved, but she turned to find her fork, used it to cut through the cheesy layers on her plate, and delivered a bite to her delectable mouth.

Disappointed, but far from ready to give up, he slid into the chair across from hers and lifted the lid off his own plate. The mouthwatering aroma of well-seared beef made him reach for his utensils and saw off a healthy-sized bite of his ribeye.

She didn't comment on his meal, but he noticed she kept her eyes averted from his plate and the puddle of bloody steak juice pooling at its center.

"So are you vegetarian for moral reasons or health reasons?" he asked.

"Both," she said. "But honestly, I just don't like the taste."

"Perhaps you've had the wrong kind of meat in your mouth. Maybe some trouser sausage would be more to your liking."

She pursed her lips and held them together until she got her grin under control. "Does that line actually work for you?"

"All my lines work." Though he seldom needed them. He only had to show a bit of interest in a woman, and he got what he wanted. Of course, he'd become quite the expert at spotting easy lays over the years, and he'd gotten himself into a pattern of going after that type of women, so why was Roux such a draw for him? She didn't seem overly receptive to a little casual sex. Perhaps she'd be more interested in a lot of it.

"I'm not going to sleep with you, Aimes," she said, cutting into a thick slice of eggplant with the side of her fork. "It would be a stupid idea to get involved with you while on tour, and I won't be responsible for causing problems for my band."

He swallowed another bite of steak and washed it down with a swig of beer. "Why would sleeping with me cause problems for your band?"

"This tour could make or break our success, and I'm the jealous type." She shrugged and lifted her amazing green-gold eyes to meet his. "So when you find a new piece of tail to chase, I won't take it well."

"What's to say I'll even be looking for a new piece of tail?" Maybe he was tired of all the meaningless sex. Maybe he was ready to find a more substantial relationship. One that lasted more than a few hours. The very idea had him hyperventilating, but he didn't back down.

"Guys like you are always looking for a new piece of tail."

She had him pigeonholed. He aimed to prove her wrong about him. He sure as hell wasn't prepared to admit she was right.

"You seem to be speaking from experience," he said.

"I've dated some men in this business. I know what can happen on tour." She held his gaze steadily. "And I know how you treated your first wife."

Ah, so she believed the stories that had been printed during his nasty divorce.

"I treated her like a goddess," he said, and he wasn't exaggerating.

"That's not what I heard."

Bianca had once been his entire world. And if she hadn't found someone new, she still would be. Of course, the tabloids had placed an entirely different spin on their breakup—little of it true. Recently discovering that she headed one of those tabloids made Steve wonder if she'd planted those initial false leaks all those years ago to make him look bad and herself the victim. He'd been too heartbroken to even attempt to correct the stories, not even in court during the divorce proceedings. He'd heard the tales of his infidelity so many times that even he sometimes believed they were true.

For some reason, that undeserved nasty reputation had helped his sex life, not hindered it, but the effects on his love life? He hadn't had one of those since Bianca left. He'd never believed her capable of betraying him, hurting him, but at least by taking the blame he hadn't been publicly humiliated. Only those closest to him knew the truth. He hadn't been man enough to keep her from straying. He hadn't been enough to love.

His appetite suddenly lacking, he pushed his half-finished meal aside and watched Roux eat. He wasn't sure why he decided to open his mouth; it was probably better that she thought he was a complete ass. Those types of opinions kept women at a safe distance, where he wanted them to stay.

That was what he wanted, wasn't it?

Maybe not.

"Shit does happen on the road," he said, choosing his words carefully, "but sometimes it happens back home when a band's on tour. Exodus End has had a long-standing rule about bringing significant others on the road."

"You see," Roux said, dabbing at a bit of sauce at the corner of her mouth with her napkin. "That kind of policy makes it easier to fool around."

"Having your woman on tour makes it hard to focus on the job twenty-four hours a day. Logan's recent girlfriend-caused lobotomy is proof of that. The four of us have dedicated our lives to our fans for the past fifteen years, and when we're on tour there's no time for anything else."

"I completely agree."

"So maybe Bianca was lonely." Steve shrugged. "I understand how it could have happened. Maybe my phone calls and gifts and spending as much time with her when I wasn't touring wasn't enough. That's why I went home to surprise her when a show got canceled due to the stadium's flooding. That's how I caught her with another man in our bed."

Roux's eyes lowered. "I guess she figured what's good for the gander—"

"I never cheated on her."

"But the tabloids and ET and . . . Hell, I think it's even on your Wikipedia page!"

He snorted. "You believe everything you read on Wikipedia?"

"Mostly," she admitted. Her lashes lifted, and she met his eyes. "If it's a lie, then why haven't you set the story straight?"

"Because the truth makes me feel impotent."

She rubbed her lips together and reached across the table to rest her fingertips on the back of his hand. That simple touch sent a jolt like lightning through his system, setting every cell in his body into a heightened state of excitement.

"I know how that feels."

He lifted an eyebrow. "You know how impotence feels?"

"Yes," she said earnestly. "I had a boyfriend once who could never get it up. I'd suck on his dick for hours and . . . *pfft*." She turned her thumb downward. "Nothing."

She laughed, and then her expression stiffened into seriousness again. He instantly missed her laugh. Her smile. Her teasing.

"I'm sorry. Your impotence isn't funny."

"I'm not impotent. I can prove that to you at this very moment." And he couldn't believe any man would have difficulty getting hard for this woman. He was more likely to have the opposite problem—to always be hard for her. "Did you really date an impotent guy?"

"I don't think you're impotent—no need to prove it. And no, it's not true. That was a joke. I don't know how impotence feels. I know how it feels to be cheated on. How worthless it makes you feel. How unwanted. How unattractive."

"You're beautiful."

She flushed, and her fingers stroked the back of his hand. Just once, but the sensation sizzled up his arm. He tightened his thigh muscles to keep from springing from his chair and dragging her to the bed. He refused to let his oversexed libido give her an excuse to push him away.

"You're beautiful," she said. "When you're not being an ass."

He snorted. "So you have to qualify my . . . *beauty*?"

"Oh, you're always hot, sexy, and too gorgeous for your own good, but just now, when you let me in here . . ." She reached across the small table and tapped the center of his chest. "You *were* beautiful."

His hands slid to cup her lovely face, framing it and those soul searching eyes of hers between his palms. She made him feel something he never thought he'd feel again. Hope. Hope that someone on this dark and twisted planet might be able to see him for who he truly was and love him because of it, not despite it. Her lashes fluttered to conceal her eyes, and she strained toward him, her mouth too tempting to be denied. He kissed her, trying to keep the caress of his lips on hers sweet and tender. He didn't want the heat of his desire to drive her away. Not yet. Maybe not ever. It had been so long since he'd allowed himself to feel anything but lust for a woman, that emotion clogged his throat.

Her tongue tentatively touched his lip, and he came completely undone, his admittedly limited self-control scattering like dandelion fluff in a hurricane. He devoured her mouth, drawing on the fiery heat of the passion he knew she kept hidden just beneath the surface.

She moaned, the sound deep and aching. Her lips parted to allow him to taste her.

He needed her completely bare before him. Not just the body he so desperately craved, but her heart, her soul, her thoughts and dreams. He wanted all of her out in the open, free and uninhibited. No constraints or limitations. No fear.

Her hand pressed against his chest, and she pulled her mouth from his. "We can't do this."

"You don't want me?" He knew she did. He was prepared to call her a liar and prove to her that she did.

"So much. Too much." She stood, her chair skittering across the floor behind her at the haste in the motion. "But I can't get involved with you, Aimes." She smoothed his hair back and kissed his brow. "Stay beautiful," she whispered before backing away.

And she fucking left him there, with a hard dick, an aching heart, and half a cold steak on a colder plate.

CHAPTER 7

WHY AM I so fucking stupid? Roux clutched the bottom of her corset and allowed herself another glimpse of Steve, who was currently in the satellite radio studio rocking out with his drumstick against a wooden block as Exodus End played an acoustic version of "Bite" for the station's lucky listeners.

"Don't look so depressed," Iona said, nudging Roux in the ribs with her elbow. "The station couldn't get a piano for you to play under such short notice and, well, a keyboard isn't technically acoustic, so you can't play that. And that xylophone suggestion?" Iona cringed. "Yeah, no."

Roux wished not being able to play during their live acoustic satellite radio spot was the reason she was miserable, but that was just disappointing. She was utterly depressed because she'd done the sensible thing last night and walked away from that beautiful, sexy, shockingly sensitive drummer instead of taking him for a long, invigorating, undoubtedly satisfying test ride.

When she'd said hi to him earlier, he hadn't even looked at her. He probably thought she was a cock tease, a frigid bitch, or worse, not interested. She glanced around the small booth at her sisters/bandmates and reminded herself that she'd pushed Steve away for their sakes. The last thing Baroquen needed was trouble on this tour, and she had no doubt that getting involved with Steve would bring nothing but trouble, trouble that she would willingly embrace if she were the only one who would face the consequences. But she wouldn't risk repercussions harming any of her sisters. The unaware bitches had better appreciate her sacrifice!

Roux squeezed her eyes shut, her false eyelashes digging uncomfortably into her eyelids. She wished she'd gotten some sleep last night. She was feeling more than a little testy this morning.

I should have just fucked him before I walked away. Why didn't I?

She had no answers to that question. She'd hooked up with a few guys in the past. It wasn't a big deal. She wasn't the type who expected lasting commitment from a quick and dirty fuck, but she'd connected with the ass. Liked him. That was why she wouldn't have been able to hook up with him just once. And hell, in less than a month she'd be on foreign soil and have to see him every night while they were on tour. She would get to see him, wouldn't she? She glanced into the studio again and about choked on her tongue when she caught him staring at her. He quickly looked away and said something insulting to Logan, which the host found hilarious.

"Maybe it's the hangover talking," Azura said, wincing, "but I think Steve has the hots for Roux."

Only Raven knew Roux had gone to his room last night. Only Raven knew she'd returned way too early and without sealing the deal.

"It's the hangover," Roux assured her. Azura didn't even remember Steve carrying her upstairs. Or puking her guts out into a plastic bucket in the limo.

"He does keep looking at her when she's not paying attention," Sage said.

"He totally has a hard-on for you," Iona said. "Like literally."

Roux caught him adjusting the crotch of his jeans, and yeah, looked like Iona was correct. So why had he completely blown her off when she'd greeted him earlier?

Because he's sensitive and easily hurt, her subconscious whispered to her. Nah. That couldn't be the reason. He was just horny because he hadn't had sex with five different women in the past three hours. Or maybe he had.

Not that she cared.

Ugh, why did she insist on lying to herself about the man?

She told herself he wasn't worth the time or effort, when he was so worth it.

She told herself she wasn't interested in any relationship with him—serious or casual—when she wanted *any* relationship with him as long as she could be near him.

She told herself musicians were notoriously unfaithful and that she shouldn't believe his story about being jilted by his ex-wife, when she had believed every word of it. Still believed it.

Roux scowled and turned her back to the large window that looked into the sound booth. If she couldn't see him, maybe she'd stop obsessing over him. Yeah, right.

At least she was too worried about trying not to worry about Steve to be nervous. She wouldn't be able to play during the segment, but she sang duet with Iona on most of the choruses of Baroquen's songs, so she wasn't entirely off the hook.

"I heard you won't be playing your ridiculous keyboard during your band's segment," Steve said from behind her, his voice deep. "I guess you'll have to stay out here with me."

She conjured up some anger, when she wanted to do nothing more than melt into his heat. "My keyboard is not ridiculous." She spun around and was blindsided by his cocky grin. She knew he was baiting her, but for what purpose? "And didn't you just play a wooden block? Talk about ridiculous."

But it hadn't been ridiculous. Ridiculously amazing, perhaps, but . . . Damn him anyway.

"I do enjoy your fire, Red."

He lifted his hand to touch her jaw, his thumb drawing slowly across her slightly parted lips. Well, if he enjoyed her fire, that little movement had definitely set her ablaze.

"After your segment, I have something for you."

"If it's in your pants, I don't want any part of it," she snapped, but she couldn't hold his gaze, because she was lying worse than a politician.

He chuckled softly, the sound making her belly quiver. "It *is* in my pants, as a matter of fact, but don't worry I'll take it out for you."

Entirely flustered, she stammered, "A-as if!"

"I think your band is waiting for you to join them."

Huh?

She turned to find the observation booth they'd been waiting in was now empty, with the exception of herself and Steve.

"You made me late."

"I didn't have to try very hard," he called after her as she rushed out into the sound studio.

"Sorry," she whispered, bobbing her head in the host's direction. Wow, was that really her favorite disc jockey, Jack Bryant? He was even cuter in real life. Roux cringed over her bad form.

"No problem. We're not live yet," Bryant said, his voice excitingly familiar. Roux heard it on her favorite satellite radio station almost every day.

The incredulity of her current situation suddenly kicked her heart rate into high gear. When had this become her life? A quick glance toward the glass waiting area made her life even more surreal. Steve Aimes was currently undressing her with his eyes, and he had something in his pants for her. How would she ever resist him?

On a cue from his staff, Bryant began speaking into the microphone. "With us now is the band you'll be talking about tomorrow if you aren't already talking about them today. They're joining Exodus End on their world tour next month, and there's a reason for that. We played you their latest single a little earlier on Fast Tracks . . ."

They did?

". . . and you, our loyal listeners, loved 'Starlight.'"

They had?

Roux exchanged excited smiles with her sisters, barely able to stay on her stool with the nervous energy flowing through her body.

"I'm sure our listeners wish they could see you in person, because, wow! You look as good as you sound."

Iona laughed, always completely at ease in the spotlight. "We're not quite that good looking."

"You in particular look familiar," Bryant said to Iona. "Where might I have seen you before?"

Roux forced her face to remain neutral. Iona had used her middle name when she'd been a favorite contestant on the reality television show *American Voice* a few years ago. She worked hard—and now wore a lot of stage makeup—to keep the general public from realizing who she was.

"Do you frequent the Delancey after midnight?" Iona asked.

"Been there a time or two," Bryant said. "A bit too goth for me."

"No such thing," Iona said, tonguing the corner of her black-painted lips as she stared him down. It did the trick; he turned his attention to Roux, who straightened as if her corset stays were attached to a released spring.

"You're the keyboardist, correct?" Bryant asked her, his blue eyes flicking to the swell of her breasts before settling on her face.

"That would be me. Though I won't be playing today."

"Unfortunately, we weren't able to get our hands on a piano in time, so, listeners, make sure you crank up the track as it was recorded, because that keyboard work is phenomenal."

Roux flushed. She was glad someone in the business appreciated it.

Iona met the eyes of each of her bandmates in turn, making sure that everyone was ready to rock.

"We are Baroquen," she said, "and this is a never before heard unplugged version of our latest single, 'In Lights.' "

The intro sounded hollow without Roux's keyboard, but Sage and Azura filled in beautifully enough that anyone who'd never heard the original version would get the general idea. Roux leaned in toward the microphone and sang one long note in a low sultry tone. Her voice was most often compared to Janis Joplin's. Perhaps that was why she sang backup. She didn't have a unique enough aperture to get the high, haunting quality that blessed Iona with pitch-perfect talent. Normally Roux didn't mind singing backup, but because she didn't have her keyboard to focus her attention on, she was very conscious that everyone—particularly Steve—was watching her sing. Or they were until Iona started the first verse. She didn't have her bass guitar today, so she gave her voice even more power than usual. So much so that Roux was pretty sure that opera singers would be jealous. Out of the corner of her eye, Roux caught the look Azura and Sage exchanged as they strummed their guitars. *Iona is such a show-off!*

But Iona was used to holding the spotlight. She'd almost had a solo career—probably still could if her boyfriend pressed the issue—but she said she preferred being part of the group. You sure couldn't tell that this morning. So when Roux's part of the chorus came around, she belted out the words with everything she had.

A muffled whistle drew her attention to the observation booth, which apparently wasn't completely soundproof. Steve had two fingers in his mouth, blowing whistles of appreciation while thrusting his opposite fist into the air like he was at some live concert. Roux licked her lips, unable to stop the little smile of pleasure that turned up the corners of her mouth. Steve gave Max a dirty look when he tried to shush him but switched to clapping instead of whistling. She couldn't hear his applause over the music in the sound booth, but she imagined it was loud.

The crescendo built in the middle of the song, Roux's voice and Iona's no longer competing, but harmonizing, rising together on different octaves. At the onset of Sage's subdued guitar solo—acoustic did not do it justice—Roux leaned away from the microphone and sucked in a deep breath to relieve her aching lungs.

Iona squeezed her elbow and gave her a thumbs-up. She was always encouraging Roux to concentrate more on her singing, but at heart Roux was a pianist and always would be. And though Iona played bass guitar, at heart she was a singer. She was a good bassist, but it was more of an afterthought for her rather than a focus. Maybe that was why the two of them worked so well together; they weren't competitive. Azura took the second half of the solo—her style more frenzied than Sage's wail—and it was obvious the same could not be said about their two guitarists. They were forever in competition with each other, and it made them both strive for a higher level.

Roux's smile spread as pride suddenly grabbed hold of her. The five of them had come so far from where they'd begun, and though they had the occasional disagreement, they each championed the others. It was times like these that Roux felt truly blessed for having this surrogate family full of talented and supportive women.

Lost in her happy thoughts, Roux almost missed her cue at the end of Azura's solo. She'd performed this song enough that the words came automatically, so while her sound started off a bit weak, she quickly ramped up her tone, her fingers playing imaginary keys across her knees.

It would be four weeks before their first opening show at the Download Festival in England. She couldn't wait to perform in front of a live audience. This studio performance was fun but couldn't compare to dozens of screaming fans spurring her on. Of course, she seemed to have picked up at least one screaming fan today. She covered her mic with one hand and laughed aloud at Steve's over-the-top cheering in the observation booth. He was literally leaping off the floor in his enthusiasm. She wondered if he'd still feel that level of enthusiasm once he heard the song with her keyboard. He claimed the instrument had no place in a metal band.

"Wow," the host said, clapping. "The studio version of that song is amazing, but wow." He shook his head, seeming at a loss for words. "I know I'm not alone in thinking these ladies rock."

A muffled *woo* came from the observation booth.

Bryant laughed. "Steve Aimes apparently agrees."

"Which is odd," Iona muttered, glancing over her shoulder at Exodus End's drummer. The same drummer who hadn't had a single positive thing to say about them the night before.

Sage shot a knowing grin at Roux and said, "Not so odd, really."

Iona's eyebrows drew together. A feat of strength considering the length of her false eyelashes and how much eye makeup she was currently wearing. Roux shrank down on her stool.

"I guess I missed something," Iona said.

Which was a good thing. Iona insisted that nothing but trouble could come from a romantic relationship between band members—either in the same band or from different bands—on tour together. She'd even had her talent scout of a boyfriend back her up on that one. Not that Roux was planning to break the rule they'd all agreed upon before signing the contract to go on this tour—she agreed with the rule—but she couldn't deny that she was attracted to the guy in the observation booth who'd told her just ten minutes ago that he had something in his pants for her. She straightened in her seat and tried to look as nonchalant as possible as Iona scrutinized the members of her band.

"So why don't you introduce yourselves," Jack Bryant said, nodding at Iona. "Let's start with the one with the pipes. I had chills during the chorus."

Iona brightened at his praise, which focused her attention on him and allowed Roux to relax. Roux peeked at Steve, who was making obscene kissing faces against the observation booth glass. She slapped a hand over her mouth to keep from laughing. Max had his fingers pressed to his forehead and was shaking his head at the disgrace his bandmate was making of himself.

"I'm Iona Clark. In addition to singing lead, I also play bass guitar."

"The drawback to radio is that listeners can't see you. First, trust me when I say she's as gorgeous as she sounds. They're all as gorgeous as Iona sounds. Second, each of these women is color coded."

They all laughed at that description.

"Iona is purple," he added.

Iona said, "I hope you mean that I have purple streaks in my hair and as accents in my costume. If I were purple, you might want to do the Heimlich maneuver."

Obviously charmed, Bryant chuckled. "I'd rather give you mouth-to-mouth."

"My boyfriend might take issue with that," Iona said, "unless I actually needed CPR to save my life. Then he'd thank you."

"I should have known you were all taken," Bryant said.

"Not all of us," Sage said.

"You heard it here first. One of Baroquen's amazing guitarists is single," he said, as if it were a public service announcement. "The green one."

"The blue one too," Azura said, holding up one hand and wiggling her fingers in a wave.

"Well, that has my fantasies running wild." Bryant fiddled with his shirt collar.

"As it should," Azura purred, resting her head against Sage's shoulder.

The two of them always played around like they were lovers. Thing was, Roux wasn't entirely sure their faux onstage attraction was entirely fabricated. Not that it was any of her business.

"The second set of pipes in the band wears red. What's your name?"

"Roux Williams. And as you pointed out earlier, my real role is keyboardist. I just sing backup and harmony."

"I do wish we could have gotten a piano in here for you to play. If you missed our airing of 'Starlight' earlier, you must give it a listen. The entire song is amazing, but that keyboard solo . . . Wow. I bet smoke comes off your fingers when you play that."

Roux chuckled. "Maybe a little."

"We also didn't get to hear much out of Baroquen's drummer," the host said, turning his attention to Lily. "She's the fastest chick with sticks I've ever had the pleasure of thrash dancing to."

Iona snorted, but Bryant continued his description of Lily. "Her color is white. Is that a color? Or an absence of color?"

"I'm Lily Tanner," she spoke clearly into the microphone, completely ignoring his questions about white.

"I hear you're married to someone our listeners might be familiar with."

"Yes, I've been married to Jack for a while now. Well, not you, Jack." She twirled a hand in Jack Bryant's direction. "I mean Jack Tanner."

"Drummer for . . ." Bryant inclined his head in her direction and waited for her to fill in the blank.

"The Fallen."

"He's a lucky man. And I promised I'd ask," Bryant said, "so forgive me. When are we going to get a new album from the Fallen?"

Lily pressed her lips together. Roux knew how much she hated being put on the spot about her husband's currently defunct band. "I couldn't say. Jack doesn't tell me jack shit about his band."

Bryant's scowl turned to surprise when the observation booth door swung open.

"Shut the fuck up!" Steve shouted. "You're married to Jack Tanner? *The* Jack Tanner?"

Bryant laughed. "I take it Steve Aimes is familiar with the Fallen's iconic drummer."

"You have to introduce me to him," Steve said. "He's my hero."

Max grabbed the collar of Steve's shirt, hauled him back into the observation booth, and shut the door.

"I think he's every drummer's hero," Bryant mused. "Yours too, I take it?" he asked Lily.

"Of course," she said, with a tender smile, "but not because he's a renowned drummer. He's the love of my life."

Roux's heart fluttered with happiness for her friend. Lily and Jack were meant to be together. Roux could only hope that one day she'd find someone as perfect for her as those two were for each other. For some reason she glanced back at Steve at that thought. She caught him watching her, but he didn't look away and try to hide it. Nope. He winked. With uncharacteristic brazenness, she winked back.

She knew she shouldn't encourage him, but even when he was in the next room making a complete ass of himself, he made her happy. It was not a feeling she'd experienced with many men.

The host waxed poetic about Jack Tanner and the possibility of the Fallen releasing a new album for the remainder of their segment, which was only a minute or two, but long enough to make Iona's eye twitch. As they were exiting the studio, she caught Lily's arm and hissed, "Why did you *have* to mention that you were married to Jack?"

"I didn't. Bryant already knew. He's the one who brought it up." Lily grinned, not the least bit ashamed of her supposed slip. "And if you for one minute think I'm not going to claim Jack as mine, you've lost your mind."

Iona took a deep breath. "Sorry. Not your fault. I know that. We just agreed that we wouldn't mention our significant others while on tour. We want to make it on our own."

"Just be glad he didn't recognize you as Kayla Clark, the favorite of *American Voice* three years ago," Sage said.

"I am glad."

Iona's stint on the show was one of the many reasons the band had decided to play up their costumes. They didn't go quite to the extremes that KISS had gone to disguise their identities in the 70s, but the more the members of Baroquen could keep their personal lives out of the limelight, the better. While Lily and Iona wanted to keep their love lives behind closed doors, Sage and Azura were concerned about people from their dark pasts finding them. Roux liked her privacy, and as her gaze landed on Steve, who had already drawn Lily to one side to arrange a meeting with her husband, Roux knew she could never pursue anything serious with Exodus End's gorgeous drummer because *A*, the man probably didn't even know how to do serious and *B*, her privacy would be a thing of the past.

As Roux brushed past him, he slid his hand around her wrist. There was no pressure there—she could have easily slipped out of his grasp if she'd wanted to—but she drew to a halt, her heart hammering with anticipation and excitement. She couldn't figure out why he made her feel this way. Was it because he was so famous, so gorgeous, so electrifying, and paid her attention? Or was her heart far smarter than her head, which kept telling her to keep away from him?

"I'll hold you to that," Steve said to Lily.

"He's a fan of yours as well," she said. "He'll be delighted." She patted Steve's arm and followed the crowd through the observation booth and into the studio's large outer office.

"We have a date with the Tanners," he said, his gaze shifting to meet Roux's.

"*We?*"

"Yep. I won't take no for an answer."

"Won't it be obvious that we're involved if we double-date with the Tanners?"

"So we *are* involved," he said. "I wasn't sure we were on the same page."

He shifted her slightly so that the partially open door blocked them from the direct view of anyone in the office, and bent his head in her direction. Her eyelashes fluttered, lids covering her eyes as she leaned into his kiss. His lips brushed hers for only a few seconds, but the gentle touch set her ablaze with instant need.

They were involved, just like that?

Involved.

With him so near, she couldn't begin to process what that meant. Did he mean they should find the nearest mattress and explore the unmistakable lust between them? Or did it mean he was interested in something deeper than a sexual fling? Her head was spinning almost as fast as her heart was pounding.

"You have an amazing voice," he said, his own voice deep, soothing, and sexy. "Why didn't you tell me you could sing?"

"Keyboardist," she reminded him. "I sing backup vocals only."

"But you could sing lead if you wanted to."

His voice so close to her ear sent shivers down the side of her neck. God, she wanted his mouth against her throat. Kissing. Sucking. Licking.

"Thanks," she said huskily. "But I don't want to sing lead. My heart belongs to the piano."

"At least I know who my competition is."

What did he mean by that? Surely not what she thought—*wanted*—it to mean.

God, he smelled good. She tilted her face toward his neck, wondering if his skin tasted as delicious as it smelled. The heat of her breath rebounded on her parted lips as they moved closer to his throat. Maybe she should offer his neck the kind of attention hers craved.

"Don't forget I have something for you in my pocket."

The spell he'd cast over her broke, and she stepped back. She was grateful for the high heels of her boots so she didn't have to crane her neck to meet his gaze.

"I'm not sticking my hand down your pants."

"If you don't, I'm going to kiss you again."

She placed a hand on his chest, her fingers curling slightly to urge him close again. She shouldn't want him closer—not here where they could be discovered at any moment. But she did. She missed his heat already. "Is that supposed to be some sort of threat?"

He didn't bother responding, just made good on his promise. She'd never been kissed in such a way that her nipples ached so bad that she had to rub them against a man's chest, but the tug of his mouth on hers had her pressing her body against his, and when his tongue traced her upper lip, she moaned and slid her arms around his back to pull him even closer. She probably should have slept with him last night so that they could be out of each other's system. Surely one quickie would be enough to cool this heat between them. And she really needed to get her personal inferno under control.

"Fish your surprise out of my pocket," he said, "or I'm going to do that again, but this time I'll do it with the door all the way open."

He inclined his head toward the door that was blocking them

from view, and she didn't bother challenging his intention. She knew he'd do exactly what he'd threatened.

"Fine," she said. "Just don't get cum on my hand."

He laughed. "No promises."

She leaned back and assessed the front of his pants, trying not to focus on the magnificent bulge in the center. She didn't think he was even hard. How many pairs of socks did he have rammed in there? "Which pocket?"

"Figuring that out is half the fun."

She rolled her eyes—though, honestly, this was fun—and shoved a hand into each pocket. The man's jeans had apparently been painted on his body, so she had to wriggle her fingers to delve deeper. His breath came out in a shuddering huff and he grabbed her wrists, tugging her hands free.

"We'll have to pick up that game later," he said. "When I don't have to face a room full of people."

"Am I giving you a boner, Aimes?" she teased.

"Let's just say that the socks I keep in my pants are being displaced to the left at the moment."

"Hah!" she said. "I knew that bulge was socks."

He bit his tongue and shook his head. "No, babe. That was a joke. That bulge is all me."

She snorted and rolled her eyes again.

"I'll show you sometime." He slid his hand into his pocket and pulled out a slip of paper.

"It's the title to a car!" she shouted, loving to tease this man as mercilessly as he teased her. She had no use for a car; the van she shared with her sisters had room for everyone. "I can't believe you'd get me a Ferrari. You really shouldn't have."

"If you want one, it's yours," he said, not missing a beat. "But I think you'll find this is far more valuable than an Italian sports car."

She made a grab for the piece of paper he was holding up between two fingers. He flicked his hand toward his chest, keeping her from her prize.

"Is it a winning lottery ticket?" she asked.

"Even better."

She snatched the paper from him and opened it. After scanning the ten-digit number, she lifted an eyebrow. "Is this your phone number, Aimes?"

He grinned. "I told you it was awesome."

"Can I trade it for a winning lottery ticket?" she asked.

"You don't want to do that."

She couldn't tell if he was being cocky or teasing her.

"Maybe I don't want to associate with you," she said.

"You know you do."

"You have a dirty reputation."

"The dirtiest." He grinned. "That's why you want that number. It's the real deal. The one I actually answer."

"I don't think I'll use it," she said, tucking the slip back into his hand. "I need to be thinking about my career right now, not . . ."

He leaned close to her ear. "Not how hot you feel when I do this?"

He nipped her lobe, and fire spread through her veins like napalm. Holy Jesus. How did he know what he did to her?

"If you want more, you'll call me."

"But—"

He tucked the paper into the top of her corset, his fingers grazing the inner curve of her breast. "And you want more. Much more."

She wanted to lie and say she didn't. They had no business getting involved. For one thing, Iona would murder her for potentially destroying their band's opportunity to advance. For another, she couldn't think when he was near, and if they got naked together, she was pretty sure her brain would stop functioning entirely. If she was completely brain-dead, she wouldn't be able to play her keyboard.

"If I wasn't leaving for Atlanta in ten minutes, I'd give you what you want right here," he added.

He was leaving? She tried not to pout when she shot back, "You don't have any idea what I want."

His seductive smile made her belly quiver. "I know exactly what you want, Red. It's you who's struggling with the idea."

"I . . . I'm going to be too busy rehearsing and getting ready to leave for Europe to get involved with you."

"Call me. We'll talk. A month of deep conversation will give me plenty of time to get you addicted to me before we meet again."

As if.

"Roux?" Iona called from near the partially shut door. "What are you doing? I know networking is hard for you, but—"

Roux jerked away from Steve just before the door swung open. "Oh!" Iona said when she recognized Roux was not hiding from everyone. Just *almost* everyone.

"I'm chatting with Aimes," Roux said brightly.

"About?" Iona glanced at Steve curiously.

"How much keyboards suck," Roux said.

"She's almost got me convinced otherwise," Steve said. "Be seeing you, Red." He took her hand and gave it a curt, completely platonic shake. *Call me*, he mouthed before he wrapped an arm around Iona's shoulders and directed her out into the main office. "So where did you learn to sing like that, Pretty-in-Purple?"

Roux tugged at the bottom of her corset, trying to get her head on straight more than to rearrange her clothing. The piece of paper with Steve's number shifted against her breast. She was not going to call him. That was just asking for trouble. She took a deep steadying breath and then followed Iona and Steve toward the crowd congregated in the large cubicle-filled room.

As soon as she had a minute, she'd dig his number out of her top and toss it in the garbage. If she didn't call him, she was certain he'd lose his fascination with her before the tour started. Unless Butch's advice was correct and the best way to keep Steve interested was to keep him guessing. But what did Butch know?

The man with all the answers was already rounding up his passel of stray rock stars and directing them out the door to meet the tour bus so they could head south to Atlanta for their next tour date. Butch seemed to know what he was talking about most of the time, but Roux was sure his advice to her was an exception to the rule. Steve wasn't the kind of guy who liked to be kept hanging, and Roux pretended not to notice when he offered her one last searching look before he was shoved out of the radio studio.

CHAPTER 8

STEVE KNEW he was in trouble, but seeing as Trouble with a capital T was his middle name, he wasn't afraid to pursue it. He had every confidence that Roux would call him—probably within the hour. A woman didn't respond to him with such heat and intensity unless she wanted him, and in all of his worldly experience, he'd never met a woman who could resist what she wanted for long.

"I got that information you asked for," Butch said as they made their way to the limo waiting downstairs.

Information? Steve was so distracted by a certain fiery ice princess that he couldn't remember what information he'd requested.

As usual, Butch read him like an open book. "You forgot already."

"I—"

"It's the redhead. I get it." Butch's lips twitched beneath his mustache. "You haven't sealed the deal with her, so your little head is fully in charge."

"How do you know I haven't sealed the deal with her? She was in my room after midnight, you know."

"If you'd made your move, you wouldn't have been drying humping her leg in the studio upstairs."

"I wasn't dry humping—"

"You totally were," Max said as he followed a member of their security team out of the station. A smallish crowd had assembled near the building and released an excited cheer the moment they came into view. Max waved before ducking into the waiting car.

"The information you requested I gather about Bianca and that bitch who leaked personal band info to the tabloids."

Oh yeah. Steve had asked Butch to investigate the connection between his ex-wife and the woman he believed was her sister Tamara. He really was in a lust-induced haze if that very important task had slipped his mind. He'd better get all his information straight before Roux called—any minute now—and muddled his thinking again.

"Susan and Tamara are the same person."

Steve scowled. "I knew it." Even though she'd lost at least a hundred pounds since the last time he'd seen her, there was no mistaking Tamara Brennan's hungry eyes. He shuddered at the thought of her touchy-feely hands. The woman was half octopus.

"There's more, but let's wait until we get to the bus. You never know who's listening." Butch glanced around the crowded New York City street as if he could spot a spy from a mile away. He probably could.

Steve climbed into the limo and found Trey at the mercy of his big brother's knuckle sandwich. Sinners' rhythm guitarist wasn't struggling to get away from Dare. Instead, he was laughing and looking very pleased with himself.

"We haven't had a song at the top of the overall charts for over four years," Dare said.

Trey squirmed from Dare's grasp and plopped into the open seat next to Reagan. "So I guess this means I've finally surpassed the master." He finger-quoted *master*.

"I'd tell you not to get full of yourself," Dare said, his smile ear-to-ear, "but you guys are totally deserving."

"Sinners rules!" Trey said, throwing up a set of devil horns.

Steve squished himself into a limo seat. The car was made to seat eight, but was currently a couple of people over capacity. "Good news, I take it," Steve said to Trey as he maneuvered his ribs away from Max's bony fucking elbow.

Trey proudly showed Steve his phone, which displayed a screen shot of the iTunes sales charts. Sinners' new single sat brazenly in the top spot above a pop diva's latest release.

"Nice!" Steve said, fighting the urge to reach for his own phone to see if he'd somehow missed Roux's call. He was certain she'd be calling any minute now. Any minute.

When they reached the tour bus rendezvous point on the outskirts of the city and she still hadn't called, he wondered if he should have insisted that she give him her number as well or programmed his number into her phone. He'd have lost the sexy banter session with the phone-number-in-his-pants routine he'd lain awake dreaming up, but at least he'd know she wouldn't have to make the actual effort of dialing all the numbers. Nah, that was stupid. She'd call. He just needed to be patient. It had been less than an hour since he'd seen her. This wasn't the end of the world.

Play it cool, Steve. Play. It. Cool.

He had other things to deal with anyway. Like whatever information Butch had to share with him.

As the first person out of the limo, Steve had no one blocking his way as he hurried up the bus steps and to the back lounge. He took his phone out to see if the battery was drained or if he'd silenced the device by mistake. Nope. And no missed call from Roux. What the fuck? Did she not understand that he needed to talk to her about . . . well, about anything.

Focus, Steve. Focus.

His gaze landed on the copy of *American Inquirer* that contained the story that had broken his biggest dirty little secret—the existence of his second wife, Meredith. They'd parted on good terms—after less than a full day of marriage —agreeing that an annulment was the best solution to their drunken visit to a Las Vegas wedding chapel. He hadn't seen her since, but the tabloid had made him out to be a villain, naturally, who'd taken advantage of a young woman's starstruck gullibility.

Steve's eyes narrowed at the irritating paper. Ah, yes. That was where he needed to concentrate his attention. Not on the irresistible mix of fire and ice that complicated Roux Williams. If she was too busy to call him, fine. He didn't give a fuck. He had plenty of women to keep him occupied. Steve shoved his phone back into a pocket and picked up the tabloid. He scanned a single headline about the newest member of their band, Reagan Elliot, crinkled his nose in disgust, and tossed the paper back on the low table in front of the sectional sofa.

Steve needed to get to the bottom of this thing with Bianca and her dick-grabbing sister, Tamara. Or Susan. Or whatever moniker that horrid woman was going by these days. He sat casually on the semi-circular sofa and waited for everyone to get on the bus before he called out, "Reagan. Toni. I need you two back with me here pronto."

"They're both taken," Logan said. "No threesome for you,

Aimes."

Steve wasn't interested in either woman, though he had to admit Reagan was one of the sexiest women he'd ever encountered. She was doubly taken—every night, as far as he knew—by Trey Mills and her brawny bodyguard, whose name escaped Steve at the moment. Steve had written off tapping that sweet ass weeks ago.

Currently lacking in patience for bullshit—why the hell hadn't Roux called him yet?—he settled one ankle on the opposite knee and waited for Toni and Reagan to finish teasing Logan about their potential interest in a threesome with Steve. Toni eventually came to sit beside him, and Butch entered the room behind a befuddled-looking Reagan. He was carrying his trusty clipboard and wearing a grim expression.

"So what did you find out about Bianca and Susan?" Toni asked Steve.

Steve couldn't take any credit, so he didn't. "I put Butch in charge of finding out more about this tabloid." He picked up the trashy rag and shook it.

"You were supposed to find out," Reagan said. "Not put Butch on it."

"What's the point of having a lackey if you don't boss him around?"

Besides, there was no way in hell that Steve would voluntarily speak to Bianca. Every time he did, he wondered if they should try to get back together, because as shitty as she'd treated him in the end, the rest of their relationship had been pretty fucking terrific. And though he wouldn't admit it to anyone but himself, he sometimes missed her. A lot. He also wouldn't admit that the entire reason he'd married Meredith in Vegas was because she looked and acted so much like Bianca. He couldn't claim the same about Roux, though. She looked nothing like his ex and was about as far from her in temperament as a person could be. So what was with the instant attraction? Steve gave himself a mental shake. Now was not the time let Roux—or her refusal to call him immediately—command his thoughts.

"I heard that," Butch said, writing on his clipboard. "No supper for Steve."

Steve knew the punishment would never stick. Butch loved every member of Exodus End like a son. Spoiled-rotten sons.

"So what did you find out, Butch?" Toni asked, looking cloyingly sweet in her nerdy glasses and tight sweater. The chick had tits for miles. He tried his best not to stare at Logan's territory, but it was a constant struggle.

"Not much," Butch said. "*American Inquirer* has only been on stands for a few months, which I guess is good for us, because its circulation is relatively low for a tabloid."

"That is good news," Toni said, nodding eagerly. As the person indirectly responsible for the entire mess—it had been her snooping notes about the band that had been stolen to fill the pages—she probably wanted the whole situation to be shoved under the nearest rug and forgotten.

"With some digging, I found out *American Inquirer* is actually owned by a business conglomerate. Tradespar West."

Steve's heart skipped a beat. Un-fucking-believable. He slammed his fist on the table, wishing it was their record label's face—if record labels *had* a face. "You've got to be shitting me."

Butch shook his head. "I wish I were."

Of all the crazy coincidences. Steve didn't believe such twists of fate existed. Maybe *this* was the evidence Max needed to finally drop their label once and for all.

"Max!" Steve yelled. "Get your record-label-ass-kissing self in here."

"What's going on?" Reagan asked.

"Yeah, I don't get it," Toni said. "What's Tradespar West?"

Steve snorted. "They're a vast network of entrepreneurs who own all sorts of companies, most of them in the entertainment industry. Movie studios, a publisher or two, agents, production companies, advertising giants, a modeling agency, I guess a tabloid now, and most importantly, our record label. Max!" he yelled.

"Do you have to be so noisy?" Max stood in the doorway massaging one temple.

Maybe he did. Not that it mattered. Max never listened to him no matter how loud he became, not even when Steve was right and their self-proclaimed band leader was wrong. Which was most of the time.

"You know that tabloid that published all those bullshit stories about us last week?" Steve asked.

"And this week," Reagan added.

"Not really," Max said.

"Guess who owns them?" Steve asked.

"You?"

This gem would wipe the smug out of Max. "Tradespar West."

Max crossed his arms and shrugged. "So?"

Or not.

"So?" Was he a goddamned idiot or what? Couldn't Max let go of his pride for the greater good of their band for a single second? Steve jumped to his feet and pushed a crumpled page of the tabloid toward Max's chest. "Don't you see what this is?"

Max glanced at the paper. "A page from a tabloid."

Was he dumb or just playing dumb? Surely Max could see that they'd all been played. "A publicity stunt. I bet you every article in these pages is about stars connected with Tradespar in some way."

"Every star is connected to Tradespar in some way," Max said, looking entirely unaffected by the bombshell that had just dropped. "Directly or indirectly."

"But if that's true, then why have they been so focused on Exodus End?" Toni asked.

There was only one obvious answer to that.

"Because," Steve said, "our record sales have leveled off over the years, and they're looking for ways to increase sales." And the only thing record labels cared about was dollar signs.

"And making our temporary rhythm guitarist out to be a whore sells albums," Max said, glancing at Reagan. "Is that what you think?"

Reagan's unconventional romantic life was a huge rag seller; Steve had no doubt about that. But there was a deeper connection here. He could practically taste it.

"There's something suspicious about all this," Steve said. "Don't you think?"

"I think you're paranoid," Max said.

And no amount of logical discussion would sway Max into admitting that their record label was involved in shady business that affected them either directly or indirectly, but maybe if Steve got Max involved with trying to sort this shit out, he'd see the light, and they could cut ties from the corruption of big business once and for all. Steve knew they could be successful on their own. They didn't need a record label or a manager to tell them what the fuck to do.

After several minutes of arguing, Max asked, "So what do you want me to do about this tabloid situation?"

A spark of hope. Steve could scarcely believe Max was finally willing to cooperate. Unbelievable as it sounded, Steve was tired of hearing himself talk about the issue. He wanted some fucking resolution to their problems. He'd been spinning his wheels for years and getting absolutely nowhere.

"Ask Sam what he's up to," Steve said. "Ten bucks says he's behind this entire thing." Because like their record label, their manager only saw them as a paycheck with lots of digits.

"I'll ask him," Max said. "Not sure why you think he'll admit to anything."

"Because he likes you," Steve said. "He thinks the rest of us are a bunch of idiots, but you're his best pal. He trusts you."

"What are you guys talking about back here?" Logan asked from the doorway.

"Steve's continued search for a reason to cut loose from our record label," Max said before leaving the room.

"We don't need a reason!" Steve called after him. "But we have millions of them," he said under his breath. He'd never been a patient man, and he was resolved to get to the bottom of this mess with or without Max's help. He might even have to break his personal commitment to avoid Bianca for the rest of his life. How had her tabloid ended up under the umbrella of Tradespar West? Was it *her* tabloid? *Her* idea? Or was she just the head editor? The easiest way to find out would be to call her and ask.

Which reminded him that Roux hadn't called yet.

He checked his phone one last time before shoving it aside and concentrating on what was important at the moment—winning a decade-long argument with Maximillian Richardson. Steve promised himself he would prevail. Roux's ignoring him only added fuel to his fire.

It had been days—*days*—since Exodus End had left behind New York and the stubborn female who still hadn't contacted Steve via his personal and usually coveted number. He hadn't yet found the gumption to quiz Bianca about her involvement with Sam, Tradespar West and the stupid tabloid, and Zach—Steve's lover, according to the same stupid tabloid—had been particularly vocal about Steve's cowardice. Not that Steve found that surprising. Zach knew him better than anyone and wasn't afraid to kick him in the proverbial—or literal—ass when he needed it.

Zach was a little moody because the tour was set to wrap up in a couple of days, and he was convinced this was the end of his glory days. Plus, his boyfriend was a jackass, and giving him the runaround. Not to be outdone, Steve was very moody because he'd figured out the thing that must be keeping Roux from calling him was the continued tour. As soon as he was on break, he was certain she'd call. So, because neither guy was in the mood for a big after-party tonight, the two of them had ventured off to a local bar to brood in shared misery.

"What do you think Bianca is going to do to you if you call her?" Zach asked. He took a swig of his beer before adding, "What can she do to you that she hasn't already done?"

Steve scrubbed his face with both hands. Despite popular opinion, he wasn't a glutton for punishment. Just thinking about talking to Bianca after years of no contact made it hard for him to breathe.

"I'm not sure I'm over her."

Zach coughed and scratched his eyebrow. "How can you not be over her? She destroyed you."

And the effects were long-lived. Bianca had probably been over him for a solid five years. Steve was the one who could not move on. He might have been able to finally get over her if Roux had bothered to call him, but no. The one woman he'd been willing to take a chance on, the one woman who had gotten under his skin, wasn't interested, as she'd told him several times in their short acquaintance. The problem was that he hadn't believed her. Still didn't, in all honesty. She'd cave eventually.

"Bianca didn't destroy me." Lie. Steve dipped his finger in his whiskey. His stomach wasn't strong enough for alcohol at the moment, so maybe he could absorb the mind-numbing whiskey through his skin.

"She did something to you. Why else would you be sitting here with me instead of accepting that pretty brunette's open invitation?" Zach inclined his head toward the woman at the bar who repeatedly glanced at Steve and smiled.

Not accepting that invitation had very little to do with Bianca and a whole lot to do with a certain redhead he couldn't get out of his thoughts.

"Maybe instead of calling her, you should go see her," Zach said.

Steve's heart rate ticked up at the thought of seeing Roux. "I should have gotten her number. That was stupid of me. Butch insists he can't get it, but I think he's punishing me for arguing with Max. The asshole."

"If you can't locate her, all you have to do is show up at her office. You know where she works."

Steve rubbed his tight forehead. Had Roux mentioned where she worked? He couldn't recall. "I do?"

"Uh, the *American Inquirer.*" Zach rapped on Steve's forehead with his bony knuckles. "Earth to Steve. How much pot did you smoke tonight?"

Oh. Zach was talking about going to see Bianca, not Roux. What a buzzkill.

"I don't want to see her."

"I'll go with you," Zach said. "The tour is almost over. God knows I don't have anything better to do."

"I'd rather go to New York."

"To see that woman responsible for the destruction of Twisted Element?"

"She isn't—"

"I'm joking. Don't get so fucking defensive. I know it's not her fault."

Steve couldn't help but feel guilty. Even though Zach was cool with how things had turned out, Steve was not. He'd never forgive Sam for kicking Twisted Element off the tour without consulting anyone. It was one thing to fuck with Steve and his career and his money, but an entirely new level of suck to do the same to his brother from another mother.

"How about this idea?" Zach said, leaning closer to keep his words secret. "You go see Bianca and get your shit straightened out with her and her stupid fucking tabloid and her dick-grabbing sister"—yes, Zach knew all of Steve's secrets—"and then, as a reward, you head to New York to figure out why Red hasn't called you."

Steve couldn't help but laugh. He'd barely mentioned Roux to Zach, but the fact that he'd mentioned her at all made it very clear to his best friend since-forever that he was interested. Far more interested than he was in the brunette who was slowly stroking the side of her bare thigh while she sent him seductive glances.

"We didn't have much time to live it up in New York," Steve said. "Sounds fun."

"*We?* You want me to third-wheel your romance?" Zach gave him a sidelong glance. "What's gotten into you?"

"You're never a third wheel." He poked Zach in the side. "Spare tire, maybe."

Zach ran a hand over his perfectly flat belly. He never did get the level of ab definition that Steve pulled off—and they did the exact same workout—but there was no extra flab on him.

"Is that why the ladies don't look at *me* like that?" He nodded toward the brunette who was now hiking her skirt a few inches higher. "I work out."

"It's probably the blaring wail of their gaydar keeping them at bay."

"And your overbearing heterosexuality keeps all the guys away, so I get *no* action."

"That's a tragedy," Steve said, swirling his finger in his whiskey and lifting it to his mouth for a tiny taste to test if his stomach was ready for a gulp. He knew Zach didn't want any action. At least not with anyone but his current boyfriend, Enrique—an up-and-coming film actor who was determined to keep his personal life out of the spotlight. Enrique liked that the world thought there was something going on between Steve and Zach. It took some of the pressure off him, and he knew Steve was no threat for Zach's romantic affection. Steve's love for Zach was deeper than the ocean, but purely platonic.

"Let's get out of here," Steve said, shoving his glass toward the center of the table. "I'm not in the mood for the bar scene tonight."

Zach tapped his forehead. "I wonder if we could figure out how to get Roux's number on our own. There is this thing called the Internet."

Steve stood and tossed a few large bills on the table. "You don't think I googled her?" Because he had.

"And?"

"Their band is surprisingly good at keeping personal information separate from their stage personas." Steve wished Exodus End was good at that. And there were no listings for Roux Williams anywhere in New York.

"So you have no clues. Nothing she talked about that might give you a hint as to her whereabouts."

Zach chugged down Steve's abandoned whiskey before following him toward the door.

"I know she was raised by a foster mother in Boston. All the women in her band were." But he'd searched for Roux Williams in Boston directories too. No matches. He'd even tried a few different spellings. It was as if her real name wasn't Roux.

"Sounds like something a local paper might pick up on and publish as a special interest story."

Steve slapped Zach on the back. Brilliant. Steve should have tried looking her up through her family connections. "I don't know why I asked Reagan's ex-cop boyfriend to dig up dirt on Sam. I should have asked you, Sherlock."

"I don't like to dig up dirt. I just think it's time you found yourself a decent partner, and not a single woman has turned your head except this Roux. So even if you're timid enough to let her get away, I'm not."

"Timid?" Oh, those were fighting words.

CHAPTER 9

ROUX FINGERED the rather ratty slip of paper she couldn't bring herself to throw away. She'd been incredibly busy for the past week with tour preparations and rehearsal after rehearsal after rehearsal. Iona was an incurable perfectionist, and she was determined to turn the rest of them into perfectionists as well. Roux had therefore found it easy to put off calling Steve while she was playing Baroquen's set list until her fingers were numb and singing harmony until she went hoarse. But they couldn't very well rehearse without their drummer, and Jack had all but kidnapped his wife and taken her somewhere for a few days' rest before they headed off on tour. Lily hadn't protested her abduction at all. And Roux had been envious. How great would it be to have a husband who looked after your well-being and took you away from it all when you were stressed-out beyond your limits? Roux sighed. That would be fantastic. She drew her finger down the center of the scrap of paper and over the number that she decided was too late to call. She'd missed her window of opportunity. He had probably already forgotten about her. Not that she was thinking Steve would make a great husband like Jack, but he was a worthy distraction—an off-limits but worthy distraction. She sure could use a distraction right about now. The closer their day of departure, the more nervous she became. It didn't help that Iona was constantly snapping at everyone that they weren't ready.

A key fumbled in the front-door lock, and footsteps approached Roux where she sat at the battered dining table.

Raven.

Roux knew the sound of her gait. She'd always had a strange ability to recognize a person by their step. The ability had started when she'd been young and had dreaded the sound of her father returning home after a night of drinking. She could usually even predict by the amount of his stumbling whether he would yell or hit or just pass out. As a child, she'd known the footstep of every person who'd lived in their apartment building as well and had naturally expanded her talent to include the safer footfall patterns of her sisters and Mama after she'd been brought into Mama's fold.

Roux palmed the phone number before pretending to examine the tour schedule in front of her. Great Britain, France, Italy, Russia. By the time her eyes read *Germany*, her heart was thundering with excitement.

"Pack a bag," Raven said. "We're going to Boston."

Fear gripped Roux's throat, and her breath caught. Her gaze snapped up to read Raven's expression, which didn't hold the concern Roux had anticipated. Mama Ramona wasn't exactly young anymore, and while she was in relatively good health, Roux couldn't help but worry about her. "Is something wrong?"

"Yeah. You look like a raccoon that's been punched in both eyes." Raven grabbed Roux's chin and turned her face toward the light. "How long has it been since you've had a decent night's sleep?"

Roux winced. "How long has it been since we signed that tour contract?"

"I figured as much. Going home for a few days will do you good."

A trip to the enormous brownstone—*home*—sounded like heaven to her, but . . . "Iona will never go for it."

"It was her idea, actually. We're all going. Well, except Lily, who's probably making love to her gorgeous and considerate husband on a beach somewhere, the cow." Raven's eyes rolled upward.

Roux chuckled and rose to her feet, heading for the corner of the room where three sets of bunkbeds and several mismatched dressers were situated. Their studio was basically one big room, though they'd put up a few strategic screens to separate spaces; there really wasn't any privacy to be found except in the tiny bathroom.

Both she and Raven had their bags packed before Iona, Azura, and Sage entered the apartment ten minutes later.

"Did anyone call Mama and tell her we were coming?" Iona asked, looking almost as exhausted as Roux felt. If they were in such bad shape *before* heading out on tour, what would they be like in three months?

"I sent her a text," Raven said.

"She doesn't use text messaging," Iona said.

"She replied with a middle finger emoji," Raven said with a laugh. "I'm assuming she meant the thumbs-up, but you never know with her."

"Maybe she's glad we finally moved out and really does want us to fuck off," Roux said. The woman had enough on her plate without four uninvited visitors showing up out of the blue.

"If she doesn't want us to visit, I'll sleep in some guy's dorm room at Parkline," Azura said, referring to the music college they all had attended at one time or another. "If I don't get out of New York for a few days, I'll go insane."

"I'm with you," Sage said, heading for her bunk and yanking an overnight bag out from under it. She tossed it to Azura and pulled out a second bag.

"Just let me call her," Iona said, and retrieved her cellphone from her pocket.

By the smile on Iona's face, it was obvious that Mama was more than happy for them to visit. Roux could hear the occasional exclamation in Italian from the woman she couldn't wait to see in five or six hours, depending on traffic.

"Raven said you sent her a middle finger emoji," Iona said, grinning as she teased Mama.

"What?"

Roux could hear her clearly.

"Let me talk to her," Roux said, a hand extended toward Iona's phone. "You need to pack."

"Roux wants to talk to you while I pack," Iona said. "Yes, I'll drive carefully. I promise. No, Kyle isn't coming, but he might show up while we're there." Iona laughed. "Yes, I remember the rule about men in the house. Here's Roux." She handed her phone over and hurried off to find her bag.

"Hi, Mama, how have you been?"

"Ah, mi tomato," Mama said, and Roux laughed. That nickname used to embarrass her, but now she loved it because Mama was the only one who still used it. "Iona is keeping you busy, yes?"

"How did you guess?" Roux watched their unstoppable band leader, who was currently packing with careful precision. Sage and Azura were randomly tossing stuff into each other's bags, figuring they'd be sharing living quarters in Boston just as they did in New York.

"It's Iona!"

Roux pictured Mama shrugging her shoulders as she spoke.

"Are you able to eat well? I wonder will rock stars have food for you on this tour."

Roux smiled, remembering how Mama had always gone out of her way to make sure Roux's plate was meat free, which usually meant she'd had to prepare something special just for her. Mama never once complained, and until recently, Roux hadn't realized what a bother that must have been for years.

"Don't worry, Mama. I'll eat just fine." The memory of a yummy plate of eggplant lasagna and some fine company raced through her thoughts. "These rock stars know how to take care of a lady."

"They probably try to get you drunk. You can say no. Don't be afraid to say no, mi tomato. You can be too polite sometimes. Just say no."

"I've already run into that situation."

"Aaaand?"

Roux could easily picture Mama's assessing stare. "I said no."

"What did he say to that?"

"How did you know it was a he?"

"Mi tomato's beauty will draw the attention of all men."

Roux snorted. "Uh . . . he wanted to know why I don't drink."

Mama was quiet for a moment, and Roux could practically feel the woman's enormous heart and immense empathy reaching through Iona's phone to tug at her.

"And did you tell him?"

"I did."

"Did he leave you alone then?"

"Actually, no." She glanced over her shoulder to see if any of her sisters were paying attention. The three packing were too busy trying to squeeze into the bathroom for toiletries to pay her any mind, and Raven was fiddling with Facebook on her phone. "He gave me his number."

"Oh. So you are seeing him now?"

Mama knew Roux had a hard time trusting anyone, especially men, and those who offered her alcohol in particular.

"I haven't called him. Too busy."

"But you like him."

"I don't know." She suddenly felt much younger. Like junior high age, when she'd gone to Mama for all her boy advice. "It's been a week since he gave me his number. Don't you think that's too long?"

"You have to call him and see." There was a loud crash on Mama's end, and Mama shouted, "Oh, Caroline be careful. You'll cut yourself." To Roux she said, "Have to go. See you soon."

"Love you, Mama."

"To the stars and back." Mama had always said the moon wasn't far enough away to encompass the depth of her love.

Roux ended the call and nibbled on her lip. Maybe it wasn't too late to call Steve. She had an excuse. Not a good one, but she did have one. It was sort of legitimate. But what would she say to him? And why oh why had she waited so long?

"Problem?" Raven asked.

Roux snapped out of her Steve-trance. "What?"

"You got off quick." Raven nodded toward the phone in Roux's hand.

"I think Caroline broke something."

Raven chuckled. Their youngest sister—no, Margaret, their newest sister, was younger—was notoriously clumsy. "Figures. So who have you been too busy to call?"

Roux pinched Raven's arm. "Were you eavesdropping?"

"Obviously."

"Snoop."

"Cow." Raven poked her in the shoulder. "Spill, or I'm asking Mama."

"She doesn't know him."

"It's Steve Aimes, isn't it?"

Dammit. Raven knew her too well. "No," Roux said. "Just drop it, okay?"

"You have Steve Aimes's number and you haven't called him," Raven said *very* loudly.

"Steve gave you his number?" Azura asked, poking her head out of the bathroom.

"You haven't called him?" Sage peeked over Azura's dark head.

"Stop it."

Iona shook her head. "Don't you know how to take an opportunity when it's offered to you?"

"He just wants to get in my pants," Roux said, though she wasn't convinced that was his only agenda.

"Exactly," Iona said.

"You're the one who told us not to sleep with guys on tour!" Roux reminded her, which was the main reason she hadn't called him. That, and she was sort of a coward when it came to matters of the heart.

Iona smirked. "We're not on tour yet."

Roux tossed Iona's phone at her. Luckily, she caught it. "I can't believe you! You made us pinky swear!"

Iona shrugged. Maybe her exhaustion was making her lax in her rules. "Not on tour yet," she repeated.

"You should call him right now," Azura said.

"And let us listen in," Sage added.

"Hell no," Roux said. For the first time in over a week, she didn't want to talk to him at all.

"Why did he give you his number?" Iona asked, her face screwed up in confusion. "I thought he hates keyboards."

"Maybe." Raven grinned. "But he definitely likes the women who play them."

Roux shot her a look of warning. Raven was the only one who knew about her short adventure in Steve's hotel room, and so far she'd kept the secret, but Roux could tell she was about to spill all.

"Something happened," Azura said, hurrying over to sit on the back of their worse-for-wear plaid sofa, her feet on a threadbare cushion. She settled her elbows on her knees and her chin atop her clasped hands and waited for the show to begin.

Roux had no plan to be the afternoon's entertainment.

"I keep having this strange memory of being carried in the arms of a tall, handsome man with long dark hair and exotic eyes," Azura said. "And being in a limo with you and him. And a bucket of vomit."

So she did remember that night.

"No idea what you're talking about," Roux said, turning her back to Azura and reaching for her bag. She slung it over one shoulder, ready to hit the road, but no one else moved. "We'd better get going before rush hour."

Traffic was always a nightmare, but it extended into all seven layers of hell after three p.m.

"Was Steve in the limo that took you guys home?" Sage asked, scrambling over the back of the sofa to sit beside Azura. Roux could imagine them hauling out a big bucket of popcorn to share while they watched her squirm beneath their magnifying glass.

Roux shrugged. "Maybe."

"He carried me to bed, didn't he?" Azura asked, squirming with excitement as her drunken memories wriggled free of her subconscious. "I thought I dreamt that, but—" Her eyes went wide, and she covered her mouth with one hand. "Oh God. Did I really *puke* in front of him?"

Roux could not keep a lid on that precious morsel. "Oh yeah, you definitely puked. Three times if memory serves."

"I didn't get any on him, did I?" she moaned.

"No. You hit the bucket."

"Thank God. So . . ." Azura pinned a laser-focused stare on Raven, because everyone knew Raven knew all of Roux's business. "Did she do the nasty with him?"

"Azura!" Roux stomped one foot.

"Little Miss Goody-goody?" Raven snorted and then shook her head sadly. "Nope. She made him order her a vegetarian lasagna, ate it in his room, and fucking left him with a hard-on."

Mouths wide, Azura, Sage, and Iona all gaped at Roux.

"How do you know he had a hard-on?" Roux snapped, crossing her arms over her chest.

Raven rolled her eyes. "He had one before he even got you alone in his room. It's not like I wouldn't notice a schlong that big seeking its freedom from pants that tight."

"You guys are the worst," Roux said, swinging toward the door, her bag bouncing against her back as she marched forward.

"She did kiss him, however," Raven said.

Ugh! Sisters!

"You didn't even give him a hand job?" Iona asked, falling into step behind her. "Too cruel, Roux. Too cruel."

"We talked, okay? He was . . . nice."

"Nice!" Iona laughed as she followed Roux down the steps. Roux could hear the rest of her sisters finally vacating the apartment. They were talking over each other about hand jobs on first dates. "If Steve Aimes was being *nice*, you were doing it wrong."

Roux paused on the landing and turned to look up at Iona. "And that's why he gave me his personal number, right?"

She turned and flounced down the steps, smiling at her small victory.

"Hey, little sister," Iona called after her, "I'm the band's vocalist. I'm the only one allowed to drop the mic."

Roux found her victory to be short-lived, as there was no way to spend five hours in a van with four obnoxiously nosy women and not end up calling Steve just to get them to leave her the fuck alone.

CHAPTER 10

OF ALL THE WORST fucking timing. Steve had been waiting for this call for years—so maybe it had only been a week—but there was no way he could answer while sitting across from his cruel ex-wife. And there was no other word to describe her unless it was ball-busting, demonic, evil, heartless, and too damned beautiful for her own good. So, with an internal moan of agony, Steve silenced his cellphone, somewhat contented by the knowledge that even though he'd missed Roux's call, he now had her number and could call her back after the hell on earth he was currently experiencing ended.

"Was that important?" Bianca asked with an alligator-like grin, nodding toward the phone he crammed into a pocket.

"You know nothing is as important as you are," he said.

Her brown eyes brightened. "Took you long enough to figure that out."

What did she mean? He'd always done his best to show her that she came first in his hectic life, but he didn't want to discuss that now. That would start an argument, and they'd never get to the point of his visit. How had Zach talked him into this again?

"You know why I'm here," he said.

"Because you missed me?" Her silky black hair slid across her cheek as she tilted her head flirtatiously.

Less and less, he admitted to himself, but yes, at the beginning it had been hard. "Are you working with Sam Baily?" he asked.

She flinched, her hand sliding across her desk to pick up a pen, which she began to click repetitively. Steve's instinct was to push her before she collected her story or whatever it was she was thinking about so hard, but one benefit of marriage was getting to know a person's habits and reactions. Bianca clicked her pen when she was stalling for time, which meant she was fabricating some lie, but he also knew that if he pressed for information before she settled on her story, she'd react with that volatile temper of hers. One that he used to enjoy watching explode back when he'd been under her spell. While he waited for Bianca to open her mouth, he wondered why Roux had suddenly decided to call him. He was sure it was because the North American leg of Exodus End's tour had finally ended. She did seem like a stickler for the rules, and that rule she'd spouted about not being able to date a musician on tour . . . Well, he wasn't on tour for the next two weeks. They could do a lot of damage to each other in two weeks.

"You're thinking about a woman right now," Bianca said, fire in her gaze.

The smile Steve hadn't realized had spread across his face turned bitter. "It isn't you."

"Of course it isn't."

"And since your tabloid continues to insist that I'm gay, wouldn't I be thinking about a *man*?"

She chuckled. "Is that why you're here? Your overinflated ego couldn't handle a little rumor?"

"You know Zach and I are only friends."

"Friends become lovers all the time, Stevie." She laughed.

God, he hated that laugh. It no longer carried joy, just cruelty. He also hated being called Stevie, and she fucking knew that. "You know that's not the case, but that's not why I'm here. How the fuck are you tangled up with Sam Baily?"

"Don't you cuss at me."

Steve took a breath to calm himself. She always focused on a triviality to direct his focus away from bigger issue. The difference between now and when they were married was that he recognized what she was doing, so instead of blowing a little thing out of proportion by getting into an argument about him swearing if he damned well felt like fucking swearing, he centered himself and asked again, without the added expletive, "How are you tangled up with Sam Baily?"

"You already know he owns the tabloid. You wouldn't be here if you didn't know that."

"I know his conglomerate of an entertainment enterprise owns the paper. And I recently found out that he's not just our manager but also the CEO of Tradespar West. What I don't know is how you became the tabloid's head editor."

She smiled sweetly. "I was the most qualified for the job."

"Because you have years of experience as a reporter or because you know a lot of dirt on me and on my band?"

She shrugged, clicking her pen again, her eyes trained on her thumb.

Steve didn't let her collect her fabricated story this time. "But not enough dirt, so you sent your sister to dig for more."

She snorted. "That didn't go as planned. Never expected someone as business conscious as Eloise Nichols to hire her own daughter over my highly qualified sister."

"You got Toni into a lot of trouble. Stealing her notes and publishing them."

Bianca's gaze lifted. "No one stole her notes. Her boss, her own *mother*, gave them to us."

"For money."

"Yes." She rolled her eyes, as if he were a few brain cells short of a functioning cerebrum. "That's generally how a tabloid operates."

"Sam didn't put you up to this, *any* of this? It was all your idea." He wasn't buying it. The coincidence was too outrageous to have been produced by chance, and in Steve's mind, Sam was responsible for every negative thing that happened to the band. So much so that he refused to give the man credit for any of their countless successes.

"He provided a list of struggling entertainers he wanted us to cover in the first few issues."

Struggling entertainers? Her words were a slap to the face. "And we were at the top of that list."

"A priority. Yes."

"And you don't feel the least bit guilty about making my life hell?"

She grinned. "You know I get off on it, Stevie."

And apparently Sam had known she would. "So if I tell you to knock it off . . ."

"I won't."

"And if Sam tells you to knock it off?"

"He's the boss, but . . ." She leaned forward, a snake ready to strike. ". . . he won't. This little stunt gave him the exact results he wanted."

"To make me hate him even more?"

"To help his struggling entertainers sell some albums."

Steve's stomach clenched with a mixture of rage and revulsion. "We don't need stupid publicity stunts to sell records. We don't need *him*. Or *you*." He'd lost the lid on his temper. Damn. He'd promised himself—and Zach—that he wouldn't let her get to him, but she knew exactly how to rile him.

"It's time for you to leave," she said.

He agreed with her on that point and shifted out of his chair and to his feet. He paused at the door as he remembered another question he wanted to ask her. "Are you dating Sam's nephew, Pyre something-or-other, the guitarist of that lame opening band we ditched at the start of the tour?"

Bianca's eyebrows rose, and for a second he thought he'd caught her, but she smiled. "Do you think I'd settle for *that* when I've had you?"

He couldn't tell if she'd complimented him or insulted him.

"Besides," she added, reaching for a stack of files on her desk to relay the point that he'd taken up more than enough of her valuable time. "Tamara's more the type to do whatever her man wants in order to keep him, don't you think?"

Tamara and Pyre? Steve cringed—whether it was on Tamara's behalf or Pyre's, he wasn't sure—but decided they made a perfect couple. He hoped they didn't procreate.

"I'm glad Reagan beat the pants off that dude in our contest," Steve said. The lame comment was the only ammunition he had against Pyre Vamp.

"You and me both. I don't think I could stomach watching Tamara throw herself at you while her current boyfriend looked on." She smiled smugly, as if she knew something he didn't.

"Wait . . ." So Bianca knew her sister had the hots for him? Steve had kept that bit of information to himself. He'd even left Bianca off the paperwork when he'd had the restraining order drawn against Tamara. But maybe Tamara wasn't quite that smart.

"Yes, I know she's always wanted you. You could have turned her down."

"I did turn her down."

"Sure." Bianca's face was hard and cold, and she wheeled her chair toward the computer to her right. "Close the door behind you when you leave."

"I did turn her down." He wasn't sure why he cared that Bianca believed him.

"Then how does she know about the freckle on your dick, Steve? Huh? Explain that."

It wasn't exactly a secret, but . . . "Because she's managed to get her hands on it more than once." She especially liked to employ a sneak attack when he was sleeping.

"Exactly. Go away now. I'm finished with you in every way imaginable."

He opened his mouth to defend himself further, but decided it wasn't worth the energy. Bianca had left him on a lie—a string of lies—but the hurtful truth was, she had found another man to warm her bed, and he could not forgive or bring himself to care about someone who wrongfully distrusted him with every molecule in her tight little body.

"This will all come back to bite you in the ass eventually, Bianca," he said before he let himself out of her office and quietly closed the door behind him, serving his pathological need to have the last word.

He found Zach leaning over the reception desk flirting with an overwhelmed-looking Asian American woman. Zach was an incurable flirt with either gender, but he especially liked to fluster women. Steve didn't get it, but hey, at least he'd kept himself out of trouble for the most part.

"If he's sexually harassing you, you should press charges," Steve said as he came up behind Zach and gave him a hearty slap on the back.

"Oh," the young woman said. "He wasn't. He was just saying—"

"That she has the most beautiful skin I've ever seen. It's like the petals of a perfect lotus blossom."

The woman flushed and lowered her eyes. "Thank you."

"What kind of moisturizer do you use?" Zach asked. "I need to get some for my boyfriend's ass so it's all nice and smooth—"

Steve clamped a hand over Zach's mouth. "We talked about this. No oversharing about the gay stuff."

The woman groaned and glared up at Zach, who yanked Steve's hand from his mouth.

"I meant what I said. You do have gorgeous skin. And you can trust a compliment from a queer because you know I'm not saying that to get you into bed."

The woman laughed. "I guess that's true. Unfortunate, but

true."

Zach offered his flirtee a friendly wave as he followed Steve out of *American Inquirer*'s deceptively bright office. Steve had honestly expected to enter some dark, blood-stained torture dungeon when he'd barged through the front door an hour ago. And now he couldn't get out of the place fast enough.

"So were all your questions answered?" Zach asked. "You were in there forever."

"Not really, but I did get a phone call while Bianca was busting my balls. Couldn't take it right there in front of my ex, but she finally called."

Zach brightened. "Roux?"

"I think so. Unless it was a wrong number. But it had a New York area code." And Steve refused to believe that it wasn't her finally breaking her agonizing silence.

"Are you going to call her back?"

"Eventually." Steve shrugged. "Let's see how she likes to be kept wanting."

"We're still going to New York to surprise her, aren't we?"

"Yep. The jet is waiting on the airstrip."

Zach punched Steve in the shoulder. "I like having friends in high places."

The car Steve had hired to take him and Zach from MacArthur Airport to New York's East Side pulled to a stop in front of a rather dilapidated building in the East Village near dark. Steve cringed at the dingy brick structure, wondering why the entire block hadn't been condemned.

"Are you sure this is this place?" Steve asked the driver.

"That's the address you gave me."

Steve was rather proud of the sleuthing that had secured Roux's address, but if they hadn't known Lily was married to Jack Tanner, they might never have found a link to the place. Zach found the only public mention of Lily's full legal name in her marriage license. Apparently an insanely secretive bunch, the women of Baroquen didn't used their full names in any public venues.

Steve climbed from the cab, wondering if Lily had used a fake address and if he was wasting his time. Only one way to find out.

He didn't want to leave Zach standing around on the street by himself in this neighborhood. Didn't want Roux to *live* in this neighborhood. "Stay here," he said to Zach. "Wait for me," he told the driver. "I'll be back soon." Maybe with a woman he planned to whisk away on his band's private jet. He wasn't sure she'd be impressed, but it was worth a go. He hoped she liked surprises, because he had yet to call her.

He climbed from the cab, distinctly aware of the very expensive watch he wore and his gold mugger-bait necklace, and counted the floors of the building. Roux's apartment was on the eleventh floor if her apartment number could be trusted, and the building only had ten floors. Maybe she lived in the attic. There were no lights on in those windows.

He approached a set of buzzers and saw the names Clark, Moore, Tanner, Williams, et al. next to the topmost buzzer. So they did live there. Maybe they were out. Or maybe they couldn't afford to pay their electric bill. He pressed the button and waited for a response. When none came, he glanced back at the car and shrugged at Zach, who was peering out the car window. Guess he'd better try calling her. Perhaps arriving on her doorstep hadn't been his best idea.

He called the number from the call he'd missed earlier that day when he'd been in Seattle failing to get any real answers from Bianca. After a few rings, a breathless voice answered.

"Hello?"

It was Roux. Her voice haunted his wet dreams; he'd recognize it anywhere. And he couldn't stop a smile from spreading across his face.

"Sorry I missed your call earlier. I was on a plane." A little fib to make his surprise easier to spring.

"Oh," she said. "I thought you were off tour for a couple of weeks."

"I am. That's why I'm standing on your doorstep. I couldn't wait another second to see you. Can you let me in?"

"You're outside?" He heard hasty footsteps and the creak of a heavy-sounding door opening. "I don't see anyone. Wait. Do you mean you're in New York?"

"That's where you live, right?"

"I'm not going to ask you how you got my address," she said.

He chuckled. "That's good."

"But I'm in Boston, visiting my family."

"Oh," he said, turning toward the car and taking long strides in that direction. The Boston address had been much easier to dig up.

Mama Ramona didn't guard her identity as diligently as her girls did. "Pretend I didn't call."

"What ar—"

He cut her off by disconnecting the call, opened the car door, and slid into the still-warm seat next to Zach.

"Well?"

"She's in Boston."

"Shit," Zach said.

"How far is it to Boston?" Steve asked the driver.

"Over two hundred miles."

Nope. Not taking the scenic route. "Take us back to the airstrip," he said. He'd asked the pilot to stay on call. He'd hoped they'd be heading to Los Angeles next, but it would have to be Boston.

His phone rang, and he grinned when he saw it was Roux. "I said, pretend I didn't call."

"But—"

He hung up again and could imagine he heard a frustrated growl coming from the general direction of Massachusetts.

"I'm not sure you're going about this the right way," Zach said.

"She's hooked," Steve replied, gripping his thighs as their driver attempted an Indy 500 maneuver around a slow truck. "Besides, when she recognizes how much trouble I went through just to see her, she'll—"

"Get a restraining order?"

"Naw. She won't be able to say no."

"I would get a restraining order."

"Not if you like me, and trust me, she likes me."

Zach chuckled. "You never were short on self-confidence. It borders on cockiness."

"When you've got the goods to back it up, it's not hard to be cocksure." Steve grabbed his crotch to drive his point home. Yep, still had it.

"Guess we'll see who's right on this one. I'd put money on you leaving Boston with a shiny new restraining order."

His phone dinged with the arrival of a text message. From Roux. *Will you tell me what's going on?*

He grinned and put his phone away without answering her question. "I'd put money on me leaving Boston with a shiny new woman."

"Kidnapping is a felony," Zach reminded him.

"I don't think it will come to that, but I will make her mine."

Zach settled back in the seat and watched the city pass. After several minutes, he said, "I wish some guy wanted me as much as you want her."

"And let it show by jetting all over the country for a moment alone with you?"

Zach sighed. "Yeah."

Steve was glad they were finally on the same page. "Want to change your bet now?"

"Maybe. What's so special about this girl anyway? I haven't seen you like this since you fell for Bianca." Zach slapped his thigh. "Wait. She isn't some megabitch cheating ball-buster, is she?"

"That's why I brought you along. You knew what Bianca was long before I figured it out."

"You're using me as a bitch detector?"

"And you're somewhat decent company, but don't let it go to your head."

"You know you're going to miss me while you're living it up on tour in Europe."

Truth. But Steve was sure Roux would be a worthy distraction. "I told you I'd hook you up with a plane ticket. You can still tag along."

"I wouldn't give Sam the satisfaction of knowing how much I wanted to be a part of this tour." It was dark inside the cab, but Steve could hear the hurt edge in Zach's tone. "Fuck him."

"Fuck him up the ass with a rusty-nail bat."

Zach snorted and then laughed. "Ouch."

"Anything for you, bro."

They were sitting on the airstrip waiting for clearance for their unscheduled flight when Steve's phone rang again. He bit his tongue and nodded, giving Zach a knowing look, but was surprised to find the caller wasn't Roux. It was Max. Max so rarely contacted him when they weren't touring or in the studio that a shiver of dread snaked through Steve's belly before he answered.

"What's up?"

"Did you get your fucking royalty check?" Max asked without pause.

"Not sure. I haven't been home yet."

"Where the hell are you?"

"New York, on my way to Boston."

"On our jet?"

"Duh."

"You can't use the band's jet for your private entertainment."

"Why not? We all do."

Max huffed out a breath. "I guess I'll call Dare, then. See if he got his."

"Did they not arrive or—"

"Oh, it was sitting in my mailbox as expected." Max paused for a second. "The problem is its size."

"That huge, huh?" Steve didn't really need more money, but he didn't turn it down.

"Small. Shockingly small. Like they left off half a dozen zeros small."

"We just put out a record. Our checks should be huge this quarter. Is the new release not on there, or— "

"It's on there, but there are more reserves against returns than sales—so bad, it's cut into our residuals."

"That can't be right."

"It's right here in black and white. We need to figure out what to do about this," Max said.

"About our shitty sales, or—"

"Our sales cannot be this shitty, Steve. Someone must be cooking the books."

"Sam?" Steve said slowly. Max usually blew up whenever Steve tried to lay any deserved blame at the feet of their manager, who they just found out also headed their record label and the tabloid that Bianca fucking worked for. The man was more crooked than a mountain stream.

"Of course Sam, or someone he pays. Who else could it be? When you get back to LA, the band needs to get together and have a meeting. Assuming we can get Logan away from Mexico or the Bahamas or wherever the hell he took off to with his woman."

"It will be fine," Steve said, finding it odd that he was saying those words to Max. "It's in our contract that we can audit our sales at any time, and if Tradespar West is stiffing us, we'll get it all back in a settlement."

"I'm going to get that ball rolling, if it's okay with you and the others."

Steve pulled his phone from his ear and checked it over to make sure it was real. Did Max just agree to investigate his best buddy—and the ass he kissed—for fraudulent royalty reporting? No, he hadn't *agreed* to it. He'd fucking suggested the idea.

"Steve?" Max said. "You still there?"

Steve brought the phone back to his ear. "Yeah, man. Uh, that sounds like a perfect plan to me. I'm sure Logan will go along with it and Dare too, but you should call them both and make sure."

"Will do. I hope I'm wrong about this."

"You'd rather our sales be that shitty than admit Sam Baily is toxic and a crook and has no one's interest at heart but his own?"

"Exactly," Max said.

Man, Max sure did not like to eat crow.

"I guess we'll find out in that audit," Steve said, knowing better than to pick a fight with Max. It didn't get either one of them anywhere.

"Right. Have fun in Boston, or wherever you end up, and tell Zach I said hey."

How did he know he was with Zach? Probably because Steve was always with Zach. "Will do. Keep me posted. I should be home within the next couple of days."

After he hung up, he turned to Zach. "Did you hear that?"

Zach grinned. "Sam's really done it this time. He touched Max's money."

"Nobody fucks with Max's money."

"And you can finally tell Max you told him so."

Delight shuddered through Steve's body. "You have no idea how good that will feel."

"A hell of a lot better than being fucked with a rusty-nail bat."

"Unless you're into that kind of thing."

Zach cocked his head to one side, bangs sliding to cover one eye. "Wouldn't you like to know?"

"Actually, no, I would not."

Their pilot's seductive voice came over the intercom. "We've been cleared for takeoff," Jordan said. "That means turn off your phone, Steven."

He would never tire of listening to that gorgeous British accent of hers.

Steve took a few seconds to send a text to Roux before shutting off his phone, and then he settled back in his seat for the short flight to Boston.

CHAPTER 11

SEVERAL PAIRS OF HANDS REACHED for Roux's phone when a text came through a little before nine. Sage had the fastest fingers.

"Is it from him?" Azura asked, looking over Sage's shoulder.

"Yep," Sage said, her gaze lifting to Roux's.

Roux shrugged as if she didn't care that he'd finally had the decency to text her back, but her heart had started hammering the moment the text tone had sounded.

"Well?" Mama Ramona said from the doorway between the kitchen and the enormous dining room where they were playing a rousing game of Monopoly. "What does it say?"

"See you soon," Sage read.

"He's coming here?" Iona said, eyes wide.

"I told you he would," Raven said, elbowing Roux in the arm.

"Isn't anyone else concerned that he's a stalker?" asked Mitzi, who had somehow become a high school senior when Roux hadn't been paying attention.

"He can stalk me any day," Azura said.

"He's not a stalker," Sage said, clasping her hands under her chin and fluttering her eyelashes. "He's in love."

Roux rolled her eyes. "We scarcely know each other."

"I think that's about to change," Iona said. "It's really going to suck when you have to dump him before the tour starts."

Iona's stare was hard and could easily be mistaken for a warning. It wasn't a warning, was it?

"*Puh*," Mama said, setting down the refilled bowl of chips and reclaiming her spot in front of a huge collection of Monopoly property cards. "A tour lasts but a few months. Love can last a lifetime. True love lasts even beyond death."

"Mama!" Roux said. "We scarcely know each other."

The endearing yet mischievous grin they knew so well spread across Mama's aging face. "I think that's about to change." She copied Iona's sentiment and punctuated it with a saucy wink.

"Well, maybe I don't want to see him," Roux said.

Everyone—from seven-year-old Margaret all the way up to the septuagenarian that headed their patchwork family—laughed until they were breathless. Roux wished this cat had never left the bag. Her family could be merciless when it came to teasing one of their own.

On her next trip around the board, Roux landed on one of Mama's hotels and went bankrupt, which gave her the out she was looking for. "I'm pretty tired after that long drive today anyway," she said. "I think I'll turn in early."

"I guess Steve is mine, then," Azura said. "He's the kind of guy who needs someone who knows how to party."

"This is why he likes our Roux so," Mama said knowledgeably—as if she'd met the guy and knew how he ticked. "She is good and pure inside and out. I never have to worry she will get into trouble. A man wants that when he is ready to settle down."

Azura scowled. "We can't all be goody-goody. Besides, I don't think settling down is what Aimes has in mind, Mama. Here, let me show you a picture of him." She opened up a screen on her phone and began searching online.

"Good night," Roux said loudly, getting a few mumbled responses from the girls and women crowding around Azura's phone.

"Oh," Mama said, a hand fluttering over her chest. "This one is trouble."

"Which is why I didn't call him until you all talked me into it. Now he's coming here and . . ." She couldn't freaking wait to see him. Ugh! Why? He *was* trouble. She shouldn't court trouble, but damn, she wanted trouble to court her. "I'm going to bed."

"Me too," Raven said. "Good night."

Everyone was still ogling online pictures of Steve when Raven followed Roux out of the dining room and slid shut the ten-foot-tall wooden pocket doors behind them.

"Let's get you ready." Raven grabbed Roux by the wrist and

tugged her up several flights of stairs to the room they'd shared as teens. It was still decorated with Raven's death metal posters and Roux's colorful daisies. The house had eight bedrooms, so Mama said this one would always be waiting for them whenever they needed to come home. As an orphan, Roux needed that stability. Mama had recognized that need before Roux had. She'd never met a better, more selfless, understanding person than their mama.

Raven threw open their closet. "Something sexy, but not too obvious," she said, sorting through a rack of clothes they'd left behind. They could wear the same size tops, so there was a large collection to choose from. Raven had more ass and shorter legs than Roux, so they could also share skirts and dresses, but not pants.

"I'm not dressing up for him," Roux said.

"Yes, you are," Raven said. "He's going to all this trouble to see you. The least you can do is make him realize *with a single glance* that the effort was worth making."

"Do you really think he's coming here?" Her belly quivered from nerves or excitement, she wasn't sure which. Maybe both.

"For sure. Why didn't you call him sooner, you damned idiot?"

"He's only interested in one thing, and though I'm interested in that too, sex with the hottest guy on Earth isn't enough of a motivator for me to put our careers at risk."

"First of all, yeah, it is." Raven gave her a pointed look before shoving a black T-shirt into her side of the closet and pulling out a black sweater. Raven's entire wardrobe was black. "Second, do you really think all he wants is sex? I don't think the man has a hard time getting laid."

Which did not make her feel any less nervous. She was no virgin, but she wouldn't call herself overly experienced either.

"He obviously sees something special in you," Raven continued, shoving the black sweater back into the closet and pulling out a black button-down shirt. "You just have to let it sparkle." Raven held the shirt up to Roux's chest, her head titled to one side. Her eyes lifted to meet Roux's. "You do like him, don't you?"

"I think so." Her hands clenched, and she squeezed her eyes shut. "Yes. I do. I don't want to, but I really do."

"He's scorching hot."

He was, but that wasn't what had her out of her head. "I don't think he lets many people get close to him, so he let me see parts of him that many don't get to see—"

"Such as his dick?"

Roux swatted at her. "In the short time we were together, he made me feel like I could be someone special to him. I know that sounds stupid."

Raven grinned. "I think it's cute. Take off that sweatshirt," she said. "And consider burning it. It makes you look frumpy."

"I love this sweatshirt." She'd had it for at least ten years, and it still chased away the chill that often permeated the bricks of the big old brownstone. Roux took off the ratty blue garment, but she dropped it on the end of her bed rather than setting it ablaze.

"Ugh! Not *that* bra." Raven closed one eye, lifted a blocking hand, and turned her face away from the sight of Roux's less than sexy underclothes. "I suppose your panties are equally granny."

"White cotton," Roux admitted. "He's not going to see them anyway."

"Just in case." Raven hurried to Roux's old dresser to sift through her underwear drawer. "Have you shaved recently?"

Roux snorted. "You really think I'm going to get laid, don't you?"

"Not think," Raven said, removing a rather skimpy black bra and panty set from Roux's I-never-actually-wear-these drawer. "Hope."

Well, Raven could just keep on hoping, because Steve was going to get the "we can be friends talk" if he did show up. And Roux couldn't understand why he actually would. Or how. She supposed millionaire rock stars had resources unavailable to her.

Raven was putting the final touches on Roux's makeup when the doorbell rang a little before eleven. Roux tried to sit still so a wayward mascara wand didn't jab her in the eyeball, and she forced herself to consider how rude it was to show up at someone's house at this hour, but her entire body was bursting with excitement and anticipation.

"Now aren't you glad you're going to greet him like this"—Raven waved a hand down the front of Roux's body like a game show hostess showing off a top prize—"instead of wearing a rag of a sweatshirt and no makeup, and with bed hair?"

Roux hopped off the chair she'd been sitting on for the past half hour, gave Raven a quick hug, and said, "I love you forever no matter what." She rushed to the bedroom door, yet once there, she took a deep breath, then another, to settle her suddenly jumbled nerves before turning the knob.

In the foyer several flights down, Mama was speaking in her

teacher voice—loudly and very pronounced. "It's a little late, don't you think?"

Roux couldn't help but grin. Mama would never let him get away with inappropriate behavior. She wouldn't care who he was.

"Truly sorry about that, ma'am," an unfamiliar male voice said.

Roux's elation took a tumble down the stairs. Steve had gotten her hopes up for nothing. The jerk. He must be pissed at her for not calling, and this was his revenge for her cowardice, which he probably thought was a slight. She had to admit that from his perspective, her lack of contact would seem that way.

She turned back toward the bedroom, and Raven must've read the disappointment on her face, because she gave her a sad look of pity. Her sister had gone to all that trouble to make her look presentable for nothing.

"Can I at least tell her good night?" Steve's voice carried up the stairwell, and Roux froze. "I'll come back in the morning like a civilized human being."

"Let me see if Roux's up for company," Mama said, her voice stern. "You two wait right there."

Roux gave Raven another quick hug, wondering why there were two guys in the foyer asking to see her—she'd never felt so popular—and forced herself not to race down the stairs like one of the Brady Bunch. For one thing, she'd break an ankle in the shoes Raven had talked her into wearing. For another, she didn't want to seem too eager.

Cool, calm, collected, she repeated to herself as she slowly navigated the stairs. She met Mama on the second-floor landing.

"You have a visitor," Mama said loudly enough so that Steve and whoever was with him were sure to overhear. "Would you like me to send him away?" Mama winked.

"It is pretty late," Roux said, squeezing Mama's elbow and working hard to keep the excitement out of her tone. "Who is it? Is it important?"

"I'm not sure. Some man from California. Says his name is Zach."

Zach Mercier was here! Holy fuck noodles. Roux loved Twisted Element. She licked her lips and smoothed her palms over her fitted blouse. "I don't know any Zach."

"It's Steve," he called up the stairwell. "Don't make me come up there and get you."

Mama covered her mouth to lock a laugh inside. Roux figured

they'd teased him enough and moved to the railing to look down into the foyer.

"Oh, hey, Steve," she said, her hair swinging forward to brush against her face. She pushed it back impatiently. "What are you doing here?"

He didn't respond. He just stared up at her as if a miracle were unfolding before his eyes. Had he always been this gorgeous? His dark eyes this mesmerizing? His jawline that strong? His hair that touchable? Lips that kissable? Throat that lickable? The butterflies flitting around in her belly kept her from shifting her gaze any lower. She tried swallowing them down, but that only made them spread, until even her fingertips and toes were tingling. What in the world was wrong with her? Was she having a damned stroke?

"I'll be right down," she said, stepping away from the railing and giving herself a mental and physical shake. She had not expected the silly crush of hers to intensify in his absence.

Mama squeezed her arm. "It was the same for me when I found Emilio. The rush. The yearning." Emilio was the husband Mama had lost long ago but still loved to this day. "Don't keep him waiting."

Roux had always wanted to experience such a heady romance, but the very idea of finding it with Steve Aimes was terrifying. She'd have to wait for another once-in-a-lifetime attraction to come along; how rare could it be?

She used the handrail to descend the stairs, not trusting her stupidly trembling knees to keep her on her feet. He stood at the foot of the stairs—Zach background noise behind him—and watched her, never once taking his eyes from hers. That was probably why she forgot that the bottommost step was ever so slightly higher than all the others and therefore ended up pitching forward when her foot hit the foyer floor.

Steve's hands shot out to steady her, but instead of helping her regain her footing, he pulled her body against his and tilted his face into her hair.

"Did you do that on purpose?" he murmured to her.

"What? Trip and make an ass of myself?" No, but now that she was pressed against the heat of his hard body, she was glad for her lapse of grace.

"No. Make the whole world stop so you could walk down those stairs."

An amused huff escaped her, and she leaned back slightly to look into his eyes. Her clever retort died on her tongue as she got lost in the warm brown of his gaze.

"Kiss him!" a young voice squealed from somewhere above.

"Yes, please put him out of his misery," Zach grumbled from near the front door.

"Caroline, to bed!" Mama said sharply. The scampering of several sets of feet was punctuated by copious giggling and then by two doors shutting.

Roux wanted to kiss him, but there was an awkwardness between them that she was sure was the result of too many prying eyes.

"So what brings you to Boston?" she asked, finding the mental facility, or perhaps stupidity, to stand on her own and put some space between them. His hands shifted to her lower back, not letting her get away.

"You have to ask? I'm a huge White Sox fan."

Roux grinned at him. "Our team is the Red Sox."

"You're all the red I want to see in Boston."

A strangled gagging sound came from near the door, and Roux peered around the fine specimen in front of her to find Zach Mercier trying to choke himself to death. His hair was shorn short except for a long section at the top tied back into a short ponytail that bounced theatrically with the motion. Roux laughed.

"Aren't you going to introduce me to your famous friend?" Roux asked, her gaze shifting back to Steve's face. He was still staring at her in that way that made her feel all tingly inside.

Steve blinked and then twisted to look behind himself. He waved at Zach. "That's the cab driver. He needs to wait outside."

"I told you that you wouldn't need a third wheel when you got here."

Zach approached Roux with an extended hand. When Roux accepted it for a friendly shake and Zach brought it to his lips instead, he earned a well-placed elbow in the ribs from Steve.

"I'm Zach, and you must be the gorgeous redhead who has my friend here making a complete ass of himself. You think you know a guy."

"Roux," she said, sliding her hand free of his and for some strange reason resting it on Steve's hip.

Footsteps descended the staircase behind her, and knowing Mama Ramona's familiar gait from years and years of her walking each floor to check on her girls after they were all supposed to be asleep, Roux stepped out of Steve's arms and turned. She didn't feel that she was doing anything wrong—not exactly. It was more out of respect for her foster mother and the rules that she'd followed since she was taken in that made her put distance between herself and the man. It wasn't easy, considering his energy drew her like an electromagnet.

"Perhaps your guests would like some refreshments," Mama said before she even reached the foyer.

"Right!" Roux said, spinning toward the hall beside the stairs that led to the kitchen and dining room at the back of the brownstone. She felt like a flustered teenager with the first boy she'd ever had a crush on visiting her house for the first time. She was sure that if Steve had found her at her own apartment rather than at her childhood home, their intimacy would be progressing into a heated inferno by now. So maybe it was a good thing that they had a chaperone or two. She doubted she could have kept her head on straight or her clothes on at all if she were alone with him. And she sure wouldn't be able to have the "let's be friends" chat, whenever she managed to get around to it.

"Would you like something to eat or drink?" she asked, looking at Zach. Because she was afraid she'd sound breathless if she looked at Steve.

"That would be great," Zach said, moving forward to stand beside her. He jabbed a thumb in Steve's direction. "This guy forgets to feed me when he makes me chase girls all day."

"Girls?" Roux chanced a quick glance at Steve. "Plural?"

"Don't worry," Zach said. "He only flew to Seattle to see that other woman so he could clear his plate enough to focus fully on you."

"Seattle?" Roux squeaked.

"I am going to murder you," Steve said, shoving Zach's shoulder.

Zach grinned, his pale blue eyes twinkling with merriment. "So, what kind of refreshments are we talking about here?" Zach asked, which prompted Roux into motion.

"Let's go see what we can find," she said, trying and failing not to fixate on the woman in Seattle that Zach was talking about and wondering why mentioning her would justify his murder.

"There are leftovers from yesterday," Mama said, zipping around the three of them like a road-raging driver. "Do you boys like chicken Alfredo, or are you vegetarians like my Roux?"

Zach chuckled, though Roux wasn't sure if it was because

Mama had called them boys and they were both in their early thirties, or if he found going without meat humorous.

"I haven't had a home-cooked meal in months," Zach said, quickening his pace to fall into step with Mama, which left the spot beside Roux for Steve to claim.

"Mama, I can take care of this," Roux said. "Why don't you go up to bed? You must be exhausted."

Mama paused in the kitchen doorway and turned to give Roux a look that said, *as if I'd leave you alone with two men*. Mama tended to forget Roux was a grown-ass woman who could take care of herself and had been alone in the company of men countless times, but Roux wouldn't argue. Not when she was under Mama's roof. It was an argument she would never win.

"I'd love some chicken Alfredo, Mrs. Rivera."

Roux scowled. How did Steve know Mama's last name? She'd never mentioned it to him.

Steve smiled the kind of smile that would make most women swoon. "And the delight of your company."

"Charming me will not clear the route to my daughter," Mama said brusquely before turning to enter the kitchen.

"Ah, I love her so flipping much," Zach said, slapping Steve on the arm before trailing Mama.

Roux started to follow, but Steve caught her arm. "So what's blocking my route to you? I want to know exactly what I'm up against. A string of broken hearts? Virginity gifted only in marriage?"

Roux snorted. "I'm no virgin." She flicked her gaze up to meet his. "Disappointed?"

"I'm no virgin either."

"Aw, now I'm the one who's disappointed." She winked at him, glad he wasn't a hypocrite. Worldly men who expected their women to be virgins? Yeah, no.

"Is it my partying or my love of meat or because I insulted you or—"

"Is *what* your partying or your disgusting diet or your big mouth?"

"The reason you didn't call me."

"I did call you," she reminded him.

"Why you didn't call immediately."

"I already explained it to you. I can't see you while we're on tour together."

"That's really the only reason?"

"The only one," she assured him.

"So after the tour is over?"

"We can be more than friends. If that's what you want."

A little breath—sounding like relief—escaped him. "That's definitely what I want. I thought I was going to have to try to change for you, but all I have to do is wait a few months?"

She nodded, sure they'd be the longest few months of her life, and hoped some other woman didn't turn his head in the interim. "I don't want you to change for me or anyone."

"But you are asking me to change," he said. "You're asking me to be patient, to delay gratification. When I see something I want, Roux, I don't wait. I go after it. And I want you."

His fingers slid across her cheek and into her hair. Her heart, which was already pounding from his nearness, kicked into a faster gear as he leaned in and kissed her tenderly. The heat between them surged, and her lips parted as a soft moan escaped her. He deepened the kiss, drew her closer, engaged her senses until there was only him. The sound of his breath, the taste of his mouth, the texture of his shirt, and the hardness of his back muscles beneath her fingertips—the scent of his body, the dizziness with which he unbalanced her—all made him real to her yet at the same time strengthened her fantasies, her ideal of him, because everything about this moment was all she'd dreamed of since she'd watched him walk out of that satellite radio studio in New York.

"Roux, would you like me to fix something for you?" Mama called from the kitchen.

Mama might as well have dumped a cold bucket of water over her head. Roux pulled away from Steve and called back in a surprisingly steady voice, "No, thanks. I'll just have a cup of tea."

"I'll put the kettle on."

Steve's gorgeous mouth quirked. "Should have known you'd be a tea drinker."

"And what's wrong with being a tea drinker?"

"Not a single thing."

She pressed her body closer to his, reminded again of how different they were in every capacity, yet realizing that those differences were what pulled her toward him. Turning her face into his neck, she allowed her lips to gently caress the pulse point in his throat. He shuddered, arms wrapping around her back to pull her closer.

"If you're trying to help me control myself," he growled close to her ear, "you're failing spectacularly."

"Not sorry," she whispered, rubbing her lips against his skin. She wanted to experience every inch of him with her mouth, her hands, her naked body. She'd never wanted a man this much before. It was a little frightening to realize how close she was to spinning out of control, and at the same time, the thought of letting go excited her to a new level.

She already knew that "let's just be friends" conversation was never going to happen. But they did need to have a different conversation.

"How did you know Mama's last name was Rivera?"

Steve cringed. "If I tell you, you'll think I'm a stalker."

She chuckled. "I already think that." But she wasn't afraid of him. Not even a little.

"I tried looking you up, but there's no mention of Roux Williams anywhere except as a band member of Baroquen."

Because Roux wasn't her legal name.

"So how did you manage to track me down?" There was an oversight somewhere that would have to be remedied. She wasn't afraid for herself—she had no living enemies—but she was concerned for Azura. No one could know who her younger sister really was.

"Lily's marriage certificate."

The connection still wasn't there. "Uh . . ."

"Lily's maiden name is on the license and on your lease."

They'd thought they'd done enough to hide their identities. Apparently not. But who besides Steve would know there was a connection between Jack Tanner and Azura? The link was several times removed. Roux's sister-danger sensors settled. Azura wouldn't be compromised by the association. Not possible.

"That still doesn't explain how you managed to show up here," she said.

"I found an article about Mama Ramona's altruism in an old newspaper well before I figured out where you lived in New York. I didn't want to bother your mother or scare her, so I was saving that connection as a last resort."

"She would never have told you how to find me, you know."

"Yeah, I know. The more I talk about this, the more I realize how out of line I was. I'm sorry. I was out of my head wanting to see you again, but I'd never do anything to harm you or your family. I hope you can forgive me."

Forgive him for wanting her desperately? For making her feel like the most important person in the world?

She slid a hand along his jaw. "You're forgiven." She leaned in to kiss him again.

Several sets of footsteps clambered down the stairs, and Roux straightened, her gaze lifting to meet Steve's. "I guess you can tell that there's no such thing as privacy in this house."

Steve chuckled, his palms skimming down her bare upper arms, which sent a shiver down her spine. "As a man who spends several months a year on a tour bus, I'm used to that."

His reminder of the tour gave her the strength to step away and enter the kitchen.

Behind her, Iona said, "Well, look who it is. Did you come to give us advice about the upcoming tour, Steve?"

Roux cringed. She was never going to hear the end of this from Iona.

"Nope. I'm on vacation." He entered the kitchen and caught Roux's hand. And when that simple touch made her gasp, he smiled. "Are you coming with me?"

"Where?"

"On vacation."

She wanted to jump at the invitation, but Baroquen still had a lot of rehearsing to do. Then again, Lily was going to be away for a few more days, so why shouldn't she enjoy the same freedom?

"I can be gone until Monday," she blurted. Wait, what was she saying? Even though she technically could be gone that long, she didn't typically go on extended weekend trips with men she scarcely knew. Strangely, however, she felt like she'd known Steve her entire life, even though she didn't truly know much about him at all. She wondered if that instant connection was due to his fame and notoriety, or if there was some cosmic link between them.

"I'd say we should leave at once, but my overworked pilot would probably like some sleep. Can you be ready to go in the morning?"

Yes popped out of her mouth before she could muster up a shred of restraint. "Where are we going?"

"I should go home to LA," he said, "but that can wait until Monday. Where would you like to go?"

"Surprise me," she said.

His gorgeous mouth twisted into a crooked smile. "I know just the place."

CHAPTER 12

STEVE GRINNED at the excitement on Roux's face as she watched out the jet's window. His stomach sank in protest as the wheels lifted off the ground and they went airborne. She probably thought he was taking her to some exotic, private island where they could frolic naked in the surf without a care, but they weren't going there until tomorrow. Today their destination was far more important to him, and he was certain she'd recognize that. He wanted this woman's heart, and after seeing her around the diverse group of girls and young women that she considered sisters—and the remarkable woman who'd taken them into her home and heart—he was pretty sure he knew how to win Roux's affection. Once the spiritual connection between them cemented, then he'd do something about the physical aspects of their attraction, assuming she'd allow the level of intimacy he craved. She provided him with a challenge he hadn't had to deal with in a long while, and he found her unusual mix of passion and restraint irresistible.

She turned her head to smile at him. "Won't you at least give me a little hint?"

"You said I should surprise you," he said, unable to stop himself from taking her hand, which was resting on the leather-covered armrest between them.

She turned away from the window and leaned her upper arm against his. "Now that I have you alone, tell me all about yourself."

All about himself? He didn't want to scare her off. Not when he'd finally made some progress, but he did want someone who could love him despite his flaws, maybe even because of them. Was she someone capable of that degree of devotion? He licked his lips and lowered his gaze to the cream-colored leather on the back of the seat in front of him.

"What do you want to know?" he asked.

"What's your favorite color?"

Oh. So this was about trivialities. Not the important stuff. He could handle that. He turned to her and wrapped a lock of her hair around one finger. "Red." He lifted his finger to his mouth and kissed the coppery strands of her hair. When his gaze met her gold-rimmed green eyes, he reconsidered, his hand moving to cup her face. "And green. And gold."

"Do you have indecisive tendencies?"

"*You're* my favorite color."

Her cheek warmed beneath his fingertips. "I can't decide if you say such things because you're romantic or you know exactly how to make a girl lose her head."

An amused huff escaped him. "What if it's a little of both?"

She licked her lips and rubbed her teeth over the full bottom curve of her mouth, a sure sign that she was thinking about being kissed. He'd keep her waiting a while, the way she'd kept him waiting all last week. "What's your favorite color?"

"It's always been red, but now I think maybe it's you."

She laughed, the sound delighting him deep into his soul.

"It sounded sexy when you said it, but ridiculous coming out of my mouth."

He shook his head. "Everything about your mouth is sexy." His thumb brushed her lower lip, and she shuddered, her eyelashes lowering to veil her gorgeous eyes. A surge of lust flooded his groin, and he decided if he was going to get through this entire flight with his dick in his pants, he'd have to stop touching her.

"We've reached cruising altitude," Jordan announced over the intercom. "Feel free to move about the cabin."

Steve unfastened his seat belt, and though every instinct told him to pounce on the bewildered-looking woman beside him, he stood and went to the small minibar near the closed cockpit.

"Would you like something to drink? A snack?"

Steve wasn't sure he'd ever be hungry again after that enormous breakfast Mama Ramona had insisted they eat before they left that morning. Zach had still been stuffing his face when Steve and Roux said their goodbyes and left him to his own devices among the dozen or so females at the table.

Steve opened the cabinet and flinched at the variety of alcoholic beverages inside. The fridge wasn't much better, but he was glad to find mixers like orange juice and club soda.

"We have water. Juice. Soda."

He started when a hand settled on the small of his back. He hadn't heard her leave her seat.

"You know what I want," she said.

She was not making this easy on him.

He swallowed against the sudden dryness of his mouth, wondering what in the hell he had to be nervous about. He knew his way around the female anatomy. It was the heart he had trouble with. "Water?"

"You," she said, her hand sliding down his belly.

"We might get around to that later." Her sexually aggressive behavior reminded him of most of the women in his life, and he wasn't sure if he liked it. When her hand brushed against the inside of his hipbone and his dick leapt to full attention, there was no mistaking that his body liked it, but his baser impulses never had his overall best interests in mind.

"Later? Are you really not interested in initiating me into the Mile High Club?"

He took her questing hand and shifted it to the hard ridge struggling to burst free of his fly. He groaned as lust swirled through him, shredding his limited control. He sucked in a breath, trying desperately to collect the tattered remains of control. "Does that answer your question?"

"Then what is it?" she asked. "Are you mad at me for not calling you sooner?"

"Yes," he admitted, then he shook his head. "And no. Your self-restraint is a complete turn-on."

Her sensual lips turned up at one corner. "That's funny. Your complete lack of restraint does the same for me."

The shreds of his self-control slipped entirely from his grasp. His hands rubbed over the gentle curve of her ass, drawing her hip against his aching groin. She pressed her soft breasts against his chest, lips parting as she strained her mouth toward his. Heat radiated from her center, and he shifted his thigh between her legs, seeking the fire building within her. He'd probably get burned, but damned if he lacked the control to turn away from it. Before he completely gave in to the mindless desire consuming him, he clutched handfuls of her hair. Her eyes fluttered open, the green-gold gaze smoldering and inquisitive in the same instant. A shudder raced through him.

"If we do this, everything will change between us," he said. "Are you sure that's what you want?"

"Don't try to convince me that you haven't ever had a frivolous weekend fling before, Steven Aimes."

Was that what this was to her? A frivolous weekend fling?

"I want more than that." He bit his lip. He hadn't meant to admit that to her. Such an omission made him vulnerable. He hated feeling vulnerable.

She touched his face, a gentle smile on her lips. "We can't be together during the tour," she said.

This again. "Your rule, not mine."

Her head inclined slightly. "Yes, my rule. But this weekend I have no rules, so you can think of this as a trial run. We can both figure out if this heat between us is worth pursuing after the tour is over. I thought I could wait." Her hand slid down his belly and unfastened the top button of his fly. "But since I last saw you, every minute of every day is invaded by thoughts of you, and I don't think I can function in that condition without at least knowing the constant distraction is worth it."

"And you're betting that it's not," he said, releasing the tangle of her hair, taking her hand and shifting it back to his cock.

"That's not a wager I'm willing to place without more evidence."

Steve groaned as her hand stroked him through his jeans. Why was he even trying to fight this?

He knew why. He still wanted more from her than a frivolous weekend of sex, but they could start with that and build from there. All he had to do was make sure her thoughts never cleared of him. Shouldn't be all that hard to accomplish, even on tour. Especially on tour. He felt like he ruled the world while he was on tour. There was no way she'd be able to resist him when he was in that frame of mind.

Roux tugged his shirt up his belly, and Steve leaned back to help her draw it over his head. She leaned forward to pepper his chest with kisses, her hands fumbling with her leggings as she slid them off over her butt; she kicked them, her flat shoes, and panties aside. Holy hell. Once she made up her mind, she was all in. She pressed her hands against his shoulders.

"I want your mouth on me," she said.

"We both want that," he said, sinking to his knees and lifting her leg to rest on his shoulder.

His mouth watered at the smell of her sex; his balls tightened in response to her heat. He parted his lips to draw her clean-shaven pussy into his mouth, his tongue prepared to work her swollen clit. The floor dipped beneath him, and he grabbed her ass with one hand and the countertop with his other to steady them.

The intercom crackled, and Jordan's sultry, accented voice said, "We've hit some nasty turbulence. Buckle up and prepare for a bumpy ride for the next thirty minutes or so."

Steve was prepared to ignore the warning, but Roux was struggling to free herself from his grasp. She launched herself into her seat and fumbled with her seat belt, gorgeous eyes wide, fair complexion downright ghostly. Steve ran a hand over his face, trying to find the strength to climb to his feet.

The plane dipped again, and Roux whimpered. "Come put on your seat belt," she said, grasping both armrests with a white-knuckled grip. "And bring my pants."

He grinned. He'd been on enough flights that turbulence didn't bother him much. "Come get them," he said.

"Don't be a dick. I'm half naked here."

"I can fix that." He crawled over to her seat, grateful for the immense amount of legroom in the luxury jet. Kneeling between her feet, he pulled her top off over her head and, before she could gather her wits enough to stop him, removed her bra as well.

"Now you're all naked," he said.

Every inch of her was perfection, especially the unique nuances of her flesh that most would label imperfections. He planned to get to know every part of her exterior intimately—from the round, puckered scar between her luscious breasts to the large flat mole on her hip to the pale blue paths of the vessels just beneath her fair skin—before he delved into her interior. He was especially enjoying the critical glare in her gold and green eyes as she raised an eyebrow.

"And how will the rescue crew who scrapes me off the ground after we crash explain my nakedness?"

"We aren't going to crash." He leaned forward and drew the tip of his tongue over her nipple.

"Steve, I'm not in the mood anymore."

He grinned. "I can fix that too."

His leisurely lick shifted to a powerful suction and there was no mistaking her gasp of excitement. Easy fix. He kissed his way to the scar made by the tragedy that had almost ended her and rested his lips there gently. He'd wanted to press his lips to that very spot since the moment she'd revealed her past, but now that he'd made that desire a reality, he had a hard time coming to terms with the sudden knot in his throat. To think someone who was supposed to love this treasure of a woman unconditionally had scarred her so severely—inside and out—had him pressing his forehead to the center of her chest and breathing through the tangle of emotion he was starting to relish. God, it had been so long since he'd allowed himself to feel like this. To care so much about a woman. It had been too long. And it might end up being much longer because he knew how severely it hurt when someone you loved with your entirety tore your fucking heart out.

Whoa. Step back. He hadn't even fucked Roux yet, and his emotions were bouncing around like a drop of sweat on a drum skin. He, Steve the Callous, was entertaining thoughts of love. Was he ready to take a chance? A chance with this woman he scarcely knew but felt he'd always known? Would he be able to let Roux in, the way he'd let Bianca in? Let her see all of him? Not just the cool parts that he showed the world, but also the lame parts, the twisted parts, the gentle parts, and even the vulnerable parts. He'd soon know if she was worth his confidence, his utter devotion, and the potential heartache, because he'd never learned to love any other way. He was an all or nothing sort of guy, and he knew it. The realization scared the shit out of him.

"Did you fall asleep?" she murmured.

Fuck. How long had he been resting there thinking? Feeling? Why was he so crazy about her?

"God, I'm crazy about you."

What? No. Don't say thoughts like that out loud. Why would he say such a stupid thing? Thinking it was bad enough. He lifted his head and met her eyes, part of him wanting her to freak out and tell him to leave her alone, most of him hoping, praying, that she returned his feelings. Even a little.

"Is that why you're making out with my scar instead of eating me out?"

Her delectable lips twisted into a sexually charged grin, and the answering surge of lust that flooded his groin made him light-headed.

"So you're up for a little oral?"

A smoldering look darkened her eyes. "If you're good at it"—

her tongue wet her lips—"I'm up for a lot of oral."

If he was good at it. *If.*

He hesitated, realizing she was leading him by the nose, and wondering why the fuck it turned him on so much. *If* he was good at it. He'd show her if. He'd make her come so fast and so hard, he'd be wearing her cum as a beard. *If* he was good at it. Please.

He swallowed and glanced down to her slightly parted thighs and bit his lip.

He hoped he was as good as past lovers claimed. He never could tell when a woman was inflating his ego or telling him the truth. What if every woman he'd ever touched had faked getting off?

Nah. Not possible.

Besides, why was he worried about that now? Maybe because he wanted Roux to be up for a lot of oral, not just a little. He trailed his hands up her silky bare legs, starting at her ankles, up a pair of shapely calves, behind her knees.

The plane dipped suddenly, and she gasped, fingers clutching at the armrests. "Maybe you should put on your seat belt," she said.

Or maybe he should create his own turbulence. His fingertips skimmed her outer thighs, down the fronts, up the sides again. On the downward stroke, he shifted a bit closer to her center, back up the outsides, an inch closer to her inner thighs on the next downward pass. He could just yank her legs apart and get down to feasting—he doubted she'd resist—but he wanted her to open for him. He wanted her to ask for his touch. He wanted her to beg for release. As his fingers slid down the center of her thighs, her legs parted, and it took every shred of willpower within him to hold her gaze as he continued to stroke her smooth legs rather than stare at the heated flesh now revealed to him. He turned his hands so that the backs of his knuckles grazed the outsides of her thighs, stroking upward to the crest of her hipbones now, hands turning down there to trace the sexy V that outlined her sex. A gasp escaped her, and her eyes drifted closed. She was probably expecting him to shift his fingers to her cleft, but he followed the inner crease at the apex of her inner thighs and then slowly skimmed all eight fingers down the insides of her thighs.

"Aimes," she moaned, her back arching.

"That's not my name."

Her eyelids opened, that familiar spark of fire simmering in their depths, but he repeated the same gentle motion on her now-trembling thighs, and her eyes drifted closed again.

"Steve."

She whispered the name that he wanted on her lips, but not with the sound of deep longing he was searching for, aching for. He needed to push her farther. Hands continuing to stroke up and down her thighs in a slow, hypnotic rhythm, he lowered his head and pressed a soft kiss to her breastbone. He kissed a trail down the center of her belly—slowly, so slowly—matching the cadence of his fingertips. He dipped his tongue into her belly button, and she cried out, her thighs squeezing shut on his hands. He stayed where he was, kissing, licking, suckling her navel, giving her a taste of what her pussy had in store whenever he decided to end this little game he was playing with her body.

"God, Aimes," she said, her fingers releasing their hold on the armrests to delve into his hair. "Steve. I meant Steve. Please. Just . . . I can't."

"You can't what, Red?" He nipped the sexy extra fold of skin at the top of her navel and tugged gently.

Her legs popped open wide, releasing his hands, and she hooked her knees over the armrests. The scent of her excitement had him reaching for his fly. He had his jeans unfastened and his cock free and gripped in a tight fist before he recovered his senses enough to remember it was his mission to make her lose control, not the other way around. He took several deep breaths, his excitement further fueled by the way she was pulling his hair, trying to get him to lower his mouth to her deliciously swollen, shiny, and delicately pink pussy.

The plane rolled through several belly-dropping air currents, and Jordan's voice came over the intercom. "Hold tight. It's about to get a bit rougher, but we'll be out of this system soon enough."

"Not soon enough," Roux muttered.

"Maybe I should get back in my seat," he said, blowing hot breaths against her lower belly and squeezing his fisted dick in an ineffectual attempt to calm himself.

Roux groaned. "You should, but I want . . ."

She unclasped her seat belt and shifted her entire body upward so that she was suspended above her seat with her thighs anchored firmly on the armrests. This put her pussy in convenient reach of his mouth. He rewarded her recklessness with a gentle flick of his tongue against her clit.

Her entire body buckled, and his cock jerked in response. Dear lord, was making her lose control really worth the effort of keep himself in check?

"Steve," she whispered. "Please. Lick me there."

The pleading in her tone made holding back completely fucking worth it. "Where, Red? Where do you want me to lick you?"

Her breath escaped in a rush. "My ass."

Fuck. He hadn't expected that request, but he was more than happy to accommodate her wishes. He drew the flat of his tongue over her ass, collecting her pussy's sweet, freely flowing juices as he licked upward, and stopped just shy of delving his tongue inside her. God, he wanted to tongue fuck her sweet, swollen pussy. If just that little brush of his tongue over her asshole had her panting and quaking, he couldn't wait to see her reaction when he really got down to business.

"Again," she said, staring down at him.

He moved in reverse, wishing he could watch her face while he gave her ass an invigorating tongue massage. Her flesh quivered and tightened beneath his swirling tongue.

"That's so dirty," she gasped brokenly.

He was never afraid to get a little dirty. Or a lot dirty when the occasion called for it.

He licked his way to her clit, concentrating on sucking, flicking, and rubbing that sensitive spot in the choreographed sequence he'd perfected long ago. It had never failed to send a woman flying. Or pretending to fly.

God, where was that self-doubt coming from? He'd just have to up his game and ensure he made her come.

Roux thrashed her back against her seat, making it impossible to keep true to his method. He grabbed her ass firmly in both hands to hold her still.

"I think . . ." Roux said. "I think I'm going to come." She sounded surprised. "Wait. I . . ."

Her legs shifted, closing on his head. Surprised, he jerked back, and scarcely caught the feral look on her face before she tackled him into the aisle, straddled him, grabbed his cock none-too-gently, and slipped his tip inside her. She sank down, taking him deep. He groaned, lost in her heat, and lifted his hips, holding her waist to press deeper. Her answering raspy moan made his toes curl, and he knew the next time he heard her sing, he'd be transported back to this very moment. God, her voice was sexy.

She rose over him slowly, whimpering when she sank down again. Leaning forward, she pressed her palms against his chest and took him higher and higher as she found her rhythm. Their rhythm. As expected, it was a frenzied tempo.

Damn, she felt good. He hadn't been inside a woman without protection for years. And she didn't seem like the type to forget such an important detail. The idea that she was so into him that she'd fuck him skin to skin had him clenching the carpet with his fingertips and trying hard not to come. Her rhythm was intense. Relentless. Perfect. Surely she'd let go soon so he could join her in bliss.

Maybe she needed a little help. He released his fingertips from their hold on the rough carpet at his back and lifted them to her small breasts, relishing the feel of their pebbled tips rubbing against his palms as her body shifted up and down. He pinched each nipple between a thumb and forefinger before releasing them and slowly drawing his fingertips down over her ribs, belly, and hips. When his thumbs brushed her mound, she shuddered and jerked her hips to one side. The sudden change of sensation almost sent him to the point of no return. He sucked in a deep breath and tensed every muscle in his body to hold back. She shifted so that her knees were pressed tight into his sides and rose up so she wasn't taking him as deep. She also upped her tempo. The intensity of that motion on his cockhead was too much pleasure for him to take. If she kept it up, she'd finish him off in seconds. He pulled her hips down and pressed deep, rotating his hips to try to lessen his pleasure. Wasn't working that well for him, to be honest.

"Will you just come already?" Roux growled.

He opened his eyes, surprised by her exasperated tone. "Not until you do."

"I can't. Do you want me to fake it?"

His ego whimpered like a kicked dog. "Of course not. We can take as long as you need. Do you want me on top?"

"No, I want you to come. I can tell you're fighting it."

"And I'll keep fighting it until you finish."

"I already told you I can't."

Her frustration was palpable. He reached up and cupped her face, trying to ignore the deep ache in his balls. He really did want her to come first, no matter how much his anatomy was arguing with him.

"Are you uncomfortable?" They were fucking on the floor of a small private jet, after all; maybe she was worried that the crew would interrupt. But they knew to stay in the cockpit when he had a woman onboard. "No one is going to interrupt us, if that's what has you worried."

"I literally cannot come when I'm with a man, okay? It isn't you, it's me. So just finish, will you?"

He gaped at her. "You've never had an orgasm?"

She slapped his chest. It hurt, and he liked it.

"Of course I've had an orgasm. I own a damned vibrator. It's just . . ." She looked away. "This is not the conversation I want to be having right now."

"So it *is* me."

She shook her head. "It's not. I've been with men—good lovers, not just duds, though I've had some of those as well—and I just can't let go. I don't know why. Not even when I've been with the same guy for a long time."

He was pretty sure he knew why. Trust. She had never trusted a man to have control over her body, over her pleasure.

"You almost came when I was licking you," he said. "Why did you stop me then?" He'd thought it had been because she was so turned on she couldn't wait to have him inside her. Now he wasn't so sure.

"I don't know. I was . . ." She turned her gaze to the ceiling, and he feared she was about to cry.

His dick was already crying from abuse, but he sat up and wrapped his arms around her back, dropping gentle kisses on her throat.

"Sorry," she whispered. "If you want to take me home, I'll understand."

What? Hell no. And now he was on a mission. He would make this woman come if it killed him. And as he turned her gently to her back and forced his dick to withdraw from the warm, wet haven between her long thighs, he thought he just might die before he claimed his victory.

"Relax," he said.

"Steve." She touched his hair. "We can try some other time. I know you must be hurting. Just go ahead and finish."

He grinned. "If you haven't figured this out about me yet, I'm a stubborn son of a bitch, and I absolutely refuse to come before you do."

She laughed. "Well, they're your balls. If you like them blue, that's your business."

CHAPTER 13

ROUX DIDN'T KNOW whether to be relieved or mortified that she'd told Steve her horrible little secret their first time together. She'd kept Travis in the dark throughout their entire eight-month relationship. Not because she was good at faking, but because he didn't seem to care that she never hit her peak and had never bothered to ask about it. Hell, she doubted he'd noticed. But she felt bad for Steve, because she'd gotten him all excited and hadn't been able to deliver promised release before he figured out that she was frigid. Well, not frigid exactly. She enjoyed sex. It felt amazing and made her feel close to her partner. She just couldn't let go. Not when anyone else was present. She'd planned to lock herself in the bathroom after he finished and give herself some much-needed relief, but now the pussy was out of the bag, so to speak.

"How many men have failed you?" Steve asked, drawing her attention to his sexy brown eyes. He squeezed them shut and shook his head. "Don't answer that. I don't want to know."

"A handful," she offered. Would he think that was a lot or wonder why so few?

"It's only you and me now." He buried his hands in her hair and kissed her and kissed her and kissed her until every nerve ending in her body was responsive to his strong, sensual lips and her belly was quivering like gelatin. The entire back of her body seemed to melt into the floor, while her front awakened to the feel of his warm skin against hers. Her nipples tingled with want and her pussy ached in its emptiness. Even if he didn't make her come—and she honestly doubted anyone could—she still wanted him inside her desperately.

Her hands gripped his hips, fingers digging into his firm butt to encourage him to take her. He apparently took this as a cue to begin a meticulous and highly sensual journey down her body. Her hands slipped up his back as he moved slowly downward. He kissed her neck, shoulders, collarbones, and his tongue and lips gave considerable attention to one hard nipple. She sighed, allowing herself to enjoy the sensation rather than concentrate on the disappointment that was yet to come. As he shifted to the other side, Steve paused to press his lips to the scar between her breasts. He held his lips there, the tenderness of the gesture filling her with a rush of emotion that stole her breath. She'd never had a man show that much care to the mark that scarred her inside and out, and by his doing so, the agonizing tightness that always centered in that exact spot loosened a fraction. She shifted her hands to his silky hair and cradled him to her chest for a moment. Why did this notoriously naughty rock star awaken such tenderness within her? Who knew he could be so gentle, so caring? And after a moment, when she released his head and he drew her neglected nipple into his mouth, she wondered who knew he could be so sensual, so sexy? Oh, everyone knew that.

His hands skimmed her ribs as he kissed his way down the center of her belly. She hoped he'd nip her belly button again. She'd loved the pulse of excitement his teeth had caused earlier, but with only a soft kiss at her navel, he continued down. A soft sigh of disappointment escaped her. Steve went still and then pushed up onto his hands to look down at her. She couldn't help but stare at the hard, sculpted shoulders that motion showed off.

"What was that?" he asked.

She tilted her head slightly. "What was what?"

"That sigh. You wanted something, were anticipating it, and I didn't deliver."

He'd recognized all that from her stupid sigh? "It's nothing. Continue."

"If you don't tell me, I can't give you everything you want, and I want to"—his gaze held hers—"give you everything."

Did he mean *everything*—not merely sexual satisfaction—or was she reading too much into his words? She knew she was prone to overthinking even frivolous comments.

"I was thinking how much I liked it when you bit my belly earlier." Her face went hot. She was lying naked beneath him on the floor of a jet, which didn't embarrass her in the least, but voicing that silly desire aloud made her blush? Jeez. No wonder she couldn't relax enough to come at a man's hand. Or mouth. Or cock.

"Gotcha," he said with a lopsided grin. He immediately lowered his body over hers once more.

He kissed a circle around her navel and then licked a chaotic trail in the same path. She moaned as her nipples tightened and her pussy clenched with unquestionable need. When he nipped her skin, her hips rose off the floor. He shifted slightly to one side, his arm moving between her thighs. He massaged her belly around her navel with deep, sucking kisses and a chaotically twirling tongue until she began to squirm and her breath came in excited gasps. Why did that excite her so much?

Stop thinking about why, Roux. Just feel. Enjoy it. Oh!

When he again nipped at the small fold of skin at the top of her belly button, her hips jerked on cue, and he slid two long, thick fingers inside her. She gasped, her pussy tightening around them. He rubbed her inner walls with firm, steady strokes. Her body tightened and tightened with each thrust until she thought she'd shatter. Suddenly her legs snapped closed on his hand, holding it locked into position. He didn't force her thighs apart, just went still and focused his attention on kissing her belly again. Oh, she liked that. Liked that so much. She started to imagine that same kissing, tongue-swirling motion on her clit, and she trembled, overwhelmed by the very idea. It took her a while to relax, and when her thighs finally fell open, he rewarded her by nipping her newly discovered erogenous zone and then pumped his fingers into and out of her clenching pussy.

He took her higher. Higher. Almost. Almost. Her legs shut on his hand again. Damn. She covered her eyes with both hands and groaned in frustration.

"It's okay," he said quietly. "You'll get there."

It was her own damn fault that she hadn't gotten there already. Every time she got close, she shut him down. And it wasn't a conscious decision on her part. It was just the way her body responded.

"Can I try that on your clit this time?" he asked.

She uncovered her eyes and looked down her belly at him. "Beware of bear-trap thighs on your head."

He grinned, and her heart melted.

"I'll risk it."

How could he stand to be so patient with her?

He kissed her belly again, heightening her excitement, making her want more. After a moment, her legs relaxed, and he shifted downward, licking a ticklish path down her lower belly. When his mouth reached its goal, her back lifted off the floor, and her legs tightened around his upper arms, but she couldn't close them. His body was in the way. He took his time with her. Gentle kisses, soft licks. He caressed her clit with his lips until her thighs relaxed, and then the fingers still inside her began to move—slowly at first, matching the maddening, pleasurable cadence of his lips and tongue, and then faster. Faster. Her excitement built. She lifted her head off the floor, arched her back to draw away from him—not understanding why she was trying to escape. She definitely didn't want him to stop.

"Okay." She panted. "Wait."

His mouth latched on to her clit with a tight suction, and with one flick of his tongue all the tension in her body loosened on a rippling wave of release. She cried out—the sound half surprise, half triumph—as her climax shuddered through her and carried her up into the stratosphere. Steve didn't let off her until every last aftershock of pleasure stilled in her utterly satiated body.

Now all she wanted to do was hold him against her, snuggle her face into his neck, and breathe him in. She'd done it! Well, technically Steve was responsible. She'd given up on ever being able to find release with a man.

Steve slipped his fingers from her body and kissed his way up the center of her body. When they were face-to-face, and his hips were settled between her thighs, he wove his fingers through the tangles of her hair and smiled.

"How was that?" he asked.

She smiled, her heart as happy and content as the rest of her body. "Amazing."

"You weren't faking, were you?"

She laughed. "No, I wouldn't know how to fake that. Congratulations, you're the first man to ever make me come."

"Yes." His hands clenched into fists of victory within her hair. "Now it's my turn."

"Do you want me to suck you off?" Because she'd love to offer him the same pleasure she'd just received at his expert mouth and fingers.

"Not this time," he said, lowering his head to kiss her lips. She could smell her sex all over him, and memories of all the pleasure his mouth had delivered roused her excitement once more.

"Do you want me to wear a condom?"

Her eyes widened. Oh fuck, she'd jumped on him earlier without even thinking about protection. How could she have done something so rash?

No popped out of her mouth before she could reconsider. She took birth control, so pregnancy wasn't a concern, but shouldn't she be more worried about where his dick had been? But staring up into his eyes, she realized that nope, she didn't care at all.

"I'm clean," he whispered, searching her eyes.

She believed him. "Me too."

He released her hair and shifted onto one hip, using his hand to guide himself inside her. Her mouth fell open in wonder as he filled her inch by inch. She wrapped her legs around his hips, tilting her pelvis to accept him deeper. He rocked into her, his thrusts slow and deep. All the while he stared into her eyes, stroking her hair with one hand and leaning in to steal sweet kisses whenever the constant eye contact got overwhelming. Roux had never felt so cherished, and even though something in the back of her mind kept trying to remind her that this man was Steve Aimes, notorious womanizer and career asshole, her heart just couldn't believe it. Not in this moment when he was making love to her as if she mattered to him more than anything.

"It's safe to remove your seat belts now," the pilot announced. "But we'll be landing in about twenty minutes, so you don't even have time for a quickie, Aimes."

Roux snorted, having completely lost track of time and place.

Steve kissed her jaw and said in a devastatingly sexy voice, "I guess our next intimacy challenge will have to be addressed another time."

Roux couldn't help but be overjoyed that there'd be a next time. "What challenge is that?"

He nibbled at her jaw, his thrusts faster now. "Coming together."

"I'm sure you can make that impossible dream a reality as well."

He shifted to peer into her eyes again. "I won't ever give up, no matter how many times it takes."

"That only encourages me to fight against you accomplishing your goal."

"Don't," he said with a wicked grin. "I plan to make you come by every imaginable means."

Now that was a plan she could get behind. And on top of. In

front of. Underneath. Next to.

He pressed his cheek against hers, his thrusting hips claiming her in a frenzied, feverish tempo. Her excitement began to climb again, a more primal pleasure unfurling deep inside her. His hot, gasping breaths against her neck made goose bumps rise to the surface of her skin. She kissed his throat, the saltiness of his sweat delighting her tongue. And when he thrust into her one last time, his body shuddering with release, she decided giving was almost as good as receiving.

He collapsed on top of her, and she wrapped her arms and legs tightly around him to draw him as close as possible.

"You weren't faking, were you?" she asked, unable to resist teasing him.

He chuckled. "I wouldn't know how to fake that," he answered breathlessly.

"Yes!" She slapped his ass triumphantly.

He rose up on his elbows to look down at her. "If you don't want me to fall madly in love with you, you'll have to start being a little less smart, sassy and fun, and a lot less sexy."

He thought she was smart, sassy, fun, and sexy? Her belly was full of all sorts of fluttery butterflies as she tried to come up with the right discouraging thing to say to keep him at a safe distance.

"Why wouldn't I want that?"

Yeah, those probably hadn't been the right words to drive him away. But even at the prospect of Iona's wrath, as Steve's gorgeous face broke into a devastatingly winning smile, Roux didn't much care if her career fell to pieces. She'd never make it all the way across Europe without sharing a bed with this man.

CHAPTER 14

STEVE LIFTED Roux's hand to his lips and kissed her knuckles. It felt good to let a woman close to him again. It had been much too long since he'd opened his heart to the possibility of loving someone. And she was just so damned easy to love. How could he resist?

She was gazing out the window of the rental car at the extensive cornfield they were currently driving past. "Uh, Steve," she said. "Not to complain, but BFE, Illinois, was not what I had in mind when you suggested we get away for the weekend."

"This is just a short stop. The jet needs to refuel."

Which obviously required them to rent a car and head out into the middle of nowhere. He hadn't told her why they had stopped in flyover country. If he did, and she wasn't keen to meet his family, he would have easily been persuaded to head due south, but he'd met her family already, and it only seemed fair that she should know where he came from as well. He loved his parents. They were good people. But it was his grandfather that Steve most wanted Roux to meet.

"You aren't taking me to meet your family, are you?" she asked, turning her head and narrowing her eyes.

"Some of them," he admitted with a shrug. He turned onto a familiar gravel road, nostalgia getting the better of him when they rumbled past the tree he'd planted on Earth Day over twenty-five years ago. What had once been a prickly twig in a paper cup was now a towering spruce.

"I planted that tree when I was in first grade," he told Roux, feeling a bit odd about sharing something that lame with her. Like she gave two shits about some stupid tree.

"Wow," she said, turning to watch the tree out the back window. "It's huge. You must be at least eighty if you planted that sucker."

He gave her a sideways glance of annoyance, but truly he enjoyed her teasing, even if it poked fun at his advanced age. "At least I'm old enough to legally drink."

"I'm twenty-five, okay? Just ask if you want to know how old I am. And you are?" She tilted her chin down.

"Thirty-four."

"Ancient." She winked, grinning saucily.

"Brat."

"I wouldn't have ever guessed you were a farm boy," she said, her attention turning to the big red barn in the distance. The house wouldn't be visible until they crested the next hill.

"Oh, I'm not. Never was. These wide-open spaces make me feel small. And that's why I headed to Los Angeles when I was sixteen. I met Zach my first week there."

It had been a chance meeting of two homeless teenage drummers living in cars parked illegally side by side. They'd been inseparable ever since. Steve often wondered how different his life would have been if he and Zach had played different instruments. Surely they'd have ended up in the same band.

"You went all that way on your own?" Roux asked.

"No, I packed up the entire family and we headed west." He chuckled at her wide-eyed expression. "Yes, I went on my own."

"I guess dropping out of school didn't hurt your career prospects."

Steve scratched his jaw, which was starting to roughen with beard stubble. "Actually, I didn't drop out," he said. "I graduated when I was fifteen."

She gaped at him.

"Not common knowledge," he added.

"So, you were like super-smart?"

"Am." He poked her in the side. "Don't tell anyone."

"Why didn't you go to college? You could have—"

"Made something of myself?" He snorted. "You sound like my mother."

"I was going to say gotten a scholarship. You've obviously made something of yourself. You're a living legend."

Steve smiled. He did enjoy a good ego stroke. "School was boring. I wouldn't have been able to stomach another year of it. Music has always been far more mentally stimulating to me."

They turned in at the gravel driveway of his grandparents' huge, old—and from personal experience, drafty—white farmhouse. It was shaped like a giant two-story box. Its only outstanding architectural feature was a small sagging front porch.

"I get that. I was pretty good at school," Roux said. "But I was great at the piano."

"My grandmother always wanted me to play piano," he said, "but I preferred banging a wooden spoon on every pot and pan in her kitchen."

Roux laughed, her eyes lighting with delight. "The beginnings of a metal drummer genius."

"Every living legend has to start somewhere," he said with a wink.

He opened his door and hurried around the sedan to help Roux climb from the car. She hadn't waited for him to open her door, but she didn't protest when he took her clammy hand in his and helped her navigate the rocky surface of the driveway.

"When I was a kid, I used to walk on this gravel barefoot," he said.

"Ow," she said. "Did you do that while wearing overalls and chewing on wheat stalks?"

He rolled his eyes. "No. While smoking a corncob pipe, obviously."

"I'm sorry. That was a bigoted thing for me to say. I'm not familiar with country life except for what they show on TV."

Steve heard clanking coming from the long metal-sided garage near the house. That would be where they'd find his grandfather. Probably restoring some old tractor, which had always been Pops's favorite hobby and which kept him busy now that Steve's dad and younger sister had taken over farm operations. "I need to warn you that Pops is deafer than a newborn kitten but refuses to admit it."

Roux chuckled. "Deafer than a newborn kitten? Is that country talk?"

"Yep. You'll catch on faster than a rabbit with his tail on fire."

She laughed again. "Y'all don't really talk like that, do you?" she asked, trying and failing at a southern accent.

"No. We're too far north for *y'all*."

Steve squinted as they stepped into the dim interior of the

garage, willing his eyes to adjust. Something heavy clattered to the ground with a metallic clank, and within seconds he was being squeezed in a tight hug.

"It's not Christmas, is it?" Pops asked, patting Steve vigorously on the back. The man was uncommonly strong for an old guy. "What are you doing here?"

"I was in the neighborhood and thought I'd stop in for a minute," he said loudly, directing his voice toward Pops's left ear, which was better at picking up sounds than his right.

"You got a show in Chicago this week? I'm sure my nephews would have mentioned it." His family—including third cousins—still came to Exodus End concerts when they were held within driving distance. And though Chicago was a full two hundred miles from home, it was close enough to warrant a road trip.

"I'm on a break, actually. Heading to Europe in a couple of weeks."

"What do you mean? I'm wide awake."

He had no idea what Pops had thought he'd said, but didn't bother to repeat himself, because Pops had just noticed Roux standing behind him. The old man's breath caught, and his glossy eyes lifted to Steve's.

"Who's this beauty?"

"This is Roux."

"Who?"

"Roux!"

"Woo? I'd have wooed her back in the day!"

"No, Roux. With an R. Roux."

"Was I rude? I apologize."

Steve slapped his forehead. "Not rude. Roux. Rooooooooo."

Roux grinned and squeezed Pops's arm above his elbow. "It doesn't matter," she said. "What are you working on here?" She extended a hand toward the ancient silver tractor with its unique three-wheel design.

Pops's eyes brightened. "You like my tractor?"

"Sure," Roux said, stepping closer to the rusty contraption.

"This here is a 1940 Silver King. I salvaged her from an abandoned barn down by Rolla."

"That's in southern Missouri," Steve explained, doubting that an East Coast resident would have ever heard of the small city.

"I will not put it out of its misery," Pops retorted. "I'll have her running in no time."

Roux pressed her tongue to her upper lip, her cheeks tight with suppressed laughter. She listened intently to Pops as he explained everything about his current project and held up various spare parts—most rusty—while he tried to remember which junkyard he'd found them in.

"Got this one on eBay," he said, proudly holding up an ordinary-looking bolt.

"Oh, I know all about eBay," Roux said. "I have a slight obsession with collecting coin purses."

"Yeah, I don't like paying shipping fees either. Lots of coin. You got that right."

Steve sometimes wished he could be in on the conversation that Pops heard, but he loved the old guy so much, he didn't bother to frustrate him by correcting him again. And Roux seemed slightly amused but not annoyed by the lack of communication. Steve was already glad he'd brought her.

"Go check out my Minneapolis Moline," Pops said, waving toward the fully restored tractor along the far wall. Its red wheels and yellow body brightened up the dingy space. "Steven helped me rebuild that one before he ran off to California. It's still my favorite."

Pops slapped Steve on the back, and Steve knew the reason that tractor was his favorite was because the two of them had bonded while restoring it. Most thirteen-year-old boys don't spend their free time tinkering with old tractors in their grandfather's garage. And that was a damn shame.

Pops gave Roux a complete rundown on the restoration process, telling her countless embarrassing stories about Steve, which didn't bother him, because they made her laugh. Anything that made her happy was cool by Steve. He couldn't help but compare this visit to the few times Bianca had been willing to come with him. She'd spent the entire trip with her nose in the air and a stick up her ass. At the time, he'd made excuses for her behavior because he'd been blinded with love. How could he have been so stupid? He wasn't that fool anymore, he told himself. He wouldn't let emotion cloud his common sense ever again.

Realizing that time was getting away from them, and he still had a few things he wanted Roux to see before they headed to his favorite little island off the coast of Central America, Steve approached Roux from behind and placed a hand on her lower back.

"We should head to the house. I have something important to show you."

"Do I get to meet your grandmother?"

The eagerness in her expression caused a lump to form in his throat.

"Sort of. Mams passed away several years ago."

Roux's face fell, and she took Steve's hand and even squeezed Pops's forearm. "I'm so sorry to hear that. She must have been quite a woman to put up with this guy."

She winked at Pops, who flushed and then howled with laughter.

"We're going to the house, Pops. Are you coming?"

"I like your new wife a lot better than that stuck-up bitch from California."

Roux bit her lip, and turned her face away, but not before Steve saw the mirth trying to escape her.

"We're not married," Steve said. He doubted he'd ever take a chance at that again. He'd learned his lesson with the stuck-up bitch from California.

"Yet," Pops said with an ornery twinkle in his eye.

Steve took Roux's hand and helped her navigate a pile of discarded tractor parts. They ducked under a low-hanging, partially open garage door and stepped out into the sunshine. The bright rays made Roux's hair shimmer like fire. The woman was stunning. He had to take a deep breath to keep himself walking forward when every instinct told him to go completely still and just watch her move.

"Does he live here alone?" she asked quietly. "I'm worried about him being out here by himself."

"He's too damned stubborn to move to town. My folks live down the road about half a mile. And my sister checks on him a couple of times a day."

"You have a sister?"

Those gold-rimmed green eyes of hers lit up again. Either she was going to have to stop doing that or he was going to have to start taking medication for an irregular heartbeat.

"She's a pain in the ass," he said with a chuckle. "But I'm sure you know that about sisters even more than I do."

"I'm always looking for more sisters, and now that I'm your *wife*, I get to add one more to my collection."

He knew she was teasing, but there suddenly wasn't enough oxygen to refill his lungs, and he choked.

"Too soon for wife jokes?" she asked, and a part of him didn't want it to be a joke. The stupid part of him that he quickly smashed down deep into the pit of his stomach.

"Yeah, well. You know my track record with wives. Ex-wives; two: Steve; zero."

Roux's eyes widened. "Two?"

"You don't read that in the tabloids?"

She shook her head.

"I lost a bet in Vegas. Ended with an annulment."

"Always a chance to win with the next one," Pops commented.

Steve glanced over his shoulder, wondering how the mostly deaf codger had managed to hear any of their conversation, especially when their backs were to him. Maybe he just pretended to be deaf as a form of personal entertainment. Steve wouldn't put it past the guy.

"What do you do for a living, Roux?" Pops asked, situating himself on her opposite side as they continued toward the house. "Besides being an absolute sweetheart."

"I work at an animal shelter," she said.

Steve smiled. Of course she did.

"Well, I used to," she added. "I had to quit a few weeks ago. Now, I guess, I'm a musician."

"Nothing wrong with being a beautician," Pops said.

Steve didn't bother to correct him. Because if Steve got his way, Pops would soon learn about her talent for himself. Steve had been listening to Baroquen's music a lot over the past couple of weeks. Late at night, he'd lie in his tour bus bunk with his earbuds linking him to Roux, because all he heard when he listened was her amazing keyboard work and her sultry background vocals. And yeah, he was sort of a fanboy, not that he'd admit it to her.

"Have you eaten?" Pops asked. "I could go for one of your omelets right about now, Steven." He rubbed his belly.

Roux raised an eyebrow. "You cook?"

"A little." He actually enjoyed cooking. Another thing he wouldn't be admitting. His notorious rock star reputation couldn't take many more hits.

"I figured you'd have servants for that kind of thing."

"You're thinking of Dare," he said with a twisted grin. "Dude has a damned butler, believe it or not." He knew he was intentionally directing her attention from himself, but bringing her here had made him feel more vulnerable than he'd anticipated. She was sure to find a reason to brush him off at any moment. And he didn't mean she'd brush off the guy in the mask that he showed the world. She'd be rejecting the real him.

"Dare has a butler?"

"Dare's from Beverly Hills. Rich boy, born and bred."

"Well, he's not stuck-up at all. He's awesome."

And now that she was defending his friend, Steve wished he hadn't brought Dare up. It was never a good idea to try to make himself look better by comparison to Dare. What the fuck was he thinking?

"About that omelet . . ." Pops said loudly.

"All right, Pops." Steve slapped him on the back. "You got eggs?"

"You know where the coop is. Best grab some veggies from the garden as well. My fridge is pretty bare."

Roux squirmed with excitement. "You have chickens? And a vegetable garden?"

"Over yonder." Pops pointed toward the old barn they'd passed earlier.

She was half jogging as they altered their course. Pops stopped and waved them forward. "I need to let the dogs out," he said.

"You have dogs?"

Pops laughed at her expression. "Have to. They keep the coyotes, coons, rabbits, and possums away."

"You have wild animals around here too?" She glanced around as if hoping to spot a leopard or a giraffe or some creature far more exciting than a squirrel.

"If you like animals, the barn cat had a mess of kittens week before last," Pops said. "Sure are cute little shits now that their eyes are open."

Steve thought she might faint from elation.

"Have you ever been to the country?" he asked her.

"Not really. Am I embarrassing myself?"

"You're perfect." Even though showing her the adorable beef calves on his parents' acreage might win him further points, he wasn't going to introduce her to them or she'd probably attempt a rescue mission to save cattle from their fate as tasty steaks.

Pops headed for the house, and once his back was turned, Steve couldn't resist pulling Roux close for a kiss. He'd brought her to the farm to give her a reason to push him away or to give himself a reason to be less obsessed with her, but damned if the trip hadn't had the opposite effect. Her kiss was sweet and tender. They let it linger between them, and he felt its effects deep in the center of his chest.

I'm in trouble.

And he was glad. He never thought he'd feel this way about anyone again.

Roux hugged the chickens while he scooped eggs out of their nests. The way she cradled them and spoke to them in a soothing tone had the birds calm and clucking softly, and had Steve thinking what a great mother Roux would make, which . . . no. He had to stop thinking that way. He wasn't the kind of guy who'd make a good role model for a child. Any child. Especially not his own. But maybe he was ready to settle down and stop filling the empty hours with women and booze and drugs and more women. Maybe all he needed was one woman. The right woman.

I'm in big trouble.

"You don't eat these chickens, do you?" she asked, settling a red hen back on her now-empty nest. The bird turned its head jerkily as it viewed them with one eye and then the other.

"Not when they're laying eggs."

She watched several chickens pecking around in the fenced area surrounding the coop.

"I'm glad they don't have to spend their entire lives in little cages," she said.

He couldn't stand her morose expression as she gazed at the hens. He figured they had pretty good lives for chickens. They were kept safe and well fed, but they were also tasty.

"Let's go find those kittens," he said, reaching for her hand and carrying the bucket of eggs in his other.

He carefully latched the gate behind them, and several juvenile half coonhound, half Labradors came loping up to sniff at them. They were all wags within seconds. Roux released his hand to squat down to pet them, laughing when they licked her face and nearly toppling over when they nudged her for more attention. One particularly floppy-eared pup began to bay in a hound's distinctive bark.

"About six months ago, my granddad's prize coonhound got into a bit of trouble with the neighbor's Lab," Steve said. "Pops decided to keep all the pups to remind her not to stray from the mate he chose for her, but I think he just likes the company."

"Mutts make the best dogs," Roux insisted, scratching a spotted one behind the ears. The pup gazed at her with understandable devotion.

Steve wished he knew the pups' names. The mama was Trixie and the male coonhound was Jonas, but he had no idea what Jonas's seven step-dogs were named. A pure black one was sticking his snout into Steve's bucket, trying to steal an egg.

"Get out of there!"

The dog skittered backward with his tail between his legs and his ears back.

"I should probably wash my hands before I handle kittens," Roux said, giving her fingers a hesitant sniff. "Not sure the mama cat will like the smell of dog on them."

"And the smell of chickens," Steve said.

"And of you," she said softly, her lashes concealing her eyes.

Okay, they needed to finish this visit so they could spend some time alone together on a private beach as soon as fucking possible.

He lifted the handle of the red well pump, and Roux stared at it as if it were some miracle invention. After a moment it began to gurgle, and water rushed out.

"Oh! It's a water pump." She thrust her hands beneath the flow.

"Sucks water right out of the ground."

"No fooling?"

He lifted a hand to the sky. "Hand to God."

She laughed and dried her hands on the hem of her shirt. He ushered her toward the barn, careful to shut the overgrown pups out, and set the bucket of eggs on the dirt floor. Beams of sunlight found cracks between the old warped boards of the ancient structure, illuminating dust particles floating through the air.

"Shh," Steve said, placing a finger to his lips and listening intently.

A faint mewing came from the hayloft above them. Roux laughed softly. "I hear them."

"Up there," he whispered, pointing to the ladder.

"Is it safe?" She frowned at the rickety-looking ladder.

"If you fall, I'll catch you," he promised.

"Then maybe I'll fall on purpose." A flirtatious grin teased her lush lips.

His breath caught, and he couldn't behave himself for another second. He jerked her into his arms and filled his hands with her soft ass while he kissed her. She squeaked in surprise when he shifted her hip against the hard ridge of his rapidly engorging cock.

"God, I want you," he murmured against her lips, unwilling to break contact even to speak.

"Again?"

"Always."

He felt her smile against his lips as she looped both arms around his neck and pressed her soft breasts into his chest.

"Are you in the barn, Steven?"

His mother's voice destroyed his good time.

With a frustrated groan, Steve released Roux, who dashed for the ladder and started to climb.

"Looking for kittens," he called to his mom.

The barn door creaked open. "Pops said you brought a guest. You should have given us a little warning. I could have made a roast."

"She's a vegetarian."

"Oh. Well, a salad, then." Mom gave him a hearty squeeze. "You need a roast, though. You're much too thin."

"The word you're looking for is cut. Shredded." He tightened his muscles. "Maybe ripped."

She caught his jaw in her hand and gave him the Mom-look that told him she wasn't hearing any of his arguments. "Thin. It's all those drugs you take."

He couldn't deny he enjoyed an occasional bump of cocaine, that pot kept life interesting several nights a week, and he liked his whiskey, but despite what his parents' thought, he didn't lie around all day with a needle in his arm and a crack pipe in his hand. "That's so 1985, Mom."

High above, Roux said softly, "Aww, aren't you the sweetest things ever."

"Is that her?" Mom whispered.

"Yeah. What did Pops tell you?"

"That you got married in Vegas."

Steve snorted. "Pops is hearing things again. It's nothing that serious."

"But something special."

He couldn't deny that. "I'll go up and get her."

Steve shot up the ladder, leaving his mom on solid ground staring up at him.

He found Roux sitting cross-legged near a pile of scattered straw with the mama cat purring contentedly on her lap and six small and shaky gray and white fluff balls exploring the area around her.

Filtered sunlight lit the area and made her fair skin glow.

"What's her name?" Roux asked.

"Betty. Why don't you come down and meet her?"

Roux grimaced slightly. "I meant the cat."

"That's Nightmare."

"Nightmare?" She stroked the calico on her lap, and the cat shifted belly up in surrender. "This sweet girl is named Nightmare?"

"I don't think the mice around here think she's so sweet. Are you coming?"

"I'm not really prepared for this," she said, lifting each kitten and nuzzling her nose into their fluff. They made squeaky meowing noises that their mother ignored as she looped a paw around Roux's wrist to gain herself another stroke.

"If you don't want to meet—"

"I do," she said, and those two little words made his heart skip a beat. "It's just . . . I'm not prepared."

"It's not like you need to write a speech. It's just my mom."

"First impressions are important." Having nuzzled the final kitten, Roux set Nightmare aside and climbed to her feet, brushing dust off the seat of her pants. The cat immediately started to rub up against Roux's leg, purring in earnest. Nightmare had gotten her name because she tended to attack people as often as she attacked mice, but apparently the holy terror had a new best friend.

"Hopefully you've gotten over your horrible first impression of me," he said.

Roux grinned. "You did make a complete ass of yourself."

No denying that fact. He kissed her softly, his hands moving to her ass as if drawn there by an incredible force. Four sharp claws dug into his ankle, and he winced. Nightmare did not share well.

"I'll go down first," he said. "Going down is a lot scarier than going up."

"Going down is a little intimidating at first." She glanced down at his crotch and lifted her eyebrows. "But I'll give it a go if we ever get some alone time."

He blew out a breath, wondering what he'd been thinking when he'd brought her to the farm instead of going directly to the island. Then again, her heart and soul were fully on display here, whereas if they'd started their time together on the island, he'd have focused all his attention on her body. He might have missed out on witnessing her true beauty, and right now in the dim light of a musty hayloft with a holy terror of a cat rubbing against her calf, her gentle soul was blindingly obvious to him. Though in all honesty, marathon sex was also likely to increase his admiration, considering the perpetually aroused condition he found himself in.

"Did you find Nightmare's kittens?" Mom called from below the loft.

Steve snapped out of his musing, released his grip on Roux's ass, and started down the ladder. "Six of them."

"She always has the best little mousers. I'll have to take a couple over to our place when they're older."

When he reached the bottom of the ladder, he held it steady while Roux slowly descended.

"It is a lot scarier going down," she said.

Her knees were visibly shaking. He couldn't help but notice the two man-sized dusty handprints on her butt. Mom must have noticed them too, because she giggled and then pressed her hand under her nose to hide her smirk.

"Don't embarrass me," Steve warned under his breath.

"That's what moms are for," she teased.

Once Roux's feet were on solid ground, she turned to face them, a lovely smile of greeting on her lips and in her eyes. Every time she smiled, Steve found it hard to breathe, and this time was no exception.

"This is Roux. Roux Williams."

"What an unusual and lovely name." Mom reached out and squeezed Roux's hand.

"It was my grandmother's. She was French. And also a redhead." Roux tugged at a strand of her silky hair.

"This is my mom, Elizabeth," Steve said. "Betty."

"Pleasure to meet you," Roux said a bit woodenly.

"Likewise." Mom turned her attention to Steve. "Pops says you're going to make omelets for lunch. He sent Dana to town to get cheese."

"So we have a few minutes," Steve said. He took Roux's hand, which had turned clammy since he'd last held it. "Let's go pick veggies."

He didn't miss his mother's scowl as her gaze landed on his and Roux's entwined fingers. Mom had been against his marrying Bianca—his entire family had been, truth be told—so she was hypercritical of any woman who came near him. He'd spent several months hiding out here after his divorce, so no one knew better than his family how severely Bianca's betrayal had destroyed him. But

Steve knew Mom would warm up to Roux quickly. How could she not? The woman was everything that had been lacking in his life. And if he could recognize that within weeks of meeting her, surely his wise and wonderful mother would see it almost immediately.

"Pops says you cut hair," Mom said to Roux as she grabbed the bucket of eggs and they all exited the barn, squinting as the brilliant late spring sunshine lit their faces.

Roux laughed. "No. He thought I said I was a beautician, but I'm really a musician."

"Oh." Mom grinned sideways. "I wish I could talk that man into getting a hearing aid. He doesn't think he needs one. So do you sing?"

"No, I—"

"She does and beautifully so," Steve said. "She just won't admit it."

Roux elbowed him for interrupting her, but he didn't mind. He liked bragging about her.

"I sing backup, and I play the keyboard."

"Maybe she'll play us a song after lunch," Steve said. It was the main reason he'd brought her there. "On grandma's piano."

Mom's lips wobbled almost imperceptivity. "I think she'd like that."

Roux's brow crinkled, but Steve knew the *she* that Mom referred to was her departed mother. Mams had always wanted someone in the family to play her piano with the same love and attention she'd shown the antique instrument, but no one had ever taken to it like she had.

The pack of overgrown pups followed them to the vegetable garden and then darted off after a startled rabbit that had been nibbling on the lettuce.

"Wow," Roux said. "This is amazing!"

As far as midwestern vegetable gardens went, it was perfectly ordinary. He tried seeing it through a city dweller's eyes. And then a vegetarian city dweller's eyes. He still failed to see it as amazing.

"We'll need bell peppers, tomatoes, onions, a bit of spinach, and whatever else you'd like," he said, setting her free to find the ripest specimens the garden had to offer.

"She's adorable," Mom commented with a grin as Roux exclaimed over an enormous tomato. He'd have thought it was coated in solid gold if he didn't know better. "Where in the world did you find her?"

"In a limo," Steve said. "Her band is joining ours on tour."

"That will be nice," Mom said. "If you can keep yourself out of trouble."

"I only get into trouble when I'm bored," he said. "And I haven't been bored since I met her."

Roux had spotted the strawberry patch and started picking and eating strawberries right off the plants. "You might want to wash those first," he called out. And unable to watch from a distance any longer, he left his mother's side to venture into the garden.

"I didn't think. Are they covered in pesticides? I didn't taste any."

"No. Pops believes in organic gardening, free-range chickens, grass-fed beef. He doesn't realize those are progressive, sustainable practices, so don't tell him." He crouched down beside her and winked.

"So I don't need to wash them." She found another ripe berry and plucked it from its stem before biting into it.

"They're probably dirty."

"A little dirt never hurt anyone."

She was so unlike Bianca. Was that why he liked her so damned much? But Bianca had been his perfect woman, so how could one so different from her also be his perfect woman? He spied a particularly large and ripe strawberry and picked it, lifting it to her lips to offer her a bite. Her gaze held his as she bit into it, and a flood of desire heated his groin, stirred his senses into chaos.

"We need to get these omelets made so I can monopolize your time." *And discover all the ways I can make you climax*, he added silently.

"I've got the onion," Mom called from the other side of the garden. "Do you want me to dig up some potatoes too?"

"Sounds good, Mom!"

"You want to hear something weird?" Roux asked. When he nodded, she said, "I feel like I belong here. In this place. Surrounded by all this life. With you." She lowered her gaze, a blush staining her cheeks. "I guess that was more stupid than weird."

He touched her chin to encourage her eyes to meet his. "Not stupid or weird. You do belong."

Her eyes went glossy with tears, and his heart panged with regret. He hadn't meant to upset her.

"Shh," he murmured, his thumb stroking her smooth cheek. "Please don't cry."

"I'm sorry." She pressed the back of her hand to one eye,

leaving a smudge of dirt on her brow. "It's just . . . finding a place to belong is hard for an orphan. And when you find it, but you know you can't have it, not really . . ." She shook her head and took a steadying breath, blowing it out slowly. "Let's go to that island."

But she could belong here, with his family, with him. He could give that to her. He just wasn't sure if he was ready to offer it yet.

"Omelets first, then we'll return to the airstrip." He could always bring her back at a later date. He loved the way she looked in this space—sunlight making her hair glow like fire, the breeze blowing the strands to life; smudges of dirt on her face; life all around her. She was right, she did belong here. But he wasn't sure he did. He'd always wanted to leave. Had grander plans for his life than a midwestern farm could offer. And he'd found what he'd been looking for in California, hadn't he?

"Stevie!"

Dana's exuberant cry broke Roux's spell over him, and he shifted to glance over his shoulder. God, he hated being called Stevie, and his sister knew that.

Dana was all smiles as she hurried across the yard to the garden.

"My sister," Steve said, rising to his feet and helping Roux to stand, but not before she plucked another ripe berry from an overburdened plant.

"Dana, this is Roux," he said.

Dana nodded in Roux's direction, but her attention was all on Steve. "You look good." She slapped his arm. "But you always look good."

"Not looking too bad yourself."

She rolled her eyes. "Please. We both know who got the looks in this family."

"You."

She laughed but also blushed. "Stop. Since when do you bring women to the farm?"

Dana shot a quick glance at Roux. She was probably wondering if Roux would be as mean to her as Bianca had once been. Bianca had taken to calling Dana *that hick sister of yours* and commenting on Dana's weight "problem." What had he ever seen in that woman?

"*A* woman," he said. "Just this one."

Roux shifted awkwardly and asked, "Do you get to live out here all the time? It's so peaceful."

"Boring. Steve would call it boring." Dana waved a hand at their surroundings. "But then he's always been a partyer."

"He does have partying down to a science," Roux said.

Hey. The conversation was not supposed to turn to—or rather, turn against—him. "Roux is a rock star herself."

Roux snorted. "Yeah. Huge rock star over here." She raised her hand. "That no one has ever heard of."

"That's about to change," Steve said.

"So you thought you'd corrupt her before someone else could claim that honor."

"She's incorruptible."

"Boring," Roux said. "Anyone would call me boring."

"I've never been less bored in my entire life," Steve said. He cringed when Dana burst out laughing.

"You're so cute when you're in love," she said, poking him hard in the chest.

"Shut up. I'm not in love." He was. God damn it, he knew he was. Fuck. How? Why? His gaze shifted uncomfortably to Roux, gauging her reaction to his sister's claim, and the moment their eyes met, his heart skittered several beats. He knew how. Roux was perfection—inside and out. As to why . . . Why not? He wouldn't mind settling down. Partying like a rock star was so last week.

"Did you get the cheese, Dana?" Mom asked when she joined their group. She held a pair of onions and several dirty potatoes in her hands.

"It's in the house."

"I'll go find a bell pepper," Roux said, retrieving the tomatoes she'd picked earlier and handing them to Steve.

"Good luck. It's early in the season for peppers. I'll see if the spinach is ready," he said, wanting to get this task over with so he could find that alone time with Roux.

As soon as they went inside, Roux insisted the family farmhouse reminded her of the big brownstone in Boston. Though it wasn't nearly as old or as opulent, it did have thick wooden doorframes and baseboards, a pocket door between the living and dining room, and the high ceilings of homes once heated with fireplaces and lacking air conditioning. In the kitchen, Roux helped him chop veggies while his family—sans Dad, who worked in a local factory during the day—settled around the kitchen island to talk loudly among each other. Every few minutes, Roux would glance at him, and he could practically feel the ache of longing coming from her.

"Do you have any siblings?" Dana asked Roux once she'd

finished arguing with Pops about the superiority of John Deere tractors. Pops hated the John Deere brand, and Dana loved to get him riled up over it.

"Uh." Roux licked her lips and concentrated on finely dicing an onion rather than meeting Dana's curious gaze. "I have twelve foster sisters," she said quietly.

"Twelve!"

Steve wasn't sure whether Dana hadn't heard or hadn't understood the foster part of Roux's answer, but he was glad she hadn't fixated on it.

"There are four older than me," Roux said. "Eight younger."

"She and four of her sisters formed Baroquen—the band she's in."

"That's fun," Mom said.

"I had six brothers," Pops said. "They're all gone now except one."

Roux reached across the counter and squeezed his wrist. "I've lost siblings," she said. "It's not something you ever get over."

Change the subject, Steve thought, his mind reeling to find a safe—less emotionally devastating—topic.

"So which tour stop in Europe are you most looking forward to?" Steve asked Roux. "Have you been to Europe?" He didn't know even that much about her.

"No." There was an undercurrent of *how in the hell could I afford that* in her tone. "I think I'm most looking forward to Italy. Will we have time to do any sightseeing? Iona says we'll be too busy working to enjoy our time there like a vacation."

"I'll take you sightseeing." Why not? His plans to party across Europe with Zach had been completely obliterated. "Italians know how to party, but those Germans? Bring on the beer." As soon as he spoke, he remembered that Roux didn't drink. He shrugged. "If you're into that kind of thing."

"Italy is amazing," Dana said. "But I had the most fun in Spain. Steve sent me to Europe with a few of my friends for my twenty-fifth birthday. Occasionally he can be nice and thoughtful." She nudged Steve's arm.

"Occasionally?" He circled the counter and nudged Dana back, hard enough to send her teetering on her stool.

"You hardly ever visit," she said. "I'd rather have seen you than Europe, you moron."

Steve rolled his eyes. "No need to lie to impress our guest."

Dana rolled her eyes right back at him.

With two pans on the stove, and a very helpful sous chef in Roux, Steve was able to churn out five omelets and a mess of country fried potatoes in record time. Which was good, because as much as he loved his family, he was ready to leave.

After a brief argument over who should be allowed to sit on the remaining stool—Steve insisted the guest should sit, while Roux insisted the hard-working chef should sit—Roux settled onto the stool next to his mother and took her first bite. Steve was left standing but didn't mind. He'd won.

"Mmm," Roux murmured as she chewed and then swallowed. "Everything tastes so fresh."

"Brings new meaning to farm-to-table," Steve said. He leaned over his plate to scoop a bite into his mouth.

"The garden really takes off in July and August," Dana said. "You'll have to come back and visit us then. I make a mean ratatouille."

"It's about time to butcher a beef," Pops declared. "I'm ready for Betty's prime rib."

Roux paled slightly but didn't chastise or preach. Steve had just witnessed firsthand how much she loved animals. Normally he would have paired their omelets with a side of bacon or sausage, but not even Pops had complained about the lack of meat.

After brunch Steve left the dishes to Dana and gave Roux a quick tour of the house. She liked to touch things as he pointed them out. He hoped that meant she was a tactile lover. The only thing he enjoyed more than touching a woman was being touched by one.

In the back parlor, which was seldom used now that Mams had passed away, he showed her his grandmother's cherished antique Steinway grand piano. Pops kept it dust free, and the mahogany gleamed from a recent polish.

"Oh," Roux said with a moan of longing, "it's absolutely gorgeous."

"It would mean a lot to me if you'd play it," Steve said.

"I couldn't," she said, but her fingers were already clenching and unclenching as if they were dying to press the keys.

"Jenny wouldn't mind," Pops said. "You go ahead and play her piano, sweet girl."

Steve spun around to find his grandfather smiling sadly in the doorway. Mom was at his elbow, and Dana was right behind, drying her hands on a dish towel.

Roux turned a worshipful gaze to the hulking instrument. "If you're sure," she said hesitantly.

Steve had only seen one other person gaze at that piano with such adoration. Now that he was older, he wished that he hadn't been so adamant about not allowing his grandmother to teach him to play anything more challenging than "Jingle Bells." Maybe Roux would teach him now and allow him to lay that regret to rest.

With a deep breath, Roux settled onto the bench. Memories of Mams sitting in that exact spot haunted him, and he saw his mother reach for her dad's hand, giving it a reassuring squeeze.

"What should I play?" Roux asked, flexing her fingers over the keyboard. "Something classical or more modern?"

"Do you read music?" Pops asked, hurrying over to a short bookshelf near a matching set of burgundy wingback chairs in the corner.

"Yes."

He tugged a battered notebook from the shelf, but Steve didn't know why.

"She wrote music her entire life," Pops said.

She had? That was news to Steve.

"But was too uncertain to ever share it with anyone but the family." Pops opened the notebook and set it on the music stand above the fallboard. "Seems a shame that no one but us ever got to hear it."

"I'll try to do it justice," Roux said, her eyes scanning the page of neat, handwritten notes drawn across the staves. "Very nice," she whispered to herself just before her fingers played the first note.

Steve couldn't move as a familiar song filled the room. He'd always thought some masterful composer had written that song. He supposed one had. His Mams had obviously been talented; he'd just never recognized that until now. By the time Roux came to the end of the cheerful tune, Mom and Dana were fighting over the dish towel to dry their tears.

"That was truly lovely," Roux said, flipping the page. "What else has she written?"

She'd played through half the notebook when Steve's phone rang. He wanted to ignore it and stay suspended in this moment of remembrance for a while longer but decided the call might be important, especially when he recognized it was from Jordan. But would it be such a tragedy if they had to spend the entire weekend there? Steve's libido cried out a resounding yes.

"We were supposed to be in the air an hour ago," Jordan said, sounding as annoyed as she must feel. "Where in the bloody hell are you?"

"Sorry, time got away from us. We're leaving now and will be right there."

He hung up the phone and waited for Roux to finish playing an up-tempo jig before breaking the news.

"We have to leave now," he said. "That was the pilot, and she's pissed that we've kept her waiting."

"Aw, do you have to?" Dana said, as if she'd suddenly turned into her twelve-year-old self. "I haven't seen Pops this happy in months."

The old guy did have a huge grin on his face.

"We can visit again," Steve promised, because yes, he wanted Roux in his life for as long as she'd have him. He might have suspected it soon after meeting her, but now he was absolutely sure.

CHAPTER 15

ROUX COULDN'T DECIDE if she was glad they were finally leaving the farm and Steve's family behind or miserable about saying goodbye. Steve had taken what she'd expected to be a frivolous, carefree weekend and turned it into an emotionally exhausting ordeal in only a few hours. She doubted he realized how hard families were for her to handle even in small doses, and she was currently overdosed on the Aimeses. But like any addict, that didn't necessarily mean she was prepared to stop seeking more of the same.

"I knew they'd love you," Steve said as they sped down the gravel road, sending up an enormous dust plume in their wake.

"Quite a risk you took there," she said. "They might have hated me."

"Not possible." He didn't look at her, but he grinned crookedly. "You were perfect. That was exactly the recharge I needed."

Recharge? "I feel completely drained." Perhaps she shouldn't admit something like that to him.

"You didn't enjoy yourself?"

"I did," she said. "Your family is amazing." She plucked a stray dog hair from her shirt. "A bit too amazing. I have my sisters, and Mama Ramona, but—"

"My family reminded you of all you've lost." He laid a hand on her knee, and her heart rate accelerated. "I didn't think. I'm sorry. I thought you'd like the farm—the garden, the animals."

"I loved the farm." She covered his hand with hers and squeezed. "And your family and the house and the meal and the piano. It was just a lot to absorb in such a short time. I'm glad you brought me here and let me see a side of you I'd never imagined existed."

"Not many people have seen that side. Not even my closest friends. Well, except Zach. Zach has been here with me. Dana adores him. But not my bandmates. Not even Logan."

"Did you bring Bianca often?" She wasn't sure why that thought made her tense with jealousy.

"A few times. I kept hoping it would grow on her, but she hated it."

"Did you bring me here as some sort of a test?"

His head jerked in her direction, and she knew she'd caught on to the truth.

"A test?" He laughed sharply. "No."

Right. "Did I pass?"

After pulling to a stop at the end of the gravel road, he shifted to look at her. His smile warmed his eyes and her entire body.

"With flying colors."

"You passed my test too," she said.

"What test was that?"

"You didn't laugh at me for being excited about vegetables."

"I was laughing on the inside. There is nothing exciting about vegetables."

He brushed her hair behind her ear, his gaze holding hers with such intensity that her toes curled. As much as she'd enjoyed their little midwestern pit stop, she was definitely looking forward to being alone with him for the rest of the weekend.

A semi roared past on the connecting highway and drew Steve's attention back to driving. Roux stifled a sigh of disappointment as he turned the car onto the blacktop. She was so craving a kiss from the unexpectedly complex man beside her. He wasn't anything like she thought he would be and everything she wanted.

At the small local airport, Roux could tell the pilot—Jordan—was annoyed, but she didn't yell at Steve for making them late. Roux got the feeling that she was used to him mucking up her schedule. Now that Roux knew him better, she realized he wasn't intentionally self-centered and inconsiderate, just used to getting his way.

"Sorry for making us late," Roux apologized, not sure why she felt the need to cover for Steve. "There were kittens." And a thousand other wonderful things to see.

Jordan smiled. "Steve didn't mention kittens."

"They were so adorable," Roux said. "I thought my heart would burst."

Jordan blinked, tilting her head to one side as if trying to figure out what country Roux was from. "I wondered why he wanted to stop here, but now I get it." She grinned, and after saying, "Enjoy your flight," she slipped into the cockpit.

The copilot—who looked as unprofessional in his black T-shirt and worn jeans as Jordan looked professional in her pristine uniform—pulled the outer door shut and secured it while Roux and Steve found their seats.

Roux fastened her seat belt, wondering how long it would stay on this time, and said, "Your bringing me to the family farm made me feel special, but I have to ask: How many women have you taken to this island of yours?"

He went still, and then pulled his fingers through his thick mane of brown hair. He fashioned it into a loose sloppy bun on the back of his head, accentuating his high cheekbones, strong jaw, and exotic eyes with one simple accessory. Roux was so busy staring that she'd forgotten that she'd asked him a question until he responded.

"Not many," he said, but he shifted in his seat, and she couldn't help but think that he was lying or at the very least understating his prowess. She doubted he'd ever done that before. He seemed more likely to brag about his innumerable conquests.

"By whose standards?" she asked. She was starting to fall for this guy and needed to know what she was up against. In the past she'd always been so very careful not to fall too hard for any man. Keeping them at a distance made it harder for them to break her heart, and even after what she'd been through as a child, she had to admit the tender organ was embarrassingly soft.

"By any standards. It's not my island, by the way. It's Dare's."

Her jaw dropped. "Dare's?"

"He's with his family this break—probably helping Trey get ready for his wedding—so he let me borrow it."

She shook her head at the outlandish idea of borrowing an island.

"I never expected Dare to—" She flushed. Why wouldn't Dare own an island for private orgies? She was sure he was a hot-blooded man. Just because he was introverted didn't mean he couldn't whisk some lucky woman off to a tropical paradise for a little alone time.

"As far as I know, he has never brought a woman here either," Steve said, leaning back against his seat as the small jet began to taxi.

Either?

"It's where we go to ensure we aren't recognized," he added, "to completely let down our guard and relax. To get away."

"Not to party yourself into oblivion and have wild sex orgies?"

He grinned. "What kind of perverted maniac do you think I am?"

"The right kind."

He laughed, the rich, deep sound making her heart pound. "I hope I can live up to your wildest expectations."

He already had, but he wasn't exactly what she'd expected. He was so much more. Once the plane lifted off and reached altitude, she anticipated him jumping her eager bones, but they got to talking about high school. Surprisingly, he'd been a football, basketball, and baseball jock even though he'd been several years younger than his classmates; not so surprisingly, she'd been involved in multiple animal welfare projects, many of which she continued to champion when she wasn't following Iona toward stardom.

"If I wasn't your biggest fan, I'd encourage you to go to college to become a veterinarian or a zoologist or something," he said, stroking the hand he held on the armrest between them.

"I thought about it," she admitted. "But I'm content. Inspired even. And even though I'll never make much money helping animals at a shelter, I do feel like I make a difference. That's what's important to me."

"You won't need to worry about money. Your music is going to make you a very wealthy woman."

She tried to cling to his confidence in her, and the self-assuredness that Iona tried to instill in the entire band, but she couldn't quite believe their tragic little songs would ever catch on well enough for Baroquen to have true success.

"I hate to admit that Sam Baily is right about anything," Steve said, "but he was right about Baroquen. The band is going to be a music sensation. And it's going to happen quickly. That's why I had to swoop in and claim you for myself before every man on the planet notices you and wants what I have."

She swallowed, trying not to let his words cloud her judgment, searching for a way to lessen the heaviness of his claims over her. She wanted to be his—she couldn't deny that. But this relationship—if that was where this was truly headed—was moving far too fast for her sensibilities.

"I think we—*you*—need to slow down a little," she said, even as her heart cried out that it didn't want him to slow down in the slightest.

"I've hardly touched you since we got on this plane," he said, squeezing her hand as if he refused to break that final contact.

"I'm not talking about the physical part being too fast. If anything, I wish that part was going faster. It's the emotional entanglement that's making me anxious."

"I thought nice girls wanted all the feelings before focusing on the physical."

She grinned at him. "You think I came with you for feelings?"

"I assumed they'd be a requirement."

"More of a nuisance. I just want a quick and dirty affair." She knew she was saying that to try to keep him at a distance because he was already much too close. He leaned across her seat and kissed her, stealing all rational thought with the sweep of his tongue against her lips.

He pulled away slowly, his eyes searching hers. "That's just too fucking bad, Red. I always get what I want, and our affair can be dirty, but it will not end quickly. It won't end at all."

"We can't continue this in Europe." While they'd been at Pops's farm, she'd started imagining how much fun they could have exploring all the sites in Europe, but she had to think rationally. The next three months would make or break her band, and she couldn't let herself be distracted, no matter how much she wanted this man.

"And that's the only thing making you hesitate?"

She stared into his eyes, thinking of all the reasons she should be cautious. The fact that he was the most famous rock drummer in the world was a major consideration, but his party-boy reputation held a close second, and his womanizing ways were straight at the top of her precautionary list. But the longer she stared at him, the less any of those things mattered, and yes, the tour was the only barrier that truly made her hesitate to toss her heart at his feet and give the uncommon connection between them a chance to grow.

"Yes," she said. "The only thing."

"I'm tempted to call off the entire tour," he said.

Her heart leapt into her throat. That was the exact opposite of what she wanted. Her hand flew out to grasp his forearm, but before she could beg him to reconsider, he added, "But I wouldn't do that to you."

She released her breath, her head swimming from lack of air. Iona wouldn't hesitate to murder her for destroying their big opportunity over some guy. Even if that guy was Steve Aimes.

"So the next few days will have to be spectacular enough to tide me over for three months," he said.

"That's a lot of pressure to put on a woman," she said, her voice wavering slightly. Jeez, until a couple of hours ago, she had never even had an orgasm while with a man. Did he expect her to suddenly become some sex kitten? Because he was going to be entirely disappointed.

"Don't worry," he said, brushing his fingers lightly over her cheek as he continued to stare into her eyes. She couldn't look away or even blink. "I'm already completely hooked."

"Me too."

"I'm glad. I was starting to think this infatuation was one-sided."

She shook her head. "I've always been very cautious about matters of the heart." She instinctually reached for the bullet on her bracelet and squeezed it into her palm. "Maybe because I came so close to losing it for real."

"Just thinking about that makes me ache," he whispered. He closed his eyes and pressed his forehead against hers. "The world would be a much darker place without you in it."

She cupped his jaw in her hands and tilted her head to claim his mouth. His words were so sweet that they made *her* ache with emotion, yet the moment their lips met, that ache shifted into something entirely physical. God, she wanted him. She hoped he'd ravish her soon.

He kissed her so deeply and so thoroughly that she moaned. Her trembling hands slid down his neck to his chest, exploring hard muscles concealed beneath soft cotton. Her fingers bumped over the ridges of his abs, and she silently cursed the armrest between them. Still, the barrier didn't stop her hand from sliding up under his shirt to touch the warm, smooth skin beneath the fabric. When she discovered a narrow strip of coarse hair just beneath his navel, she followed it down to the waistband of his jeans. Dare she? She peeked at his face from under her lashes and found his eyes closed, his face twisted in an agonized expression. Did he like being touched or . . . She pressed a hand against the hard ridge in his pants, and his breath caught. He pushed his head back against the seat but didn't encourage or discourage her exploration. She wasn't used to initiating sexual encounters. It was a little intimidating, but also liberating and arousing.

"Would it be okay if I . . ."

"You don't have to ask," he said, pressing her hand against his hard-on. "I'm completely at your mercy. Do as you please."

She glanced up at the lit fasten-seat-belt sign and resisted the urge to stick her tongue out at it. Still, there was plenty she could do to his gorgeous body before they reached altitude and she could free herself from her seat.

"Put your hands on the armrest and don't move," she said, half expecting him to refuse her request. When he did exactly as instructed, a thrill of empowerment raced through her. He clung to the armrests as she pushed his shirt up his belly and stroked his skin in slow, teasing motions. He squirmed but didn't protest further as she took her time getting to know the rock-hard abs he was famous for. Lord, this man had a body that should be thoroughly appreciated. The strong and well-defined muscles quivered beneath her fingertips, drawing a satisfied smile to her lips. She enjoyed building his anticipation as well as her own.

She unfastened the top button of his jeans, and an excited hiss escaped him. Hiding a wicked grin by tilting her chin down, she moved her attention back to his belly.

"I could stroke your abs all day," she said, her typically husky voice even scratchier than usual.

"There are other parts of me that would enjoy a good stroke," he said tightly.

"Let's see if I can figure out which parts you're referring to."

"You know damn well what I'm referring to."

"Maybe I should use my mouth instead of my hands," she said.

"Yes. Yes, you should."

Arching over the seat put strain on her lower back, but she managed to lock a sucking kiss to his side. His belly tightened, and he huffed out a breath, but he didn't release his white-knuckled grip on the armrests. She kissed a trail down his side, one hand resting flat against his stomach. Her lips continued their journey as far as she could reach, but until she could take off her seat belt, her exploration remained limited.

"We have a problem," she said, shifting her gaze up to his face to find him watching her. "I can't reach."

He grinned crookedly. "Just how small do you think it is?"

She remembered well that he was the opposite of small. Maybe she could reach his cock with her mouth. Well, the tip at the very least. Her hand slid down his belly to his fly, and he groaned as she slowly unbuttoned the remaining buttons there. The look of heated longing on his face made her squeeze her thighs together against a rush of achy needed. She forced her attention to where her hand was fumbling to release him from the confines of his pants, and when his cock sprang free, fully erect and straining, her breath caught. Every inch of this man's body was exquisite. Her fingertips skimmed up the smooth skin of his cock and then trailed back down, slowly, gently, over and over again, until he was panting, his muscles went taut, and his cock twitched. She hadn't realized they could do that.

Feeling a bit uncertain about her skill level—he must have gotten blow jobs from women far more experienced than she was— she bent over his lap and tentatively licked his cockhead. He gasped excitedly, encouraging her boldness. She sucked his tip into her mouth, rubbing her lips over the rim and swirling her tongue over the glans as she sucked softly. He strained toward her, attempting to lift his hips, but his seat belt held him snuggly in place. Further encouraged, she slid a hand into his open fly and cupped his balls, loving the way they slid beneath the loose skin of his sac as she fondled them gently.

His hand shifted to her head, but he didn't try to force it down to take him deeper into her mouth. He merely stroked her hair from her face with tenderness.

"That feels amazing," he said huskily.

Her original intention was to tease him for as long as he could stand it, but now she just wanted to make him come. To give him the intense pleasure he'd given her earlier. Her touch became bolder, caressing his balls, stroking his shaft. Her mouth took him deeper, suction tightening, tongue dancing against his most sensitive skin.

He groaned, his fingers tightening into a fist in her hair. The tug in her scalp each time she lowered her head seemed to tug at her pussy as well. She shifted uncomfortably, the emptiness between her thighs intensely unbearable. She couldn't wait. Fuck the seat belt.

With a groan of impatience, she yanked open the latch, jerked her pants clean off, and sat on his lap, reaching between their bodies to direct his thick cock inside her. She rode him hard and fast, clutching the seatback in front of her. God, how he filled her. She couldn't get enough.

"Fuck, you feel good, baby," Steve said. His seat belt clicked open, and he shifted forward so she could sink deeper onto his lap. "Take what you want. Lose control."

She had lost control, and while normally even the idea of losing control scared her, this lack of control was entirely rewarding. He was so hard, so thick... Their friction produced so much heat... Her excitement built, strengthening into a tight coil within her. *Just let go*, she coached herself. Let go. But the more she tried, the further release spiraled away. She was starting to fatigue.

Steve shifted against her back. "Need a hand, sweetheart?" he murmured close to her ear. He kissed her neck.

"A hand?"

His hand slid against her inner thigh, and then a fingertip rubbed up against her clit. Her pussy clenched, and she almost shot off his lap. She sank back down, not wanting him to ever fall free of her body. Not ever.

"Or maybe just a finger." His teeth sank into her shoulder, and he expertly rubbed her to explosive orgasm within seconds. Her pussy clenched hard around his cock, spasms rippling from her center outward until every cell in her body was awakened by her release.

"Don't stop," she pleaded, the up and down motion of her hips becoming jerky and less rhythmic as she gave him control over her release and trusted him to take her higher. Higher. Higher. Oh dear God, the man did not know how to disappoint.

"Not a chance," he murmured against her shoulder. "We're about to discover if you're multi-orgasmic."

She would have laughed if she could have done anything besides moan in pleasure and attempt to keep fucking him while her climax continued to rip through her. She knew she couldn't come more than once. She'd tried it on herself and had never been able to reach a second orgasm. But then she'd never realized she could keep coming long after the first ripples of release tore through her. When at last he'd wrung every shred of pleasure from her weak body, she settled back onto his lap to catch her breath. He was still massaging her clit, and the sensitive flesh began to protest from overstimulation. She caught Steve's wrist to hold his hand still.

"Enough," she panted.

"Not nearly enough."

"I can't take any more."

"You'll take everything I give you and like it." He cupped her breast and pinched her nipple through her shirt.

She gasped in surprise as her pussy tightened around his cock with excitement and renewed need.

"Your pussy already knows it," he said, the command in his

tone making her shudder. "Now I just have to make the rest of you a believer."

He wrapped an arm tight around her lower belly, grabbed the seat in front of them with his free hand, and in an incredible feat of strength, stood up with her still impaled by his cock. He pressed her front up against the back of the seat and shifted her legs so that her feet found the seat behind them. Once she had her balance, he shifted his hold to her hips, and began to thrust his hips.

He was rough as he pounded into her. She'd never had a man fuck her so hard. She never knew she could like it so much.

"Do you like to be fucked, sweet Roux?"

She caught his relentless rhythm, his brutal tempo, and rocked back to meet him. He fucked like he drummed—hard, fast, and rhythmic, putting his entire body into every beat.

"Answer me," he demanded, his fingers pressing deep into her hips.

Had he asked her something? His deep voice echoed through her thoughts: *Do you like to be fucked?*

"Yes!"

"Say it."

"I like to be fucked." Her eyes shot open as her pussy tightened on the brink of release. "I'm gonna come!"

"Yeah, you are. And I'm going to fill your hot cunt to the brim with my cum."

Her eyes widened at his crass words and widened further as her womb tightened and she reached orgasm a second time. This one felt different. Deeper. Less like ripples and more like intense spasms. She cried out, her body going stiff, trapped between the seat and his body. She would have sagged and slid to the floor if Steve hadn't had a firm grip on her hips.

"I knew you had it in you."

He patted her ass as if they were in the end zone and she'd just scored a touchdown.

"Now it's my turn."

When he pulled out, she cried out in protest. She wasn't ready to part from him. Was he going to jack off onto her back? But he'd promised to fill her with his cum. She wanted that. She wanted him. She wanted all of him.

He dragged her limp body from between the seats and settled her onto her back on the sofa that ran along one side of the aisle. He peeled her shirt and bra from her body and shed his clothes before settling on top of her. The warmth of his bare skin against hers made her heart pound. Oh, this was nice. He felt so good nestled between her thighs. She wrapped both arms around his neck and stared up into his gorgeous brown eyes. He kissed her gently, reached between them and found her opening. He eased into her slowly, never breaking eye contact.

He was surprisingly tender as he took her with slow, churning strokes, peppering gentle kisses on her lips, her eyelids, her neck, and caressing her body as if she were a priceless work of art. Even as the heat between them rose and their skin became slick with sweat, he made her feel treasured and more than a little overwhelmed by the emotions swirling through her. His emotions were close to the surface as well. She could see the turbulence mixed with passion in his eyes. His raw vulnerability made her want to hold him and never let go. This was so much more than she'd bargained for. A gift, she realized, as he lifted her hand to his mouth and kissed her palm and wrist. How was it possible to love a man she barely knew? Not that she could tell him her feelings. He'd think she was stupid or insincere or wanted something as trivial as his fortune. But she only wanted one thing from him. She moved her free hand to the center of his chest and relished the feel of his heart pounding hard beneath her fingertips. His heart. That was what she wanted. His true heart. She knew he wouldn't give it lightly. Not after it had been so thoroughly shattered by his ex-wife. But Roux vowed to never hurt him. Just love him and dare to believe he could someday love her in return.

He stroked her hair from her face and kissed her lips, and then he lifted his head to stare into her eyes again. "It's been so long since I made love to a woman, I forgot how good it could be," he said.

Her Steve-is-perfection fantasy bubble burst, and she jabbed him in the chest with one finger. "Liar."

"Not a lie," he said, capturing both her hands in his and pressing them to the sofa on either side of her head. "I fornicate, I fuck, I screw, but I don't make love. Not like this."

Now she felt bad. She blinked back tears and nodded, at a loss for words but wanting him to know that she understood this encounter was special to them both. She shouldn't have belittled his sentiment. He kissed a drop of moisture from the corner of her eye and grinned down at her.

"Time for the grand finale."

But she never wanted this to end. What if this was their last time together? What if it never felt this good again? What if her rational mind convinced her emotional one that all these feelings were just a product of physical attraction? What if, what if, what if... Her doubts scattered when Steve rose up on his knees, lifting her hips by supporting her lower back with one hand and placing the other over her mound. His thumb brushed her clit, and her entire body jerked in response.

"Ever come with a man?" he asked, the familiar cockiness in his tone a relief after all the overwhelming emotions he'd been stirring within her.

"Like having simultaneous orgasms?"

"Exactly like that."

She quirked an eyebrow. "Obviously not."

"Well, you're about to," he said.

Doubtful. She'd already managed two explosive orgasms. He didn't really think she was capable of a third, did he? Before she could even form a snarky comeback, he began to thrust. The shift in position had the head of his cock rubbing hard against her front wall. She gasped in surprise as an unfamiliar pleasurable sensation rocked through her pussy. That might not have been enough to send her flying on its own, but then his thumb began to massage her clit and within seconds she was thrashing in torment as he brought her to another peak.

"Yes," she cried out. "Yes!"

She shattered, and he followed her over the edge. His hands shifted to her hips, pulling her hard onto his cock as he pushed into her.

"Oh God," he groaned, his entire body quaking. He pulled out a couple of inches, but pressed balls deep again, still shuddering. "Mmm." He pulled out all the way, and she felt a spurt of cum against her opening before he thrust into her one last time.

With a whoosh of breath, he shifted his legs out behind himself again and collapsed on top of her, squeezing her so tightly she could scarcely breathe. But she didn't mind. She hugged him even closer.

They lay intertwined, breathing raggedly, for a long while.

Roux drifted in and out of sleep, not sure how much time had passed when the intercom crackled and startled her to full alertness.

Jordan announced, "We'll be landing in about an hour. The persistent fasten-seat-belt sign is your punishment for making us late, Aimes. We have clear skies all around, and there's a magnificent sunset forming off the right wing."

Steve lifted his body off Roux's and peered out the window over the back of the sofa. "She's right," he said. "You need to see this. It's spectacular."

She stared up at him, her heart pounding at his gorgeousness. "It sure is."

He grinned when he recognized that she was staring at him and not at anything as mundane as a sunset. "So we've accomplished multiple orgasms and simultaneous orgasms this afternoon," he said, settling over top of her with his weight supported on his elbows. "What should we tackle next?"

He stroked her hair from her face and kissed her brow. She melted into the sofa and released a contented sigh.

She had no idea what came next, but whatever it was, she was confident that he could deliver and that she'd enjoy both the journey and the ride.

Chapter 16

IT WAS NEARLY DARK when the plane made its final approach toward the landing strip on the small, tree-covered island—an island that Dare claimed was shaped like a guitar, but which Steve thought looked more like a dick and balls. The main portion was rounded at the bottom and roughly oval-shaped, with a long peninsula that extended far out into the sea. There were even a few rocks jutting up from the ocean at the tip of the peninsula, which could be construed as drops of jizz, but Steve had discovered long ago that Dare didn't think owning a dick-shaped island was funny in the least. It was a guitar, damn it. So Logan and Steve joked about Dick Island behind Dare's back, but never to his face.

"What does the island look like to you?" Steve asked Roux, who was sitting next to the window and gazing outside with a flush of excitement on her fair face. The woman was an absolute goddess.

"A tropical paradise."

"I mean its shape. Does it remind you of anything?"

She nibbled her lip and then said, "A baby rattle."

"What?" He stretched over her to point. "The long part is obviously a dick and the round part is the balls."

"Those would be some huge balls and a disappointingly thin dick," she countered.

True. He was glad his junk wasn't shaped like that, but still . . . "It doesn't look anything like a guitar, right?"

She tilted her head, giving the rapidly enlarging island another look. "About as much as it looks like a dick and balls. It's a baby rattle."

"Do babies even play with rattles anymore?"

"Or it could be a spoon." She looked at him with wide eyes, as if seeking approval.

He still thought it looked like a dick and balls, but said, "Yeah, I can see that." He stroked a silky lock of her hair, realizing that he had an unquenchable need to touch her hair as much as possible as well as to touch her lovely face and the rest of her. God, the woman was deep under his skin. He leaned in for a kiss, but the plane touched down and they bumped foreheads.

"I don't know about you," he said, rubbing the spot on his head with one hand and the one on hers with the other, "but I'm ready to get the fuck off this plane for a couple of days."

"Oh, I don't know," she said. "I had a pretty good time on this plane."

"Just pretty good?"

"Best time of my life."

She gifted him with that sexy little smile of hers. As usual, it made his balls tighten.

"But somehow, I think we're going to top it."

He squeezed her hand. "Count on it.", He'd usually heap on the island fun by getting plastered and high and then dance naked on the beach until he passed out, but with exception of naked beach time, that scenario held absolutely no appeal to him when he was with Roux. He couldn't decide if the sudden shift in his idea of fun was a good thing or a bad thing. He had his notorious rock star reputation to uphold. But not here with her. Here with her he could be anything he wanted to be. Even lame.

There were two main dwellings on the island and a caretaker's cabin. They left the air crew of two to enjoy their weekend at the larger, more luxurious house near the landing strip that ran the length of the peninsula. He and Roux climbed aboard one of the sports quads to make their way to the smaller, more secluded beach house that could be reached only by driving through the jungle or by boat. The small headlights cut through the darkness to guide them on a path that was difficult to navigate even in the daytime. The underbrush had a way of overgrowing and blocking the narrow road within days of it being cleared. Steve guessed that the day's notice he'd given to Dare hadn't been enough time to alert the island's caretaker to cut back the brush.

"Are there monkeys in this jungle?" Roux asked excitedly as she peered into the dark under-canopy around them.

Normally Steve would have the vehicle at full throttle and be barreling through the underbrush in pursuit of Logan, who was a total adrenaline junkie. But he took it slow, concerned for Roux's safety. He'd never realized jungle underbrush could put him in a romantic mood, or maybe it was the feel of her hands on his waist and her warmth at his back that had him considering their surroundings as something other than a nuisance blocking his way to the beach. The eerie call of some night creature piqued his curiosity rather than making him want to get out of the foliage as soon as possible.

"Monkeys? I don't think so," he said. "Birds maybe. We can explore in the daylight and see what we can find."

"I thought you'd been here before."

"I have," he said, suddenly feeling embarrassed by his total disregard for the potentially amazing wildlife on the island. All he'd ever cared about before was that the bar was well stocked and that no one complained about how loudly he blared the music on the beach. "I just stuck to the beach. Never ventured too far into the trees." At least not at a rate of speed that he'd have been able to see anything but a furry blur.

Roux slapped herself hard, and he jumped.

"Well, there are definitely mosquitoes on this island. Do I need to worry about malaria?" she asked, slapping herself a second time.

"I hope not. I'll go a little faster so the thirsty buggers can't catch us. Hold on."

Her arms tightened around his waist, and he decided his going fast with her was the best decision he'd ever made—and he wasn't thinking about the speed of the ATV.

A few minutes later, he pulled to a halt under the beach house—between its sturdy stilts—and a motion sensor switched on the security lights.

"Oh my," Roux said, peering up at the underside of the tiny cottage. "What a charming little house."

He wasn't sure how she could tell from this vantage, but it truly was cute and cozy. Painted blue with white trim, it had a nautical theme inside and out.

"This cottage was original to the island when Dare bought it," Steve said, sliding off the ATV. "He added the landing strip and the ridiculously expensive mansion-type house at the base of the dick after he bought it."

"It's not a dick, it's a spoon handle," Roux corrected with a grin.

He sighed and shook his head. "You're too sweet for your own good, Red." But he was okay with that, because her nature drew out qualities in him that he'd forgotten he possessed, and she was wonderful to be around. He couldn't imagine a single day in his future without her in it.

She slapped her neck. "Apparently the mosquitoes agree."

"Let's hurry inside before your sweetness attracts a swarm."

Feeling unabashedly chivalrous, he scooped her off the quad and into his arms. He carried her to the open-backed wooden stairs that led to the deck that faced the ocean. The warm onshore breeze stirred her hair against his face and was a welcome relief after the cloying heat of the jungle. It was also an effective mosquito deterrent. Roux wrapped her arms around his neck and leaned into him, breathing deeply.

"I figured I'd have to get throwing-up-in-a-bucket drunk to experience this for myself," she said.

He puzzled over her words until he remembered that he'd carried her friend Azura to their hotel room the night of the after-party. He also remembered having to jack off that night for the first time in years because Roux had left him with a raging hard-on and no desire to seek alternate pussy for relief. "No drinking required. I'll carry you anywhere you want to go."

"To the top of Mount Everest?"

"If that's what you desire."

She pressed a kiss to his neck. "This is all I desire. I was so jealous of Azura that night."

"She puked in a bucket. Nothing to be jealous of there."

Roux chuckled. "That's true. She just realized yesterday that you were not a figment of her imagination and were present for her total disgrace. She was mortified."

"I'll have to tease her mercilessly the next time I see her," he said.

"Only fair."

He refused to let Roux know he was winded by the time they reached the top of the stairs. She wasn't heavy; the stairs were especially steep. "I'll have to set you down to open the door."

"Kiss me first. I want this fantasy to be complete."

He loved that she'd fantasized about him and wondered if she'd like to know how much he'd fantasized about her over the past two weeks or if she'd think his infatuation was creepy and a little desperate. He kissed her deeply, lips caressing hers, tongue seeking her taste. By the time they parted and he set her on her feet, he was breathing hard for an entirely different reason than carrying an adult woman up a flight of stairs. She watched him fumble with the lockbox that held the key, though he wasn't sure why Dare kept the place locked. It was highly unlikely that anyone would rob the place. Then again, fans and paparazzi had been known to do some bizarre things to get close to the members of his band.

"Would you be totally scandalized if I spent the entire weekend in my underwear?" Roux asked. "This breeze feels fantastic."

"If I have anything to say in the matter, you'll be overdressed in your underwear."

She glanced over her shoulder and caught her first sight of the ocean view. She gasped and raced to the railing to peer out at the water. A half-moon rose over the inky, shiny surface of the choppy ocean. Waves lapped at the shore along the pristine sand of the beach, which was peppered with large coconut trees and some sort of flowering shrub that perfumed the entire area.

"Oh!" she said, hopping up and down at the railing. "It's gorgeous. Can we swim? Or are there sharks out there?"

"We can swim. The sharks stay farther out, around the reef."

"There's a reef? You didn't mention a reef."

He would have if he'd known she'd be so excited about it.

"It's fairly small. Nothing like the Great Barrier Reef. You'll probably be disappointed." He finally fished the key out of the lockbox, but instead of unlocking the door, he pocketed the key and joined her at the railing.

"Have you actually been to the Great Barrier Reef?"

Her wide eyes caught the reflection of the moon, and he wouldn't have been able to keep his hands off her even if she were covered in pig shit and thorns.

"I have." He wrapped both arms around her and drew her heat close, rubbing her back as he wished for more light so he could examine her face without shadows. "Would you like to go snorkeling there?"

"It's always been a dream of mine." She grinned and shook her head. "I have so many dreams and so little means."

"I've got the means, and I'd love to share your dreams, if you'll let me."

She lifted her hands to her face and pressed her fingers against her cheeks. "Are you trying to spoil me, Aimes?"

Nothing would make him happier. "You deserve to be spoiled. You're wonderful." *I love you already*. He swallowed as the sentiment ricocheted through his thoughts. She really would think he was creepy and stalkerish if he started blurting out love confessions this soon, so he savored the knowledge in his heart, allowing his affection to grow with each passing second.

"Being with you makes me happy." She wrapped her arms around him and pressed her face against his chest, snuggling into him. He cradled the back of her head and pressed her closer. He had so many things he wanted to say but could only muster one breathless word.

"Same."

He'd fallen, and he hoped he never got up.

He held her for a long moment, too absorbed in the feel of her against him to even watch the waves or count the stars that glittered overhead.

"I do think we're overdressed for this," she murmured.

He didn't need to be told twice. He peeled her shirt off over her head, and she helped him out of his. Both landed somewhere on the deck. He unhooked her bra, and she yanked it off before pressing up against him again. The warmth of her skin against his, the softness of her breasts, and the smooth texture of her back as he caressed her slowly made him crave more, yet he was in no hurry. They had all weekend, and after the European leg of the tour, they had a lifetime to get to know each other.

Her hands began to explore his back, and her lips caressed his chest with soft kisses. That, together with the onshore breeze, gave him goose bumps. A shiver raced down his spine.

"Have you ever been skinny-dipping?" he whispered into her ear.

"Yes," she said, and a pang of jealousy twisted his heart. He wished he could share every unique life experience with her, but that was just stupid. "But never in the ocean," she continued, kissing her way up to his neck. He shivered again as she discovered one of his erogenous zones. "And never with a man."

The moonlight lit her face as she gazed up at him. He couldn't resist the allure of her slightly curved lips and leaned in to take the kiss he craved. His hands moved to the waist of her pants and eased them down over her hips. "I hope you weren't planning on going to bed tonight."

"We'll get there eventually," she said, unfastening his jeans.

"But I wasn't planning on sleeping in it."

Naked, they hurried down the steps to the beach and dashed, hand in hand, toward the water. When the waves washed over Roux's feet, she squealed, and he scooped her into his arms, giving her a twirl as the water sloshed against his calves.

"It's warm," she said, wrapping her arms securely around his neck. "I was expecting it to be cold."

"In June?"

"I'm from New England. I thought all oceans were cold. Or at least cool. You can put me down."

"In a minute." He kissed her thoroughly as he waded deeper and deeper into the water. When the churning surface was about thigh high and he was sure there were no sharp shells or rocks to hurt Roux's feet, he allowed her to slide down his body, partly because she felt so good against him, but also because he wanted her to become aware of how turned on he was by her.

"Wow," she said, grinning up at him. "Is that a log of drift wood you've got there, or are you happy to see me, Aimes?"

His retort died on his tongue as she wrapped a hand around his shaft.

"Let me help you with this," she said. She sank down into the water.

He groaned when she gently sucked the tip of his cock into her mouth and gave himself over to sensation. Waves lapped repetitively around his upper thighs, washing over his balls with just enough regularity to increase his anticipation. One of Roux's hands stroked his length, the other caressed his ass, the breeze cool against the wetness she left on his skin. Strands of his hair tickled his neck and shoulders as they danced on the wind. But her mouth—Lord, her mouth—was delightful in every capacity. Whether she was singing, speaking, smiling, or sucking, he was completely enamored by that mouth of hers. He was torn between wanting to kiss her and encouraging her to suck harder so he could fill her mouth with his cum.

"Can I come in your mouth?" he asked, hoping she'd agree, but not cruel enough to do it without her permission. She was vegan after all, and he was all animal.

She nodded slightly, and he threw all restraint aside. His hands moved to her hair, wet fingers dripping water over the silky strands. He shifted his hips forward, eyelashes fluttering as her tongue caressed the underside of his dick and his head brushed the roof of her mouth. When he felt her throat tighten involuntarily, he retreated slowly and allowed her to regain her composure. He knew women who bragged about not having a gag reflex, but the sensation of it triggering around his cockhead never failed to undo him completely, and Roux's gag reflex was particularly strong. He had to experience it again.

"I'm sorry," he groaned as he thrust into her throat again, and was gifted once more with her throat constricting around his tip. His balls tightened. He was already close. So close. Being brought to his limit so quickly was a little embarrassing for a man known for his longevity, yet at the same time, it was glorious. Roux had done this to him. Roux. Her name echoed through his thoughts, making his heart pound. Roux.

He pulled his hips back and looked down at her face shining pale in the moonlight. Her eyes were closed, nostrils flared as she sucked air into her lungs through her nose. She had surrendered to his need, showing no signs of resistance. He almost felt bad for taking advantage of her generosity and thrusting into her throat again and again. Dear God, he'd found utopia.

When she couldn't take anymore, her hand tightened around his shaft, and he groaned as his release caught him by surprise. She jerked back, her eyes opening wide as his cum wet the side of her mouth. Her eyes met his as she opened her mouth wide, stroking his length to accept his load as promised. The pleasure of his release was so intense, he had to struggle to keep his eyes open, but he doubted he'd ever witness anything more sexually gratifying in his life than Roux's wondrous mouth filling with his cum.

And then she swallowed.

"Fuck," he growled, bending to grab her by both arms and lift her out of the water. He pressed her length against his, her wet body cool against his heated chest as he wrapped one arm tightly around her back. He cradled the back of her head with his free hand, pressing her face against the rapid pulse in his throat. He was completely overcome with emotion—breaths coming in harsh rasps, eyes watery with tears—over a fucking blow job. What the hell was wrong with him?

"Did I do it right?" she asked, her tone uncertain.

He couldn't help but laugh. "You were perfect. *Are* perfect." *I love you, sweetheart. You have no idea how much.* He wished he had the guts to tell her now, but revealing the depth of his feelings would have to wait until after the tour ended and they were free to be together without reservation. But even if he couldn't tell her, he could show her.

"It's time to find the nearest bed," he said.

"It's a little early to go to sleep," she said. "But it has been a long day."

"You won't be sleeping." He slid a hand down to cup her supple ass. "You'll be too busy coming to sleep."

"Sounds great," she said, "but can we eat first? That protein Slurpee reminded me that we haven't had dinner."

He chuckled and squeezed her butt. "Priorities, Red. The only thing I want to eat right now is you."

Chapter 17

ROUX SNUGGLED CLOSER to the warm body beside her. A smile formed on her lips before she even opened her eyes. The sunshine streaming across her face made her eyelids glow red-orange, but she wasn't ready for last night to end. Not yet. She was almost convinced it had been a dream—a very erotic wet dream that had no place in reality. She shifted her hips and could still feel him inside her. Her skin was still sticky with a mixture of their sweat and saliva and cum, and as much as she wanted to lie beside him wasting the day away, she needed a shower. She usually took one right after sex, but after Steve had finished with her, she'd been too exhausted and satisfied to even consider anything more involved than a quick pee and a wash in the sink.

Steve shifted beside her, and her smile widened as his lips brushed her jaw. "I was dreaming about you," he murmured. He kissed her chin before nibbling his way toward her ear.

A shiver of excitement raced through her. Her body already knew what was to come and was eagerly onboard for Steve's next adventure.

"A good dream, I hope," she said, stroking the smooth skin of his back.

He shifted her body beneath his and settled between her legs. She gasped when the hard length of his cock pressed against her tender pussy. She was going to be so sore after this weekend. She'd probably need those three months apart to recover. Her arms tightened around him, heart aching at the thought of their separation. She could only imagine how hard it was going to be to see him every day but keep her distance.

"That is not a rabbit in my pocket," he said. "Or driftwood. I'm really happy to see you."

She giggled. "I'm happy to see you too."

"Are you too sore?" he asked, his thoughtfulness touching her. She never expected him to be that way and had almost convinced herself that he did treat her special. She couldn't ask him if he was this considerate of every woman. "If you are, I can just jerk one out on your tits."

Now *that* was something she'd expect of him. "I am a little tender," she admitted. "But I still want you to fuck me gently before you jerk off on my tits."

He groaned, shifting his hips to press his cock more firmly against her. "You are my favorite person, Red."

She never thought she'd say it and mean it but she said, "You're my favorite person as well, Aimes."

His breath caught, and he lifted onto his elbows. She could feel his gaze on her, so she forced her eyes open, blinking in the bright daylight until his tousled gorgeousness came into sharp focus. She'd never seen him with beard growth before. It made him even sexier, if that was possible. What she wouldn't give to wake up to this glorious vision every morning.

He held her gaze and licked his lips, as if struggling to find words. After a long moment he shook his head and murmured, "Still too soon," before leaning in for a deep kiss.

By the time he pulled away, Roux's heart was aching. She'd never been kissed by anyone the way Steve kissed her. There was something deeper than passion between them. It was as if her heart, body, and soul had found all their missing pieces in one naughty, raunchy, notoriously bad-boy womanizer. Her head was the only part of her that found the idea preposterous.

She sighed as he began to kiss and suckle his way down her chest. The roughness of his beard stubble added a new layer of sensation to the mix. She groaned in protest when he shifted his cock away from her body so he could suck her nipples.

"You do want some dick this morning, don't you?" he teased.

"Only yours," she protested. It wasn't as if she woke up each morning craving whatever dick was unoccupied at the moment.

"Happy to hear that." He licked her nipple. "But you're going to have to wait until I've tasted your cum first."

She cringed. It wasn't that she didn't want his mouth on her, but she wasn't exactly sanitary down there this morning. "Maybe I should shower first."

"I prefer my morning pussy dirty," he said, slapping her ass.

She tried not to think about how much dirty morning pussy the man had enjoyed in his lifetime as he nibbled his way down her belly.

He didn't stop until he reached the juncture of her thighs. He inhaled deeply through his nose. "Your scent drives me crazy."

Probably because he had to hold his breath and no oxygen was getting to his brain, but all traces of her mortification vanished when his mouth began to work its magic on her clit and lips. He'd been phenomenal at exciting her from the start, but somehow he became even better each time they touched. He was learning her body. She'd never had a man care enough about her needs to work so hard at pleasing her.

His tongue teased her clit so gently, she could scarcely feel it. The light touch drove her absolutely crazy, and just when her hips began to writhe with unfulfilled need, he changed tactics, sucking hard and flicking her clit with the tip of his tongue. The instant her body tensed as climax approached, he returned to his crazy-making feather-soft teasing. Each round took her higher, brought her close to orgasm more quickly, until she was calling out to God and her entire body was quaking. Steve finally gave her what she wanted, sucking her clit to orgasm, and while she was shaking with blessed release, shifted his tongue to her opening—thrusting and swirling it inside her as she clung to his hair with both fists and arched toward the ceiling.

When his tongue slid over her asshole, she nearly catapulted clean off the bed, her heart thudding wildly in her chest.

"What was— Why did— I was not prepared for that!" she squeaked.

He rose on his elbows and grinned in a way that made her think she was sleeping with the devil himself. "Someone needs a little ass loving."

Her jaw dropped, and her already rapid pulse surged to new heights. "I know you're not talking about me."

His grin widened. "I am."

He grabbed her hips and flipped her onto her stomach. She lifted up on her knees and tried to scramble away, but his warm wet tongue brushed her asshole, and it was as if she was completely paralyzed. She couldn't move except for the quivering in the muscle his tongue was massaging.

Oh God. Her eyes rolled, and her jaw went slack. Why the fuck did that feel so good?

"So dirty," she murmured.

His tongue breached her ass for a scant second, and her body went rigid. He sank his teeth into her butt cheek before rising to kneel behind her. She moaned as he filled her hot center with thick, hard dick. And she did want some dick this morning. She wanted a lot of dick, to be honest. And Steve had a lot of it to give.

His thrusts were almost brutal, and it turned her on that his control had slipped. He was still with it enough to reach around and rub her clit with his hand, the ridges and valleys of his stiff fingers stimulating.

"Am I hurting you, sweetheart?" he asked, though his thrusts didn't gentle.

"I'm a little sore," she admitted, but she liked that she felt their previous times together with each new penetration.

"Want me to make your ass sore too?"

She shattered at the mere thought, moaning as ecstasy rippled through her. He slapped her ass, which made her tighten around his cock, and he followed her over the edge.

"Later," he promised as he held himself deep inside her, fingers digging hard into her hips. Her inner muscles gripped the hard length of him in seemingly endless waves as she drew his orgasm into hers.

After a long moment, he collapsed onto his side and drew her close, spooning her back tightly to his chest.

"It's only going to get better between us," he murmured close to her ear.

She wasn't sure how that was possible, but she was looking forward to finding out if he was right.

After an outdoor shower that used water from an overhead reservoir of collected rainwater, they picked ripe tropical fruit off the trees for their breakfast.

"You're going to get sick of fruit," Steve said as he handed her a papaya. "There's not much food stored here that you can eat. We usually fish for our supper, if we aren't too drunk."

"I'll be fine," she insisted, spotting an avocado tree on the edge of the clearing around the little beach house. "Better than fine." She loved avocados, especially with eggs. "Dare needs to get some chickens."

"Then you'd prefer his island to my farm."

"I prefer being with you," she said as she tried to figure out which avocados were ripe, "wherever that happens to be."

Steve drew in a deep breath, his bare chest broadening. "How do you feel about obnoxiously large mansions in Los Angeles?"

"I'd prefer someplace a little cozier, but—"

"Good. Dare's the one with the ungodly huge mansion. I live in a tiny cottage in Venice Beach."

She wasn't sure why he thought he was in competition with Dare, but she recognized a male ego in need of stroking when she saw one. "I can't wait to see it," she said, before realizing she was getting ahead of herself. There had to be a reason why he'd brought her to Dare's island for their weekend together rather than to his own house. "I mean if you ever want me to visit."

"Probably not a good idea," he said, reaching over to place a hand on her bare back. "I'd probably do something stupid like ask you to move in with me."

She laughed off his admission, partly because she figured she'd probably say yes, and that would be ridiculous. They scarcely knew each other. At least other people would see it that way. She felt like she'd always known him.

A loud squawk made her jump. Roux spotted numerous colorful birds in the jungle behind the little beach house, but no monkeys. There probably weren't any. It was unlikely that they'd be able to reach the island from the mainland, but that didn't stop her from wanting to explore.

"Can we check out the jungle after breakfast?" she asked, squinting into the dim interior of the thick undergrowth.

"I was hoping you'd want to check out my body."

"I can multitask." She turned toward the house carrying several papayas and avocados, and a bright purple fruit she didn't recognize but that Steve had insisted was edible.

The only thing more delightful and delicious than the fruit was the company. Steve had an endless stream of humorous tales about Logan's ceaseless search for a new adrenaline rush and how he somehow always convinced Steve to join him.

"So he's dangling from the top of the tree with one hand, throwing these coconuts down at me with his other like projectile missiles, when he decides we can use the tree as a springboard to jump over this little cliff into the ocean."

Roux covered her eyes with both hands. "Please tell me you didn't agree to try it."

"He dared me."

She shook her head. Boys!

"So I shinny up the tree, and the dang thing bows all the way to the ground under our weight. Logan pushes me off onto the beach, and the trunk pops up and sends him flying."

She tried not to laugh, because someone probably got hurt, but Logan Schmidt flying off the end of a tree had to have been a sight to behold.

"Dare's just standing there with his finger on speed dial for emergency medical transport."

"And Max?"

"Max is yelling that he hopes we break our stupid necks."

"It sounds like you guys have a lot of fun together," she said.

A crease formed between Steve's brows. "Yeah, we used to," he said. "But now we spend most of our time arguing."

"What about?" She was expecting the usual "creative differences" response. That was what most bands argued over. Especially one as successful and long-lived as Exodus End.

"Sam Fucking Baily."

"Our manager?"

Steve's lip curled, and storm clouds built in his gorgeous brown eyes. She hadn't known a person's mood could shift so swiftly.

"Should I be worried?" she asked, because she wasn't experienced enough to know when to worry about having a powerhouse of a manager versus when she should feel grateful for having one.

"I won't let him hurt your career," Steve said. He took her hand and squeezed it before pointing to her lips. "You have a little something there."

She licked at the corner of her mouth but couldn't find traces of anything unusual. "What?"

He leaned forward and kissed her. "My lips."

"Mmm," she said, sliding a hand to the back of his head to keep him from moving away. "I think I'll keep those there for as long as possible."

It was near noon when they finally ventured out of the house again. Roux was slathered in sunscreen and bug spray and wearing a semi-transparent cover-up over her green string bikini. The sun had never been kind to her skin. She burned quickly and severely if she wasn't careful. She envied Steve's tan and the fact that he could wear nothing but a pair of shorts in the muggy heat.

"Are you sure you want to go into the jungle?" he asked. "It's a jungle in there."

She rolled her eyes at his lame joke. "Just for a little while," she said. "I've never been in a jungle before."

"You were in one last night."

"I can go by myself if you don't want to protect me," she said.

That did the trick. He took her hand. "I'll always protect you. Do you want to walk or take the quad?"

She wore little tennis shoes and Steve wore sandals. She wasn't sure how rugged the terrain would be but feared the noisy quad would scare off any wildlife.

"Walk. Is that okay?"

"Whatever you want, Red. This is your adventure."

She soon discovered that the farther they got from the beach, the hotter and more humid the air became, until she was pretty sure they'd somehow ventured into the steam room at the gym. Steve pointed out several brightly colored birds in the trees, and Roux discovered that cute furry shrews lived in the leaf litter and munched on the many bugs that populated the area. They didn't find any monkeys.

"I've seen a few sea turtles on the beach," Steve said.

She figured he was less than enthused by their jungle walk and was trying to entice her back to the much cooler beach. Or maybe he knew she loved sea turtles.

"I'm ready to head back," she said. "Maybe we'll find more interesting wildlife on the beach."

A large iridescent green beetle landed on Steve's shoulder. He shouted, his body jerking as he wildly flailed his arms. Roux laughed and plucked the beetle off his skin before allowing the shiny creature to run over the surface of her hand.

"My hero," she said.

"It startled me."

The beetle spread its wings and took flight toward Steve, who ducked and swung a hand at it.

"You're not afraid of bugs, are you?" Roux asked.

"No. I just don't like them touching me. Or flying around me." He grinned. "Or existing."

"Don't worry," she said. "I'll protect you."

He poked her in the ribs, and she yanked away, giggling. She started toward the beach by carefully stepping over a fallen tree, but Steve caught her by the arm. "It's this way." He jerked his head in the opposite direction.

"Are you sure?" She wasn't. Sometime during their walk she'd lost track of direction, and here under the forest canopy, she couldn't see the sky except in occasional small patches. As she looked up hoping to catch a glimpse of the sun, the branches overhead swayed and rustled with the strong breeze and the interior of the jungle darkened.

"I'm sure," he said, and she stepped back over the log to stand at his side. "I'm also sure we're about to get soaked."

"How—"

A single rumble of thunder announced a sudden downpour. The dense leaves overhead caught the rain, but the load was soon too much, and water drenched them in seconds. The cool rain felt refreshing after the cloying air, so Roux turned her face up and closed her eyes, allowing the water to cascade over her cheeks. She even stuck out her tongue for a taste. She gasped in surprise when she was suddenly gripped by both arms and pressed against a sturdy tree trunk.

"You don't have any idea how beautiful you are, do you?" Steve asked, cupping her face and rubbing water from her cheek with his thumb.

She opened her eyes and crinkled her nose. "I'm pretty sure I look like a drowned rat at the moment." Though *he* looked irresistibly sexy with his dark hair clinging to his face and neck and water dripping from the strong contours of his jaw to trickle down his throat and broad, muscular chest.

He shook his head. "I want you."

"Now?"

"Always."

In that case, she couldn't resist leaning close to lick the water from his collarbone or kissing a trail up his neck. She always wanted him as well.

One of his hands squeezed her breast while the other worked its way beneath the fabric of her bikini bottoms. His fingers were cool against her heat. With a few rapid strokes against her clit, he had her wet and moaning. She fumbled with his shorts to free his cock and took a moment to appreciate the silky skin that covered the length of his hard shaft. With his continued teasing of her clit, her own need took precedence, and she tugged him forward, lifting her leg and nudging her bikini bottoms aside to direct him into her. He needed no further encouragement. Steve grabbed her ass to lift her higher, leveraging her back against the tree so he could thrust deep.

Her heart pounded furiously as he began to move, his strokes as frenzied and wild as the storm raging against the trees above. His fingers dug into her ass, and she wrapped her legs around his hips. The tree against her back was hard and unyielding as his body drove into hers again and again.

"Oh God. Oh God," she cried as he pushed her closer and closer to her peak.

"Steve," he corrected with a soft chuckle in her ear. "I can't take credit for all existence."

At that moment, she was pretty sure he could. "Oh, oh G— Steve. I'm coming. Don't stop."

She shattered, her body shaking and arching as she claimed her release.

"Ah fuck, baby. I'm done too." Steve groaned and buried his face against her throat as he shuddered in bliss.

Roux relaxed against the tree, clinging to Steve's shoulders and squeezing his hips with her legs as she tried to catch her breath.

"I'm never going to achieve my goal of making you come three times if I keep losing control like that," he said.

She grinned, loving that she made him lose control. "I'm rather fond of the simultaneous orgasm thing," she said, noticing that the rain had stopped, and the wind had settled down.

"We're becoming experts at that," he said.

He shifted her away from the tree, and she winced as air brushed against her back. She was sure she'd have scratches for days, reminders of him after they parted. Would he really be able to wait for her for three months? Not that he'd promised not to be with other women during that time. At the thought, her chest squeezed in agony.

"Did I hurt you?" he asked, stroking her forehead.

"Not yet," she whispered, breathing through her emotions.

He smirked. "Do you want me to?"

"Not especially."

"Good," he said. "Because I don't think I'm capable of it."

She was certain he was.

ROUX HAD TO ADMIT that the beach was far nicer than the jungle. The cool breeze made the heat pleasant rather than unbearable, and Steve had decided to do a little offshore fishing in the nude, which made the view spectacular. She didn't even care that they had yet to spot a sea turtle. She sat in the shade to protect her fair skin and pretended to read a paperback she'd found in the beach house. But the flexing of certain back and butt muscles each time Steve cast his line was far too distracting to allow her to comprehend a word she read. Her gaze kept drifting out to the waves and the unexpected center of her universe standing bare-assed for her enjoyment. Feeling bolder than usual, she removed her cover-up, and then, after a few moments' hesitation, her bikini top. She'd never felt sunshine on her bare breasts before, so she ventured from under the shade tree to sit closer to the shore.

Steve snagged another fish and reeled it in. Now that she was closer, the view was even more spectacular. Who knew fishing could be such an entertaining spectator sport? He turned to show her the size of his prize—and she caught a glimpse of the size of his package—and he immediately dropped the fish back into the water. The size of his package grew.

"Did you put sunscreen on your pretty pink nipples?" he asked.

She laughed, not sure if she should be offended that he was able to worry about something like sunscreen when she was sitting topless on the beach or touched that he was concerned for her well-being.

"I figured they wouldn't be exposed for long," she said. "Not when your mouth is empty."

"Good point." He grabbed the bucket of fish sitting in the waves and carried that and his pole toward shore. His other pole was standing at full rigid attention. Roux's mouth watered, but she played it cool, closing her eyes, tossing her hair back and arching her back to show off her bare breasts. She felt daring and liberated and beautiful. Those were not things she felt often and certainly never all at once.

Cool water dripped on her foot, and a shadow blocked the heat of the sun from her body. Her nipples hardened as if they knew Steve was admiring them.

"I wonder if anyone would notice if we stayed here forever," Steve said quietly.

She opened her eyes, thankful for the sunglasses that kept her vision clear. His cock was at eye level, and any thoughts she'd had about the length of forever scattered on the breeze.

"Come on my tits," she said, squeezing her thighs together as the image of him doing it entertained her thoughts. "Right here. Right now."

His naughty grin had her rocking her pussy against the sand. "I can't do that on demand," he said. "I'll need a little help."

"You can't help yourself?" Because if he kept looking at her like he wanted to devour her, she was going to have to help herself real soon.

"It's been a while," he said, one hand moving to circle his cock. "Two weeks to be exact. But I think I remember how."

When his grip tightened around his shaft, her entire body spasmed with longing. She couldn't take her eyes off him as he stroked himself, and she could almost feel him inside her, thrusting into her with that same rhythm. She thought the anticipation and longing were almost as good as being fucked, until his breath quickened with excitement. Then she decided this was a total waste of cum.

"Wait," she said.

She tugged his hand away from his cock. She placed a gentle kiss on its tip, her tongue snaking out to flick against a small freckle that decorated his skin just beneath his rim. Steve's breath came out in a huff.

"I changed my mind."

"That's not very nice."

"I want to ride you."

She glanced up to catch his wide grin. "I take it back. That's much nicer than doing this manually."

She tugged his arm gently, and he dropped to his knees beside her, cupping her face with both hands and kissing her gently.

"I still want you to come on my tits," she said, shoving at his solid shoulder to coax him onto his back. "Don't come inside me this time."

He groaned. "But I love coming inside you."

She grinned and slipped off her bikini bottoms. "I love it too."

"Careful not to get sand between us. It chafes like a bitch."

She stepped away from him and brushed the sand off her butt and thighs, and then straddled him. "You put it in," she said. "I have sand on my hand."

"I must say, I like this bossy side of you, Red."

"I like all sides of you," she said, her heart hammering at

admitting something so binding. She pressed the bullet dangling from her bracelet into her belly to soothe her suddenly jumbled emotions.

"I like all sides of you as well." His tip nudged her opening, and she shifted to accept him inside her. "More than like."

"I more than like you too."

He laughed, his eyes bright. He looked blissfully happy.

She sucked a breath through her teeth as she slowly lowered over him. Damn, she was tender. How many times had he been inside her in the past twenty-four hours? A dozen? Still she wanted more.

He moved his hands to her hips, pulling her down as he thrust up to penetrate her fully.

She placed her palms on his chest, the bullet on her bracelet between her flesh and his. He didn't complain about the discomfort. He covered that hand with his and pressed down as if he wanted that little bit of metal that had nearly ended her life to brand him permanently.

"I more than like you so much," he whispered. "I thought feeling this strongly about a woman would be terrifying, but it's a relief and a joy."

"Shut up before you say too much," she said. "This is a frivolous weekend affair, remember?" But she knew it was so much more than that as she began to rise and fall over him. He had her heart, and she knew it. He also gave her hope that she could one day have his.

"Well," a deep voice said behind her. "What do we have here?"

CHAPTER 18

STEVE LIFTED HIS HEAD OFF the sand and glared at Logan while Roux attempted to cover her spectacular naked body with her hands.

"It sure is easy to sneak up on you when you're getting laid," Logan said, his dark blond hair ruffling in the ocean breeze like he didn't have a care in the fucking world. Of course, he wasn't the one with his wet dick in the air.

Steve sat up, his entire body protesting its sudden loss of pleasure, and Roux scrambled behind him, crouched into a ball with her head pressed against his back. He spotted her bikini bottoms and scooted them in her direction. A dainty hand snaked out to grab them, and he did his best to shield her from prying eyes while she wriggled into them.

"How the fuck did you get here?" Steve asked. The jet was still on the landing strip. He would have heard it take off since the flight path went directly over the beach house.

"I rented a boat. You didn't hear the engine?" He pointed toward the pier just visible at the end of the deep bay. Sure enough, a speedboat was docked there. "We came in from the other direction."

"We?"

"Me and Toni. She's over there trying to regain her land legs." He laughed. "Poor thing never did get her sea legs."

"Is that Steve?" Toni asked as she rounded a curve in the beach.

Roux pressed up against him from behind, her soft breasts flattened against his back, and used both hands to cover as much of as his softening cock as possible.

"Sorry to ruin your fun," Logan said. "When I asked him last week, Dare said it would be fine if I brought Toni here during the tour break. He didn't mention you'd be here."

Funny. He hadn't mentioned that Logan would be here either. It might have slipped Dare's mind, but more likely he was getting revenge for something one or the other of them had done to annoy him. The guy could be incredibly passive aggressive sometimes.

"It's fine," Steve said, though he'd never wanted to strangle Logan more than he did at that moment. If Roux hadn't been watching, he probably would have tackled him to the beach and choked him. "We were going to stay at the greater manse tonight anyway and fly out tomorrow."

"We were?" Roux asked.

"You look familiar," Logan said to her. "Have we met?"

Steve could feel Roux's body move behind him. He wasn't sure if she was shaking her head or nodding until she said, "No. I don't think so. I'm . . . uh . . ." She extended one of the hands that had just been on Steve's dick, and Logan raised his eyebrows. Her hand dropped back to Steve's lap. "I'm Katie. Katie Williams."

Steve covered his puzzlement with a poker face. Why had she given a fake name? Or was it fake?

"You have real nice tits, Katie."

Steve kicked sand at him, but Logan just chuckled.

"What did you say?" Toni asked, still a little crooked as she stood next to Logan with her hands on her hips. She bobbled to the side, and Logan steadied her with one hand.

"She's naked," Logan said. "I couldn't help but notice."

Toni gave Steve the twice-over. "Steve is looking mighty fine as well."

Logan scowled and kicked sand at Steve. "Put some damn pants on."

"I might if I had any."

Toni rummaged around in a brightly colored bag and drew out a beach towel, which she handed to Steve. She didn't so much as glance at Roux. Embarrassed for her, maybe? Jealous? He couldn't tell. Steve shook open the towel and draped it over Roux behind him. When she shifted her hands to collect the ends, he stood, fully naked, and leaned over to help her cover herself. Toni's little gasp made him grin, and he chuckled at Logan's growled, "Goddammit."

"We should probably get you out of the sun," he said to Roux.

The woman who he more-than-liked, the one who more-than-liked him in return, smiled up at him, and his chest expanded, filling with tenderness. He didn't care if they stayed there naked on the beach or scoured the jungle looking for nonexistent monkeys or relaxed in the hot tub at the mansion on the other side of the island; as long as he could be with Roux, he was happy. He helped her to her feet, fully aware that he was free-balling it and Toni was getting an eyeful.

"Will you stop staring at it?" Logan complained.

"Sorry. I can't help it." Toni spun around to face the beach house. "Oh, it's cute. I was expecting something bigger."

"That's what she said," Logan joked.

"The beach house is perfect for *two*," Steve said testily.

"If you want us to go to the other house, we'll start walking," Logan said. "Oh wait, you have a quad here." He pointed at the ATV parked under the house. "We'll just take that."

"I already said we're heading to the main house tonight. You're not taking the quad."

"It's not yours, it's Dare's. If I want to borrow it, then—"

"Hello!" Roux said loudly, holding the towel securely around her with one hand. "I'm Katie." She extended a hand toward Toni, who stared at it uncertainly. "And you would be?"

Toni pushed her glasses up her nose with the back of her hand before accepting the offered handshake. "Toni."

"Nice to meet you. You'd probably like to freshen up now that you're on dry land."

Toni nodded. "Yes, that would be wonderful. Thank you, Katie."

Steve watched the two women wander up the beach toward the house. Logan tapped his arm and leaned close. "That's the red chick from Baroquen, right? The one you have the hots for. I thought her name was Roux."

"I don't know why she said her name is Katie." No sense in hiding facts since Logan was already on to her.

"Maybe she doesn't want anyone to know she's with you."

That was probably close to the truth, and it stung more than a little to recognize that.

"You weren't really planning to head up to Dare's ludicrous beach palace, were you?" Logan asked. "We can make room here for all four of us. Won't be the first time we've been packed in like sardines."

"I only get one more full day with her before we have to go back to our regularly scheduled lives. So we'll hang out here with you for a while, but two's company, four's—"

"An orgy?"

Steve grinned and slapped Logan on the back. "I know you think you're teaching Toni how to become more sexually aware, but if I so much as laid a pinkie on her, you'd freak the fuck out." Steve had seen how Logan had reacted to Dare just teasing about touching Toni. Steve wasn't looking to gain a matching bloody nose. Maybe this clusterfuck was Dare's way of getting back at Logan for that sucker punch. If so, it wasn't fair that Dare had ruined Steve's good time as well. Steve hadn't had anything to do with that fiasco.

"Damn straight." Logan clasped his hands together. "I was thinking more about Roux touching her while I watch."

Steve lifted a brow. "And where do I fit into this scenario of yours?"

"You can wait on the boat until they're finished."

Steve laughed. "You're back to two's company. You realize that, don't you?"

"Yeah, but I'd be watching."

"You didn't happen to bring any tofu with you, did you?"

At first Logan's eyebrows shot up in surprise, but then they drew together. "Some new kink I'm not aware of?"

And people thought *Steve* had a one-track mind. "Roux is a vegetarian. I figure she's getting hungry with nothing but fruit to eat. I caught some fish, but she won't eat those either."

"I'm sure there's plenty of vodka and tequila in the house. They're made from plants, right?"

"She doesn't drink." Not wanting to get into the reasons why, Steve turned toward the waves and crossed the sand to his bucket of fish. Logan followed.

"You're dating a vegetarian who doesn't drink?" Logan asked. "You?"

Dating? Were they dating? He wanted them to be dating, but would Roux even consider a serious relationship with him? Perhaps after the tour ended they could come out officially as a couple. Damn, it was going to be a long three months without her. Maybe they could act like friends and at least hang out. He enjoyed being with her. He didn't have to touch her, kiss her, make love to her if she was near. They could be together for three long months in a completely platonic capacity. Sure.

"You really like her, don't you?" Logan asked.

It was that obvious? "She's amazing."

Logan shoved him in the shoulder, because admitting to romantic feelings and bros should not mix. Especially when one of the bros was still entirely naked.

"I caught plenty of fish. You and Toni are welcome to have some."

"Only if you gut and clean them," Logan said. "We'll throw it all on the grill. We brought burgers."

"But no tofu?"

Logan shook his head.

"Eggplant?"

"Seriously?" Logan snorted. "Why the fuck would I bring eggplant? I think we have a tomato for the burgers. One."

Steve was going to have to plan better the next time he brought Roux to Dick Island. The poor woman was going to starve to death at this rate.

He found her—now wearing her bikini top and gauzy coverup—standing under a grapefruit tree, trying to reach a ripe-looking fruit. He plucked it from the branch and handed it to her.

"Not that I don't love the view," she said, a hand sliding over his bare flank, "but I'd rather other women didn't get to enjoy the same privilege."

Steve spotted Toni next to the papaya tree trying not to be obvious about stealing glances. "Hey, Lo!" he yelled. "Could you tell your woman to stop ogling my junk? R— Erm, Katie doesn't like it."

Roux smacked his ass, which made his junk even more interesting to ogle when his cock stirred to life.

"I meant that you should put on some shorts," she said.

"Hey, I was here first. I should be able to walk around naked if I want."

Roux covered her mouth with one hand and spoke just loud enough for him to hear. "I don't share well with other women. Remember?"

He did recall her saying that, but she didn't have to worry about sharing him. He had no interest in Toni or any other woman. But he did want Roux to be comfortable.

She patted his butt. "Now, please put on some shorts before I jump your bones and forget to entertain our guests."

"I didn't invite them. And I'm sure they'd be entertained if you jumped my bones."

"And Logan could get another good look at my tits," she said.

Steve scowled and went to rinse sand from his body in the rainwater shower beneath the house before donning a pair of shorts for Toni's benefit. Logan took the quad to pick up supplies from the boat and bring them to the beach house, while Steve fired up the grill. Toni was upstairs in the house nesting in what had been his and Roux's cozy, private space, and Roux was gathering more fruit. He tried not to be too obvious about watching her, but the woman was breathtakingly beautiful and so at ease with the natural world around her. He remembered how uncomfortable she'd seemed at the after-party in New York. Would she even like being on tour? He ate up every minute of the attention and craziness that surrounded the concerts, but Roux was all about tranquility. When she was near, he felt relaxed and at peace with the world he usually raged against.

"Take a picture; it will last longer," Logan said behind him, and he jumped at the unexpected intrusion.

"What?"

"You're staring at her."

"Can you blame me?"

"She doesn't seem your type at all."

Logan knew Steve's usual type quite well. Steve gravitated toward party girls—loose and loud with no boundaries and no filters. Even Bianca had pursued a perpetual good time. Back then he'd thought being with someone like himself was ideal. He'd been wrong.

"Maybe that's what I like about her so much," he said. "She's different from me. Besides, you can't talk." He gave Logan a hard shove. "You're dating a geek."

"Toni isn't a geek."

"She's totally a geek. And so sweet my teeth ache when I look at her."

"She is pretty sweet." Logan grinned and bent to open the cooler at his feet. "You better get busy cleaning those fish."

He figured Roux wouldn't want to watch him eviscerate any animal, so he gathered his bucket of fish, a cutting board, and a knife and carried it all down the beach to where the strip of land bent sharply toward the dock. He'd be out of sight there.

By the time he returned to the others, Roux was standing next to Logan at the smoking grill, dropping thick slices of fruit on the grill top and laughing at something he'd said or done. Logan was likely telling her stories about his and Steve's misadventures, adding the usual bias in his own favor. Steve frowned, but then shrugged. He didn't have anything to hide. Especially now that Bianca's stupid tabloid had dug the biggest skeleton out of his closet. Roux seemed okay with his brief marriage and subsequent annulment to Meredith. He'd been more than a little drunk when they'd taken Zach up on that bet. Who hadn't done some incredibly stupid things when they were drunk? Roux. That's who. Maybe she was too straight and narrow to fit neatly into his crazy life. He wasn't looking for a neat fit, though. He just wanted her.

"What have you been telling her?" Steve asked as he joined them at the grill.

"Stories of you acting stupid when you're drunk."

Well, that could provide endless entertainment.

Steve set the board of cleaned fish on a small table covered with various barbeque tools and everything he needed to season the fish perfectly. He and Logan took grilling seriously. He sloshed olive oil and a splash of white wine into a bowl and gently rolled each fish in the mixture to coat both sides before setting them aside to marinate.

"Are you really going to eat something that's *staring* at you?" Roux asked, cringing at the fish that still had their heads. And their eyes.

Steve began chopping fresh herbs to stuff inside the fish once they'd sat in the oil for a while. Fish could be tricky on the grill if they stuck to the grate and flaked apart. "Yep, and I'm going to enjoy every bite. Would you mind slicing up some lemons?" he asked.

"They don't have eyes."

"But potatoes do," Logan said. "Do you eat potatoes?"

Roux stuck her tongue out at him. "Yeah, I eat potatoes."

Toni deposited a bag near the table, darted over to Logan's side, and looped her arm through his. She rose up on tiptoe and looked at him all doe-eyed. Logan kissed her until something fell through the grate and sizzled in the coals.

"Save me some of that for later," Logan said, his grin crooked as he patted Toni's butt before he turned back to the grill.

"The grilled mango is ready," Logan said, rescuing chunks of fruit and dropping them onto a waiting platter before they ended up in the coals as well. "This actually looks better than I expected, um, Katie. Now I wish we had a pineapple to grill."

"Mmm, pineapple does sound delicious," Roux said, slicing lemons on the end of Steve's cutting board.

He loved how her arm brushed his as they worked side by side.

"Did you really bring only one tomato?"

"I'll grill half of it for you. How does that sound?"

"Heavenly," Roux said, offering Logan a friendly smile. "I love fruit and all, but that's all I've had to eat today."

"Technically, tomatoes are fruit," Toni said.

"If you want to get really technical, tomatoes are berries," Roux said, reaching for a second lemon to slice.

"I didn't know that," Logan said with a little snort.

Steve looked up from the fresh thyme he was dicing and noticed Toni giving Roux the evil eye. He wondered what he'd missed while he'd been down by the water cleaning the fish. Or maybe Toni didn't like to have counterpoints tossed in her direction. Whatever the reason, he got the distinct feeling that Toni didn't like Roux, which made absolutely no sense, because Roux was kind and charming—the epitome of perfection.

"Are you on the rag or something?" Steve asked, pointing at Toni with the tip of his knife.

Toni's jaw dropped. "What kind of question is that?"

"Just wondering what you're so cranky about." Toni was also typically kind and charming, but she was coming across as downright prickly this afternoon.

"I'm not cranky."

"I think she needs to get laid," Logan said, slapping burgers on the grill. They sizzled and sent flames shooting upward, which Logan doused with beer from an open can.

"Logan!" Toni said, planting a fist on both hips. "You don't really think I'm cranky, do you?"

"Well, you didn't want to have sex on the boat. Maybe I should hand the grill over to Steve and take you upstairs to remedy that cranky problem now."

She glanced at Roux for some inexplicable reason and then turned a death glare in Logan's direction. "Is that all I am to you, an easy lay? You, you, incredible ass!"

"My ass is pretty incredible," Logan teased.

Toni set her jaw in a harsh line and stomped off toward the beach.

"What did I say?" Logan said, handing Steve his spatula as he hurried after Toni. "I was just joking. Of course you mean more to me than an easy lay."

Steve lost track of their argument when the ocean breeze kicked up and scattered their voices. "So . . ." he said as soon as they were out of earshot. "Why did you tell them your name is Katie?"

Roux didn't even bother to look guilty for lying. "That's the woman who leaked that shit about the band all over the tabloids, isn't it?"

"Yeah, but apparently someone stole her notes, so it wasn't her fault."

"She should have protected you guys better," Roux said. "And if she can't protect your secrets, why would she protect mine?"

"You want me to be a secret?"

She shook her head. "No. I want the fact that I'm the 'red one' in Baroquen to be a secret. And my name isn't exactly common, so if I introduced myself as Roux, she'd put two and two together."

"She'll put two and two together as soon as she sees you on tour in Europe." Especially since Logan had already figured it out and could keep a secret almost as long as a typical five-year-old.

"Not if she never sees me out of makeup and costume."

Steve flipped a burger, decided he should let the others cook a bit longer before flipping them, and offered Roux a contemplative stare. "What are you cooking up, angel?"

"A way to have my cake and eat him too."

She winked at him, and his heart stumbled over a beat.

"So you better get used to calling me Katie. It's my real first name, by the way. Roux is my middle name. I switched to using it after . . ." Her fingers moved to the center of her chest and caressed the scar there. "Well, just call me Katie in public when I'm not in costume."

Roux didn't look that different when she was all dolled up as the "red one" in Baroquen. Surely Toni would recognize her. But he wouldn't argue. Not if she got to have her cake and eat him too.

Chapter 19

ROUX'S JAW DROPPED when she stepped over the threshold and into the island's main house. The structure appeared rather sterile from the outside—all sharp angles and glass—but the interior was both inviting and opulent, with abundant natural light and views from every angle. It was almost like being out on the beach, but with air conditioning.

"Wow," Roux said. "Is Dare loaded, or what?"

Steve bit his lip. "Do you like this kind of thing? I thought you'd prefer the cottage."

"I love the cottage," she said, patting his arm and venturing into the stunning foyer that spired several stories high. "But who wouldn't love this? Wow!" She couldn't even imagine how much it had cost to build a house like this on an island where all the building materials and construction equipment would have to be brought in from the mainland.

"Dare came from money, so he knows how to invest it and is not ashamed to spend it."

"He doesn't seem like a rich boy," Roux said, but even the furniture and artwork screamed affluence. "He's so quiet and kind."

"So because he's quiet and kind, he can't be rich?"

"No, I just didn't expect this. Not from Dare. Max maybe." She slapped her lips with the tips of her fingers. "Do you hear me? I sound so judgmental. Tell me to shut up."

"Shut up, Roux, and enjoy Dare's only vice." He laughed. "We all do."

"You are not making me leave early, are you?" Jordan asked in an exasperated tone. She wore a postage-stamp-sized yellow string bikini which looked stunning against her bronze skin and held a bright, fruity cocktail in her hand. "I don't think I'm fit to fly." She took a long sip of her drink. "And if I am now, I won't be when this third mai tai kicks in." She giggled.

"No plans to leave early. I figured you were getting lonely without me," Steve said. "So Roux and I are spending tonight and tomorrow here."

"Plenty of room," she said, her voice slightly slurred. "Lee and I are all settled on this side of the house." She pointed a finger behind her. "So if you want company, the smallest bedroom is still available. Or if you want privacy, the entire second floor is yours."

Roux hoped Steve opted for the second floor and privacy. Not that she didn't like Jordan and Lee, but if she'd wanted to spend time with other people, they could have stayed at the beach house with Logan—who was an absolute doll—and Toni—who thought Roux was Steve's slutty groupie entertainment for the weekend. Roux had not bothered to correct the misconception. It made the other woman leery of Roux's intentions toward Logan, but also kept her from getting too friendly and made it more likely that Toni wouldn't recognize who Roux really was. And keeping her identity secret from journalist-types was Roux's ultimate goal.

"Would your rather—"

"Upstairs," she blurted.

He grinned and said to Jordan, "We'll sleep upstairs, but we want private time access to the hot tub and pool for a few hours tomorrow night. Let Lee know he's not invited."

"Good luck getting him out of the hot tub, Aimes," Jordan said. "I think his bare ass has taken root."

"That's twenty-four hours' notice, plenty of time to dislodge his ass from the seat."

"You're the boss." Jordan smirked and saluted him with one hand before tipping her drink into her mouth with the other. "If you're hungry, there's food in the fridge."

"We had fish," Steve said.

"*You* had fish," Roux reminded him. "I could eat." If there was anything in Dare's kitchen she felt comfortable consuming. She hadn't even been able to stomach much of the grilled fruit with everyone else's dinner staring at her.

"You're probably starving." Steve rubbed her back through her airy tank top. "I was so preoccupied with the thought of finishing what we started on the beach hours ago that I can't think straight."

The tendency of her hands to stray while she clung to him on the back of the quad might have had a little something to do with that as well.

"Like anyone is surprised you're thinking with your dick again, Aimes." Jordan tutted and shook her head. "I'm heading back to the pool. I'll warn Lee that one of the boss men is around and he should be on his best behavior."

Steve laughed. "Lee's best behavior is still pretty bad."

"Look who's talking." Jordan waved farewell as she carried her drink toward an open lanai door.

Roux could just see the sparkling blue water of the swimming pool beyond. She also noted the thong bikini bottom Jordan was wearing. If Steve noticed the woman's perfect bare backside, he hid it well.

"Let's go find you something to eat," he said. "I thought maybe you just weren't very hungry today. You hardly touched dinner."

"Because your fish was staring at me. I thought I was going to puke."

"Why didn't you say something?"

"Because I promised myself I would never be one of those vegetarians. The ones who preach ethics and try to sway everyone to their way of life."

"You won't ever convince me to stop eating meat. I love the stuff. But if it bothers you to look at my fish's head, I can hack it off before I eat it."

She appreciated him trying to make her more comfortable, but *eww*. "If I cooked you a vegetarian meal, would you try it?"

"You cook?"

She nodded. "I'm pretty good at it. I had to learn how to make food that you omnivores would actually eat since my sisters and I rotate cooking duties each night. I'm usually Thursday."

"Do you think you can handle cooking on a Saturday?"

"I'm not sure."

She followed him toward the back of the house, where they stepped into a chef's dream kitchen. She was glad that Dare's vice was living in abundance. She didn't need a six-burner stove or a refrigerator the size of a minivan, but she had to admit both were marvelous. She found the refrigerator mostly empty, but the freezer was packed full of frozen veggies of all sorts. The texture wouldn't be as good as if she had fresh vegetables to work with, but there was a little bit of everything. The pantry was well stocked with canned goods and other nonperishables. She could eat well there for months.

"Oh my God, yes," she said, grabbing a jar of sundried tomatoes and cradling it against her chest before reaching for a box of whole wheat pasta.

"You know, if I could think with something other than my dick when I'm around you, I would have thought to raid Dare's pantry before we left for the cottage."

"Do you want to go back there?" He seemed a little uncomfortable, and she wasn't sure why.

"No, I want you to eat so you can start thinking with something other than your stomach."

"Like what? With my vagina?" She grinned and reached for a can of crushed tomatoes.

"Now you're thinking like I'm thinking."

"You have a vagina?"

"No, I just think about it a lot and am hoping you'll share."

She laughed and handed him several containers of dried herbs and spices. She noticed a jar near the back of the shelf and pulled it out. "Artichoke hearts. Oh God, yes!" She rolled her eyes in exaggerated bliss.

"Maybe I like you thinking with your stomach after all," he said, his arm snaking around her waist and his mouth seeking hers.

Her body awoke with instant need. Her grip slackened on the artichokes, and she almost dropped them before coming to her senses enough to realize what she was doing. She pulled away from him and looked up into his gorgeous face. He burned for her. She could see it there in his smoldering dark eyes. And she'd wanted to cook?

"Hold that thought," she said, setting her jars and cans down on a nearby shelf. She took the spices he held between splayed fingers and returned them to the shelf as well.

"I thought you were hungry."

She slid the walk-in-pantry door closed, enveloping them in darkness except for a thin ribbon of light shining under the door. "Turns out I'm thinking with my vagina right now, specifically about sharing it with you."

She reached up, seeking his face in the darkness, and cupped his jaw, using touch to guide her mouth to his. When their lips met, he sucked in a deep breath through his nose and began fumbling with what few clothes they were wearing. She kissed him hungrily as he stripped them naked, not even relenting when he turned her so that her back was pressed against the only available wall space next to the pocket door. She cringed as she bumped the back of her skull and jerked her head to the side when their teeth smashed together. He grabbed her ass and shifted her higher up the wall.

"Help me find you." His lips caressed a tender spot just beneath her ear.

Trusting him not to drop her, she reached between her splayed legs and found his heated skin. Her fingers glided down the ridges of his belly, seeking the treasure she wanted buried inside her. She found his shaft and circled it with her hand, rubbing the head against her clit and the wetness of her opening. His body quaked as he waited for her to press him inside her, and his breaths came in hot excited bursts against her neck.

As she rubbed his tip into her opening, he shifted her hips forward slightly and pressed up into her. Oh yes, that was what she wanted. She pulled her hand from between their bodies, and he stepped closer, thrusting deep. Holding her securely in both hands, he pulled her away from the wall, and she clung to his shoulders, her heart hammering wildly as she feared she'd fall. He shifted her upward and pressed her against the wall again, settling her into a more comfortable position.

"I won't drop you," he promised.

"Sorry." She loosened her grip on his shoulders.

"I am going to fuck you, though."

He pounded into her hard and fast. Excitement spread between them, driving her toward a peak that in the past she never would have expected to reach. But something had changed within her. The more she trusted Steve—the more she opened her heart to him and the more comfortable she became with him—the easier it was to reach orgasm. So she held nothing back—didn't worry about what he thought of her flaws, didn't care if she was making too much noise or not enough, didn't wonder if it felt good for him. She knew it did. And as always, he delivered.

She cried out, her body straining toward him, as she found release. An instant later, he stiffened, breath catching in his throat.

"Damn," he muttered. After a few more strokes, he held himself deep within her and quaked as he climaxed. He held her pinned between his body and the wall as he caught his breath. The gentle kisses he pressed to her neck made her strangely misty-eyed as she toyed with the stray hairs at his nape that had escaped his man bun.

"One of these days I'll be able to hold back when that sweet pussy of yours tightens around me. When you come, it's *like oh my God, that feels fucking amazing.*" He shuddered. "I have no choice but to come with you."

She grinned and kissed his jaw. "I don't want you to hold back."

"That's good, because I don't think it's an option when it comes to you. And I'm not just talking about sex."

She hugged him close, feeling the exact same way, but cursing fate. Why did she have to fall for him now? It was the worst possible timing.

They were both quiet as she prepped the meal. He sat at the enormous kitchen island, which was about twice as big as Roux's bathroom back home, and he watched her with a soft smile on his lips and in his eyes. She made enough pasta primavera for four, and asked Jordan and Lee if they wanted to join them. Both members of their aircrew were fairly drunk and more than a little loud. Roux did her best to hide her unease. She couldn't stop herself from fiddling with the bullet on her bracelet, however.

Steve took her hand under the dinner table—always perceptive, always kind and steadying and empathetic. Was this really the same man that had mistaken her for a hooker at their first meeting?

"I don't think I've eaten anything but pretzels today." Lee lifted his plate to his face and inhaled. "This looks a bit too healthy."

"It won't kill you," Jordan said. "You could stand to consume a vegetable on occasion."

"I don't know. My system might go into shock."

Roux smiled, her unease fading as she recognized neither of their dinner companions were angry drunks. Unbalanced drunks? Definitely. But not threatening. She squeezed Steve's hand appreciatively and released it before picking up her fork. She was pleased that her first bite was delicious. She was even more pleased when Lee asked for seconds several minutes later.

"If anyone is getting seconds, it's me," Steve said. "I'm the one who was smart enough to bring her here."

"You wouldn't have even made it here if it wasn't for me," Lee insisted.

Jordan's eyebrows shot up. "I can easily fly that plane without you."

"Aw, man."

"Roux should get any leftovers," Steve said.

"I'm full," she said, polishing off her final bite. "There isn't much left anyway." Perhaps she should have made more.

Both men rose, plates in hand, and made a mad dash for the stove. There was a bit of a scuffle, but as Steve was bigger and not unsteadily drunk, he ended up the victor.

"There's a bit of sauce left," he told Lee as he headed back to the counter with the remains of the pasta on his plate. "You could lick it clean."

"Don't mind if I do," Lee said. He lifted the pan to his face and cleaned it with wide sweeps of his tongue.

"I'd like to blame that behavior on his drinking, but he's always a slob," Jordan said, crinkling her nose.

Roux laughed. "I'm happy he likes it so much."

"You know what would have really taken this dish to the next level?" Lee asked. "Meatballs."

"I thought it was perfect without them," Steve said, and he smiled at Roux.

Roux's need to touch him undeniable, she pressed her elbow against his. His arm slid behind her back and urged her to lean into his side as he shoveled in his last few bites of pasta.

"Lee will do the dishes," Jordan said, hiding a knowing grin with a ducked chin.

He set the pan down on the stove with a loud clank. "Aw, man."

"Have you shown Roux the view from the second floor?" Jordan asked, nodding toward the staircase between the open kitchen and great room.

"We haven't made it that far yet," Steve said, sliding his plate toward the center of the kitchen island. "Are you ready to go upstairs?" he asked Roux.

"Can I have a bath?"

"You can have whatever you desire."

She slid off her stool and took his hand, tugging him along behind her. "Then you'll have to come with me."

THE VIEW FROM THE BATHTUB WAS BREATHTAKING. A bright moon lit the night sky, reflecting off the dark ocean water and casting a surreal glow over the lengthy beach. But Roux didn't waste much time staring out the floor-to-ceiling window, because the view in the bathtub was far superior. Bathwater hid everything below Steve's sculpted chest, but he'd let his hair down from the bun he'd sported all day, and the way it moved across his shoulders was utterly distracting. Not quite as distracting as the way his large, strong hands looked massaging her foot. She'd always thought of her feet as big and bony, but nestled between his palms, her foot looked delicate and feminine, and pale in contrast to his bronze skin. She did envy his skin tone. His thumbs rubbed the pad under her big toe in hypnotic circles, and she moaned in bliss. She'd expected something different when he'd climbed into the tub with her, but now she could say she'd never been gladder to have feet.

His dark eyes held hers as his hands worked toward her ankle. Shifting closer, he lifted her foot higher out of the warm water and nipped the pad of her big toe. She gasped as a thrill of excitement shot up her leg and ignited a primal passion within her. Mesmerized, she watched him nibble and suck her toes, wondering why that felt so good and looked so sensual. They were just toes, for heaven's sake.

His thumbs switched to massaging her instep in delightful arcs. She relaxed into the steamy water, her eyes drifting closed.

"I'm starting to think you have a foot fetish," she murmured dreamily.

"I have only one fetish," he said.

Her eyes flicked open.

"You," he said.

"I don't think I can be a fetish."

"A fetish is an obsession necessary for sexual gratification," he said, grinning. "That sounds right. I definitely have a Roux fetish."

She flushed. "I guess by that definition, I have a Steve fetish."

"I won't argue that logic."

She splashed water at him, and he wrapped a hand around her ankle to tug her closer.

"What do you want to do tomorrow?" he asked.

"Besides sex?"

"We don't have to have sex at all," he said.

She begged to differ. "Isn't that the entire reason you brought me here?"

"No. It's some of the reason," he said, "I can't deny that. But I want to be near you and get to know you better."

"You've already sealed the deal, babe. You don't have to say things like that to get into my pants."

"But it's true. Sex with you is the best I've ever had."

She snorted. Sure . . .

"But I could have sealed the deal without going to these lengths."

She wished she could say he was full of himself, but she'd never been good at lying. "So why did you go to all this trouble?"

"Easy. To make you fall in love with me."

Her breath caught. "Why would you want that?"

"Because I'm ready to be in love."

"But I'm not," she said without conviction.

"Then I have more work to do." He smiled and lifted a wet hand to her cheek.

When he kissed her, she decided he didn't have much work to do at all, but for Baroquen's sake, she had to fight her developing feelings.

CHAPTER 20

STEVE MISSED HER ALREADY. The entire plane trip back to Los Angeles, Zach blathered on about how much fun he'd had jamming with Azura and Sage that weekend, and how Raven had dressed him up goth and taken him to some club, where Iona had let her guard down and turned out to be pretty cool to hang with. Steve was glad Zach was his typical talkative self and didn't require much reciprocal conversation, because he doubted he could string a complete sentence together.

"Sorry your weekend didn't turn out better," Zach said as they collected their luggage from beneath the plane.

"It was perfect," he said, the ache of longing in his chest spreading. God, he'd forgotten how much he hated that awful feeling of separation.

Zach scowled. "Really? She didn't even kiss you goodbye."

"We've decided to keep our relationship entirely secret until after the tour ends." And he would try to do exactly that for her sake, but he was already miserable. How could he possibly endure three months, pretending he wasn't completely in love with the woman?

"That doesn't sound like you," Zach said.

Steve shrugged. He didn't want to talk about it, but he could tell by the understanding look on Zach's face that he did. "I have to go," Steve said. "Max called a meeting."

"I thought that was tomorrow."

It was. They had to wait for Logan to make it back from Dick Island.

"Yeah, but—"

"Yeah, but you're in a funk because you can't see your new girlfriend. I get it. And I don't want to go home because I'm pretty sure Enrique is going to break up with me."

"What? Why?" Steve latched on to his friend's romantic problem because he didn't want to dwell on his own any longer.

"He was pissed that I spent the weekend in Boston instead of with him."

"That was my fault, not yours."

"I am capable of booking a commercial flight."

"So why didn't you?"

"I guess I'm tired of the secrecy. Of feeling like I'm not worth much to him if he won't even claim me as his."

Steve slapped him on the back. He was in a similar situation, but for a different reason. "If he kicks you out, you can always stay with me."

"Give up the luxurious mansion to stay in that tiny shack you call a house?"

"Hey!" Steve happened to love his Venice Beach shack. And so did Zach. Zach always said he'd rent the place if Steve ever wanted to move someplace bigger.

"People will talk about us."

Steve snorted. "Like they don't already do that."

"So do you want to go hang out at the Brig?"

"At two o'clock in the afternoon?" It had been four days since he'd last had any alcohol. He licked his lips, suddenly parched. "Yep."

An hour later he was deep into his third whiskey sour, surrounded by familiar faces, noisy conversation, and loud music, when he got the sudden urge to call Roux. He wasn't supposed to call her. It had been one of their rules, but fully sober Steve had agreed to that bargain. Buzzed Steve thought their deal was probably the stupidest thing ever.

She answered after several rings. "What's wrong?" She sounded breathless.

"You're not here."

"Where are you?"

"Some bar near my house. How soon can you get here?"

"I'm rehearsing. I'll be rehearsing all week. I asked you not to call me unless it was an emergency."

"This is an emergency. I miss you."

Zach sniggered. Four or five of their bar buddies, who'd joined them at their regular table, burst into fits of laughter. Perhaps Steve should have taken the call outside.

"I miss you too, but I have to work. Please don't call me unless it's a real emergency."

"But I can text you, though, right?"

"I need this time to prepare for the show, Steve. You promised you'd give me space."

He had. But he hadn't realized how hard being without her would be and how quickly he'd need to see her again. "I'll try to control my impulses." Which was never going to happen when he'd been drinking.

"It was good to hear your voice," she said.

He smiled.

"But I don't want to hear it again for a week."

He frowned. There had to be some way he could get her to break her stupid rules.

"I'm hanging up. I still more than like you."

A fluttery feeling filled his chest. "I more than like you too."

When he hung up, he noticed that his typically noisy companions were completely silent and gawking at him.

"Steve has a woman?" Mike's eyes were wide as he glanced at Zach and back at Steve. "I thought you two . . ."

Zach rolled his eyes. "Have you been reading the tabloids, dude?"

"I thought it was odd, because Steve is usually surrounded by more pussy than he can handle."

"I can handle it," Steve claimed, downing the remains of adult beverage number three.

"But maybe that's just a cover for the truth," Mike added.

"You hang out with us all the time," Zach said. "Do you honestly think we're more than friends?"

"I knew that story was complete bullshit," Matt said. "And the one about you and that pretty boy actor, what's his name?" He looked to Mike to fill in the blank.

"Enrique something or other."

Zach dropped his drink. "Fuck."

While several guys grabbed tiny napkins to stop Zach's drink from reaching their laps, Steve grabbed Zach's arm to keep him in his chair.

"Which tabloid did you read that in?" Steve asked Mike. "Was it the *American Inquirer*?" Because it was one thing for Bianca to fuck with him and an entirely different thing for her to fuck with his best friend.

"It's online," Mike said. "Viral even."

"Fuck!" Zach said, shrugging off Steve's hold and jumping to his feet. "He's going to kill me."

"Why? You didn't do anything." Steve rose and grasped Zach's shoulders. "Take a breath."

"I promised no one would ever find out."

"You mean it's true?" Mike shouted.

The bar, which wasn't overly crowded at that hour, went completely silent, and all eyes turned toward them.

"Mind your own business," Steve snarled. He directed Zach out of the dimly lit bar and into the bright Southern California sunshine.

"He must not know," Zach said. "He'd have called me if he knew. Do you think it would be better if he heard it from me first?"

Zach's phone rang. He closed his eyes, and Steve felt his dread in the pit of his own stomach.

"If he really cares about you, he'll claim you as his and stand up for you."

Zach pulled his phone out of a pocket and checked the screen. He released a relieved breath. "It's only Toby." The lead singer of Zach's band.

"S'up?" Zach answered and started to walk toward the beach a few blocks away. Steve followed. "Yeah, I just heard about it." He stopped walking and pressed his fingertips to his forehead. "No, I don't think he'll star in our next music video." Zach rolled his eyes at Steve. "I'm not going to ask him. He didn't want anyone to know about us in the first place." Zach breathed out a frustrated sigh. "Yeah, whatever. We would have never gotten to tour with Ex End this summer if it weren't for me, so you can shove your guilt trip straight up your ass." Zach hung up on Toby and gestured to Steve. "Vocalists."

Steve grinned, knowing exactly what Zach was dealing with. Max was also the sort who'd do anything for fame.

"Do you have a plan?" Steve asked.

"Hide out at your place and pretend I'm dead."

Steve slapped him on the back. "Good plan." Of course, he would have said that about any plan Zach devised. While Steve understood Zach's issues with Twisted Element's overzealous vocalist, he had a harder time knowing what it would be like to be in love with a dude who refused to come out of the closet. Or what it was like to be in love with any dude, for that matter. He and Zach didn't go into details about their love lives.

They started to walk in the direction of Steve's house. It was only a few blocks away from the bar, which was good, because neither of them had any business driving.

"I can't believe you called Roux in front of the guys," Zach said, snorting on a laugh. "*I more than like you*," he mocked, darting away when Steve took a swing at him.

Steve knew Zach was trying to divert his thoughts from his own problems, so he didn't take his teasing too hard. "Would you rather me tell her I love her?"

"Don't you?"

Steve allowed his fist to drop to his side. "Yeah, I think I do."

"Hopeless romantic." Zach fluttered his lashes at him.

"No one would ever believe that about me," Steve said. "Everyone knows I'm an asshole with a different woman in my bed every night."

"I know better." Zach scrunched his brows together. "Though you do bang a lot of chicks."

"I did, but now I have someone I care about. I won't bang any chicks but her."

Zach chuckled. "We'll see how long that lasts when you're in Europe."

Steve had dealt with quite a few sexually aggressive European women on past tours. He typically loved the type; he didn't even have to try to seduce them. Was that why he got so tangled up in Roux, because she was the opposite of what he was accustomed to?

"And without me to keep you in line . . ." Zach shook his head piteously.

"Since your romance is on the rocks, you might as well come to Europe as my personal assistant."

"Your personal assistant? No way in hell."

"Beer caddie?"

Zach grinned. "Do you tip well?"

"Nope. But you should call Enrique. Maybe he's figured out he can't live without you."

"I'm thinking probably not." Zach blew out a heavy breath. "Love sucks."

Not when it was shared with Roux. But did she love him? Or

just more than like him?

"If you're not going to call Enrique, maybe I should call Roux."

"Didn't you just talk to her?"

"Yeah, but she didn't have time to talk to me then." He wouldn't allow himself to entertain the notion that she didn't *want* to talk to him. "Maybe she does now."

Zach laughed and shoved him in the back. "Dude, you aren't a hopeless romantic. You're just fucking hopeless."

Steve waved at his neighbor as he passed the small walled garden the man was tending. Jim had a way with climbing roses. The entire front of his little house was covered in blooms of various colors, sizes, and scents. Steve was certain Roux would love the place. His own plain house next door? He wasn't as sure about. His house was small and modest with cedar shingle siding painted a soft sage green. A pair of large palm trees rustled on either side of the brick walkway. The rock garden that made up the entire tiny front yard had a few low maintenance spiky succulents grouped in clusters, but he simply didn't have the time or attention span to have a more elaborate yard. He'd bought the house—which had been a falling-down shack then—over fifteen years ago, before Venice Beach had become outrageously expensive, before Exodus End had exploded in popularity, before he'd married Bianca. As a wedding gift, he'd bought her the big, fancy house of her dreams in Malibu, but he'd rented out the Venice Beach place because he couldn't bear to part with it. In the divorce she'd gotten the Malibu mansion and he'd gotten the hovel. He couldn't have been more pleased with that outcome.

After his months of solitude back on the farm, this was the home that had welcomed him back to his life in California. He'd since invested some money into fixing it up. It was no longer a falling-down shack, but it was still modest, and the designer he'd hired had been from Venice Beach. She'd understood the landscape, the culture, the quirky artistic nature of the neighborhood, and the décor reflected all that. Steve's little house was an artist's—a musician's—dream. But it had only one small bedroom. Zach would have to take the couch.

The house was stuffy from being closed up for months, so he opened the windows, which faced the ocean breeze, in the small but functional kitchen. He inhaled the crisp air that flowed inside. He'd missed the smell of the ocean. He might have been raised in the middle of the country, but this was home to him.

"Where are you going to put all your kids when you marry Roux?" Zach asked, ducking his chin to hide a grin.

"Bunk beds to the rafters." He pointed toward the roof, which, after the remodeling that had removed the low ceilings, was all exposed beams. The beams had been painted black against a pitch-sloped white background to add "architectural interest" to what had been a claustrophobic box before the drywall had been removed. The silver crescent-shaped blades of the high ceiling fans became a blur as he turned them on with a remote control.

Zach had gone still. When Steve looked at him, he was scowling.

"You're really serious about this woman, aren't you?" Zach asked.

"Was there ever any doubt?"

"Things are going to change again," he said. "Like they did when you were with Bianca."

Steve had been so busy trying to make his marriage work that he'd neglected his friendship with Zach for those years. Zach hadn't replaced his best friend with another, he'd just become incredibly lonely. He was the kind of guy who didn't let many people get close to him, and those he did, he loved fiercely. Forever. Steve wondered if Zach had allowed Enrique to get that close to him. If he had, Steve predicted devastation in his near future, and he'd be taking Zach to Europe with him for sure.

"Roux is nothing like Bianca. Her true beauty is on the inside."

Zach lifted his gaze to the rafters.

"Don't get me wrong. She's absolutely gorgeous on the outside, but I've been with plenty of beautiful women, and she outshines them all."

Zach pressed his lips together and snorted. "If I wasn't so damned happy for you, I'd knock some sense into you. You've known her for only a few weeks."

"Hey, when it's right, it's right."

"I'm going to call Enrique now."

"And break up with him?"

"I'm going to try to convince him that he can't live without me."

"Did he even call you once while you were in Boston?"

Zach shook his head. "And I didn't miss him much. I was too busy listening to the incessant nagging of women. You left me there with a dozen of them for two days."

Women adored Zach by default. Steve figured he'd have a good time with them. Zach hadn't really complained about his time with Mama Ramona's girls until now, but maybe he had been nice for Steve's benefit.

"So they drove you nuts?"

Zach grinned. "Naw. They made me feel like a new man. I hadn't realized how down I was about being kicked off the tour. But Ramona has this way of healing emotional wounds. You need to sit down with her and have a talk someday. I thought maybe she was a head shrink or something, but do you know what she used to be?"

Steve sorted through things Roux had mentioned about her foster mother. "Music teacher," he blurted.

"A music professor, actually."

"Professor?" Well, that sounded important.

"All the girls she's raised play an instrument. It's remarkable how she's healed them all and made them whole. Each has a tragic past, but good luck trying to get any of them to talk about specifics."

Steve's heart panged at the thought of the real-life nightmare that had destroyed Roux's biological family. She'd talked to him about her past right away. Had she known he was a sucker for that kind of thing? Or had she been hoping to scare him away?

"I think that's what makes Roux and her sisters so strong. So beautiful on the inside."

Zach slapped him on the arm. "I wish I'd had more time with your girl," he said. "If she's anything like her sisters, you've scored a top prize."

"You're assuming she'll want to continue being with me after she sees how I act on tour." Well, usually acted. But he had the feeling he'd be too busy chasing after a certain woman to pursue his typical diversions.

"Are you nuts? Of course she'll still want to be with you. I saw the way she looked at you when she didn't kiss you goodbye." He winked at Steve.

This was the main reason Zach had always been his best friend. Steve didn't have to play the macho bullshit card with him, but he played it constantly with every other guy he hung around with. Everyone but Zach would be completely flabbergasted if confronted by Steve's deeper, gentler side. He guarded his tender heart like a Rottweiler; Bianca's betrayal could be blamed for that. But Steve figured he'd finally be able to get past that and give the guy he used to be a chance to come back into the light after so many years of being shoved into a dark corner and left to die. Roux's love could be blamed for that.

"I suppose I should order some comfort food," Steve said.

"For me or for you?"

"Both of us. Pizza?"

Zach nodded and then walked over to the sliding door that led to the backyard, which had nothing remotely resembling grass. Round pebbles in various earth tones and grays peppered the entire area around cement paths, and some bushy vine that refused to die provided the suggestion of shade as it creeped up the pergola as if trying to break into the house. Steve watched Zach through the glass as he settled into one of the Adirondack chairs in the shade and stared down at his phone. When he took a deep breath and dialed, Steve turned away to give him privacy and to order that pizza. They both typically ate healthy—junk food just wasn't worth the icky feeling and extra hours at the gym—but sometimes even a health-conscious man needed pizza and beer without guilt. He'd just order one with a veggie or two among the processed meat bits.

With pizza promised within the hour, Steve couldn't stop himself from replaying that Baroquen song where Roux sang most of the melody and had an amazing keyboard solo. The sound hit him in the gut every time, but now that he knew her better, now that he could picture her at his grandmother's piano playing the music the woman had written but had never taken credit for, the song turned him inside out. How was he going to survive the next week without seeing Roux? They'd promised to keep their distance on tour, but at least he'd be able to see her. *Not* seeing her was hell.

Impulsively he sent her a text message, unsure if she'd answer. *Miss me yet?*

Her reply was almost immediate. *God, yes.*

Forget the tour and run away with me. We can disappoint millions of fans together.

Millions of fans in your case. Tens of fans in mine.

He laughed out loud. *But if you run away with me, you'll have your biggest fan right beside you.*

You're such a groupie. She punctuated her message with the eye roll emoji.

Can I get a backstage pass? Pleeeeease. I'll do anything you want.

Tempting, but no. I have to go. Iona is going to think I passed out in the bathroom and hunt me down.

So that was why she was free to text him. She was using the

bathroom. He knew well what it was like to have such a busy schedule that even finding time to take a piss was an ordeal, so he cut her a little slack. He didn't want to be the guy who made a nuisance of himself. He just wanted her to think about him at least half as much as he thought of her.

Promise you'll text me next time you take a dump.

Steve!

He laughed again. *Promise.*

I promise.

I already have you trained.

You wish. I really am going now. She punctuated that with a kissing emoji, which he copied in his answer.

Steve was buzzing with all sorts of excited, happy energy when he set his phone aside. The woman already ruled his world, and he knew it. He just hoped she didn't send him crashing and burning the way Bianca had. Falling hard and fast was risky, but lord, it felt good. He glanced out toward the backyard and saw Zach sitting with his elbows on his knees, arms stretched out, and his phone gripped loosely far in front of him. His head was low, gaze on the ground between his feet. Steve's heart sank for the guy. He wasn't as good at being a sounding board as Zach was, but he slid the door open and sat in the chair next to him, waiting for Zach to say something if he wanted to. Steve wouldn't pry, but he knew his friend well enough to know he liked to talk about his problems. A lot.

"He doesn't want to break up," Zach said after a moment of uncomfortable silence.

"So he's coming out publicly?"

Zach snorted and ran a hand through the long half of his hair, which was hanging loose today. "No. His publicist is doing damage control on the online rumor. Why do these rumors keep springing up about me? First with you, which was false, and now with Enrique, which isn't."

"Maybe you should try hanging out with less famous dudes." Steve elbowed him in the arm.

"You're not that famous."

"More famous than you are."

"Not after this, I'm sure."

"Maybe we should call Sam," Steve said. "I'm sure he'd know how to use your sudden notoriety in your favor."

The only person who hated Sam more than Steve did was Zach, and he didn't even flinch at the suggestion.

"Great idea. Maybe he'll rehire Twisted Element for the next leg of the tour. I just have to sell my soul to the publicity devil. It isn't worth much anyway."

"We both know you wouldn't do that. What are you going to do about Enrique?"

"Give him another chance."

Steve cut off the sigh that tried to escape him. He knew better than to try to fix someone else's relationship. It was hard enough navigating his own.

"I hope it works out." And he meant it if Enrique made Zach happy. But if the bastard made his friend miserable, Steve hoped the fucker got hit by a train.

Zach smiled slightly. "Me too. Is the pizza here yet? I'm starved."

"You aren't running back to him tonight?"

"I'll crash here with you, if you don't mind. He thinks I should stay away for a few days. Wouldn't want to get caught with me on his property while the paparazzi are so thick outside his house."

Steve bit his tongue, but only for a second. "And you're going to put up with that bullshit?"

"It's just for a few days." His gaze turned to the pebbles that covered the ground. "Or weeks. Or however long it takes for suspicions to die."

And when they did, Steve hoped Zach didn't plan to jump when Enrique beckoned.

"I'm taking you to Europe with me. You don't have to be my personal assistant. You'll be my guest."

"I can't go. I need to be here—"

"When Enrique decides you're worth his time? Fuck that. You're going."

"But—"

"If he wants you, he'll come find you."

Hope flickered behind Zach's gaze, but it was quickly squelched as he started thinking too hard about it. "He won't do that."

"Then he isn't worth your time. Move on."

"Easy for you to say! You just met the woman of your dreams."

"She wouldn't hold that status for long if she pulled the crap that Enrique pulls."

"Whatever. I'll just crash at your place while you're gone."

"You're going to Europe."

A knock at the front door drew Steve to his feet.

"You're going," he added as he stepped into the house through the sliding door.

He opened the front door to a smiling delivery man. Almost immediately the smile dropped off the guy's face, and his eyes widened in shock. The pizza box tipped precariously and would have landed on the floor if Steve hadn't made a grab for it.

"Y-you're Steve Aimes."

Steve smiled. *Not that famous, my ass*, he thought smugly. "Last time I checked."

"You're Steve Aimes."

"I thought we already covered that." He tried passing a fifty to the dumbfounded delivery guy, but the fluttering bill was completely ignored.

"Oh my God, you're Steve Aimes!"

"I hope that's the pizza," Zach said, peering over Steve's shoulder. "I'm about to die over here."

The delivery guy's gaze shifted from Steve to Zach. "Y-you're Zach Mercier."

Zach beamed. "You know Twisted Element."

The man's head shake was almost imperceptible. "Steve Aimes's best friend."

"I do need to hang out with less famous people," Zach muttered under his breath.

"Can I get a picture with you?" Delivery Guy asked.

"What's your name?"

"Chris."

"Yes, Chris, you can get a picture with me, but only if you get one with Zach too. He's a little bummed. Needs to feel important."

Zach slugged him, almost unseating the pizza box from Steve's palm.

"Yeah, yeah, of course." Chris fumbled with the pocket of his baggy cargo shorts, pulled out a phone, dropped it, picked it up, dropped it again. He took a deep breath and retrieved his phone from the doorstep once more. "Sorry. I'm kind of nervous. Holy fuck, Steve Aimes!"

Steve backed into the house and set the pizza on the tiny dining table that could seat two uncomfortably.

"Come on in," he said, beckoning Chris with one hand. Steve flipped open the box, and Zach descended upon the pie as if he hadn't eaten in the past century. "Got time for a slice and a beer?"

he asked Chris. As far as Steve was concerned, all fans were friends and welcome—one at a time—in his house. He didn't have room for a crowd. That was what the beach a block over was for.

Chris looked back at his car parked at the curb and the pizza delivery sign affixed to the roof. "I am going to be so fired," he said, but he stepped into the house and closed the door.

Chris stayed only for one slice of pizza—refusing the beer because he couldn't afford to get fired from another job—and half a dozen pictures of him and Steve, and him and Zach, and Steve and Zach, and the Neil Peart autographed drumhead on the wall that was "too cool."

"I'm a drummer too, you know," Zach muttered.

"I guess I need an autographed drumhead from you to add to my collection," Steve said, smirking at Zach, who wasn't usually the type to feel sorry for himself. It was Sam's fault that Zach's ego had taken such a hit. The ass had called Zach's band mediocre. That was as bad as being told flat out that he sucked. It was their bassist who sucked. Steve gave Logan a hard time about how replaceable he was, saying that he was only a bassist, but without a good bassist, the music was hollow. Zach's bandmates were too loyal to send Gavin packing. Steve had stopped pressing the issue a long time ago, but maybe now that they'd been fired as an opening band, they'd be more open to suggestion. Not in front of Chris, though.

"For the pizza," Steve said, slapping a fifty into Chris's hand as he gave it a hard squeeze in farewell. "Keep the change."

"Thanks! You rock so hard!"

In that case . . . Steve pulled out a hundred. "This is for any pizza that got cold while you were in here bullshitting with us. And you can keep the change on that one too. Now, I have one rule for new friends. Don't stop by without calling first."

Chris's wide smile faded slightly. "But I don't have your number."

"Exactly. Hope to see you around sometime. At a bar. At the beach. Not here, though, unless I order a pizza." He hoped Chris got the message as he closed the door behind him.

"You're just asking for trouble," Zach said, picking up Steve's discarded pizza crust and nibbling on it.

"Haven't had any yet." Which was mostly true. He'd had to get stern with a few fans who'd found out where he lived and loitered in front of his house for days. But he just had to make them feel entirely uncool for doing it, and they left him alone. Fans didn't want the rock stars they idolized to think they weren't cool.

"Didn't Dare have some naked chick in his pool one time?" Zach bit off another bite of crust.

"I'm sure he's had lots of naked chicks in his pool," Steve said. "But yeah, he had a stalker who invited herself for a skinny-dip without his permission." Dare had called the cops. Steve most likely would have banged her first. Good thing his yard was too small for a pool.

Zach was in fairly good spirits for the rest of the evening. They sat in the backyard sipping beers and talking most of the night. Often Steve's thoughts drifted toward the East Coast and one redheaded babe who lived there, but he didn't mention Roux. He was certain Enrique was on Zach's mind, and he didn't want to rip open recent wounds by talking about their love lives. Sometimes it was nice to forget the outside world existed and just chill with a trusted friend.

"So what's your band meeting about tomorrow?" Zach asked.

Steve wondered how long he'd been chewing on that question.

"Some audit our accountant did on the record label."

"So they *have* been ripping you off. That tiny royalty check of Max's wasn't a fluke."

Zach had that right, but Steve shrugged. He'd been warned about the nondisclosure agreement that was in their contract. They were not allowed to tell anyone that royalties were improperly handled, even if the record label was at fault. But if they had to sue the company, it would all come out. If the label agreed to pay without a fight, no one would ever know but the parties involved, and that meant they wouldn't be able to warn other artists about Sam Baily and his crooked corporation. He hoped they could take the case to court. He went so far as to cross his fingers for added luck. He'd love to see Sam destroyed due to his own greed.

"You wouldn't be having a band meeting about it if everything was in the clear, would you?" Zach pressed.

"I can't say."

"I'm not an idiot, Steve."

"I literally cannot say. There's a nondisclosure agreement in the contract to protect the corporation's reputation." Steve scratched at his beard stubble. He often let his facial hair grow on tour breaks, and it was currently at that annoyingly itchy length.

"You can tell me. I won't tell a soul. How much money are you guys out?"

Steve pressed his lips tightly together and shook his head. He wasn't going to tell him anything. He refused to mess up this golden opportunity to finally fuck Sam Baily as hard as he'd fucked dozens of musicians in the industry.

"I bet it's millions. Have you seen that guy's shoes? Genuine fucking alligator. Probably made from the newborn babies of some endangered reptilian species. One pair costs more than I made all of last year."

"There are things more important than money."

"Like not being a greedy, cruel son of a bitch?"

Steve bumped his knuckles against the back of Zach's hand, which was resting on Zach's chair arm. Lazy bro tap, they called it. He was glad that Zach was always on the same page as he was when it came to Sam Baily. Perhaps tomorrow Steve would finally get Max and Dare to admit that they'd been wrong about him for the last ten years.

Steve snorted at the thought.

CHAPTER 21

THE NEXT MORNING, STEVE FOUND ZACH SITTING at the breakfast table staring into a bowl of soggy wheat flakes. Steve didn't recall having cereal or milk on hand, so Zach must have done some middle-of-the-night shopping.

"You're up early," Steve said, wiping the sleep from his eyes.

Zach glanced up. His drooping eyes were surrounded by dark circles. "Late," he corrected. "I never went to sleep."

Steve had slept well after a short midnight call from Roux. She hadn't even been taking a dump to hide her flouting of the no-contact-with-each-other plan, but she had gone outside on the fire escape so she wouldn't wake Iona.

Steve was sorry Zach wasn't having a better time.

"After this dumb band meeting"—which Steve was so looking forward to—"we'll grab Logan and go surfing. How does that sound?"

"Enrique loves to surf."

Ugh.

"He's not invited."

"I thought he'd call or text or . . ." Zach's gaze returned to the gloopy bowl of cereal. ". . . show up here in the middle of the night and demand I come home with him."

Steve moved to stand beside Zach and squeezed his shoulder. He didn't know what to say. It was too soon for the "he's not worth your time, you're better off without him" speech, though both were true. Zach turned his face against Steve's belly, his body quaking. Steve pressed a hand to the back of Zach's head and let him cry it out. He'd have to change his shirt before he left—he wasn't prepared to explain a tear-soaked belly to his bandmates—but he knew this emotional letting go would let Zach sleep, and he'd be thinking much more clearly after he caught some shut-eye.

Suddenly Zach pushed away, rubbing the tears off his face with both palms and then lifting the hem of his shirt to do a more thorough job. "I'm sorry. Fuck, I don't know what's wrong with me."

"Don't worry about it. I won't tell the press that you cry like a baby." Steve shoved him none too gently.

Zach released a breathless huff. "Well, I will tell them that you snore. Dear God, I thought a lumberjack was clearing a forest in your bedroom last night."

Steve grabbed Zach by the head and hugged his face tight against his belly. "It will be all right," he said quietly. "I know it doesn't feel that way now, but you'll get through this even though you'd rather not."

"If you make me cry again, I'll kick your ass."

Steve shoved him away, almost toppling Zach's chair over backwards in the process. "I'd like to see you try."

"I'm going to sleep in your bed while you're gone," Zach threatened.

"You'd better not." Though he hoped he would. There were blackout shades on the windows in his bedroom, and it would be a lot easier for Zach to sleep there in the middle of the day. "Are you going to finish that cereal?"

Zach spooned up a glob of slimy-looking disintegrated wheat flakes and let them plop back into the bowl. "I made breakfast for you," he said, grinning.

"I think I'll pass." He peeled off his shirt and tossed it into Zach's face. "You should wash that for me since you got it all wet."

Steve expected him to fire off some witty quip, but he lowered his head and pressed the shirt against his chest.

"Yeah," he said. "Thanks for that, by the way. I do feel a little better."

"And you'll feel like a new man after you get some sleep. You look like hell."

"If Enrique shows up with me looking like this"—he raked a hand through his hair—"I don't stand a chance."

Steve stifled an inward groan and reminded himself that this breakup, which he was sure would become permanent at some point, was fresh. Zach wasn't ready to give up yet.

"Exactly," Steve said, heading back to the bedroom for a cleanish shirt. When he returned, Zach was shoveling the remains of the cereal into the garbage disposal. "I'll see you later this afternoon. Get some sleep while I'm gone. I don't want to have to put up with a pansy ass when I get home."

"I'll try."

ALMOST AN HOUR LATER, STEVE TURNED his Kawasaki into Dare's driveway, and straddling the bright green fast-as-sin motorcycle, he pressed the intercom button to be let inside the gate.

"Do I know you?" Dare's voice came through the speaker.

"Depends on if you need a new vacuum cleaner." Did door-to-door vacuum cleaner salesmen still exist? Steve wasn't sure.

"I do, as a matter of fact. I hope it's ridiculously overpriced."

The gate rattled open, and Steve revved his engine and took off with a rush of speed and the accompanying adrenaline.

Logan had turned him on to dirt bikes almost a decade ago, but while his friend liked to jump the damned things and jar the shit out of his knees and hips, Steve just liked to go fast, so he'd eventually opted for a street bike and healthier knees. The front tire popped off the ground as he cranked the accelerator. And soon after it touched down, the back tire bounced up as he braked hard and came to a sudden stop at the front door.

"Show-off," Dare said.

"Just blowing off a little steam."

"I figured you'd do that on Guitar Island."

"You mean Dick Island?"

Dare shook his head and turned back into the foyer of his ridiculously huge mansion.

"Where's your butler today?" Steve asked. He'd always thought it was stupid that Dare had an honest-to-God butler, but Dare did need someone to take care of the ridiculously huge mansion when he was away. Apparently his housekeeper, pool boy, and gardener couldn't handle the task alone. At least Harold was Dare's only live-in servant. Steve couldn't have fit Dare's hired help inside his house, but he was more than okay with that. Steve also couldn't fit a car in the small shed he used as a garage, hence, an extra benefit of having a motorcycle.

"He's on vacation while I'm home."

Steve crossed the threshold into the crisp, air-conditioned foyer that was all marble and opulent furnishings. He was pretty sure that one painting was an authentic Degas and the chandelier, real crystal.

"Then who wipes your ass after you take a shit?" Steve asked

"That's why I invited *you* over."

"Am I the first one here?" If so, that was weird, because Steve, as usual, was at least ten minutes late, and Max was more punctual than an atomic clock school bell.

"Max has been here for several hours showing me spreadsheets."

Dare picked a corridor off to the left of the foyer. Steve was used to heading to the right wing of the house where the music studio was located. He knew that the kitchen and entertaining area were straight ahead, but he'd probably been down the left hall only once. He didn't even remember what rooms were located in this direction.

"Sounds like a blast," Steve said. "Sorry I missed it."

"He's not dealing with this well. Maybe you should consider not tormenting him today."

But where was the fun in that? "I'll try to keep my I-told-you-so's to a minimum." Mostly because he didn't want to piss Max off so much he decided to side with Sam no matter what he'd done just so he was in disagreement with Steve. It had been known to happen. "Did Logan make it in?"

"He's on his way. Jordan sure is earning her paycheck this month. How many flights has she done for you just this weekend?" Dare asked, his passive-aggressive way of telling Steve to knock it the fuck off.

They passed several guest bedrooms on their way down the long hall, footsteps echoing off polished marble.

Steve shrugged. "A few."

Dare lifted his brows.

"More like six," Steve admitted. "But it was for a good cause."

"Your libido?"

For his heart, actually, but he said, "Yep."

"Oh, I almost forgot. We're playing at Sed's reception this weekend, so don't wander too far from town. We'll need to rehearse."

"Sed's *wedding* reception? Why the fuck would we do that?" He liked the lead singer of Sinners just fine, but was a little surprised he'd even been invited to the wedding. He didn't know Sed all that well.

"Trey asked, and I told him we'd do it."

That explained everything. Trey had his big brother wrapped securely around his little finger.

At the far end of the hall—which was starting to remind Steve of that lengthening hotel hallway from some horror film—Dare slid open a pair of twelve-foot-high wooden pocket doors to reveal a den larger than Steve's entire house, including the yard. The mahogany woodwork gleamed from floor to thirty-foot ceiling. A balcony ran the perimeter of the room adjacent to shelves stuffed full of books. Steve's jaw dropped. He would have remembered the gorgeous room if he'd ever been in it. It looked like some library from an exclusive private school. Max sat at an enormous round table in the center of the room. He looked up when they entered, and his hand immediately crumpled the page resting beneath his palm as he made an agitated fist.

Not dealing with it well, was that how Dare had put it? The guy looked like he was about to climb out of his skin and use the discarded casing as a noose.

"Hey," Steve greeted. There was no way he was goading Max today. Wow.

"Did Logan arrive yet?" Max asked, glancing at the open door behind them.

"He's on his way," Dare said. "Should be landing within the next half hour."

Max looked slightly ill and then beckoned Steve to sit beside him. "I'll get you up to speed while we wait."

Steve refused to point out that it would make more sense to wait for Logan and explain everything to them both at the same time, but yeah, whatever Max wanted at the moment was okay with him.

Steve settled into a heavy upholstered chair and tried to pay attention.

"It started off small," Max said, shuffling through papers until he found the one he was looking for. "The year we signed with the label and were given the opportunity to work with Sam Baily."

They'd all been excited to work with Sam in the beginning. He'd had good success getting several hair bands in the 80s and grunge bands in the 90s to the top of the charts, but everyone thought that metal was a dying genre. Exodus End had proven the naysayers wrong. Steve had to admit that Sam played a part in their initial success. As a publicity wizard, Sam had helped them get recognized.

"So this was set up so royalties are deposited directly into a common account. After we pay all band expenses, including tours, employees, instruments and equipment, jet fuel"—Max's sidelong glare said Steve had been using an unfair share of fuel that weekend—"Etc., etc., the remaining money is divided equally between the four of us."

Steve vaguely remembered deciding that setup was the fair way to handle income. He nodded.

"So here's the balance sheet for our first year, the numbers we were given—our gross income, deducted expenses, the royalties we were eventually paid."

"Like a partnership." It was all coming back to Steve now. Max had fretted about all these details from the beginning, making sure no one got screwed over and that the band was treated like a business. Steve had agreed at the time just to get him to shut up, but now that he was older and wiser, he could see that Max had been looking out for more than just himself by drawing up articles of incorporation. He'd been looking out for all of them.

"Exactly. The auditor ran all the numbers and then ran them again and again, and this was what *he* came up with as the figure for reported expenses."

Max flipped another page in front of him. Steve's eyes widened. "That's a ten-thousand-dollar difference." Exactly ten thousand dollars.

Max snorted. "We're just getting started. The discrepancy goes up every year."

"Who controls the expense account?"

"Our manager," Max said, eyes narrowing.

"Oh."

"Our gross royalties go up every year." He flipped pages in front of Steve in rapid succession. "And that discrepancy goes up along with it. This was at the peak of our career."

Steve's jaw dropped. "Seven million dollars!"

Dare crossed his arms over his chest and leaned against the table beside Steve. "And we didn't notice, because we were bringing home fat stacks then."

"Now we're in a decline," Max said. "And the discrepancy shrinks. A lot. I think he was starting to worry that we'd catch on."

"You're sure Sam is taking the money."

"Not for himself. Not all of it. Our auditor got his hands on Tradespar West's books too. Small-time bands with not enough royalties to pay their expenses have money appearing out of nowhere."

"So he took money from us to help other musicians." That wasn't so bad. Steve didn't need the cash, and he knew how hard other musicians struggled in the business.

Max slammed his fist on the table. "Exactly! Can you believe this shit?"

Oh, that was what he was mad about. Steve put on a stern face. If it got rid of Sam, he could pretend it pissed him off too. If Sam had been using the cash to buy his ridiculous shoes, that was one thing, but if it was too help fellow musicians succeed, Steve felt differently about the situation. Would Baroquen have gotten a deal if Sam hadn't fiddled with the books a little? Or rather, a lot?

"I've known he was a weasel for a long time," Steve said. "This just proves it's all about dollars for him."

"*Our* dollars," Max bellowed. "No one fucking steals from me and gets away with it."

"Right." Steve nodded. "I wonder if they're even reporting the right royalties."

"Not for the past three years. The bastard started skimming from the top instead of the bottom when our record sales declined."

"He's been taking a higher percentage of ticket sales as well," Dare said. "I thought it was weird that the ticket prices had been raised and we're still selling out stadiums, yet we're seeing lower profits."

Dare was the financial wizard of the band. Why hadn't he caught on to this series of scams sooner? Because Dare was a trusting bastard, that was why. It was very hard to get on Dare's bad side. Steve's distrust of Sam had always been personal. He couldn't stand a guy who put money-making above every other consideration, including creative license, the personal lives of the band, and the happiness of the fans.

"What are we going to do?" Steve asked, preparing his foot to kick Sam's ass out the door and into the gutter where he belonged.

"We'll decide when Logan gets here," Dare said, ever the diplomat.

"How much does he owe us?" Steve asked. "If he pays it, we can't take him to court." And that was what Steve preferred even over a simple return of funds—to get the jerk out of the business entirely. But what would happen to all those less popular bands who couldn't afford to fund their own tours? If Exodus End got some of their money back, maybe they could sponsor up-and-comers out of their pocket. They'd probably been doing that for years already without knowing it, and Steve had everything he needed. Why not help out struggling musicians?

"Going on thirty million," Dare said.

Steve blinked. That couldn't be right. "He won't be able to pay that." Steve clenched a victory fist under the table. This guy was so screwed. They were going to drag his name through the mud in an ugly legal battle. They wouldn't have to resort to fabricating stories in some stupid tabloid to make him look bad, not like Sam and Bianca had done to Steve and his bandmates, including poor Reagan.

"He better fucking pay it," Max said. "Plus interest."

His jaw was held in such a tight line, Steve feared it would shatter.

"We should have had an audit done years ago," Dare said. He shook his head. "I completely dropped the ball on that."

"No blame lies with you, man," Max said. "It's all Sam."

A loud whine blew over the house, announcing Logan's arrival. When they weren't using the jet, it was kept on Dare's private landing strip. It was no wonder that the guy didn't notice a measly seven or eight million of his dollars missing. Even Steve hadn't noticed.

"Wait," Steve said. "If we do get reimbursed, will Bianca be entitled to a cut?"

She'd taken him to the cleaners in the divorce, but some of that missing income had been made while they'd been married.

"If so, she won't be entitled to much," Dare said. "The big chunks were taken after you divorced."

Steve released a relieved breath. He hadn't minded her getting a large settlement in the divorce as, at the time, he'd still loved her, but he was past that now. She continued to be a thorn in his side all these years later, and, frankly, he no longer cared if she couldn't pay her credit cards or if her Mercedes got repossessed.

"Does this mean you're finally going to move out of that tiny hovel you call a house?" Max asked.

"I'll never leave Venice Beach," he said. Unless it was to be closer to Roux. He wondered how she'd deal with the news of seed money for her band coming illegally from Exodus End's royalties. He hoped Baroquen weren't mixed up in this mess. He wanted them to succeed even if it was at his expense. They deserved their time in the spotlight.

"It's a cool place to visit," Dare mused.

"Are you putting on airs, Mills?" Steve lifted his brows. "Don't want to rub elbows with the common folk?"

"That's not it. Venice Beach is just . . . *busy*."

Dare was a solitary creature by design and by choice. He'd likely never leave his walled-in, gated mansion or his distant private island if he had a say in the matter. And he didn't have a say, because Exodus End would not exist without their talented lead guitarist.

"We won't have to cancel the tour, will we?" Steve asked.

Max went still, his face slightly ashen. "I-I hadn't thought that far ahead."

Steve knew the only thing Max loved more than cash due was the stage's spotlight.

Logan arrived not long after, and, as always, accompanied by Toni.

"Not to be rude, but she can't be here," Max said.

"Why not? I'm going to marry her someday."

Toni flushed prettily and pushed her glasses up her nose with the back of one wrist.

"Because we have a nondisclosure agreement on this crap," Steve said, "and we aren't going to fuck up this opportunity to destroy Sam Baily because of some lame technicality." He shifted his gaze to Toni. "Why don't you explore Dare's mansion? We'll try to find you when we're done here. You might want to leave a trail of breadcrumbs."

"Is your groupie girl here?" Toni asked.

What groupie girl? Oh, she still thought Roux was his groupie when the opposite was closer to the truth.

"Nah. Why would I bring her?" Steve shrugged as if thoughts of the woman in question weren't currently tugging at him in all sorts of uncomfortable places.

"You seemed to like her pretty well."

"I like all my groupies." And as much as he liked Toni, he didn't like being questioned by someone with ties—even if indirect—to a damned tabloid.

Logan pulled Toni aside, kissed her for an obscenely long time, and whispered to her. She smiled brightly and nodded, then left through the set of monstrous pocket doors. Logan slid them closed behind her.

"Does she always do your bidding?" Steve asked as Logan settled into the chair next to him.

"Putty in my hands. I told her to make me a sandwich."

"And she wasn't offended?" Dare asked.

"She likes taking care of me. And I like taking care of her." He wiggled his eyebrows. "In the bedroom."

Steve rolled his eyes. He seriously doubted Toni was making Logan a damned sandwich. Then again, she was a bit of an odd duck. A sweet, loving, and sensitive duck, but definitely odd.

"What's this meeting about?" Logan asked. "And why was it important enough to ruin my much-needed vacation?"

"Bassists don't need vacations," Steve teased, because he just couldn't resist. "All they do is play one note repeatedly. Hell, they can't even handle a full six strings." That earned Steve a kick to the shin, but he loved giving Logan a hard time.

"Someone—most likely Sam—has been embezzling money from our account since we signed on with our label twelve years ago," Max said, righteous anger flushing over his face once more. "And more recently, our royalties have been underreported."

"Don't forget about ticket sale profits," Dare said.

Steve's phone vibrated in his pocket as a text message was delivered. Roux? Maybe Zach, though Steve hoped he was sleeping. Everyone else likely to text him was in the room. Already bored with Max's repeated spiel, Steve pushed his chair back. "Can you draw me a map to the nearest toilet?" he asked Dare.

"Second, no, third door on the right. Or use any of the guest room on-suite bathrooms."

"Just how many bathrooms does this place have?" Steve asked.

"Nine, I think." Dare shrugged.

Nine? The dude had probably never used most of them.

"Don't make a decision on Sam Baily's annihilation until I get back," Steve said.

Max lifted a hand to let him know he'd been heard, as he continued to show a bewildered Logan his never-ending stack of spreadsheets.

Steve slid open the door and eased it closed behind him. He spotted Toni a few doors down the hall gaping at an enormous painting in a gilded frame. She turned in his direction at the sound of his footsteps.

"Is this thing real?" she asked.

Steve glanced at the painting, sure he'd seen it before but not recognizing the artist. "It probably is. Dare likes nice things."

"Obviously. Is Logan's house like this?" She tilted her chin down and whispered, "I'll be afraid to touch anything."

"His place is real nice, but nothing like this. It's up in the hills surrounded by dirt bike trails. You'll love the view."

Toni's shoulders dropped. "Do you think the band would be open to including something about your private homes in the book? I think the fans would love knowing how you live. This place is so impressive!"

She was always thinking about that book. He wondered if there'd be a chapter on Logan's skills in the sack since she had plenty of experience with that.

"No one will be impressed with my little house," Steve said.

"I bet it's grand."

"Not in the least. You wouldn't have happened to run across a bathroom around here, would you?"

She shook her head.

Remembering Dare's instructions, he counted three doors on the right and opened the door to a small powder room. "Here it is," he said. "You'd better get busy making Logan that sandwich." He winked at her.

"It will probably take me a month just to find the kitchen."

She really was going to make him a sandwich? Maybe she was putty in his hands. "When you make it to the foyer, take the center hall."

"Thanks," she said.

He closed himself in the bathroom and pulled his phone out of his pocket. When he saw the message was from Roux, a surge of adrenaline kicked up his heart rate. What would the guys think if they knew even the slightest hint of attention from her sent his hormones into a frenzy and made him giddy with a flood of happiness? What did he think about that?

"I'm putty in her hands," he admitted aloud.

Her message read *I don't think I can survive for three months without you inside me. Not sure I can make it three more minutes.*

He answered, *It's not nice to give me a hard-on in the middle of an important band meeting.*

He unzipped his pants and found his text was no joke. He took several calming breaths to relax enough to take a piss.

Tell me about the meeting. Maybe it will take my mind off your hard-on.

He flushed the toilet and washed his hands before answering.

Maybe I don't want your mind off it. I'd prefer your hand on it, though.

She sent him a series of short messages that arrived one after the other.

I'd use my lips first.
Then my tongue.
My mouth.
My hand only to guide you inside me.

Wow, Dare's bathroom was overwarm. He probably needed to call an HVAC technician pronto. Steve's mind was churning up a thousand scenarios to follow her start, but damned if none of that kinky adventurous stuff sounded more exciting than simply being inside her.

Once I'm inside I don't even want to move, he responded, his heart aching over her absence even more than his balls did.

I'd like you to move a least a little. The words were punctuated with a winking heart-kiss emoticon.

What are you doing this weekend? I need a date for a wedding reception. Which he'd be performing at, according to Dare.

I'm sorry. I'd like to go. I really want to, but I can't. I have dress rehearsal every day for the next ten days straight.

All work and no play . . .
Makes Roux a dull girl?

Makes Roux's boyfriend horny and lonely. He held his breath, waiting for her response to his using the term boyfriend for the first time. His nerves were raw, his belly jumbled, his heart raced. He couldn't remember getting this worked up over hot chicks in high school, and he'd been a giant cauldron of sex hormones back then. This was fucking ridiculous. But he wouldn't change it. This high was far better than any drug he'd ever tried.

It felt like ten years had passed before her response dinged his phone. *I will be sure to make it up to him the next time I see him.*

"Yes!" He made a victory fist. She was ready for the next step.

Next time you see me? Not in three months? he texted back. He should have just called her. Or better yet, used FaceTime so he could see her lovely face. Damn, he missed her.

He could practically hear the amusement in her response. *Three months? Yeah, no. Not happening. Didn't I say I doubted I could make it three more minutes?*

Well, you must have. I've been texting you for at least ten. And he was bound to be missed soon, though Max could probably bore Logan with his spreadsheets for at least another half hour.

Nope. I've been touching myself this entire time.

"Fuuuuck." He hoped Jordan didn't think she was getting a day off anytime soon, because he was going to need to go to New York even if it was just for a quickie against the wall in an airport bathroom.

You are evil, he texted, followed by, *I don't think I can continue this conversation.* And then, *You're going to make me come down my leg if you keep talking like that.*

Too late to make that simultaneous.

She'd come while texting him? "Fuck!" he said again. He was no stranger to dirty talk or sexting, but with Roux, it was like he was completely inexperienced. Everything was new and exciting. He wanted more. He wanted her. Now.

He sent her one last text. *See you soon.*

What? What does that mean?

He didn't respond. She was going to find out what happened when she pushed him to the limits of his scanty self-control.

CHAPTER 22

ROUX SHOWED the text she'd just received from Steve to Raven, the moron who'd suggested Roux try sexting with him, probably to get her to shut up about him for a few minutes.

"Does this mean what I think it means?"

Raven grinned. "You lucky bitch! He's totally in love with you."

Roux's heart rate kicked up several notches, but she rolled her eyes. "Whatever. He's just horny." He wouldn't really see her soon. Like, not in person. Maybe he meant he'd FaceTime her or something. She hadn't slept a wink because she'd been so busy thinking of him all night. How had he gotten so far under her skin so quickly? He was perfection, that was how.

"If he were just horny, he'd grab the nearest groupie and get his rocks off. It isn't like the guy couldn't find a willing substitute."

"We promised we wouldn't screw around with anyone else."

Raven nodded. "When I'm right, I'm right. Totally in love with you."

Roux hopped up from the chair she'd been sitting in while Raven had been pretending to touch up her makeup so she could sext with Steve in the middle of the day. She paced the length of the small room, reading and rereading the string of messages they'd sent to each other. She was almost positive his final three-word message meant he was coming to see her soon. But how was that possible? He had important band meetings and, and some wedding to go to, and, and, and Zach's heartache to help mend—she loved that the two were so close. Her sisters had had nothing but great things to say about Zach, who'd blended in with the family of women and girls as if he'd grown up in the brownstone with them all. Mama Ramona adored him. Especially when she unwittingly asked him which of her girls he planned to marry and he assured her that only the top prize—Ramona herself—would do. Anyway, Steve was much too busy to fly clear across the country to see her. She wouldn't have time to entertain him anyway. Iona was already growing suspicious that even though Roux had assured her there was nothing remotely serious between her and Steve, things were a tad more complex than anyone was letting on.

"What am I going to do, Raven? If he shows up here, Iona is going to flip. I promised her there wouldn't be any fooling around between me and Steve during the tour."

"But you aren't on tour yet," Raven said, fingering the hoop that pierced one nostril as she watched Roux fidget.

True! Roux hugged Raven tight, hoping that she would get to see Steve again before they had to do the distance-keeping thing for real. She'd be devastated if she'd misinterpreted his message and he didn't show up. "You're right; we aren't on tour yet. I love you!"

"But you love Steve more," Raven teased.

Roux released Raven and turned her back to her. "Not more. Different."

"That's a relief," Raven said. "I wouldn't want to keep you awake all night, too uncomfortable in your wet panties to sleep."

"It isn't just the sex between us that's making me crazy." She pressed her fingertips to her lips, trying to find the words to explain her feelings but coming up lacking. "He's so . . . not what I expected. He has a huge heart."

"And the huge dick is just a bonus."

Roux laughed. "Exactly!"

For the rest of the day and evening, Roux's gaze kept darting to the wings of the stage as if she expected Steve to be there. First of all, even if he'd commandeered the jet the second he'd stopped texting her, the distance was too far for him to get there this soon. Second of all, he wasn't really coming. What kind of crazy guy would drop everything just to see a woman he'd met only weeks ago? Third . . . Her bandmates were staring at her. She clenched her fingers, which were no longer moving across the keys.

"You okay, Roux?" Sage asked.

"My fingers cramped up," she lied, flexing her hands as if trying to work some circulation through them. "I can't imagine what yours must feel like. Are they bleeding yet?"

"I could use a break," Lily said from behind her drum kit. She was drenched in sweat. "I need to rehydrate too. I feel a little dizzy."

"Yeah, yeah, and my throat hurts, but we have only a week to get this right!" Iona said. "From the top." She strummed the first bass note, but the rest of them only stared at her. "I said, from the top." She repeated the note, but again no one joined her.

"I'm calling it a night," Lily said, placing her sticks on her snare and groaning as she stood from her stool. She pressed both hands to her lower back and stretched it back and forth. "If you kill us all before the tour actually starts, you won't ever attain that fame you so desperately want."

"I don't want it for me. I want it for all of us," Iona said.

"But none of us wants it the way you do," Sage said, lifting her guitar strap over her head and setting her green guitar on a stand near the edge of the stage.

"Speak for yourself," Azura said. "I want it all." She played a fast series of notes on the blue guitar that matched her hair and clothing accents.

"We can have it all without killing ourselves," Lily said. "We got this." She joined Iona, who looked half sick, and wrapped an arm around her shoulders. "This isn't like that show, Iona. You aren't alone; we're with you. There's no competition here. You're just doing something you love."

But everything was always a competition with Iona. It was simply how she operated. They all knew that about her, and they all loved her because of that internal drive, not despite it.

"If you're not careful, you'll lose your voice again," Roux said. Iona went a shade paler. "You need rest too."

"We'll be back tomorrow," Sage said. "It's not like we're finished forever. We all know we still have a few kinks to work out of the set."

"And I have a few kinks to work out of my back." Lily groaned and bent over, rounding her back to relieve the tension.

"And I'm sure Iona has a few kinks to work out on her man," Azura said, removing her guitar and setting it aside. "When do I get a chance at some kinks?"

"Maybe we should go to the Delancey tonight," Sage said. "Any kink you're looking for will be there."

Azura brightened. She loved going to their favorite goth nightspot in New York, but her shoulders sagged after a brief moment. "I'm too damned tired to even consider it."

Roux draped a cloth over her instrument to keep the dust off the keys and followed her sisters off the stage. Looking around at the current setup, she was struck by how lucky they were that Sam had found this place for them to use for the next week. Most of their equipment was on a barge headed to England, so renting all this stuff couldn't have been cheap. It also was within walking distance to their apartment. The sun was already going down, and they lived in a neighborhood where it wasn't safe to walk alone at night, but the six of them together felt secure enough to goof around and gossip as a bit of relief from a long day of attempting to turn their fun hobby into a grueling job.

"I guess he isn't coming," Roux said quietly to Raven, who was answering messages as she walked.

"Give him time. He's not the boy next door."

That was true in multiple ways, but that point didn't make Roux feel even a little better. She missed him like crazy. Maybe he was right and real rock bands didn't have keyboardists. She could quit now and become a desperate groupie begging for his attention. *Right.* That was simply her hormones talking. As soon as the nuisance giddiness wore off, she'd regret such a stupid decision for the rest of her life. She needed to get a grip. Especially since she was certain the reason he was even remotely infatuated with her was because in the beginning she'd pushed him away and now she continued to lay ground rules even if she wasn't very good at keeping them.

Stay strong. She tried a self-directed pep talk. *You don't need a man to be happy and successful and to live a fulfilling life.*

But having Steve beside her would sure make those dreams all the sweeter when they became her reality.

She was halfway up the fourth flight of stairs to their apartment when her phone dinged with a text message. She whipped the phone out so fast, she nearly chucked it down the stairwell. She clutched it to her chest, heart hammering wildly, and then peered at the message through the slits between clenched eyelids, as if reading it that way would lessen her disappointment.

Meet me at Republic Airport in six hours.

Six hours? That would be two thirty in the morning; was he crazy? She glanced at her sisters, realizing they'd all be asleep—with the exception of Raven, who rarely slept—and wouldn't know if she snuck out in the middle of the night. They'd never know she'd been unable to keep her word about not seeing Steve for less than forty-eight hours.

And so she impulsively texted back. *I'll be there. How will I find you?*

You'll figure it out. Putting my phone in airplane mode now.
Wait. I have questions.

But he didn't answer.

"Damn," she muttered under her breath. It would serve him right if she stood him up. Oh, who was she kidding? She'd be there to meet him even if she had to crawl through the New York City sewers on her hands and knees.

When Roux tiptoed out of the apartment hours later—Raven silently locking the door behind her—her belly was quivering with a mix of nerves and excitement. What kind of crazy guy had she gotten herself mixed up with? The right kind of crazy. She grinned as she hurried down the steps in her bare feet, carrying her sandals by the straps until she was safely, quietly, out of the building. Once outside, she sat on the rain-wet front step and slipped into her shoes. A soft drizzle fell, giving the cement an earthy smell that instantly relaxed her. She stood from the stoop to make her way to the nearest subway station but stopped before she'd managed a single step. A white limousine was parked at the curb. Red flower petals lay scattered on the pavement before the back door, which a stern-looking man opened. He stood watching her.

Was Steve already here? Was he waiting inside the limo?

She approached the car warily. Mama had warned her never to get into a stranger's vehicle. Unless it was a limo. Stranger-danger rules didn't apply in such situations.

"Miss Roux Williams?" the driver said, his voice far more comforting than those shrewd-looking eyes of his.

"Y-yes."

"I'm to take you to Republic when you're ready."

She'd given herself a couple of hours to get there because she figured she'd have to take public transportation. Iona monitored the mileage on the van for tax purposes, and she was determined not to get caught.

"You are?"

"Yes, miss. The gentleman instructed me not to bother you and wait at the curb until you came outside."

"He did?"

"Yes, miss. I can take you anywhere you'd like to go as long as we make it to our destination before two."

"I guess we can take the scenic route," she said with a shrug.

He smiled, and his eyes softened. "As you wish."

He took her elbow to help her into the car. More red rose petals carpeted the floorboards. She wasn't sure of their significance, but as she settled into the wide comfortable seat, she scooped a petal off the floor and brought it to her nose. She closed her eyes as she rubbed it over her lips.

"Help yourself to any refreshments you desire," the driver said. "If you need me, lift the phone handset there." He pointed to a phone affixed to one wall.

"Wait!" Roux said as he started to close the door.

He ducked his head into the open door. "Yes, miss?"

"I didn't catch your name."

He smiled again. "It's Arnold, miss."

"Thank you, Arnold. You saved me from a walk in the rain." The light sprinkles were already turning into heavier drops. She had no doubt that she would have been completely drenched by the time she reached the subway.

"My pleasure, miss."

The door closed, and within a few moments the car pulled away from the curb. In the seat across from her sat three boxes of various sizes, each wrapped in bright floral paper. She stared at them as if they might jump off the seat and tear out her jugular. She hadn't received many gifts in her lifetime. Holidays and birthdays had been special under Mama Ramona's care, but not lavish. Instead of buying presents for each sister, her family had done a gift exchange at Christmas and pooled their money for a single birthday gift, so in her memory she'd never gotten three gifts at once. Not even before she'd been saved. She licked her lips nervously and turned her attention elsewhere.

On the central console stood an open bottle of champagne chilling in a bucket of ice, chocolate-covered strawberries arranged artfully on a platter, and various hors d'oeuvres on tiny plates. Upon closer inspection, she found the treats were vegetarian friendly, and unable to resist sampling each variety, she also discovered they were all very tasty. The champagne turned out to be non-alcoholic sparkling grape juice, so she poured herself a glass, feeling slightly ridiculous to be sitting in the back of a limo alone sampling rich-people food and drinking juice on her way to meet a rock star in the middle of the night. She felt like an imposter in her own life. She hoped Steve didn't make a habit of this frivolous kind of adventure.

While it was wildly romantic, and she couldn't help but feel special, this little rendezvous was wasteful and over the top and unnecessary. Well, seeing him did seem as necessary as breathing, but the limo and the refreshments and the gifts she was afraid to touch and the drive around downtown New York made her uncomfortable. Indebted. But yes, very special. She couldn't stop smiling. Maybe it was the delicious sparkling grape juice. She'd certainly enjoyed enough of it by the time she found the courage to open one of the gifts. The box was flat and square. She carefully peeled off the tape as if she planned to rewrap it, so no one would know she'd opened it. She set the paper aside and lifted the lid. Inside a layer of red tissue paper, she found the skimpiest, most transparent pair of black panties ever made.

She flushed, checking over her shoulder for observers before lifting them out of the box and holding them at eye level. "He doesn't expect me to actually wear these, does he?" There was nothing to them but a few strings and a patch of gauze.

A white card lay at the bottom of the box. On it was typed *Imagining you in these gets me through my next breath without you. Steve.*

Emotion threatened to choke her. She checked the interior of the limo for onlookers, squinting at the dark glass to search for prying eyes, and after deciding no one would see her, she slipped her hands under her skirt and peeled her sensible panties down her thighs, replacing them with the ones Steve have given her. She quickly wadded up her discarded drawers and stuffed them into her purse.

Hooked already, she reached for the second box. This one was rectangular and made a clunking sound when she turned it over looking for tape. She wasn't quite as careful with the wrapping on this one, and cringed when it tore, but she soon had the paper tossed aside and lifted the lid, her belly tight with anticipation. Inside were two small bottles of fragrance. She lifted them out and unscrewed the tops, giving each a sniff. The first was sweet smelling—a mix of honeysuckle and some citrus fruit. The second smelled spicier, musky. At the bottom of the box she found another neatly typed message.

Sweet or sexy? You're both to me. Chose what you want to be for me tonight. Steve.

She inhaled a whiff of each fragrance again, deciding she loved them both. How could she choose? She decided she didn't have to. She dabbed a bit of the sweet fragrance behind one ear, and the sexier scent behind the other.

The final gift was the smallest and a long, thin shape. She hoped good things did come in small packages. Wanting to savor this one, she took her time removing the wrapping. Her heart thudded when a black velvet box was revealed. She was going to have to tell Steve not to buy her things. She knew he could afford it, but what could she ever give him in return? She was broke.

Fingers shaking, she opened the hinged lid to find a diamond tennis bracelet with a large ruby heart in the center. She touched the red stone and sucked her lips into her mouth. It was gorgeous, but she could never accept such a lavish gift. She'd just put it on for a second to see how it looked, and then put it back in the box and ask him to return it. Her heart was thudding as if she'd stolen the thing as she released it from the fasteners securing it to a satin-covered interior and then wrapped it around her wrist. The bracelet she always wore—the silver one with the bullet dangling from it—even looked good next to the extravagant string of diamonds, as if the two were meant to be paired. She fastened the clasp and held it up to the light. It glittered prettily on her wrist. Oh God, she loved it!

"You're not making things easy on me, Aimes," she muttered under her breath, running a finger over the faceted diamonds and tracing the ruby heart. And he had exquisite taste. Or was some Exodus End lackey responsible for choosing her gifts? She discovered another neatly typed card caught in the lid of the bracelet's velvet box.

Not sure if you're ready to give me your heart yet, but when you are, wear this, and I'll know you've given me the greatest gift I could ever receive. More than like you, Steve.

She blinked against the sudden rush of tears, dabbing at her eyes with the back of her hand to save her makeup from utter ruin. She fingered the clasp, knowing she should take off the bracelet, especially since he'd attached such significance to the gorgeous piece of jewelry, but . . .

She was ready to give him her heart. It had likely been his from the moment he comforted her on the balcony when she'd told him about what had happened to her family. She was ready to love him, but was she ready for him to know? She knew how much he liked the chase.

She was still wearing the bracelet when they arrived at the airstrip a few minutes before two. The limo pulled to a halt, and after a moment, Arnold opened the door. She wondered if she was supposed to tip him. She had only a few dollars on her and figured that lowly amount would insult him. All her worries about proper tipping etiquette vanished as she stepped out of the limo onto more red rose petals. Feeling as if she were walking into a dream, she absently handed her champagne flute to Arnold, diamond bracelet glittering in the hazy light from street lamps, sexy new underwear riding uncomfortably up her ass crack, a mix of fragrances swirling about her face ... and followed the trail of rose petals into the building that served as a hub for private flights. The place was deserted. Even the customer service counter had been abandoned. She could see a few small planes out along the airstrip, but it was too dark to tell if one of them belonged to Exodus End.

The rose petals continued down a corridor and around to the right into a shadowed hallway illuminated by a trail of burning candles along the floor. Her heart rate increased with each step, with the anticipation of discovering what lay at the end of the path—*Steve*—as she remembered him saying she'd know how to find him once she got to the airstrip. Was he here waiting for her? Or was she early? The trail of rose petals and candles ended at a closed door. She read the placard beside the door and snorted. The men's room? All this fanciful flare to lead her to a *men's room*? Only Steve would come up with something so—

The door eased open, and there he stood, so gorgeous in a white button-down shirt with his hair swept up into a bun and his dark eyes burning with desire, he stole her breath.

"Fancy meeting you here," he said with a disarming grin.

She swore the earth stopped turning and that all of existence vanished except for the man before her. She couldn't find enough air to speak, so she stared at him, lips parted with longing, and then she reached out to fist her fingers in the front of his shirt. A desperate moan escaped her as he shifted her into the bathroom and pressed her back up against the cool tile of the wall beside the door.

His kiss seared her inside and out. Sparks of want and need crackled between them as his lips caressed hers fervently. Her fingers were at the buttons of his shirt, releasing them as fast as her fumbling hands could manage. When her palms smoothed over the warmth of his hard chest, he pressed his thigh between her legs, lifting her up on her toes. She cried out, squirming against his leg in search of relief. Too many clothes, she thought, glad he could read minds as he pulled her top off over her head and flung it to the floor.

"Only you do this to me, Red," he murmured in a low growl

that made her nipples tighten and strain toward him. His teeth scraped the edge of her jaw, and he bit down just hard enough to send a jolt of excitement down her spine.

"I didn't do much," she said, refusing to take the blame for this encounter, but eager to claim the benefits.

"You just have to exist."

He hiked her skirt up to her waist and ran a finger along her hip under the string that was posing as underwear. "I've been imagining you wearing these for hours, and now I'm too turned on to even look." His breathless laugh twisted her into knots. "God, I've missed you."

"I've missed you too." She stroked his stubbled cheek. She was completely aroused, but her deepest longing wasn't for the pleasure she knew his body could give her, it was for the bliss of being with him.

"Is that . . ." His breath hitched. He turned his face into her palm and kissed the ruby heart of her new bracelet. "Please tell me you read the note before you put this on," he said, his voice wavering with emotion.

"I didn't," she admitted. She refused to lie to him about anything.

He sagged against her, pressing her into the wall. "Oh. That's okay. It's yours to wear regardless."

"I read the note after I put on the bracelet and figured I should have you return it. I'd have to be crazy to feel that strongly about anyone after such a short time knowing someone."

"I knew it was a long shot."

She threaded her fingers through the loose strands of hair framing his face and stared into his eyes. The hurt behind his gaze tore at her heart. She really shouldn't torture him by going into long-winded details.

"But I'm glad you wore the sexy perfume," he said, pushing his fingers beneath the scrap of material that barely concealed her pussy. When he touched her throbbing clit, she jolted several inches up the wall.

"Are you sure?" She turned her head so he could smell the sweet perfume beneath her ear.

"Sweet?"

She smiled. "That's the part of me that got giddy because you attached heavy significance to this gorgeous bracelet and told me to wear it anyway."

"Does that mean what I think it means?"

Yes, but she wasn't quite prepared to blurt out her deepest feelings when she was pressed up against the wall of a men's room. She turned her head the other way, and he inhaled the second fragrance she'd applied in the limo.

"I was right," he said. "I did smell something sexy."

"That's the part of me that wants your hard cock pounding into me at this very moment."

She held her breath as he unzipped his pants and then let the air out in a gasp of excitement as he shifted his hips and guided himself into her. He didn't pound into her, though. He took her slowly, carefully, wetting his length with her juices as he thrust in and out, claiming one inch of new territory at a time. He never took his eyes off hers, not even when he'd filled her completely.

"I love both parts of you, sweet and sexy," he said, and the way that he was looking at her, as if she was his entire world, kept her from questioning the depth of his feelings. "I love all parts of you, Roux. I love you."

Gravity ceased to exist. She clung to Steve's shoulders, certain that if she hadn't been anchored to the only reality in her universe, she would have drifted into outer space. "I love you too." She hadn't meant to say it, but she'd never spoken truer words.

He released a small gasp before claiming her lips. The passion behind his kiss made her toes curl, the emotion behind it made her chest ache, and when his hands gripped her ass and he began to thrust his hips, a deeper connection was cemented between them. Sex became more than pleasure, more than fun, more than heady excitement and inevitable release. And maybe it had always been that way between them, but she hadn't recognized the emotional entanglement before.

Their souls were touching. She felt him everywhere, with every part of herself, and it scared the hell out of her.

Why had she let him get so close? What if someone took him from her? Who would put her back together if she lost him? Her survival instincts told her to push him away, to run, to close herself off completely. So why was she holding him so close? Steve was the problem, not the solution. If she didn't love him, she wouldn't be destroyed when her father put a bullet in him.

Crazy, she told herself. *Daddy's dead. He can't hurt Steve.* She knew that, but reality didn't stop the fear from rooting in her heart. And even if the sick bastard couldn't rise from the grave and take love from her again, someone else could.

"What's wrong, baby? You're shaking."

"Don't stop," she pleaded.

But he already had. She'd been so wrapped up in her personal demons that she hadn't recognized he'd gone still.

"You're sorry you said it, aren't you?" He spoke quietly, as if he didn't want to voice his concern.

Her arms tightened around his head, drawing him to her chest. Could he feel how hard her heart was beating and how it ached?

"No, I'm not sorry. I do love you." She took a deep breath. "And that's why I'm so scared."

"What's scary about love? There's no drug that can match this euphoric feeling. I should know, I've tried them all."

"Naughty," she said, slapping at his shoulder.

"Tell me why you're scared. I won't betray you, not ever."

"I know that. I trust you. I honestly do. It's other people I don't trust."

"I can handle myself. If some woman comes on to me, I'll turn her down."

He thought this was about infidelity. She supposed that made sense considering how cheating—or being accused of it—had destroyed his marriage. "I'm not worried about you cheating on me."

"You're not?" He lifted his head and looked into her eyes. "I'm getting too old to attract horny women, is that it?"

She laughed. He was so gorgeous, he made her eyes hurt sometimes. How could he think he wouldn't attract even the most prudish of women?

"I'm certain you'll have to be extra careful to make sure you never cheat on me," she said, her breath starting to calm now that her mind wasn't stuck in a loop about losing him.

"I will be more diligent than a straight-A student," he said. He kissed her briefly. "Now tell me what's bothering you, since I obviously projected my fears onto you."

"You think I'm capable of cheating on you?"

He grinned and shook his head. "I'm more worried that you said I love you only because I did."

She never would have guessed that Steve Aimes was so vulnerable and uncertain about himself when it came to love, and that vulnerability somehow managed to make her love him even more. When it came to sex, drugs, and rock 'n' roll, he was the epitome of a confident man. And that was the guy the world knew, the one she'd thought she knew because of interviews and videos she'd seen and stories she'd read. She wouldn't have fallen for *that* guy so quickly, but wouldn't he be that character when they were out on tour?

"I didn't say it because you did. I said it because it's true. I love you."

He smiled a boyish little grin that had her thinking about having his adorable babies. What the fuck? She dashed that foolishness aside at once. She didn't have time for babies. Not even ones who'd be as perfect as their father. Their scheduled quickie against the bathroom wall was not going according to plan.

"So what has you trembling?" He shifted his hips and thrust into her, reminding her that their rendezvous was far from over. "You can tell me anything."

Where her fears had been so raw before, she now felt silly for having them. "It's nothing. What does a woman with a hard cock inside her have to do to get fucked around here?"

"Say no more."

He angled her hips so he could pound into her, drawing her toward release so quickly, her head was spinning. Seconds before she shattered, her feet touched the floor and he pulled out. She groaned in protest—so close—and he turned her to face the wall.

"Sorry, Red, but I don't trust my strength to hold you like that anymore. We spent too much time talking and not enough time fucking."

Before she could form a reply, he gripped her hip and tugged her backward, filling her with one deep thrust. She pressed against the wall with both hands to hold herself steady while he took her. When his finger brushed her asshole, her entire body tensed. Steve moaned somewhere behind her. After a moment, her body relaxed, and his finger slipped inside her. She tensed again, his invasion unfamiliar but sexy.

Steve went still behind her. She peeked over her shoulder to find him standing there with his eyes closed, lip caught between his teeth as he struggled to breathe. Hmmm . . . So he liked when her pussy clamped down on his cock. It was a purely involuntary reaction on her part. Or it had been. She drew in a breath and held it as she squeezed him inside her as hard as she could.

"I'm trying not to come back here," he said breathlessly.

She relaxed her muscles before squeezing him again. She loved to make him come. Loved more that he always seemed so surprised that they climaxed together so easily. He slapped her ass, and she tightened further. When he began to thrust through her tension, her thighs gave out and he had to keep her on her feet by wrapping his arm around her waist. Soon his fingers went exploring and found her clit, rubbing and rubbing as he filled her and withdrew, at the same time stretching her tight asshole with a circling finger. She had no choice but to come. She cried out as release shattered through her. He answered with a sexy groan as her clenching pussy pulled him over the edge with her.

After they caught their breath, she hovered over the toilet to pee and they both cleaned up a bit in the sink, quietly completing the task. She wondered how long he could stay but was afraid to ask. She was sure he'd have to leave soon. Maybe he could stay the night. Or forever. She was already feeling weepy over the thought of having to say goodbye to him again.

His clothes mostly back in order—though his shirt was still unbuttoned and giving her a breathtaking view of a narrow strip of his chest—he leaned against the counter beside her.

"I have to ask, even though I already know your answer," he said as he crossed his arms over his chest.

She met his eyes and saw the same anguish over parting that she felt in her own chest and belly.

"Come to LA with me," he said.

"I can't. I want to." And for a few seconds she almost faltered and told the world to fuck off. She didn't need a career or friends or to do the right thing. But she couldn't be that kind of person. "You have no idea how much I want to." She squeezed his forearm. "You could stay here with me."

"I'm enough of a selfish asshole to do just that," he said.

She grinned. "No, you're not."

He opened his arms, and she stepped into his embrace, settling her face against his beating heart. He hugged her close. His voice rumbled deep against her ear as she snuggled even closer.

"Can't you get away this weekend? Or even one day? Sed's getting married. My invitation says *plus guest*. Don't make me look like a loser by forcing me to bring Zach."

She chuckled and squeezed him tight around the waist. "I'm sure the tabloids would love to print that story. How's Zach doing? Did he get things sorted out with his boyfriend?" She still couldn't believe Enrique Sanz was gay. He'd dated a fair number of A-list actresses over the years. Roux had had quite a crush on him at one time.

"Zach's heartbroken. Refuses to get out of my bed."

"Um . . . I'm sure the tabloids would love to print that story too."

He kissed the top of her head. "I'd rather them print the one about how I ran off and eloped with the sensational keyboardist of the up-and-coming band Baroquen."

Her breath caught, and she pulled away to gape at him. Was he serious? His grin told her that he couldn't possibly be. She slapped his arm. "Don't joke about stuff like that."

"I'm not joking. I have a jet at my disposal. Say the word and we're in Vegas getting hitched in a matter of hours."

Her heart thundered out of control, and she stepped away. "You are moving way too fast for me."

"I'm moving way too fast for me too," he said, capturing her upper arms in both hands. "I just don't want you to get away."

"I'm not going anywhere."

"You're sure?"

She nodded.

"You seemed pretty freaked out about saying I love you."

"That isn't what freaked me out." But she didn't want to discuss her silly, irrational fears. "Is Exodus End really going to play at Sed's wedding reception? That's crazy."

"Don't change the subject. Tell me what had you so afraid."

She shook her head and turned her back on him, fingers automatically going to the bullet dangling from her old bracelet. "It's nothing."

His arms slid around her waist from behind, and he rested his cheek against the top of her head. "It isn't nothing. Tell me."

Having those thoughts return now caused the familiar panic to rise up her chest and into her throat. She couldn't breathe. She had to get out of the bathroom. There was no good place for them to hide in there. She pulled free of his grasp and bolted for the door, opening it and almost crashing into Jordan who had a fist up ready to knock on the heavy wood.

"Oh good," she said, "you're done. We have to get in the air if we're going to make it back by morning."

Roux dashed past her, sadness over Steve's leaving crowding out her silly panic. She didn't know whether to scream or cry, so she hurried to the huge window that faced the airstrip and clutched the waist-high windowsill, settling her forehead against the cool glass and sucking deep breaths into her lungs. She knew the instant that Steve stopped beside her. She could feel his presence.

"I thought you said you weren't going to try to get away." His tone was teasing, and she was glad he was trying to lighten the mood, because she couldn't take any more heaviness pressing in at her from all directions.

"I'm not trying to get away from you."

"You just won't tell me something as important as why you're afraid. You don't think I can handle it?"

She could see him struggling not to reach for her. He went so far as to shove both hands into his pockets.

"I don't want you to think I'm silly," she admitted. "My fears are completely irrational. I know that. But it doesn't make them feel any less real."

He watched her closely but didn't crowd her or say anything. Maybe that was why she couldn't keep quiet.

"When I realized that I love you, my first thought was that my father would shoot you too. Take you from me like he took everyone I loved. I couldn't stand to lose another person I love that way."

Steve wasn't so special in that regard. Sometimes she still worried that some asshole with a gun would kill her sisters or Mama Ramona, but she hadn't experienced crippling panic over those kinds of thoughts for years. It must be because loving Steve was so new. She simply hadn't had time to convince herself that the chances of him falling to the same tragedy that had taken her family were slim.

Steve took one step closer, but still held himself stiff, listening closely to what she was saying but not interrupting. He must think she was a fucking lunatic. She didn't want him to think of her that way, so why the hell couldn't she shut up?

"There was no good place to hide in that bathroom." She pointed toward the dimly lit hallway that led to the bathroom. "If someone came in there, we'd be sitting ducks." The fear of huddling in that dark closet, the sound of Daddy's gun firing again and again, the feel of his hand wrapping around her ankle and of being dragged out into the open, the strange acceptance of knowing she was about to die—all those sensations were as vivid and real to her now as they had been when she'd experienced them over a decade ago. She covered her chest with her hand, as if that would have stopped the bullet that almost ended her life, stopped it from affecting her life to this day.

"Good point," Steve said.

Huh?

"I didn't think of how something like that might affect you."

He wasn't going to tell her that no one would have tried to attack them in a million years? Not tell her she was being irrational and not to worry, that they'd been perfectly safe? That was what she was used to hearing, and none of those words made her feel more secure or less panicked. Mostly they just made her feel stupid.

"Are there certain places that make you feel vulnerable?" he asked, taking another step closer.

She licked her lips and shook her head. "It wasn't the place," she said. "It was a feeling." She huffed out a laugh. "And not a feeling I'm willing to give up now that I recognize it." But a feeling she'd been avoiding for years. She just hadn't realized why she never allowed herself to fall in love in any of her past relationships. Steve hadn't given her a choice. She *had* to love him. She would have to find a way to cope, because she refused to let her father's actions take love from her now that it was hers. "I love you. That feeling is what makes me feel vulnerable."

"I can't just stand here and not hold you right now," he said.

Her heart twisted, and a tear leaked from her eye to course down her cheek. She remembered the first time he'd said that to her out on the balcony when she'd tried to scare him away by telling him about her past. Was that the moment she'd started falling for him? She took a step closer, and he threw his arms around her, pulling her securely against his chest. Here she felt safe. Only here.

After a moment, Steve stiffened and looked over his shoulder. Jordan was standing behind him, tapping him on the back. He had to leave. Roux knew he had to, and she forced herself to be grateful for the moments they'd stolen rather than bitter that the time had already slipped away from them.

"It's only a week," she said, more to herself than to him.

"But we can't see each other on tour either," he said. "Your rule."

"We can if you're dating Katie Williams—unknown fangirl—rather than Roux Williams—unknown rock star."

He laughed and drew her in close for a tight hug. "Are you sure Roux won't be jealous?"

"She'll be too busy being fabulous to be jealous."

Jordan cleared her throat, her arms folded over her chest, and her foot tapped against the floor. "Any day now," she grumbled under her breath.

Roux had wanted to surprise Steve with her idea to lead a double life on tour. She was convinced that no one would ever figure out that Katie and Roux were the same person. She looked totally different in stage makeup and costume. That was how she'd have her cake and eat him up as much as possible. She'd learned long ago that compromise was the best way to get more out of life.

"Call me, text me, send me nude photos," he said, kissing her several times before drawing away an inch.

"I won't be totally nude," she said, giving him a stern look. She smiled when he scowled, and then she lifted her arm to catch the light in the bracelet he'd given her. "I'll be wearing this."

"And the panties? I never did get a good look at them."

"Maybe." She kissed him once more and then lightly pressed on his chest. "Now go before Jordan taps a hole into the floor with that foot of hers."

"This foot of mine is about to land squarely in the center of a certain drummer's backside," Jordan said. "You promised you wouldn't dally if I did this for you, Steve."

Steve held up one finger and then turned to gaze deeply into Roux's eyes.

"I love you," he said, his words making Roux soar.

"I love you too."

The instant he pulled away and she was no longer cocooned in his aura, she felt the loss. She forced herself not to run after him, not to get on the plane, not to give in to what she truly wanted. They had plenty of time to be together. This parting was only temporary. Of course, one never knew when one's time was up. She fiddled with the bullet on her bracelet. *He'll be safe*, she told herself. *No one is going to hurt him*.

"Wait!" she gasped just before he followed Jordan out a door that led to the tarmac.

She unfastened the bracelet she always wore as she hurried after him. "Here," she said, pressing the bullet into his hand. "Keep this with you. It will protect you."

He lifted his brows. "It will?"

Of course it wouldn't. That was silly, but . . . "I want you to have something of mine." She pressed her hand to his chest. "Something of me."

"Your love is enough," he said, but he squeezed the bracelet into his fist and pressed it against his chest. "But I'll treasure this and return it to you when I see you again."

He kissed her once more, and then he was gone. With her forehead pressed against the glass door, she watched him hurry to the plane. Some unseen force tugged at her gut, trying to pull her toward him. Even after he turned and waved and she waved back, that feeling didn't go away. Nor did it leave her when the jet's door was shut or even when the plane was taxiing. The link between them was strong, and it was going to be one long fucking week without him.

CHAPTER 23

STEVE COULDN'T STOP SMILING. Even Zach—who was stuck in a pathetic self-loathing loop—noticed.

"Did you just graduate clown school or what?" Zach grumbled. "All that smiling gets creepy after a while."

Steve wiped the grin off his face for almost a full second before it returned. "Can't help it," he said. "I'm happy. And I know your misery would like some company right now, but too bad."

A car pulled to a stop at the corner where they were waiting for their Uber, but it didn't fit the description of their ride.

"You could have left me to wallow in my misery alone," Zach said.

"You're not spending another day in my bed. It's starting to smell like you. Talk about creepy."

"If you want me to go home, I'll go home."

"And where would that be? Did you find an apartment when I wasn't looking?"

Zach crossed his arms and turned his face away. "I have a place."

"I'm not going to let you go begging to Enrique for a place to stay," Steve said.

"If I don't have anywhere else to go, he'll have to take me back." His miserable look was momentarily replaced with a hopeful one.

Steve resisted the urge to punch him. He knew Zach still wanted Enrique, but he needed to get over him and move on. Zach needed someone who would lift him up, not bring him down, and he sure as hell wasn't going to find that someone moping around Steve's house. That was why Steve was taking him to the dumb wedding reception rehearsal.

They'd been practicing the songs for a couple of days, so Steve didn't see the need for an on-site rehearsal. Not that he didn't like hanging out with his band when he was on a tour break. What was he thinking? He fucking hated it. They needed to get out of each other's faces for a week or two. He'd much rather be spending his break making a nuisance of himself at Baroquen's rehearsals in New York. He absently rubbed the bullet dangling around his wrist. He'd had to get a chain extender so he could wear Roux's bracelet, but he was grateful for the constant reminder of her. He needed to send her something special today so that she knew he was thinking of her.

Their ride finally arrived—driver apologizing profusely for making them wait, but traffic was what it was.

"If you'd let me pick up my bike," Zach grumbled, "we wouldn't have to wait or *pay* for a ride."

"We tried that, remember?" And Zach had fallen apart at the gate of Enrique's estate when the ass refused to even speak to him. Zach had completely forgotten his entire reason for going there until it was too late to choose a less desperate strategy. "If *someone* had picked out something a little less custom for his birthday, we wouldn't have to wait or pay for a ride either."

Zach's birthday wasn't for another seven weeks, and the bike Steve had gotten him on a whim—mostly to cheer him up, but also to replace the one at Enrique's house—would probably be delivered after the fact.

"You spoil me, is the problem," Zach said, smiling for the first time that day.

"Character flaw," Steve said before he slid into the back seat of the Mini Cooper. His knees were immediately in his face.

"You don't have to buy people things to get them to love you," Zach said, flopping the front seat back into Steve's shins.

Tiny cars and long legs did not go well together. He should have made Zach take an Uber, and he could have ridden his bike, but Zach probably would have gone back to Enrique's house and had a mental breakdown on the street. There were still photographers milling about the area, and the latest story from Enrique's publicist was that Zach was some deranged fanboy whose misguided obsession was not returned by the actor. Enrique wouldn't even admit he knew him. Steve would really like to punch the guy in the balls. Assuming he had any. Fucking coward.

Zach made small talk with the driver while Steve used his phone to order an enormous bouquet of flowers to be sent to Roux. He wasn't sure if she liked flowers. Maybe he should send her a puppy. He knew she liked those. He settled for mentioning the puppy on the message card and imagined their future life together in his tiny house and surrounded by dozens of rescue pets.

"What are you smiling about now?" Zach asked when he let Steve out of the back of the Mini Cooper at the reception venue. "Let me guess. Roux."

"I need to get used to calling her Katie," Steve said.

"She doesn't look like a Katie. Are you sure you want to hide your relationship? It didn't work out so well for me."

"We aren't hiding it. Just not letting any outsiders know what she does for a living."

Zach rolled his eyes. "That's kind of a big deal."

"It will be fine," Steve said.

The guys were all there waiting when Steve entered the room. Their minimal stage setup reminded Steve of their early days before they hit the record charts and could pull a crowd. He had only one bass drum, a snare, and a few toms and cymbals. On what, exactly, was he supposed to expend his copious energy? The set list—which included Elvis, Neil Diamond, Chuck Berry, and even Madonna—reminded him of nightmares he'd had about playing the wrong song in concert before a huge, pissed-off crowd. He still wasn't sure how they'd been talked into doing this. Curse Dare for being so damned likable. It was impossible to stay perturbed at the guy, even when he made promises to his brother's bandmates that prevented Steve from enjoying his week off.

Dare looked up from the tuning peg he was adjusting. "Wow, only thirty minutes late."

"You're lucky I showed up at all. Don't you guys have better places to be?"

"I gave Jordan the next week off," Max said, "so if you need to run off to New York again, you'll have to fly commercial."

Steve cringed. That would make it loads easier to stay away from Roux for the next seven days. He hated flying commercial.

"Hey, Zach," Logan said. "Steve isn't planning on passing his drumming duties off to you, is he?"

Now there was an idea.

"He's put me on suicide watch." Zach grinned. "Doesn't trust me to be left alone."

"Don't even joke about that," Steve said. "Your task is to help take the metal out of my drumming."

"Why the fuck would I do that?"

"Because someone has a soft spot for his little brother, which results in lame gigs." Steve lifted an eyebrow at Dare, who didn't bother to deny it. "Speaking of your little brother," Steve continued. "He wouldn't happen to know a nice guy to get Zach here out of his funk, would he?"

"I'm not looking for a new man," Zach said before Dare could respond. He went off to sulk in a corner.

Before Steve managed to settle behind the underwhelming drum kit, Reagan dashed into the room carrying an armload of papers. More sheet music, Steve presumed. She'd been given the task of gathering up any missing songs from Jessica's absurd idea of a playlist. Steve scrutinized the scores for "Twist and Shout" and "Crazy for You," discovering that both had minimal drums. He yawned as he sat on his stool and picked up his drumsticks. He'd done more intricate drum work on Mams's pots and pans as a toddler. Why was he there? They could have hired a chimp to cover this crap.

"Sorry I was so late," Reagan said as she passed out more pages to each underwhelmed band member. "I was . . ."

She flushed, and Steve began to imagine what a woman who was dating two men was probably doing. Her engagement ring caught the light as she shuffled through her stack of music, reminding Steve that she'd recently become engaged to Trey and was in a huge rush to marry him. Did that mean Ethan was free? Maybe he could get Zach out of his funk. Ethan was tall, dark, and hunky. Not exactly Zach's type. Zach gravitated toward more feminine-looking men. Steve glanced at his friend, who was on his phone—probably cyberstalking pretty-boy Enrique on Instagram again. Steve wanted Zach to be happy yet wasn't sure how to help him get back to that state. Maybe when they got to Europe Zach would have so much fun, he'd forget all about that stupid actor.

"I've got the set list here for each of you." Reagan passed out a printed list of songs to each band member. Steve placed the paper on the floor by his foot. "You're starting with 'Can't Help Falling in Love.' Don't metal that one up like the others. That's Sed and Jess's song, and it has to be perfect." She smiled like a fool in love.

Steve wanted to find a song with Roux. Would any song truly

capture how he felt about her? He suddenly felt less cranky about playing at a wedding reception, even if the first song didn't use a bass drum at all. He yawned again. Logan had a more complicated part on bass than Steve did on drums, for fuck's sake. What was an underchallenged drummer to do?

Improvise.

"From the top," Max said into his mic. The cheap sound system wasn't doing his deep voice any favors.

Steve started out drumming the repetitive *tap*, *tap*, *tap* on his snare and cymbal, but two measures in, he added a few extra taps, and then the bass, and then a progression around the toms. It took him a moment to realize his entire band had stopped and were staring at him.

"What are you doing?" Dare asked. "She said we can't make this one metal."

"Maybe not. But no one said it had to be boring," Steve said.

Max grinned. "You're right."

Max admitting that Steve was right twice in one week? Steve stared up at the ceiling, expecting a meteor to come crashing through. Dare brought Steve's attention back to earth when his fingers ripped out the signature riff from "Layla." Now why couldn't *that* song have been on Jessica's lame playlist?

The rest of the afternoon was spent making sure every overplayed Top 40 song they were performing the next day had been transformed into a pure metal masterpiece. By the end of rehearsal, Steve had worked up a sweat, and even Zach was smiling.

"This is going to be the most awesome wedding reception in history," Zach said. "Almost makes me want to get married."

"You guys will play at my wedding next weekend, won't you?" Reagan asked. "Trey would love that."

"Of course," Dare volunteered without consulting anyone.

"I wasn't invited," Steve reminded her.

"Me neither," said Max.

"Uh." Reagan flushed. "There wasn't enough space in the chapel after we invited all the reporters to cover the event, but you all can come to the reception." She licked her lips. "If we have one."

"Why the fuck would you invite reporters?" Steve asked. "Don't celebrities usually do everything in their power to keep the press away from their special day?"

"Not when they're trying to cover up the truth about their unconventional relationship," Dare said.

He leveled Reagan with a disapproving stare. She looked away, but Steve caught the sick look on her face. She didn't comment; just hurried from the room before anyone could press her for details.

"So she plans to keep both guys even after she marries your brother?" Max asked.

Dare closed the lid on his guitar case and lifted it by its handle. He wasn't trusting enough to leave such a valuable instrument at the venue overnight.

"Yep," he said as he headed for the exit.

Steve guessed Ethan wasn't available to fuck Zach out of his funk after all. That was unfortunate. Zach was already frowning again.

THE NEXT DAY, WITH THE EXCEPTION OF ERIC KICKING Steve off his drum kit for the initial song, and Sed singing the nonmetal version of "Can't Help Falling in Love" to Jessica while they swayed to their first dance, the amped up set list went over well with the reception's guests. They partied well beyond the time when the happy newlyweds left on their honeymoon. The worst part about having to play at the reception was that Steve didn't get to take advantage of the open bar. Zach, on the other hand, had drunk enough for himself and all the members of Exodus End combined.

"Drunks really *are* annoying when you're sober," Steve said, half carrying, half dragging Zach to Max's pristine white vintage Rolls Royce. He'd offered them a ride, which made Steve wonder if Max had an ulterior motive. He wasn't known for taxiing people around.

"If he pukes in my car, you clean it up," Max said, hoarse from singing for hours.

"With your shirt."

"I never throw up," Zach said, his voice slurred. "You can . . ." He blinked, blurry-eyed. "You can count on me . . . *hic* . . . boss." He saluted Max and fell sideways into the back seat.

Paparazzi had been milling about outside the venue all evening, and they didn't miss their opportunity to snap pictures of the spectacle. *Do not engage*, Steve repeated to himself in a silent mantra. As much as he hated the leeches that made their living on more famous people's misery, he'd learned through his own trials with the jerks that the best way to be left alone was to be as fucking boring as possible.

"Is it true that Exodus End played live at the reception?" some reporter yelled.

"That is true," Max said, as always, maintaining his cool.

Steve sometimes thought that Max liked the attention of the press, which was baffling.

"We even took a few requests. For your safety, please step back from the car. We need to get our friend home." His winning smile plastered on his face, Max slipped into the driver's seat and shut the door.

"Is Zach Mercier drunk because he's torn up over Enrique Sanz denying their relationship?" a different reporter asked. He was standing close to Steve—within punching distance—and had a look of concern on his face. That didn't stop Steve from despising him.

"He just came from an awesome party," Steve said. "Why wouldn't he be drunk?"

"Is it true that Zach is living with you? Are you two finally ready to expose the depth of your relationship?"

"We're best friends," Steve snarled. "That's the entire story." He hopped into the passenger seat since Zach was lying facedown across the back one.

Max cranked up the stereo and waved at the mingling reporters as he slowly and graciously did not run over any of them. The paparazzi spotted Reagan leaving with Trey and scrambled over to make her life miserable.

"I don't know how you can stand those people," Steve said to Max, watching Reagan walk very stiffly down the steps, her head held high and her mouth sealed shut.

"The paparazzi?"

"No, bathroom attendants." Steve rolled his eyes. "Yes, the paparazzi."

Max shrugged. "We need them."

"Just like we needed Sam." No one would ever convince Steve of that.

"We did need Sam. And we might still need someone like him, but we're taking him down." Max's eyes narrowed as he scrutinized the light traffic in front of him.

"Do you really think replacing one blood-sucking leech with another is the best idea?" Because, no, it wasn't. It wasn't even a mediocre idea. It sucked.

"Your goal is to concentrate on making music, right? The fame, the fortune, the fun—none of that is important to you."

Steve hadn't realized that Max paid attention to such things. "Not particularly." He scratched his nose and crossed his arms over his chest. "Well, the fun, maybe."

"If we have to sell our own records, when will we have time to make music? We need someone like Sam to get our product out there so we can concentrate on what's important to us."

"Getting your ass kissed?" Zach murmured from the back seat. So he wasn't unconscious? Steve was surprised.

Max smirked. "A definite perk of the gig."

"I didn't know you swung that way," Zach said. "I've got mad ass-kissing skills if you're interested." He made lewd sucking noises that made Max cringe.

"I'll have to take your word for it," Max said, stopping at a red light. He peered into the back seat through the rearview mirror. "How are you still conscious?"

"My liver has had lots of training," Zach said.

Steve snorted and pretended not to notice the car full of attractive women that stopped beside them. It was doubly hard to do so when the driver flashed her boobs at them. Steve tried to remember what they'd been discussing before their conversation had gotten derailed.

"You know our records will sell themselves at this point in our career," Steve said to Max, who was not ignoring the ladies in the next car. He was smiling at them while probably doing the math on how to engage all three of them at once. Steve cared about Roux too much to even consider it. He wondered if he'd have time to take a commercial flight to New York to see her for a few hours.

Damn, he really did have it bad.

"That remains to be seen," Max said, rolling down the front passenger window with the button on his armrest. "Are you ladies having a nice evening?" he asked, as if they weren't squealing like a set of bald tires. They totally knew who Max was. Had probably intentionally followed him. That sort of thing happened to Max all the time. He wasn't likely to engage, though. Steve wondered what had Max acting out of character.

"You interested in a small orgy?" Max asked Steve quietly.

Zach sat up in the back seat and peered into the car beside them. "No guys. No guys at all." He flopped back down on the seat.

"Is that Zach Mercier in there with you?" the driver of the car shouted. The other two ladies shrieked with excitement. Their interest made Steve miss Roux even more.

"I call dibs on Zach," said the brunette in the back seat.

Apparently she hadn't been reading the tabloids about Twisted Element's drummer and his sexual preferences.

"I couldn't get it up for you if I tried, lady," Zach muttered to the seat his face was squashed against. "And I'm too tired to even try."

"I'll take a pass on this, Max," Steve said. "You aren't seriously considering it, are you?"

Max laughed, and sped forward when the light turned green, leaving the car of women behind as he took a risky left turn at the next yellow light. "I knew it!"

Steve raised an eyebrow. "Knew what?"

"I've never known you to turn down ass under any other circumstance. You're in love with someone."

"And what made that so obvious?" After all, he couldn't deny it. "Was it all the flights to New York or me taking a woman to Dick Island?"

Max laughed—a deep, mirthful, genuine laugh. Steve could not remember the last time he heard Max laugh that way, at least not in relation to him. There had been so much tension between the two of them over the past few years that they had barely tolerated each other. What had changed all of a sudden? Steve was pretty sure the difference wasn't in him.

"You still call it Dick Island?" Max said. "God, that must piss off Dare."

Steve smirked. "Why do you think we call it that?"

Max laughed again, and then hit the brakes hard when the car in front of him stopped abruptly. Steve's seat jerked forward, and Zach tumbled onto the floorboard behind them.

"I'm going to feel that in the morning," Zach said, groaning theatrically.

"You didn't damage anything important, did you?" Steve asked, peering over his shoulder and down at his barely functioning best friend. He was starting to think drinking was as stupid as doing recreational drugs. Steve wasn't sure he was ready to give up either completely, but he was sure where that idea had come from. A certain woman had a lot more influence over him than he cared to admit.

Zach groped around his crotch. "Everything seems to be in tip-top shape," he said.

Steve shook his head. "I meant your brain or maybe your hands, but I see what's important to you."

"I haven't had sex in weeks," Zach said as he pulled himself up onto the seat again. This time he sat in it properly and even fastened his seat belt. "Priorities change when you're dying for a good piece of ass."

"I can drop you off at one of your clubs," Max offered. "I'm sure you could find a solution to your problem."

Zach lifted an eyebrow—probably at Max's use of *your* to modify clubs—but he let the mild offense drop. "There's only one good piece of ass on the planet as far as I'm concerned."

Steve was in the same camp at the moment—though his only piece and Zach's did not belong to the same person. Maybe Zach truly loved Enrique. The actor didn't deserve Zach's devotion—no matter how attractive or famous he happened to be—but that didn't make Zach's feelings any less real than Steve's. Maybe Steve should try to help Zach get Enrique back rather than trying to help him get over the fuckhead. Ugh, Steve hated that asshole. Or more precisely, he hated how he'd hurt his friend.

"That piece of ass doesn't belong to someone in this car, does it?" Max asked, peering at Zach in the rearview mirror.

Steve couldn't tell if Max was joking, concerned for his own ass, or indirectly asking if Zach had a thing for Steve, an assumption they ran into often. A lot of people had a hard time believing that a straight guy and a gay man could be best friends without sexual attraction entering the equation, just like a lot of people claimed that a heterosexual male and a woman couldn't be platonic friends for the same reason. Both claims were complete bullshit. It was humanly possible for a man to think of something besides sex.

"No," Zach said quietly. He closed his eyes and leaned against the window. He might have passed out finally, or he might have wanted to shut down the direction the conversation was moving.

"So who's the lucky girl?"

Steve almost blurted the entire truth right there, but he remembered Roux's worries just in time, so he supplied the half-truth they agreed to share with the public. "Her name is Katie." It felt so weird to call her that even though it was her legal name. "She, uh, works at some animal shelter in New York."

"Are you going to be seeing her on tour or not? She plays keyboard, if I'm not mistaken."

Steve's head whipped around. How had Max pieced that

together so easily? They'd never keep her identity a secret at this rate. "You'd better wipe that smirk off your face before I wipe it off for you."

Max laughed again. "I didn't realize it was supposed to be a secret."

"She doesn't want anyone to think her band scored a spot on the tour because she's sleeping with me." He wasn't sure Roux cared about that at all, but for some reason her sister Iona was adamant about it.

"People are going to think what they're going to think."

"Agreed."

Max shifted in his seat. Apparently their sudden tendency to agree on anything, much less everything, was as uncomfortable for him as it was for Steve.

"But if it puts her at ease to be called Katie in public," Steve continued, "and to pretend her life in the spotlight can be entirely separate from her personal life, I'll do what makes her happy. You are going to pretend you don't know who she is when I introduce her as Katie, aren't you?" Because he would throttle anyone who messed this up for him. The flimsy façade Roux had decided to hide behind was the only way she'd allow him to see her on tour. If it fell through, he'd have to turn to more obnoxious tactics, and he wasn't sure how she'd take outlandish displays of his love.

"I don't have a problem with it." Max was silent for a moment as he navigated traffic. "I wanted to ask you . . ." He licked his lips and glanced briefly at Steve, as if hoping he didn't actually have to speak his request and Steve would magically know what he wanted.

"What?"

"Would you be willing to fire Sam? I've been trying to think of the words to say, but I just . . . freeze up.

Steve frowned. Max was never short on confidence and had been so pissed at Sam when they'd decided to fire him that Steve was surprised Max didn't literally set fire to their soon-to-be ex-manager. "It would be my pleasure," Steve said. "Why the cold feet all of a sudden?"

Max sighed and rubbed a hand over his face. "He's been like a father to me for so long."

He had? Was that why Max had always defended him?

"I'm mad at him. I feel betrayed and used, but . . . he made us who we are. I can't forget that."

Steve wanted to shake sense into him. "We were not made by

anyone, Max. We were discovered."

Max worried his bottom lip with his teeth. Why was this so hard for him? Had Sam brainwashed him?

"How about I call him right now?" Steve said, reaching into his pocket for his phone. "Get that toxic piece of shit out of your life for good."

Max's hand shot out and knocked the phone out of Steve's hand. It landed somewhere on the floorboard at Steve's feet.

"After the European tour. We agreed on that much."

They had, but now Steve was worried that somehow, with three months to let his anger cool, Max would convince himself—and maybe Dare and Logan—that they still needed the thieving, backstabbing son of a bitch to rule their careers.

"Is money really that important to you?" Steve blurted, because dropping their label would naturally cut into their finances, at least temporarily. Even with the guy skimming money off the top, bottom and both sides, he did know how to promote a band and help them make buttloads of cash.

"It's nice to have."

Steve knew Max had been poor growing up, and maybe he hadn't had the most loving family to make destitution somewhat bearable, but he had to know that there were things more important than driving a Rolls Royce and having a big house on a hill.

"I'm not exactly rolling in cash these days," Max said quietly.

Steve gnawed on his lip. This was news to him. Maybe he should talk to Max more often. "If you're having problems, maybe Dare could—"

"Save me from my own stupidity? Yeah, no. I don't even want him to know about it."

But he was confiding in Steve. The two of them had never been especially close. Not rivals, exactly, but tension always stood between them. Steve wasn't sure if anyone was truly close to Max. He wasn't the type of guy who let people in. He had a certain outgoing persona he shared openly with their fans, but it was superficial, and he never maintained it when he was out of the public eye. Very few people knew Max well. Dwelling on that fact now, Steve wondered if the reason Max always tried to protect Sam was because their manager was one of the few people Max had allowed to get close. Steve had always been baffled as to how anyone—especially someone as savvy as Maximillian Richardson—could be so blind to Sam's shortcomings, that he'd never even considered the reason why Max defended him.

"I know you think we're going to fail without the label backing us," Steve said, "but we're pretty amazing dudes."

Max chuckled at that, but didn't deny it.

"I think we can succeed without any record label at all," Steve said, knowing they'd agreed to shop around for a new label before going full indie—which was what Steve really wanted.

Max shook his head. "You're such a rebel."

"He just doesn't like anyone to tell him what to do," Zach mumbled from the back seat.

Steve had thought Zach was out; how much had he overheard? Not that Steve worried about Zach blabbing secrets, but Max might. "Unless it's some woman that he's in love with. Then he's a doormat."

"I'm not a doormat." He just liked his woman to be happy and didn't care if it was at his own expense. So far, Roux hadn't taken advantage of that tendency in him, but Bianca sure had.

"Total doormat," Zach said. "That's why he needs me on this tour, so his new girlfriend doesn't take complete advantage of him."

If thinking that Steve needed him for that reason got Zach to Europe, Steve wouldn't argue. But he couldn't stop himself from defending Roux. "She's not like that," he said. "She won't take advantage of my generosity."

"Well, if you guys are brave enough—or stupid enough—to actually go indie, you'd better watch your cash flow a bit closer, dumbass."

"True. I probably shouldn't have bought a friend of mine a new custom motorcycle for his birthday," Steve said, drawing a finger to his lip. "Maybe I should cancel the order."

"I'd still love you," Zach said.

Steve decided that Zach had slipped into advanced drunkenness, where he became extremely sentimental. Max did not need to witness that. It could get too mushy to tolerate in a matter of seconds.

"You're the only thing good in my life," Zach said in a shaky voice.

"You only say that because it's true," Steve teased, reaching over the seat to punch him and help Zach check himself. He also gave Zach a silent warning to keep his distance, because he doubted that Max would understand if they hugged it out.

"Maybe we should try going indie for a year or two," Max said, as if completely deaf to the conversation around him. "And if it doesn't work out, I'm sure we can find a new label."

Steve stomped his foot as if he had a brake pedal on his side of the car and jerked his head around to gape at Max. "Are you serious?" he sputtered.

"It's just a couple of years," Max said, shrugging.

Steve had no idea what was going on with Max to suddenly make him so open to change, but he thanked God for it, whatever it was. Afraid he'd change his mind, Steve didn't push him for details or even hug him in a stranglehold. He wrestled down the euphoric excitement coursing through his veins and said, "That sounds reasonable."

"Do you think Dare and Logan will agree?"

"I know Logan will," he said. He and Logan had discussed going indie dozens of times.

"I'll talk to Dare," Max said. "See if he thinks this is the best course of action."

Now wait a second. Max wasn't going to take credit for this idea of going independent. Steve had been championing that goal for years. He tried not rocking the boat for at least three seconds before he blurted, "If this works out, this was all my idea. But if it fails, it was yours."

Max laughed and said, "Either way, it was yours. Everyone knows that."

And Steve could do nothing but stare in disbelief. He'd never known Max to be reasonable about risk or change. Maybe he had an identical less-evil twin who had assumed his identity when no one was looking. Steve wondered if the guy could sing. He'd sure like to keep him around.

CHAPTER 24

ROUX SETTLED INTO THE BUSINESS CLASS SEAT in which she'd be spending the next eight hours and tried to calm her nerves. She'd expected the excitement, the surreal feeling that this was finally happening. She'd even expected the overwhelming eagerness to see Steve when they landed in the UK. What she had not anticipated was feeling like she was going to toss her American cookies/British biscuits (she'd been practicing her British English) as the scope of the adventure squeezed in on her from all directions. She reached for the bullet on the bracelet around her wrist and found only the gorgeous diamond and ruby tennis bracelet that Steve had given her. She admired it for a moment, loving the significance it represented, but it did not calm her nerves. If anything, it made her more nervous. Not only would she be in the spotlight and making sure her performances were nothing short of perfect, but she'd be trying to figure out how to juggle a romantic relationship on top of that. She wouldn't change any of it, but she was worried that she'd make a spectacular mess out of her career, her life, her romance.

Taking the seat beside Roux, Iona fastened her seat belt. Roux looked around for Raven, who was supposed to sit next to her, and found that she'd been stuck next to some stranger. Raven shrugged as if she didn't care. Had Iona finally realized that Roux was avoiding her so she couldn't let slip the plans she'd made with Steve for the next three months?

"Wasn't it nice of Sam to spring for business class?" Iona stretched her feet out far in front of her. "Look at all this legroom."

Roux knew about Sam's treachery with Exodus End—not every detail due to a strict nondisclosure clause. Steve had forbidden her to even mention their troubles with their manager until after they officially split with him, but she was worried about how Exodus End's crisis with Sam would affect her own band. Every instinct told her to warn them, but without Sam, they wouldn't be where they were at all. Her need to protect her boyfriend by keeping quiet, and her sisters by blabbing everything she knew was tearing her in two.

"I'm not sure Sam is a good fit for us," Roux said, hoping that statement was vague enough to keep Exodus End out of legal jeopardy while seeding a kernel of doubt into Iona's head. Her second-eldest sister was a shrewd businesswoman at heart, and if Iona believed they had better options, she wouldn't hesitate to pursue them.

Iona snorted. "Yeah, being successful and pampered rock stars is so out of line with our goals. We'd never want to tour the world opening for an incredible band like Exodus End. We enjoy starving and not being able to pay our rent. Sure."

"He's just a little too slick in my opinion."

"And that's why he's so good at what he does." Iona patted her arm. "I know you're not interested in the business side of music, and that's okay. Stop worrying, sweetie, and let me figure out how to get us to the top. You concentrate on being the best keyboardist in rock and roll today and leave the logistics to me."

Roux bit her lip to keep from blurting that Exodus End was going to fire Sam in a few months. She didn't know why they were getting rid of him, but Steve had been so excited about ditching their manager that he'd told her they were firing him even though he couldn't share any details. Surely Sam had done something truly awful to get himself axed. But maybe she was worried about nothing. Maybe Exodus End just wanted a change. The knots in her stomach weren't buying her attempts to rationalize the situation.

"So, how's Steve?" Iona asked.

Roux knew her well enough to read her true question: How are you going to keep from seeing Steve on tour? Roux hadn't shared her plan to see Steve as Katie. She doubted that Iona would think it a good idea. But the days she'd been separated from him had been pure hell, and she knew she wasn't strong enough to keep him at a distance when thousands of miles were no longer between them.

"Excited about the tour, I think," she said, fiddling with her diamond bracelet. She had never realized how often she'd used the bullet on her bracelet for comfort until she'd loaned it to Steve.

Iona grinned. "I think he's more excited to see you. I've never known any man to send a woman two or three gifts a day."

Roux's face flushed with heat. He had been a bit over the top with the gifting. Few of the items he'd sent had been expensive—oranges after she mentioned she liked them, an electric fan for her keyboard when she'd said the stage lights were hot, a CD with a song that reminded him of her, a vibrator when she whispered she missed having him in her bed. Her protests against the extravagance had gone ignored, so she'd started to anticipate what he'd send next—and especially those short, written sentiments that accompanied every gift—rather than feel guilty for accepting his generosity. She only wished she could afford to reciprocate. He assured her that it was better to give than to receive, but damn, how many blow jobs did she owe him now? Her jaw ached just thinking about it, but she planned to make him a very, very happy man when she saw him tomorrow. He had invited her to join Exodus End on their private jet, but she couldn't abandon her band on their first transatlantic flight. Besides, Logan's girlfriend would be on that plane, and Roux figured it was best to not spend hours upon hours in her company. Toni was a smart woman. She'd eventually figure out that Katie and Roux were the same person, and though Steve trusted Toni with their secret, Roux didn't. It would also be rather difficult to convince Iona that she'd be keeping her distance from him if she hopped on his jet the first day.

"He's very good to me," Roux said, tucking her hair behind her ear.

"It's going to be tough to stay away from him while you're on tour."

Roux knew that was Iona's passive-aggressive way of reminding her she wasn't supposed to be in contact with Steve.

"Yeah," she said vaguely, glad the flight attendant had started the safety demonstration as the plane backed out of the gate. She could pretend to concentrate on how to survive a crash and avoid inevitable questions from their leader. Iona wasn't even the oldest—Lily was—but she definitely had the right personality to head the band.

"Three months isn't so long." Iona squeezed Roux's hand, which rested on the armrest between them. "And you'll be so busy, the time will fly by."

"Mmm hmm." Roux's stomach was starting to twist into knots.

She'd never kept a secret from one of her sisters. She didn't like the way it felt. But she liked the feeling of not seeing Steve even less. "I wish we could have talked Mama into coming to see a show." Perhaps changing the subject would help Roux feel a tad less guilty.

"Maybe when we get hugely famous we can afford to invite all the younger girls along as well. She'd have to say yes then."

Roux could have asked Steve to foot the bill for transatlantic flights for eight more members of her family, but even though she knew he wouldn't hesitate to bring her that joy, she could never ask it of him. Baroquen would make it. Probably not as quickly as Iona envisioned, but Roux had faith that with hard work and persistence, they'd get to where they wanted to be. She knew that every one of them wanted the band to be a success, but their reasons were entirely different. Iona wanted to be a superstar, a household name, and to never have to worry about money again. Lily wanted everyone she loved to be proud of her, so she'd already gotten that wish whether she realized it or not. Sage's main goal was and always had been to support Azura, who just wanted to have as much fun as possible, and who could possibly have more fun than a young, beautiful, and famous rock star? Roux struggled to identify her own goal. Did she really care about fame and fortune? She loved playing the keyboard and sharing Baroquen's music with people—touching their lives in some small way and bringing them moments of joy. She supposed her goal was to make everyone happy. Deep down, she knew that wasn't possible, but she could bring smiles to as many faces as possible, and she supposed the more well-known Baroquen became, the more she could fulfill that wish. More fans equaled more people made happy by their music. So yes, she did want to become famous, but not for the same reason as Iona or her sisters.

Iona spent most of the flight writing lists and ideas in her ever-present notebook. Roux figured it must be hard to be that ambitious. She didn't think Iona's mind was ever quiet. Part of her drive came from an endless tap of internal motivation, but she'd become even more obsessed with success after she'd started dating Kyle. He'd given Iona the self-confidence she'd needed to go after her dreams, and she hadn't slowed down since. Roux was surprised that Kyle had been so scarce since Baroquen had signed with their new label. She hoped it didn't mean that Iona and Kyle's relationship was faltering.

"How are things with Kyle?" Roux asked.

Iona dropped her pen in her open notebook and scowled.

"That good, huh?"

"He's so stubborn. I asked him to give me these three months to focus on my career, and he acts like I never want to see him again. Men!"

"He loves you. I'm sure the thought of being without you for that long is devastating."

"It's not devastating when he's the one too busy working to take a weekend off."

"Do you really want him to back off for three entire months?"

"It would make things a hell of a lot easier." She picked up her pen, her scowl shifting into a lopsided grin. "But no, I don't really want him to back off. I love that he's stubborn. I hope that he shows up and demands to see me. I'm crazy that way."

Roux giggled. "I sure hope he's a mind reader."

"Nope. He's a man." She sighed loudly. "He'll think I meant what I said. Which means if I want to see him, I'm going to have to swallow my pride and invite him to visit."

"Pride is highly overrated."

Iona squeezed her arm affectionately and then picked up her pen to scribble more notes. Roux tried to concentrate on reading a novel but found herself so distracted by thoughts of finally getting to see Steve again that the words didn't make sense. Her attempts to take a nap were equally fruitless, so she watched an inflight movie, not sure what it was called or what it was about. She'd never been this crazy over a guy before. She wasn't sure that she liked the feeling. She liked *him*, no question. It was the can't-concentrate, the can't-sleep, and the-can't-live-without-him feelings he evoked that she would happily relinquish.

"You're not going to last five minutes," Iona muttered as the plane made its final descent into Glasgow to catch their connecting flight to Nottingham. Roux was straining to peer out the window at the dreary overcast day, not looking for landmarks but for Steve. Like she'd recognize him from this altitude. She wasn't even sure he'd be landing there. Exodus End's jet would likely land at a different airport and not have a connecting flight at all. But he was closer to her here than when they'd been on opposite sides of the United States.

Oh my God, Roux. Get a fucking grip.

She turned to find Iona smirking.

"I won't last five minutes at what?" Roux asked.

"Staying away from Aimes."

That obvious, was she?

"I might as well tell you that I do plan to see him," Roux said, surprised she'd kept her plans to herself as long as she had.

Iona opened her mouth, but Roux raised a hand to stop her outrush of words.

"Hear me out. He's promised never to interact with me in anything but a professional manner when I'm in costume, but when I'm not, we're going to be together. He's even going to call me Katie." Iona drew in a breath to again start her scolding, but Roux blurted, "No one knows who I am when I'm not in my makeup! They won't figure out that I'm part of Baroquen, so they won't think any of us fucked our way onto the tour."

"Are you finished?"

Roux lowered her eyes and nodded. A strange mix of anxiety and relief warred within her. She knew Iona would be mad, but facing her wrath would be easier than lying to her.

"You should have said something sooner. We can help you see him," Iona said. "Protect you both from snooping paparazzi."

Huh?

She must have looked as perplexed as she felt because Iona chuckled and patted her hand. "It's obvious that you love him. If you were just fucking him for fun, I'd feel differently, but I would never stand in the way of your happiness, sweetie."

Roux hugged Iona's head awkwardly, her seat belt cutting into her hips. "I should have just come clean from the start." She felt loads better. "I love you."

"I love you too," Iona said. "I'd love you more if you weren't trying to break my neck at the moment."

"Sorry." Roux released Iona's head and hugged her arm instead. Roux was truly blessed to have her sisters. They might not be blood, but they would do anything for her, just as she would do anything for them.

"I wonder if he'll be waiting for your arrival," Iona said, smiling to herself.

"I think his flight lands later. They had to fly all the way from LA and stop to refuel in New York." That was where Steve had suggested she meet him to join his flight, and lord, had she been tempted. But she was glad she got this time with Iona. It would feel good to love him freely around her sisters, even if she couldn't love him openly in front of the world just yet. She'd love to show everyone on the planet how wonderful the two of them were together. Not to brag, exactly, but to show that love was real and that it could last no matter what the circumstances. She'd always dreamed of having the kind of romance she could share with anyone, a romance that people would sigh over the same way she sighed over couples who were obviously in love and not afraid to show it.

"Well then, maybe you should be waiting for his arrival."

Roux smiled, realizing that her sisters really could help her with her romance. They were thinking far more clearly than she was. She likely would have just gone straight to the hotel and paced the floor until he came to retrieve her.

Roux tried out her British accent. "Smashing idea!"

Iona raised an eyebrow. "*Smashing*?"

"When in Britain . . . ?"

"Don't be a git, Katie." Iona's British accent was only slightly better than Roux's, which was surprising since she heard Kyle's accent all the time.

It felt weird to hear Iona call her Katie, but she supposed they'd all better get used to it. Iona leaned forward and stuck her face between the seats in front of her.

"Be sure to call Roux Katie when she's not in her stage makeup and costume," she whispered to Azura and Sage.

Two pairs of eyes peeked back at them from between the seats. Azura's and Sage's heads conked together as the plane touched down at that exact moment. "Ouch!" they cried in unison and rubbed each other's foreheads.

"Why?" Azura asked.

"I'll explain later, but don't forget. Pass it on."

Sage leaned forward to spread the word to Lily and Jack, who were sitting in front of them. Iona hadn't protested when Jack insisted he accompany them for the duration of the tour. Maybe that was why she was willing to help Roux see Steve. Maybe Iona was getting soft. Or maybe it was because she was in love herself and knew love wasn't easy to find. Or maybe it was because she didn't want any criticism when she asked Kyle to join them and he actually showed up.

They had only a short layover in Glasgow, so they didn't have time to venture out and explore, but their third tour stop was in Scotland, so they'd be able to see the sights then. Having sprung for international cell service before leaving the states, Roux texted Steve as soon as they landed. She assumed he was still in flight when he didn't respond to her text blitz: *Can't wait to see you. Are you in Donington Park yet? Where can we meet? I miss you. It's foggy here.* Their second flight was much shorter and more cramped since there was no business class, but she sat next to Raven, who couldn't wait to deliver her *I told you so.*

"I told you Iona would be happy for you. She's not as scary as you seem to think she is."

Roux scowled. "I'm not scared of her." Much. "I just didn't want to disappoint her."

"You're too much of a people pleaser. I say fuck them. Fuck them all."

"You have been working at that."

Raven shoved Roux's arm. "I have not!" But she had broken up with her boyfriend just in case she wanted to continue the job while in Europe.

Roux had always envied Raven's ability to have casual sex without regret. It seemed like fun. But now that Roux had Steve, she was too hooked on their emotional connection to want anything less.

"I guess this means I'll be occupying our shared room alone." Raven grinned, looking pleased with herself.

Roux's heart rate doubled. Would she be able to spend nights with Steve? She hadn't really considered that option. She'd figured they'd be stealing limited moments together, enjoying some sex-free sightseeing, and watching each other perform on stage. And all of those things would have been enough, but to be able to spend every night with him? That would be sheer bliss.

"I sure hope so," Roux said, wiping her suddenly damp palms on her thighs.

When they landed, Roux checked her messages and found Steve had responded soon after they'd taken off in Glasgow. *I have a little business to take care of first, but meet me in my room. I told the clerk at the hotel desk to give Katie Williams my spare key.*

Raven squealed when she read the text. She hugged Roux's arm as she said, "He is going to tear you apart when he sees you."

"And that's a good thing?" She knew it was and squirmed in anticipation.

As the band and their accompanying guests climbed into the shuttle van that would take them to the hotel, an overabundance of excitement spread among them. They'd arrived—figuratively and literally—and would be performing onstage at one of the biggest hard rock festivals in the world. They weren't yet renowned enough to play on the main stage like Exodus End and Sinners, but that didn't dampen their spirits or their enthusiasm.

"I remember my first Download Festival," Jack said with a nostalgic smile. He clenched his hands in his lap when he added, "And our last."

Lily squeezed his knee. "You know everyone is waiting for your comeback. Say the word, and that stage is yours."

"I'm happy teaching," he said, kissing her lips gently. "And being yours."

"And I, yours."

It would be spectacular if The Fallen returned to the music business, but Lily never pushed her husband. Roux smiled to herself, silently vowing to be as supportive of Steve as Lily was of Jack. Especially amid all the professional turmoil that might be in his near future. Would Exodus End seek a new manager or go it alone? Surely Steve could tell her that much without breaking any contracts. She'd have to ask him if she could think straight while in his company, unlikely as that seemed.

The hotel had been recently constructed, its lobby modern and spacious. Iona marched up to the front desk and checked in for all seven of them, getting their room keys and distributing them to each set of roommates. Roux hung back out of sight of the desk, sending Raven to collect her key from Iona because she wanted to limit her time in public with the rest of the band. Out of costume, she couldn't be recognized as one of them. It had been her plan for weeks, but now, separating herself from the group tore at her insides. She was proud to be a part of Baroquen, and pretending she wasn't did not sit well with her. Azura offered her a wink, Iona a knowing smile, Raven slipped her room card into her pocket as she passed, and Sage waved imperceptibly, but none of them made it obvious that they knew her. Roux hadn't felt so alone since she'd been orphaned and not yet assimilated into Mama Ramona's patchwork family. But if she wanted to spend time with Steve incognito, this was how it would have to be.

She waited a few minutes, pretending to check out the artwork in the lobby, and then went to the desk.

"May I help you?"

The pretty clerk's British accent sent a thrill of excitement through Roux. She was in England!

Her excitement fluttered with additional nervous energy when she said, "My . . . uh, *boyfriend* . . ." She took a breath and squared her shoulders. "My boyfriend said to pick up a key to his room at the front desk."

The clerk didn't so much as bat an eyelash. Didn't she realize that this was new ground for Roux? She'd never done anything like this before.

"Name?"

"Ro—Um, Katie. Katie Williams. I'm staying with Steven Aimes."

An eyelash did bat at that name. "You're his third girlfriend today," the clerk said.

Roux's jaw dropped. "What?"

"Fortunately, you're actually expected. I have your name right here, but I will need to see identification."

Roux released a relieved breath, wondering about those other two girlfriends of Steve's. Did they know him, or was that just their story to try to get into his hotel room?

Roux produced her passport and driver's license, both which had her given name, Katherine R. Williams. "I go by Katie," she told the clerk as she carefully inspected her ID.

She apparently passed the test, because without additional questions she was given a keycard and assigned a security guard to see her up to the room. She couldn't help but notice the muscled hunk was not only tall and dark but definitely handsome, and also claimed in excess; he wore not one but two wedding bands on his left ring finger. He also looked familiar. She stared at him rather rudely while she tried to place him.

"The tabloids," he said on the elevator.

"What?"

"That's where you've seen me before."

Roux's cheeks went hot, and she lowered her gaze. "Sorry for staring."

"Hey, at least you didn't call me an asshole for destroying Trey and Reagan's relationship."

"Oh!" Roux said. He was that guy. Reagan Elliot's bodyguard. Steve had mentioned the couple's unusual yet perfect commitment ceremony which had taken place only days ago. Or would that be the *threesome's* ceremony? How did one refer to an illegitimate marriage between three people?

"I've been entrusted with your secret identity," he said. "Steve told me your plan, so you can relax, Katie. I'll keep the sharks at bay." Under his breath he said, "Even if I couldn't manage to do that for Reagan."

"Thanks, uh . . . Sorry, I don't recall your name."

"Ethan."

"Thanks, Ethan." She wondered how much of those tabloid stories were true. Probably little, she decided, but refused to pry. It was none of her business.

When they reached the proper floor, Ethan escorted her to Steve's room. There were several additional security members on this floor—all wearing matching orange shirts—and none of them questioned her presence, presumably because Ethan was with her.

Ethan entered the room ahead of her and checked the bathroom and closets. "All clear," he said. "Have a good time. He must be crazy about you."

Roux smiled. "The feeling is mutual." Ethan closed the door behind him and left her to fend for herself. She hoped she didn't have to wait too long for Steve to arrive. She wasn't sure how much time they had before she'd be required to prepare for tomorrow evening's show. She would like to check out the venue and meet the other musicians—all while in costume, of course. But that meant she'd have to keep her hands to herself around Steve, and seeing as it had been an eternity since she'd last touched him, chances were slim that she'd be able to keep her distance.

Roux glanced around the room, smiling at the king-size bed she hoped would get excessive use in the near future, and noticed three colorful boxes sitting in a neat row across the dresser. More gifts? She hated to presume anything, so she checked for a card. Her heart fluttered when she found one addressed to *Katie* sitting in front of the presents. It read *Pick your fantasy from one of these boxes, and make all of mine come true. With love and anticipation, Steve.*

She lifted the lid off the first shiny box—midsized and white—and found a gauzy pink negligee with faux fur trim and obscenely tiny matching panties. Also inside were fur-lined handcuffs, vanilla-scented candles, pink rose petals, and one of Steve's signature cards. *If you're feeling nice and need a little convincing to be naughty, pick me.*

She scrambled for the second box—the enormous black one—lifting the lid and peering inside. Her jaw dropped at the crotchless leotard, the thigh-high black leather boots, and the restraints. There were no scented candles or rose petals, but there were several wicked-looking implements that made her quiver with both excitement and anxiety. The enclosed card read *If you're feeling extra naughty and think I need a little convincing to behave, pick me.*

Fingers shaking, she opened the smallest box—red—and

found it empty except for a card. *Answer the door in this if you'd rather improvise.* Answer the door in what? She checked inside the lid in case she missed something. There was nothing in there. Oh. She grinned. Nothing. Answer the door in nothing.

While she was feeling nice and extra naughty—and would insist they shouldn't let his other gifts go to waste—something told her to choose the red box. Red was her color, after all.

She heard voices coming up the hall, and though the sound was muffled, she recognized that one of those voices belonged to Steve. She didn't have much time. She kicked her shoes off and yanked her top off over her head. Bra, jeans, panties, and socks soon found the floor. She checked her appearance in the mirror and cringed. Damn, she definitely looked like she'd spent the better part of a day on an airplane. She combed her fingers through her hair to give the flat locks a bit of volume. While she kicked her discarded clothes under a nearby chair, she licked her teeth, wishing she had time to brush them before . . .

There was a knock at the door. "I hope you're indecent in there," Steve said from the hall.

She hurried to the door and said, "And if I'm not?"

"I'll still love you."

She was flying higher than any aircraft in existence when she reached for the handle and opened the door. Struck immobile at the sight of him, she just stared. She'd forgotten how gorgeous he was. That sexy little smile of his. The strength in the lines of his handsome face and strong jaw. The lump of his Adam's apple. The way the light caught mahogany highlights in his silky brown hair. The admiration in his exotic dark eyes. He'd been working out, she decided, fingers lifting toward the hard contours of his upper arms, and he'd gotten some sun since she'd last seen him. His complexion was a shade darker. And while she loved the beard he wore while off tour, she preferred his face smooth as it was now. There was no hiding his expression when he was clean shaven.

"Looking good, Katie Roux!" Logan called from behind Steve.

That was when she remembered she was naked. Before she could cover herself, Steve stepped into the room and closed the door. She expected a moment of awkwardness after their separation, but the second he touched her, there had been no lost time between them, no distance. Physically, yes, they hadn't touched, but their soul-deep connection had never severed or even thinned.

"I missed you," he said, wrapping his arms around her and

pulling her securely against his chest. His hands slid up to cradle the back of her head as he leaned his face close and kissed her hair. She could feel his heart thudding beneath her cheek. Hers answered in a hard, almost uncomfortable rhythm.

"I missed you too."

"You chose the red box," he murmured.

"I didn't really have time to choose anything else," she said, her hand flattening on his belly. She could feel the definition of his world-famous abs under his T-shirt. She wanted to nibble and lick every one of those eight ridges.

"If you want, I can wait."

"I can't," she said breathlessly, sliding her hand up under his shirt. Her fingertips rubbed the smooth skin of his belly, bumping over the contours, circling his navel.

"Can we make this last forever?" he murmured.

Their reunion? The inevitable sex? Their feelings? What did he mean? She needed him to be more specific. "*This*?"

"All of this. You. Me. Together. Never to part."

"Yes," she said with confidence. She could do forever with him. "I never would have guessed you were so romantic, Mr. Aimes." But she was so glad that he was.

"I love being in love," he said with a soft laugh. He drew her back slightly and smoothed her hair from her face with one hand as he gazed into her eyes. "With you in particular."

She fleetingly wondered if he'd been like this with Bianca, and then decided she didn't want to know. She wanted to believe that his love for her was special. Needed that to be true.

"I love being in love with you too."

"Have I told you that I missed you yet?"

Smiling, she nodded.

"God, I missed you." He lowered his head and captured her mouth in a searing kiss. Heat and emotion flooded her, swirling feelings of love and lust, of want and need, into one indecipherable mess. She was drowning in him and didn't care if she ever drew a sound breath again. She tugged his shirt up, needing to feel his bare chest against her hardened nipples. She wanted every inch of him melded against every inch of her. And once they were one, she didn't want to move. Just be. With him.

He helped her pull his shirt off over his head and then drew her against him quickly, as if they were of one mind and the thought of any space between them was unbearable after their time apart.

She struggled to find air as she kissed him, but somehow his lips against hers were far more important than getting enough oxygen. She shivered as his hands stroked her back and slid lower over her butt, pulling her against the hard ridge of his cock. Groaning against his lips, she unfastened his jeans, and pushed them down his thighs. His answering groan sent fire coursing through her veins. She needed him inside her. She really couldn't wait.

"Steve," she pleaded.

It was enough to send him shuffling toward the bed, kicking his shoes and the nuisance of his jeans off as he dragged her along with him.

"I've been mentally coaching myself all day to take my time with you," he said.

She tumbled back onto the bed and he followed. She opened for him, not wanting him to take his time.

"My coaching skills apparently need more work."

He reached between their bodies and rubbed the tip of his cock against her clit. She gasped, her back arching off the mattress. "Steve," she pleaded again.

He entered her slowly, gaze locked on hers as he filled her inch by inch. Buried to the hilt, he relaxed against her, lowering his belly against hers and cocooning her in his arms. She'd never felt more cherished, more connected, more content. Her lashes fluttered as he lowered his head and kissed her, claiming her mouth with the same care he showed as he took her body. Emotion clogged her chest until she couldn't breathe, and panic began to set in. Now that she knew what a love this perfect felt like, how would she go on if she lost it? If she lost him?

Her breath quickened, and she pulled him closer using both her arms and her legs—squeezing him so close she was likely hurting him. He didn't protest. Instead he shifted his arm and pressed something hard against her side. Her bullet, she realized with a flood of relief. He was wearing it on a bracelet. She released her tight hug and found his wrist, gripping the bullet in her hand until her panic began to subside. It didn't take long. Only a few deep breaths. *It's getting a little better*, she told herself. But maybe that was a lie.

"I wondered if it was me or your lucky charm you were missing," he said, and she opened her eyes to find him smiling kindly at her.

"You," she said without hesitation. "It's the thought of losing you that makes me reach for this." She squeezed the bullet in her hand and then released it to dangle around his wrist so that her arms were free to hug him close again.

"I know." He kissed her softly, not promising what he couldn't promise. Just validating how she felt. Giving her exactly what she needed to find the stability she still lacked. "I will never willingly leave you."

She smiled and squeezed him tighter. That was all she could ask of him. "I'll never willingly leave you either."

He shifted onto his elbows, and she slowly released her death grip, settling into the mattress and gazing up at him. He rocked his hips, moving inside her, and her eyes drifted closed as pleasure radiated outward from their joining.

"Part of me thought you wouldn't accept my invitation," he said.

"I couldn't get here fast enough."

He kissed her neck, his strokes no faster than before, but oh so deep. Her toes curled, and she arched into him.

"Am I presuming too much if I keep a toothbrush and some clothes in your room?" she asked.

His hands skimmed over her shoulders, her breasts, her waist.

"You already have a toothbrush in the bathroom. It's the red one."

Her smile faded into an opened-mouthed gasp of pleasure as his lips caressed her jaw, her throat, her earlobe.

"But you won't need any clothes here," he added.

Her smile returned. "I might need them when I leave."

"You just promised me that you won't do that."

And she wished she never had to. She touched his face. "I'll have to leave eventually. I have a job to do."

"Make me happy?"

"Yes, but—"

He kissed her silent. "Watching you perform will make me happy too."

"So you aren't planning to chain me to your bed?"

"Now there's an idea."

She lost her train of thought as his strokes hastened. She surrendered her pleasure to him, trusting him to bring her higher, higher.

"Steve!" she cried as she shattered, her enter body shaking with power of her release.

"I win," he said, grinning down at her.

Still quaking in bliss, she needed a moment to register his words. . She sucked in a breath and asked, "What do you mean, you win?"

"Made you come first." He beamed with pride.

She laughed. "I think that makes me the winner."

"Nope. Me."

"I want a rematch."

"Maybe you'll score second place, but I think I have that victory in the bag as well."

"We'll just see about that."

But when he kissed his way down her body, spread her legs wide, and set his mind—and mouth—to claim another victory, she forgot to even try to win. Besides, she was the one claiming orgasms. She was pretty sure that made her the real winner.

"Steve: two," he said. "Roux: zero."

"I'll try harder," she promised. But he flipped her over onto her knees and entered her from behind. Being taken fast and rough after the care he'd shown her before sent her body reeling into a new dimension of pleasure. And when he reached around to rub her clit while he fucked her, she couldn't help but allow him a third victory. Though, really, if this was what losing was like, he was welcome to tattoo a giant *L* on her forehead.

"I'm on a roll," he said.

She managed to get him on his back, and took his cock into her mouth, sucking him and caressing his cockhead with her tongue. When his breath started to hitch in excited gasps, she decided a four-to-one loss wouldn't be so bad. She shifted up his body to straddle his hips and slid him inside her with her hand. Using her weight to drive him deeper, she moved her hips in grinding strokes to rub her clit against his body. Steve seemed okay with her throwing him another point as she worked her way quickly to orgasm. He waited for her, sitting upright the moment she shattered to wrap his arms around her and hold her tight against him as he let go inside her.

"I changed my mind," he said as he collapsed backward onto the bed, pulling her down with him. "Coming is definitely winning, not losing."

She giggled. "I do know what I'm talking about sometimes."

"I'll never doubt you again."

When Roux's cellphone rang a while later, she was dozing peacefully in Steve's arms. She groaned, knowing before she even looked at caller ID that it was Iona and it was time for her to pretend she had a real job. Though she took her second career—making Steve happy—very seriously.

"Do you have to go?" he murmured.

She climbed from the bed before that sexy-sleepy voice of his made her consider a permanent career switch.

"I'll be back as soon as I can," she said, leaning over the bed and kissing his lips softly. She knew she couldn't spend the entirety of the tour in bed with him. Knew that, but hated it was true.

"I need my rest anyway," he said, looking even sexier than usual with his eyes all drowsy and his hair tousled from their earlier activities. "I'll miss having you tucked against me while I sleep."

She lifted a brow as she retrieved her clothes from beneath the chair and began to dress. She knew how he slept, all sprawled out on his belly with scarcely an inch for her. She ended up less tucked against him and more clinging to the edge of the bed so she didn't wind up on the floor.

"You are a total bed hog."

He grinned. "Guilty. I'll work on that. But only for you."

Now dressed, she kissed him again, forcing her feet to move toward the door. "I love you," she said.

"Love you," he murmured, eyes now closed.

She released a sigh, quickly committing the look of him to memory before opening the door. Roux took note of the middle-aged, mustached security guard in the hall who was arguing with some burgundy-haired woman. She recognized him from the after-party in New York as Butch, the head of Exodus End's security team and the guy who'd given her wonderful advice about making Steve fall for her. Roux kept her head down as she passed the pair, still worried about hiding her alter ego from strangers. The woman paused in her diatribe about all-access press passes as Roux hurried past them and to the elevator. Her neck prickled beneath the iciness of the woman's glare as she hammered the down button, as if that would get the car to the floor quicker. Something about the woman was familiar, but Roux couldn't figure out where she might have seen her. She seemed out of place, yet not her looks. She looked every inch a rock star aficionado—from her chunky leather boots to her short burgundy hair to all the piercings and tattoos in between. But Roux felt that she didn't belong there. Maybe it was because Butch obviously didn't want her there. As soon as the elevator opened and Roux stepped inside, the woman began berating the poor guy again.

"Sam assured me that I'm allowed on this floor and there's nothing you can do about it, Butch."

Ah, Roux thought. *That's what's off about her. She has an American accent, and we're in England.*

"I'm not bothering any of them on your account," Butch said sternly. "I don't give a single fuck what Sam says."

Roux smiled. She did like Butch. The elevator door slid shut, and she pressed the button for her floor. When the door opened, the scene was quite a bit different. Where Exodus End's floor was quiet and orderly and had security, the floor where the opening bands had rooms was utter chaos. Two young women streaked by in their underwear, paying Roux no mind as a chortling naked musician with a hard-on chased them into an open hotel room. Someone tried to pass her a half-empty bottle of whiskey, which she politely declined, and music was blaring from two different rooms. The songs were both loud and heavy but didn't play over each other with any harmony. She eyed her keycard, hoping she'd gotten the floor wrong. She'd never be able to concentrate amid all this noise and confusion. Her sisters would likely have a blast in this environment, but Roux coveted peace and quiet.

"Whatever made me think I could be a rock star?" she muttered to herself as she found her room at last. With dread, she realized that everyone in the hall had seen her without her stage makeup on. She should have planned better.

She knocked to alert Raven that she had arrived and inserted her keycard into the slot.

"I'm coming in," she called.

"Is that you, Katie?" Raven called back. At least she'd remembered to call her Katie.

"Yeah. Is Roux ready to go to the venue?" she asked loudly before shutting the door.

"Not looking like that, she's not," Raven said with a laugh. "You must have gotten laid. You're glowing."

"I saw Steve; of course I got laid." She hurried to her suitcase and found that Raven had already taken her costume out and had hung it to help smooth the wrinkles. "It's crazy out in that hall."

"If it was anyone but musicians acting like that, someone would have called the cops by now."

"We do get away with a lot of troublemaking." Well, not her, but *real* rock stars who behaved badly did. And Steve happened to be one of those.

"Do I have time for a shower?"

"Are you all covered in rock star cum?" Raven tutted. "Poor dear."

Actually . . . "And sweat. And saliva."

"Hurry up," Raven said. "And don't get your hair wet."

Minutes later, a cleaner Roux was shimmying into her costume while Raven came at her with her wig and false eyelashes. They hurried to complete the transformation, but the rest of the band was left waiting while they applied the finishing touches to Roux's costume.

"You're going to have to leave Steve's bed a little earlier next time," Iona said, checking her wrist as if she were wearing a watch.

"You can't talk," Azura said. "I barely got you to leave Kyle's side."

"Kyle's here?" Roux asked, her heart filling with joy for her sister. So the man was a mind reader after all.

Iona smiled. "He took some time off to be supportive."

Azura snorted. "He took some time off to get sex."

Iona slapped at her. "And he wanted to visit his mum in London." She went a bit pale. "Introduce me to his family."

"Isn't his mum like a hundred years old?" Azura asked. "She's going to think you're a child."

Iona cringed. "Maybe she has cataracts and won't be able to see me clearly."

Roux was glad she'd already gotten her "meet the family" out of the way with Steve. She hoped they visited them again after the tour was over so she could meet his father too. She'd had fun at the family farm and longed for that weird but wonderful feeling of home she'd experienced.

"You know what Roux's situation reminds me of," Sage said, changing the subject completely, as she was prone to do. "Hannah Montana."

"*Ew*. No." Raven shook her head so vigorously, her chin-length black hair went flying out in all directions. "More like Jem."

"Jem?" Sage scowled.

Raven looked at her as if she were daft. "That rock star chick from the eighties?"

Sage lifted her brows and shook her head, obviously not following.

"It's a cartoon," Roux said. Raven was a huge fan of anime and cartoons, and because they'd shared a room since puberty, Roux had little choice but to know about those things. "This would be a hell of a lot easier if I had Jem's hologram earrings to help me change personas, but I'm ready now. Let's go."

Roux followed her sisters into the hallway, yelling, "See you later, Katie," into the empty room before she shut the door.

The entire band stared at her oddly.

"It's sad to leave Katie here by herself," Roux said, widening her eyes and nodding to get them to play along.

Raven snorted. "Yeah, that's what's sad about this." She began to sing the theme song to the Jem and the Holograms cartoon as she made her way to the elevator. After Raven's sixth repeat of the chorus, Sage finally told her that she remembered the show just to get her to shut up about how truly outrageous Jem was.

They were shuttled via a small bus to the festival grounds. Several other bands were also on the bus—all friendly and welcoming and very loud. Roux mostly observed, finding the various personalities fascinating to watch. Iona had found a fast and ambitious friend in the lead singer of Killer Monkeys, and Azura and Sage were talking shop with several guitarists—all male, yet respectful of their female counterparts. Poor Lily was being harassed—as usual—about when her husband and the Fallen were going to make their comeback. It occurred to Roux that she was the only keyboardist present. That made her a bit of an oddity in and of itself, but she was also a quiet soul, and rock music was so loud and in your face. Maybe that was what she loved about the genre and the people who gravitated toward it. For her, the music filled a void in her otherwise serene existence. Sometimes a quiet girl just needed to rock.

"So how does it feel to debut as opener for Exodus End and Sinners?" a deep voice said behind her.

Roux turned. She knew that the spiky-haired man was in Killer Monkeys, but wasn't sure what his name was. He must have realized that, because he extended a hand.

"Kevin. Bass player."

Roux smiled and took his hand, giving it a firm shake. "Roux. Keyboardist."

His smile faltered a bit, but then widened. "Are you about to shit yourself? I'd totally be shitting myself if we had to open for two huge bands right out of the gate."

"Aren't you kind of opening for them here?" Roux asked.

Kevin shook his head. "Festivals are different. We play on a side stage and people come and go as they please, but at a venue?" He widened his brilliant blue eyes and shook his head. "Everyone who bought a ticket to see superstars is stuck watching you." He shrugged. "Unless they don't show up until the headliners go on."

A new fear niggled at Roux. What if *no one* showed up until the headliners went on?

"Sorry. Didn't mean to make you nervous," Kevin said. "I'm supremely jealous of your luck."

Luck? Not skill. Or talent. Luck.

"But yeah," he added, "if I was in your shoes, I'd be shitting myself big time."

The guy beside him elbowed him hard in the ribs. "That's because you have bowel issues, Kev. If I was in her shoes, I'd be dancing in the clouds." He had long, dirty blond hair—the kind that could use a good washing—and kind, dark eyes. He extended a hand, and she smiled a greeting before shaking it. "Todd. Another bassist. So you play keyboard? I don't think I know any keyboardists."

"I'm a rarity." Hence Steve giving her a hard time about it at the beginning.

"I know one." Kevin lifted a finger and then added a second digit. "Well, two now. Is it hard to head bang while you're playing that thing? I think it would be hard to head bang."

Roux chuckled. "I don't head bang."

"Do you dance around?" Todd asked. His gaze shifted to her chest. She waited for him to recover his manners and meet her eyes before she answered.

"Maybe. Perhaps you should come check us out if you're curious."

"I am definitely checking you out," Kevin said, giving her the twice-over.

Roux expected to be checked out when she was in costume; Baroquen didn't dress in corsets and short skirts and sky-high heeled boots to be ignored. She did feel a bit uneasy when the attention was this up-close and personal, however. Especially since she was outnumbered. She really wished Steve were sitting beside her at that moment.

"I meant our music," Roux said, careful not to put too much iciness in her tone. She wasn't here to make enemies either. The other members of her band would have taken this opportunity to flirt. Roux had always had a more difficult time with that part of their act. "Check out our music."

"Consider it checked," Todd said, staring at her chest again.

"My boobs will be onstage too," she said, tilting her head. His attention snapped to her eyes.

"Sorry, sorry. I'm just not used to being around such . . . nice . . ." His gaze started to drift downward again.

"Keyboardists," Kevin said, slapping Todd's arm.

"Right."

"It's mostly dudes around here," Kevin added. "Total sausage fest."

"Feel free to consider me just another dude," Roux said.

Todd shook his head. "Not humanly possible."

She laughed, relaxing slightly as she realized he wasn't a threat. He thought she was attractive, and that was okay. She was supposed to be attractive while in costume. That was the whole idea.

The bus pulled to a stop, and all the men waited for the members of Baroquen to disembark before scrambling out after them. Everyone wanted to show them around and introduce them to people and be seen with them. It was kind of bizarre how well they were catered to. Was it because they would continue their tour opening for the top two headlining acts of the entire festival? Or was it because their boobs looked spectacular in their costumes?

"Everyone is so nice," Raven said, smiling happily and hugging Roux's arm. "I never expected this warm welcome." She might not play an instrument or join them onstage, but Raven was definitely part of the band.

"It's your costume design, I think," Roux said with a laugh.

"Happy to be of assistance," she said, adjusting a red-ribbon stay at Roux's back. "But I think it's more than that. You're something special."

Roux rolled her eyes. "And you're too partial to judge."

"Partial, yes, but also a good judge of star presence. And you've got it."

Roux wasn't so sure that she did, but her sisters—Raven and the ones back home included—were all superstars in her mind and heart. She supposed Raven felt the same way.

A crowd of crew and musicians had congregated near the main stage. The excitement that had been surrounding Baroquen for the past hour shifted to the four men standing in the pit. Exodus End. Now there were the real superstars of this operation. Roux forced her face to remain impassive as her eyes sought and found the tall, lean—and inexplicably shirtless—form of the man she loved but had to pretend she barely knew. He stopped laughing at something some guy she didn't recognize had said to take a swig from a half-empty bottle of bourbon. Was he drunk? She'd seen him less than two hours ago, and he'd been almost asleep. Now he was halfway through a bottle of Jack, walking around shirtless so anyone could see that gorgeous body she so coveted, and having a grand old time.

Check yourself, Roux. He's on tour and playing a part just like you are.

She wasn't a huge fan of him starring in this particular role, and that confused her. That guy over there who everyone was idolizing was Steve, a man who sent her silly little gifts and always knew exactly what to say in the messages that accompanied them. A man who promised to take his time satisfying her but who managed to send her flying almost instantly. A man who claimed he was her biggest fan and groupie after making a big scene about keyboardists sucking. A man she loved so much that the very idea of losing him gave her panic attacks. He lifted his gaze and met hers across the distance. For a moment that familiar look of love crossed his handsome features, but he blinked, and his expression was replaced by impassive disinterest. He was doing exactly what she wanted him to do, so why did his indifference cut so deep?

A woman ran up to him—a member of the crew, according to her T-shirt—and began to gush. He smiled and talked to her as he signed a particularly sexy poster of himself. Roux's hands clenched into little balls of fury as she watched.

"Tone down the jealous vibes," Iona said near her ear. "And stop staring at him. You're being completely obvious right now."

With a frustrated sigh, Roux whirled to face the opposite direction and took several deep breaths. She would have to avoid him entirely in public because she *sucked* at acting like she didn't care.

"We have to go greet them now," Iona said, taking her arm. "Steel yourself."

Roux took one more deep breath and squared her shoulders before forcing her feet to follow Iona and the rest of her band toward the pit. *Don't gush. Act friendly but impersonal. Smile. Not too much. Oh God, there are so many people watching.* She should have practiced this interaction beforehand.

"Hello," Iona said to Max. "It's nice to see you all again. We've been working hard to prepare for this tour. I know we won't disappoint you."

"Well, if it isn't the talentless bitches who got Zach's band kicked off my tour," Steve grumbled.

Say what now?

CHAPTER 25

STEVE WAS CAREFUL TO KEEP DISDAIN IN HIS EXPRESSION even when shock registered on Roux's face. He hoped she'd forgive him for being an ass toward her band in front of everyone. He hadn't had time to explain to her yet that Tamara was sniffing around with an all-access press pass, which was going to make it incredibly hard to keep their relationship a secret. Best to let everyone think he hated them, he'd decided. He was rethinking that decision when Iona flinched and Roux stared at him wide-eyed, as if he'd physically assaulted her sisters. Perhaps calling them bitches had been a bit much.

"Get over it, Steve," Max said, He smiled at the members of Baroquen. "We're happy you're here and know your performances will be sensational."

Relief registered on every face—not just the ladies'—and Steve wanted to kick himself. He hadn't realized how bad his words would sound until they'd crossed his lips, but it was too late to take them back now, so he took another swig of whiskey and growled, "Not as amazing as Twisted Element would have been."

"Forgive him," Max said, sending him a warning with his eyes, even though that fake-ass smile he'd perfected was firmly in place. "He's just a little bitter about the whole Twisted Element thing."

"A little?" Roux blurted.

Steve lifted his brows, thinking how gorgeous she looked in her rock star getup, yet still preferring her without all the makeup and sexed-up clothing. "Got a problem with me, Red?"

She crossed her arms over her chest. "You're being a jerk."

"Just living up to my reputation." He turned on his heel and stalked away.

That had not gone as planned, but when he saw Tamara lurking around a collection of empty equipment cases, trying to be discreet about watching him, he knew he'd done the right thing. There was no way he'd get her off his ass. Best to make her think he was enemies with Roux, but damn, it sucked. He obviously didn't want to hurt Roux, but he also liked her sisters and he was a huge fan of their music. He was glad Zach would be arriving soon. He needed someone to vent to, and while Roux was in costume and hanging with her band, it couldn't be her. Maybe Logan could be convinced to leave Toni's side for a few minutes. He could confide in him, unburden himself of the weight crushing his chest, but not if Toni was around. Though knowing Logan, he'd probably spilled Roux's secret to her long ago. Steve took another swig of whiskey, wondering how the bottle was almost empty already. He hadn't drunk nearly as much as usual over the past weeks and was starting to feel the liquor's effects. Apparently it made him act dumb as fuck and screw up something phenomenal with a single sentence.

"Fuck." He should apologize. Not in front of everyone, but definitely in private.

"This must really be eating you up inside."

He turned to find Tamara following him.

"What?"

"Is it because they're women? Is that why you can't stand the thought of them being better than Zach's band?"

"Their gender has nothing to do with this. I happen to think Twisted Element are a better fit for the tour, is all."

"You just can't live without Zach, is all." She smirked.

Steve scowled, knowing she was the one who'd come up with that story about why Twisted Element had been replaced on the tour. Well, either her or her equally bitter sister, Bianca. "Why am I even talking to you? Get lost."

Tamara examined her nails. "You make this so easy."

"I make what so easy?"

"Making you look bad." Her eyes lifted, catching his gaze. "I don't even have to dig." She snatched the bottle out of his hand and took a drink. Then she tried to glare him down.

"Whatever. I don't care what you print about me." He did want his bottle back, though.

"But you do care what I print about the people you care about.

Who was that pretty redhead who snuck out of your room a couple of hours ago?"

Shit. Tamara had seen Roux leave his room. Steve's heart was thundering, but he pretended confusion. "I don't know what you're talking about."

He reached for his bottle and jerked it out of her hand, very pointedly wiping her spit off the opening on his jeans before taking another drink.

"Surely you weren't so high and drunk that you don't remember the last woman you slept with."

"She was just some stupid groupie." More accurately, the love of his life who probably hated him now.

"You don't let groupies into your private hotel room. You've always fucked them in the dressing room or a supply closet. Maybe on the tour bus *if* they're lucky."

She had him there, but he shook his head. "Things change." He turned and started walking with no destination in mind. "Do not follow me," he called over his shoulder. "If you want to talk to me, schedule an interview." Which he would not so politely decline.

"Good seeing you. I'll tell Bianca you said hi."

"You do that," he said and walked away.

Would he ever be free of his ex-wife? Not with her annoying fucking sister on tour with them. Whose idea was it to give Tamara an all-access press pass? Oh yeah, that had been Sam's brilliant idea. Some new publicity stunt of his. Butch had filled him in on the details soon after Roux had left his hotel room. Steve could not wait for the day when the band fired Sam. He hoped Max still wanted him to do the honors, because it would be a major highlight of Steve's life.

He wished they didn't need Sam for the tour. It would be a logistical nightmare to dump him now, but Steve figured any complications would be well worth being rid of him. And Sam could take Tamara—and the rest of the paparazzi on his bankroll—with him.

Deciding it was best to keep down appearances when he was in such an aggravated state, Steve went back to his hotel room. He sent Roux a text telling her that he was sorry for calling her and her sisters bitches in front of a crowd—that had been excessively asshole-ish even by his standards—and that she should be careful around Tamara. The reporter was already sniffing around like a bloodhound on a scent trail. He also told her that he still wanted her to stay the night with him, but would understand if she feared discovery and kept her distance.

Her reply, which came almost half an hour later, made him smile. *That's who that was! I saw her in the hallway earlier and couldn't place her. Fuck her. I'll come see you as soon as I can get away. Sam's making us attend a dinner to impress some music executives from London. You're supposed to be here too, you know.*

Don't care. I'm not fit for company.

Except yours, he amended in a second message. Or he would be after he slept off a bit of the alcohol he'd consumed. Damn, his head was pounding, and the room was spinning. He doubted he could stand up at this point. Apparently taking a few weeks off drinking had lowered his tolerance of the stuff. He'd prefer to sleep his intoxication off with Roux in his arms, after he sweated some of the poison out during some hot and dirty sex. But he wasn't even sure he could figure out where her vagina was located in this condition. Fuck, he was wasted. Couldn't ever remember feeling so wasted.

He received another message from her a few minutes later. He blinked at it, trying to decipher words that blurred together and made little sense to him. *This dinner is actually pretty funny. Kyle is fucking with them all so hard. You would be amused.*

Kyle?

Iona's boyfriend Kyle Schultz. The sexy British entertainment scout from American Voice. Surely you've heard of him.

Everyone had heard of him. He was notoriously tough on the show's contestants. He made most of them cry. Especially the men.

Iona is dating him? How had she even met him? Wasn't he like twenty years older than she was?

Yeah. I never mentioned that?

Nope.

Forbidden to. But if he's here as her date, it's sure to get out, am I right?

Is that why Iona has been so insistent that our relationship stay a secret? Because hers is?

That wasn't really fair.

IDK. TTYL.

Due to his inebriated condition, he translated her abbreviations with some difficulty. *I don't know. Talk to you later.*

Well, that sent a clear message. She must be getting herself into trouble and could no longer talk to him. So now he waited. He'd never been the kind of guy who waited around for a woman to get her priorities straight. If the roles had been reversed and he knew she was waiting around to see him, he would have made his excuses and left the dinner at once. But they were not at the same point in their careers. She wasn't in a position to blow shit off when she felt like it. Still . . . he would have done it for her.

He stretched out across the bed, turned on the television, amused that even the commercials were British, and drifted off to sleep. Or more accurately, passed the fuck out.

He had no idea what time it was when she showed up, but he couldn't even open his eyelids when she began to remove his jeans. It was weird. He could feel her hand and mouth on his cock, but it was like it was happening to someone else.

"R-r?" He tried to say her name, to open his eyes, to lift his head off the pillow, but he was too far gone. He couldn't even keep his dick hard, but she was doing her damnedest to help him with that. He was scarcely aware of her bare breast in his hand, in his mouth. Why couldn't he open his eyes? He'd gotten fucked up on some serious drugs before, but he never remembered feeling this wasted. What the fuck was wrong with him? When she kissed him, he tried to work his mouth to kiss her back, but it was useless. He was useless. And why was she so insistent on fucking him? Couldn't she tell he wasn't doing well here? He was starting to think he might need medical attention but felt so disconnected from his own body that he couldn't ask for help.

Completely numb, he felt consciousness slip away just as she straddled his hips.

SOMETHING WARM AND WET BATHED his face, his neck.

"Steve." Roux's voice. "Open your eyes, sweetheart. You're scaring me. What did you take?"

"Nothing," he said. Maybe. He tried to say the word but wasn't sure if he spoke it or just thought it.

"How much did you drink?"

"Not as much as usual." Hey, his mouth was working again! And so were all the pain receptors in his head. Fucking hell, his brain was going to explode.

"When I came in, I thought you were dead." She dropped over his bare chest and hugged him tight. "I was so scared."

"That didn't stop you from trying to jump my bones." He laughed, but nausea suddenly gripped him. He groaned and reached for a pillow to block out the glaring light.

"No idea what you're talking about. That must have been some dream."

Not a very good one. He hadn't been the least bit aroused. More like repulsed.

"I feel like shit," he said. "Maybe the booze over here is more potent or something." But he'd never had that kind of reaction when he'd been in England before, and his brand of whiskey had been imported from the US.

"It's probably a good thing that you threw up."

He'd thrown up? He didn't recall that. Yet now that his senses were coming back to him, he smelled the evidence.

"Promise me you won't drink that much again. It's dangerous."

He never *wanted* to drink that much again—not if it made him feel that horrible in only a few hours—so he nodded his promise.

"Let's get you cleaned up," she said. "Can you stand?"

How utterly humiliating to have her discover him in such a state. Naked, unconscious, and covered in his own puke. Lovely. And on the same day he'd been such an ass to her band in front of all the musicians they'd want to respect them while they toured Europe. He was batting a big fat zero today.

"Do you need a new car?" he asked. "What kind do you like? Expensive ones, I hope. Didn't you mention a Ferrari the day I gave you my number? A red one. I definitely think it should be a red one."

She lifted a puzzled eyebrow as she helped him haul his unsteady body off the bed. "Could you think of a more useless vehicle?"

"Useless? You'd look hot in it. What kind of Ferrari do you want?"

"You are not buying me a Ferrari."

"Something less flashy then. How about a Corvette?"

"No. No car. At all."

"Please let me. I messed up. I messed up bad."

"Yes, you did." She wrapped his arm around her shoulders and helped him hobble toward the bathroom. His legs were still a bit wobbly, and his head was still pounding, but he was upright. That was a marked improvement over ten minutes ago.

"I need to make this up to you," he said, "and show you how sorry I am."

"Not with a car."

"A yacht?"

She chuckled. "The only way you can make this up to me is by taking better care of yourself so I don't have to worry about you."

Strange request. He was sure most women would rather have the car.

"I love you," she said. "Your self-destructive behavior hurts me too."

Self-destructive behavior? Was that what she thought this was? "I didn't aim to get that drunk."

She pursed her lips and made him sit on the toilet while she turned on the shower.

He caught her arm. "Under no circumstances will you clean up that mess I made in the bed."

"It's no big deal. I'd do it for anyone."

He knew she would have. He didn't know what he'd done to deserve such a selfless woman in his life, but he was determined to keep her in it. Not by coercion or force or guilt or bribery, but by making her as happy with him as he was with her.

"Call Butch and tell him you need a discreet cleanup in my room," Steve said. "He'll know what to do."

"Butch?"

Steve smiled. "You didn't think his only job was heading the security team, did you? He runs interference for us while we're on tour." And spent more than a fair share of time dealing with Steve's mishaps. "Also, ask him for some painkillers. My head is fucking killing me."

Steve hauled himself into the shower, leaning against the wall when he feared his legs wouldn't support him. That had been some whiskey. Maybe his liver was starting to fail him. It would be best to lay off the booze entirely for a few days.

Roux handed him soap, shampoo, a toothbrush, toothpaste, and several washcloths. "I'll call Butch and then help you clean up. Assuming you want my help."

Her help? He always wanted her help and wasn't too proud to admit it. "I'd appreciate your assistance."

"Did you eat anything for dinner?"

He shook his head.

"I'll order you some food too," she said. "Something that'll be gentle on your stomach."

He wasn't sure if it was the aftereffects of the alcohol or what, but emotion suddenly flooded him, choking him up. "I don't deserve you, Red," he said, "but I'm glad you're mine."

She pointed at him, a stern expression on her lovely, makeup-free face. "Don't make this a habit, you hear me? I won't put up with this bullshit."

He nodded, thinking what a great mom she would make, and then wondering if she even wanted kids. He'd have to ask her sometime.

She left the bathroom, and he stuck his head under the flow of water, brushing his teeth first. How had she known his mouth tasted like ass? She'd probably smelled his breath, he thought with a wry smile. She definitely hadn't offered him any kisses. Had he really dreamt that she'd come and undressed him earlier? It had seemed so real at the time. So real that he'd stripped off his own pants while he'd been dreaming about her. Or maybe he'd taken them off before he'd passed out on the bed. Had he shut off the television? He couldn't remember. He shrugged, spitting foamy toothpaste into the drain. Hallucinogenic drugs had made him do some weird shit in the past, including climbing out of a five-story-high window when he'd wrongly thought his hotel room was on fire, but alcohol had never had such an effect on him. It made his head hurt to puzzle through the past couple of hours, so he reached for the shampoo and pushed his thoughts away. He'd actually done a pretty good job of not getting vomit all over himself, but he scrubbed his scalp vigorously just in case.

He heard a deep, muffled voice in the bedroom. Butch wasn't only discreet and efficient, but also quick to respond. Steve figured when they fired Sam, they could offer Butch the guy's exorbitant salary. Butch deserved to be better compensated for all the shit—and vomit—he had to deal with.

A few minutes later, Butch entered the bathroom with Roux right behind him.

"Hey, man, you okay?" Butch asked. "Your lady is really worried about you."

"I'll be fine as soon as I get some painkillers for this headache."

"I'm not giving you anything until you tell me what you took."

Butch focused on Roux for a moment. He probably wondered if Steve would be honest about his drug usage in front of her.

"I didn't take anything. Just drank some Jack. Quite a bit of it. But I didn't mix it with anything."

"You're sure? You don't usually react to alcohol that way."

"I'm sure."

"I won't be responsible for giving you a painkiller that will react with whatever you took earlier. You're absolutely positive that you didn't take anything else?" Butch spoke slowly, as if Steve didn't understand English.

"Positive."

Butch sighed loudly, but palmed him a couple of pills, which Steve tossed into his mouth and swallowed. They got stuck in his throat, so he tilted his face into the shower flow and forced down a drink of warm water.

"Thanks," he said.

"You're lucky I love you, you fucking pain in my ass," Butch grumbled before slipping past Roux and out of the bathroom.

"Love you too, errand boy!" Steve yelled after him, and even though he couldn't see into the bedroom, he knew that Butch was extending a middle finger in his direction.

"Maybe we should take you to the ER," Roux said. Both hands were twisted in the hem of her shirt. "Just to make sure you're okay."

"I'll be fine. I have the liver of a rock star. They're indestructible."

She didn't look convinced.

"Now are you going to get in here with me before I use up the hotel's entire supply of hot water?"

She smiled. "I suppose we have time before your soup arrives."

She closed the door and had just shimmied out of her leggings when Butch called, "Your soup is here. I'm leaving now."

"Thanks, Butch," Roux shouted through the door. "I'll take care of him."

"It's about time I got some help around here," Butch yelled.

"You know you love the challenges only I can offer you," Steve hollered back, smiling to himself. He gave Butch a hard time, but the man was one of his favorite people, and not just because he saved his ass on a regular basis.

Roux slipped into the shower behind him and wrapped her arms around his waist, resting her face against his back. Her fingers sought the bullet on the bracelet he now wore around his wrist, and he could only imagine how upset she'd been when she'd discovered him unconscious. He knew she was afraid of losing him. He had to be more careful in the future not only for himself, but for her as well. He never wanted to cause her pain of any sort.

"Are you sure you don't want a car?" he asked as guilt churned in his belly, and she laughed.

"No, I don't want a stupid car. I want you, Steve. Only you."

"A car is better," he assured her.

"Not in my opinion."

Silence stretched between them as she washed his back with a soapy washcloth. He sighed in bliss, the impotence problem he'd dreamt about while unconscious no longer an issue. He turned to face her and tilted his head, lifting his brows and then lowering his gaze toward the erect issue she'd created with her touch.

"Yeah, that's not happening tonight," she said, stepping out of the shower.

"What do you mean that's not happening tonight?"

"I mean sex. It's not happening."

"Are you on your period?" His gaze dropped to look for traces on her inner thighs. "Because I don't mind."

"Now that you're not dying, I realize that I'm pissed at you. *Supremely* pissed."

He'd thought she was over her anger already. "I said I was sorry." Had he? He couldn't remember if he'd actually issued an apology or had just felt it. "I'm really sorry, Roux. This *might* not ever happen again."

Apparently his joke didn't amuse her. She scowled and wrapped herself in a fluffy towel before scooping her clothes off the floor and hurrying into the bedroom. He didn't bother to rinse off or grab a towel before following her.

"Roux, don't be mad. It's our first night together in Europe. It should be special."

"Well, maybe you should have thought about that before you drank yourself to unconsciousness."

He moved to stand in front of her, gingerly lifting his hands to cup her shoulders. He'd never seen her mad and didn't know if she was biter. "I didn't mean to."

"I don't know if I can do this." Tears sprang to her eyes, and she dropped her chin.

His heart froze in his chest. "Can do what?"

"Be with someone who drinks." She pressed the heels of her hands to her eyes and took several deep and shaky breaths.

"If that's how you feel," he said.

She whimpered, and her arms shot outward, wrapping tightly around his back. He took it that she thought he meant they should break up.

"I won't drink around you again," he said, "and since I plan to be around you at all times, I guess that means I won't drink at all."

"I can't ask you to give up drinking for me." They both knew those kinds of promises rarely worked anyway.

"To be honest, I didn't enjoy drinking at all today. I swear I won't miss it." He usually drank to alleviate boredom, or to allow himself to behave like the jerk everyone expected him to be, but when Roux was with him he was never bored, and the last thing he wanted to do was behave like a jerk. His big fat jerk of a mouth had already upset her once today. "But I'd miss you. I've been missing you all day. Forgive me?"

She smiled and nodded.

"Give me another chance?"

She nodded again and then stretched up on tiptoe to kiss him. His head was still pounding—though slightly less than before—but the bed was freshly made, and her towel was quite simple to remove. With the slightest brush of his hand, the corner of the terry cloth slipped free and the whole towel dropped to the floor. She pulled away and squatted to retrieve it.

"I'm still not having sex with you," she said, glaring at him through narrowed eyelids. "Until you eat your soup."

She grinned, and his entire world brightened.

"And go rinse that soap off," she added. "You're all sticky."

"Yes, my lady."

After claiming a lengthy kiss from her pliant lips, he returned to the bathroom to rinse off. He even turned off the water and wrapped a towel around his waist. He vowed to be on his best behavior until his soup was gone, and then they were going to dig into the contents of the big black box still sitting on his dresser. When he returned to the bedroom, he discovered that Roux was of the same mind. She was already wearing the black crotchless, braless leotard and was slipping her shapely leg into a leather boot. His dick decided his thighs were a bit overwarm and lifted the front of his towel.

"The faster you eat your soup, the faster I can begin your punishment," she said, not bothering to look at him as she reached for her second boot. "That is, if you think you're up for it."

"Oh, I'm up," he said. He hurried to the covered dish on the table in the corner. He lifted the lid and tilted the bowl to his mouth, downing the entire contents in several deep gulps.

"I guess you're feeling better," Roux said, an amused smile twisting her lush lips.

"I am now that you're wearing that."

"Not sure what to do now that I have it on."

She rose to her feet and planted a fist on either hip, staring down at her body as if it belonged to someone else. Her tits looked fantastic, her waist appeared exceptionally tiny in the clinging black leotard, her clean-shaven pussy was exposed just enough to tease, and the few inches of her thighs that showed above those boots made him incapable of speech. He stared with mouth-watering anticipation.

"You're not much help," she said with a disarming grin.

His heart skipped a beat, probably because it was overstrained from pumping all the blood in his body into his painfully engorged cock.

God, he was in love with her. He prayed the feeling lasted forever.

"Have you been naughty?" she asked.

"No more than usual," he said, surprised he'd strung a coherent sentence together.

She approached him, and his legs trembled as if he'd just done ten thousand squats at the gym. An aftereffect of his binge drinking? Or did this woman make him weak in the knees?

"A simple yes will suffice," she said, her normally soft voice laced with an iciness that made him shiver.

"Yes."

She took his hand and tugged him toward the bed. "Come with me."

"I love to come with you."

"Not tonight. You're being punished." She fastened a restraint around his wrist and pushed him to sit on the bed.

"I have the feeling that you're a particularly vicious mistress."

She smiled an evil little grin. Lord, what it did to him.

"You have no idea. Your safety phrase is *I'm coming*."

"That's not a very good one. I'll probably say it when I don't want you to stop, not when I do want you to."

She didn't respond, just fastened a restraint around his other wrist. He scrutinized the headboard and found it was one of those fake padded things designers anchored to walls. Damn. Hotel rooms should be required to have headboards with sturdy rails. He'd request such from Butch for the remaining stops of the tour. Luckily for him, his woman was as smart as she was talented and beautiful. She took a flat sheet from the pile the cleaning crew had left behind—presumably in case he had another vomiting incident or two in the night—and slid one diagonally under the mattress at the head of the bed and the second under the mattress at the foot. This gave her four sheet corners to tie him down spread-eagle. He probably could have ripped himself free if he tried hard enough, but he had no plans to struggle.

She tossed aside the towel that was crumpled around his hips, leaving him naked and ready for whatever she had in store for him. He was sort of surprised that she hadn't tied him facedown so that she could paddle his ass. It could use a good paddling. He hoped she didn't get too rough with his more vulnerable front side, though he was already seeping precum at the thought of her hurting him.

"Remember your safety phrase," she said.

"I'm coming."

She nodded and climbed onto the bed between his open thighs. "Thank you for spoiling me with all those gifts while we were apart," she said, looking so sweet—even in her devilish attire—that it made his teeth and his heart ache. "It helped me realize that you were thinking of me as much as I was thinking of you. I've been trying to come up with a way to repay you."

"You already have."

She shook her head slightly and then lowered her face. When her first soft kiss pressed against his inner thigh, he jerked, pulling against his restraints. They held easily, and he wondered if he actually could get away if he needed to. He was in an awfully vulnerable position and . . . Dear God, what was she doing with her tongue?

She kissed and sucked and licked the insides of his upper thighs until he thought he'd die from unfulfilled desire. His hips thrust gently in an instinctual rhythm as his cock was given none of the attention it deserved. If this was her idea of repaying him . . . Her mouth moved to his balls. He groaned, head pressing back against the mattress, every muscle in his body tight. Her tongue was gentle as she sucked and licked every inch of his sac. His toes curled, and his hands fisted around the sheet attached to his wrist cuffs.

"Dear God," he moaned.

She nibbled his taint, and if he hadn't been restrained, he would have launched off the bed and through the ceiling. When her hand circled his shaft, a violent shudder ripped through his entire body. She didn't stroke his length the way he craved, just held her hand around the base of his cock while she continued to pleasure his balls. She was getting precariously close to his asshole with that tongue of hers. God, how it made him twitch.

"Wha-what are y-you . . . What are you doing to me?" he asked, his breath hitching.

"Punishing you for being so, so good to me," she said.

"I promise I'll never do it again."

"You don't like this?"

The uncertainty in her tone tore at him. "Of course I do," he said. "It's the best torture I've ever endured."

She giggled, and her breath tickled against his wet balls. Oh fuck, he couldn't take much more.

"Suck my dick now. Please."

She lifted onto her elbows, and her lovely face came into view. Unfortunately, she was scowling. "Did you just tell me to suck your dick?"

"I said please!"

"Not yet."

She resumed torturing him with more pleasure than he could stand. He thrust his hips, trying to get that hand circling the base of his cock to brush the head. Just a little, and he could endure more of those maddeningly soft kisses and licks of hers, but no. Her hand followed the movement of his hips and didn't slide up his length even a centimeter.

"Please, Roux. Please. I can't take — I can't take it anymore."

"You will. Because I'm giving you more."

More?

Her tongue swirled over his asshole, and his mouth dropped open. He went completely still. It wasn't his first rim job, but by God, in his current overexcited state, it was by far the best. She retreated quickly.

"I hope that was okay," she said. "I've never had the courage to try it before."

"A-OK," he said, more than willing to be her test subject in anything she wanted to try. "Have you ever tried . . . sucking my dick?"

She laughed. "Is that what you want?"

"Yes, please."

"Not yet."

Fuck! What else could she possibly do to him that— His breath caught as she stuck her finger in her mouth.

"I heard that you can make a guy come by massaging his prostate. Is it true?"

"I'm guessing you're about to find out."

She grinned. "Is it okay?"

"You have me tied down. You can pretty much do whatever you want to me."

"But I wouldn't do anything you didn't want me to."

"Yet you won't do the thing I really want you to."

"Suck your dick?"

He nodded eagerly.

"Not yet."

Damn! "You're an evil, torturing brat."

And then her finger was in his ass.

"What am I feeling for?"

"Deeper." He shuddered when she complied. "Forward. Toward the front." She followed his instructions, and blinding pleasure shot straight up his dick. "Holy fuck!"

"Found it." She had the gall to suck his balls while she rubbed his prostate until he had no choice but to come.

"I'm coming," he groaned.

Her lips released the nut she was kissing, and she said, "Finally," before she sucked the head of his cock into her mouth.

She'd been waiting for the safety phrase? He'd have yelled it twenty minutes ago if . . . Oh fuck, he really was coming. She fingered his ass perfectly as she swallowed his load down her throat, wringing out every ounce of release his body had to give. When he went still, completely spent and unable to move, she climbed up to straddle his hips and pressed his still-hard cock inside her. He forced his eyes to stay open as she leaned back, giving him a perfect view of her cock-filled pussy as she rubbed her clit, bringing herself to orgasm. She rode him as she came, still stroking her clit and straining for more stimulation as her inner walls tightened around him in hard spasms.

When her tremors stilled, she dropped to lie beside him. Immediately, her hand circled his softening cock, gently stroking its length as he twitched in overstimulated misery.

"The torture continues," he murmured.

"It's only beginning, my love. You called my sisters bitches."

CHAPTER 26

THE DAY OF BAROQUEN'S FIRST CONCERT had finally arrived. Roux was glad she'd managed to catch a few hours of sleep after punishing her naughty lover for most of the night. The man had been tough to break, but by the end she'd had him yelling "I'm coming" every time she touched him. Still naked, she peeked out the hotel window. The overcast sky didn't match her current sunny disposition, so she jerked the curtain closed and went to rouse Steve.

He looked so at peace lying sprawled across the bed on his stomach, one arm dangling off the edge of the mattress and the other angled over his head. The covers were tangled around his upper thighs but didn't hinder her appreciative appraisal of his perfect tan backside. Why was his ass tan anyway? Did he sunbathe in the nude? He must. There was no other explanation.

She needed to get back to her room and get ready for the day, but once she was in costume, she wouldn't be able to interact much with Steve. He'd taken their pretend disdain for each other a bit too far the day before, but she understood that he didn't want Tamara to catch wind of their relationship. No telling where the reporter would take that golden nugget of information. Maybe it would be easier to come clean and get this all out into the open. How bad could it be? Plenty of famous people flaunted their romances on the Internet, and people loved it. But there were also those who were relentlessly ridiculed for the same.

She was more worried about pissing off Iona than suffering through whatever public opinion she'd have to endure when the story broke. She didn't much care what people she didn't know thought of her, but she did care that it would upset her big sister. She leaned over the bed and kissed Steve's forehead. He didn't even twitch.

"Wake up, sleepyhead," she murmured. "I need to leave, but I'm craving one of your toe-curling kisses before I go."

She shrieked when his arm shot out and caught her around the waist, tumbling her onto the bed and pulling her beneath him. He kissed her deeply, curling her toes as requested. After a moment, he lifted his head and smiled sleepily down at her. His hair curtained their faces in silken waves. Damn, he was gorgeous. She got all fluttery and flustered just looking at him.

"I'm craving far more than a kiss," he murmured, and she squirmed to spread her legs. She hoped the more he craved involved deep penetration; she was already wet for him. He kissed his way down her body, stopping along his journey to suck a nipple, nibble her navel, delve into her cleft with his tongue. He spread her legs wide and muttered, "Breakfast of champions."

Her body jerked as his tongue gathered her fluids. He licked and suckled her clit until she found release, and then replaced his mouth with his fingers, rubbing her to prolong her orgasm as he guided his cock inside her with his free hand. He kept her coming as he pounded into her, pulling her higher, to a new level. She couldn't help but cry out as her body responded to his touch, his thrusts. Was it possible to have a clitoral and vaginal orgasm at the same time? Dear God, the man knew exactly how to get her off. Her pussy gripped him in hard spasms, quickly pulling him over the edge with her. He shook as he spent himself within her, and then, breathing hard, he collapsed on top of her.

"Well, that was a glorious wake-up call," he murmured, kissing her ear. "I'll be sure to ask the front desk for another one of those tomorrow."

She wrapped her arms around his neck and squeezed tightly, so full of love and laughter she felt like she could fly. "I love you, Steven Aimes."

"I love you, Katie Roux." He patted her flank. "Now you'd better get your ass up. You've got a big day ahead of you."

"I wish you could spend it with me."

"I could," he said. "It's your stupid rules preventing that, not mine."

"I know. I'm going to talk to Iona. See if she's willing to bend those rules." Especially since it had been obvious at dinner the night before that she and Kyle were more than professional acquaintances.

"Why do you do what Iona says at the expense of your own happiness?"

"Because I'm happiest when those I love are happy."

Steve smiled and brushed a lock of hair from her face. "Well, you must be the happiest woman on the planet when you're with me, because I'm deliriously happy when I'm with you."

She grinned. "Why do you think I can't keep away from you?"

"Because I have a big dick."

She rolled her eyes. "Yeah, okay. Can't get enough of that enormous dick. That's totally it." She kissed him and then squirmed off the bed. "I can stay with you again tonight, though, right?"

"I won't be able to sleep without you beside me."

"Are you sure? Last night I was certain you wanted me to sleep on the floor."

"I'll work on that."

She'd heard that before.

A knock sounded on the door. "Wake-up call. Ten minutes to gym." Roux was pretty sure the voice shouting from the corridor belonged to Butch.

"I'll be there!" Steve yelled. He kissed Roux before climbing out of bed. "It was nice while it lasted."

Roux followed him to the bathroom. "What was nice?"

"Butch minus his schedule clipboard."

When Steve stepped up to the toilet to pee, Roux backed out to offer him some privacy.

"Got to get my piss break in now, or I'm shit out of luck," he said. "Actually, I should probably take a shit too. I don't think you want to witness that."

"I'm leaving," Roux said. "I love you."

"Love you too. See you tonight. I'll be the obnoxious fan in the mosh pit at your performance. Wouldn't miss it."

Her stomach took a nose dive as reality grabbed her by the throat. Today was the day that the world got its first real taste of Baroquen. "I'll be sure to catch yours as well," she said.

"We're on tomorrow. But we can see Sinners together tonight. If you want to."

"Of course I want to. I love Sinners."

She shuffled into her shoes and headed for the door. The second she stepped into the corridor, a flash went off in her face.

"Ah, the mystery woman returns," Tamara said, falling into step with Roux as she speed-walked in the direction of the elevator. "Are you a local? Are things between you and Steve serious? How long have you been spending the night with him?"

Roux kept her eyes down and her lips sealed. When Tamara followed her onto the elevator, she pushed the button for the lobby instead of her original destination. No way was she going to her hotel room to get ready for the day with an obnoxious paparazza tail clinging to her ass.

"I'd have thought you were just another one of his endless string of willing vaginas, but spending the night twice in a row?" Tamara's eyebrows rose toward her burgundy-colored hairline. "There's something between the two of you. What's your name?"

Roux considered telling her that she was Katie Williams, but feared even that was too much information. The nosy reporter was going to figure this out. It was one thing to try to keep a curious bystander in the dark and quite another to fool a member of the press and keep her from figuring out the connection between Katie and Roux. Fuck! The elevator door opened to the lobby, and Roux was greeted by the smell of the complimentary breakfast offered by the hotel. Well, at least she had a good excuse to be here. Still refusing to give Tamara a direct stare, Roux headed for the breakfast room. Her bandmates were already inside, laughing together at a nearby table in full costume. Iona saw her first—good thing, because she was quick to notice details. A flicker of recognition crossed her face, but was quickly replaced with an impartial mask as her gaze settled on the woman still following Roux.

"I wonder what's taking Roux so long," Iona said as Roux grabbed a plate from the end of the breakfast bar. There was no way to get breakfast without passing close to her sisters' table. Azura, who was sitting to Iona's left, jumped suddenly and rubbed at her shin beneath the table.

She scowled at Iona, who was eyeing Roux sidelong. Luckily, Tamara was too focused on making a nuisance of herself to notice the table of rock chicks struggling to make excuses for their absent band member. After all, there were plenty of more famous, and therefore more interesting, musicians scattered around the dining room.

Roux scooped eggs onto a plate, bypassed all the processed meat products, including something she feared was the blood pudding stuff she'd heard they ate in England—gag!—and opted for toast, yogurt, and a plethora of fresh fruit. She glanced around for an empty table and cringed when Logan waved at her excitedly. Toni pulled out the chair beside her in welcome. Shit. Now what should she do? She shook her head slightly, giving a subtle nod in Tamara's direction, and scanned the overcrowded dining room hoping to locate an empty table so she could eat in relative obscurity.

She knew the exact moment that Logan recognized she was being followed by Tamara. His cute and normally friendly face darkened with rage. He approached them so fast that Roux cringed and almost dropped her plate.

"Get the fuck out of here," he said to Tamara. "Stop harassing Katie."

Well, at least he had remembered to call her Katie, but now Tamara knew for sure that she had a deeper connection to Exodus End other than being some nameless pussy that Steve had enjoyed two nights in a row.

"I have a pass," Tamara said, flashing a plastic tag that was dangling from around her neck. "You know her?"

Logan's fury was replaced with hesitation. He obviously wasn't sure what he should say. Toni took Roux's elbow. "I saved a seat for you," she said to Roux. "Did you want some juice? I'll get you a glass. Sometimes assistants need a little assistance themselves."

Assistant? Roux wasn't sure where Toni was going with this, but she said in her poor attempt at a British accent, "Cranberry juice would be lovely, darling."

Darling? What was she doing? She sounded like an idiot. She hurried over to the table that Logan and Toni were sharing with Dare—who looked mostly asleep this morning—and sat down.

"Why did you bring the witch down here with you?" Dare grumbled into his cup of black coffee. "It was bad enough having her in my face the moment I emerged from my room this morning."

"Sorry," Roux said. "She followed me. I'm not sure how to handle this."

"I'll give you the same advice I give my brother. Own who you are. If people can't handle it, that's their problem, not yours."

"It's not that I'm ashamed or anything. My band doesn't want anyone to think we're on tour with you guys because I'm . . ." She noticed that Tamara was within hearing range and dropped the conversation, focusing instead on her fruit salad.

Dare scowled over his shoulder. Roux adored Dare and his quiet introspection, but Tamara put him in such a bad mood that

Roux was relieved when he made his excuse to leave.

"Logan, I'm heading to the gym before Butch gets his panties in a twist about us fucking up his schedule. Are you coming?"

"Yeah, I'd better." To Tamara he said, "In case it isn't clear, you're not welcome here." He kissed Toni quickly before following Dare out of the dining room.

Toni deposited a glass of cranberry juice next to Roux's plate and sat back in her spot across from her.

"I never knew Steve needed an assistant." Tamara sneered at Roux, apparently unable to comprehend what Logan meant by she wasn't welcome. "What are you assisting him with exactly? His hard-ons?"

Well, technically, yes, Roux did help him with those. "He's uh . . . working on a project." Her fake accent was more Australian than British this time. Damn . . .

Tamara stepped closer to the table. "What kind of project?"

"A good one."

"You know it's none of your business, Susan," Toni said. *Susan?* Wasn't the woman's name Tamara? "Go bother someone else."

"And how do you know Katie, Toni?"

She saw me topless and screwing Steve on the beach at Dick Island, Roux thought wryly. *I didn't exactly make a good first impression.* She wondered if Toni now knew that she was a member of Baroquen or if she disliked Tamara so much that she was willing to breakfast with the woman she thought was Steve's current favorite groupie.

"She's a friend," Toni said.

"Everyone knows you don't have any friends, An-*toni*-a."

Toni lowered her gaze. Roux got the feeling that the animosity between the two women was not new. "Maybe. At least I'm not a raving bitch."

Tamara chuckled. "Better a bitch than a doormat."

"Get lost, will you?" Roux said, not wanting to join in on an insult-throwing match, though she had a few for the obnoxious woman who was harassing Toni. "There is no interesting story here."

"I disagree, but I already have an interesting story about Steve. You aren't the only woman he had in his bed yesterday." She smirked before waving smugly and venturing out of the breakfast area.

"God, I hate her," Toni said, pushing her glasses up her nose with the back of her wrist. "I didn't think I was capable of hating anyone, but I guess I'm not as good a person as I thought I was."

"I don't think it's possible to *like* her. She's completely insufferable." Roux speared a piece of melon with her fork and popped it into her mouth, trying not to let herself dwell on the lie Tamara had just spewed about Steve's bedmates. He obviously hadn't had anyone else in his bed the day before. Roux had been with him most of the day. Though she had found him passed out naked. Alone. But naked.

"Try having her as your boss." Toni groaned and curved inward, both arms wrapped around her narrow waist.

"Is that how you know her?" she asked, continuing to munch her fruit salad.

"She worked for my mom's company as an editor. She was supposed to be the one writing the book about Exodus End that I'm working on, but luckily I talked my mom into sending me in her place. That's why Susan hates me. I screwed up all her plans. Somehow she managed to get close to the band anyway."

"Why do you call her Susan? I thought her name was Tamara." Though Roux couldn't criticize anyone for using an alias, considering she now went by Katie in certain circles. Including this one with Toni.

"She was Susan when she worked for my mom; I think she didn't want Exodus End to realize who she really was. But she was Steve's sister-in-law, for crying out loud." Toni rolled her eyes and pulled the wrapper off a muffin before breaking off a piece. "Yeah, she'd lost a lot of weight since they last saw her, but just how stupid does she think he is?" She popped the bite of muffin into her mouth.

"Steve's actually very smart," Roux said, unable to stop herself from defending her man. "Except when he drinks. Then he's a fucking idiot." She laughed and opened her yogurt, stirring the fruit up from the bottom with a spoon.

Someone bumped into the back of Roux's chair, and startled, she glanced up to find her sisters standing there.

"Oh, sorry," Iona said, not sounding sorry in the least. "I was just in a hurry to get to the shuttle bus and wasn't watching where I was going."

"Roux better hurry up," Sage said pointedly, "or we're going to have to leave without her."

"Keyboardists!" Azura rolled her eyes as she passed the table. "No consideration for anyone."

"I'm sure she has a good reason for keeping us waiting," Lily said.

That was Roux's cue to get off her ass and change into her stage costume. She excused herself from the table, dropping her dirty dishes into a bin, and scoped out the lobby for signs of Tamara. After determining she wouldn't be followed again, she headed to the elevator.

As soon as she knocked on the door to her own room, Raven opened it wide and yanked her inside.

"Azura texted and told me you had the press following you around this morning." She was already trying to tug off Roux's shirt before the door had even shut.

"Yeah, it sucked." Roux kicked her shoes off. "I didn't want the snoop to follow me to our room, so I had to go down to the lobby to get breakfast as a diversion." She jerked off her pants and stepped into the black satin and lace dress that Raven was holding out for her. "Then Logan starts waving at me and I thought for sure I was sunk, but Toni told her that I'm Steve's assistant, so the reporter sort of backed off."

"Oh, what a tangled web . . ." Raven adjusted Roux's breasts in her bodice and grabbed the corset off the bed. Raven laced the corset up Roux's back while Roux rubbed foundation into her face.

"I'm sorry to keep doing this to you," Roux said.

"I like the excitement," Raven said. She fit the nylon cap over Roux's hair, tucking in stray locks, before taking her long black and red wig off the foam head on the dresser and placing it on Roux's head. "I feel like the pit crew at a racetrack."

Roux laced up her boots and put on her jewelry while Raven worked on the rest of Roux's makeup. She was halfway out the door when Raven called, "Wait. You forgot your petticoat."

A few costume adjustments later, Roux was racing for the elevator. Her sisters looked happy to see her when she reached the lobby.

"Did you oversleep again?" Iona chastised her.

"Sorry." Roux released an exaggerated sigh. "My damn narcolepsy strikes at the worst possible times."

"I hope you grabbed a snack. You don't have time for breakfast," Azura said, her sly grin telling Roux that she was actually enjoying the farce.

"I'm good. Thanks," Roux said. "When will the shuttle be here?"

"We missed the first one," Lily said. "But another will be along shortly."

"I'm sorry I made us late." Would she have to give up her nights with Steve? All because that stupid reporter wouldn't leave them alone? Was it really asking too much that she could have her time with Steve and keep up appearances with her band as well? The plan had gone so smoothly in her head.

The camping sites and outer festival grounds were already crowded, even though the main gates didn't open for another hour. Baroquen wasn't playing until later that afternoon, but they all wanted to experience as much of the atmosphere as possible. Well, Iona mostly wanted to network, but that was easy enough to do when dozens of bands were congregated.

"I had a dream last night that only four people showed up for our set," Sage said as they meandered through the parked tour buses.

"Did they throw buckets of piss at us?" Azura asked.

"No, they liked us," Sage said. "But there were only four of them."

"That makes four more UK fans than we had before the show." Azura patted Sage's shoulder just beneath the lower curved edge of her black and green wig.

No one knew who Baroquen was over here. They didn't have many fans in the US either, but in Europe they were completely unknown. What if Sage's dream turned out to be a prophecy? What if no one showed up?

Some musician stumbled out of a tour bus, nearly knocking Iona on her ass. She greeted him and smiled but was entirely ignored. Maybe it was just too early for him to be friendly. Roux was too amped up to be jet-lagged, but not every traveler was chipper in the morning.

Iona watched the guy walk away as if she didn't exist. "Maybe instead of trying to rub elbows with our better-known peers we should be rounding up some fans."

"Like out there?" Sage pointed toward the main gate, which wasn't visible from their current position.

"It's where the really important people are," Iona said.

"Do you think that's wise?" Lily asked. "Jack said I should be careful. These festivals can quickly get out of hand."

"We'll be fine," Iona said. "And I'm sure Sam would approve. He's always talking about how important it is to get a loyal fan base. How better to gain loyalty than by meeting potential fans one-on-one?"

Roux had to admit Sam was right, but she wasn't sure that the door-to-door-salesman approach was their best bet. "You don't think that will make us seem desperate?"

"We *are* desperate," Iona said. "This won't be like our arena shows opening for Exodus End. We have to draw our own crowd. We can't depend on them to do it for us."

"It reminds me of our basement gig days," Azura said. "How many flyers did we have to hand out to get thirty people in the door?"

"So many trees were sacrificed," Sage said.

"But once we got those thirty there and showed them a good time, they told their friends and we had to pass out fewer and fewer flyers until we didn't have to pass out any. Eventually we had to turn people away."

"But we don't have any flyers," Roux pointed out.

"I have an idea," Iona said. From the bodice of her dress, she pulled out a pack of multicolored permanent markers. "Don't judge. I was hoping someone would ask for my autograph."

Roux laughed but didn't refuse the red marker that Iona handed her. "What are these for?"

"Turning people into flyers," she said. "If they'll let us."

It was a long walk to the main gates, which were set to open in less than half an hour. Eager attendees were standing in line waiting to enter the concert area. Those at the front of the line were the most eager *and* the most bored—they'd been waiting a long time. Iona—who didn't have a shy bone in her body—walked right up to a young couple who were watching their approach with interest.

"I know you've never heard of us," Iona said, "but we're hoping you'll come see us at three this afternoon on the second stage."

"Who are you?" the man asked.

"Baroquen."

"What now?"

"Baroquen. B-A-R . . . Here, let me write it on your arm."

And the guy actually extended his arm over the barrier. Security was watching closely, but they didn't intervene. Iona took the cap off her purple marker and wrote *Baroquen* across his forearm, with the time and place beneath.

"Are you like their roadies or something?" he asked, staring down at his walking billboard of a forearm.

"No, we're in the band. We're opening for Exodus End this

summer, but we're new, so—"

"Exodus End! Have you met them?" The guy's eyes were wide as he glanced from one member of Baroquen to the next. Roux wondered how excited he'd be if he knew how truly close she'd become to one member of the band.

"Yes. They're great guys. Very supportive of newbies like us. We hope we can count on your support as well."

"If Exodus End supports you, count me in." He grabbed the arm of the woman with him and pulled it over the barrier. "Do hers too. And like, maybe autograph it or something."

Iona grinned like she'd just won the lottery and signed her much practiced autograph on the guy's arm.

Azura stepped forward to mark the woman's arm with their band name, and the time and location of their performance. Naturally, she wrote the message in blue, which matched her costume and undertones of her wig. A few men behind the couple leaned in to see what was going on.

"They're a new band from America," their first new fan told the men. "Opening for Exodus End this summer."

"Are they any good?"

Someone in line had already downloaded one of their songs onto their phone and played it for nearby spectators. Roux couldn't believe that Iona's crazy plan was working. Well, unless they hated their music. Then they were sunk.

"That sounds pretty badass," some guy said. "A mix of Black Veil Brides, Marilyn Manson, and Nine Inch Nails."

Uh, okay. If he said so.

"And every member of the band is a hot chick?" another man asked. "I'm so there. Write on my arm!"

Roux was closest to him, so she uncapped her marker and wrote their flyer message on his arm. "Are you the guitarist?" he asked.

"Keyboards," she said, her voice slightly muffled by the marker cap she held between her teeth. She placed it on the top of her marker, seeing as it looked like everyone in line now wanted a forearm message. "Azura and Sage are the guitarists." She nodded in their direction. "The blue and green ones."

"I want them to autograph my arm too. Their dueling guitar solo is lit."

Lit? Was that a good thing?

That guy's trend quickly caught on. Everyone wanted not one

autograph beneath their flyer message, but one in every color. The gates opened, and people behind the initial entrants stopped to see what was going on. Not everyone was interested in being marked, but enough people were, and most of them insisted on hearing a sample of music before they agreed to being written on with permanent markers. The best part was that once a skeptical person was introduced to Baroquen's unique sound, they always wanted to be included.

"*Ahh*," Iona said, writing her purple messages and autographs much more rapidly than in the beginning. "I don't care what any drug addict says. *This* is the best kind of buzz."

Roux grinned, once again recognizing that her sister was a publicity wizard.

The fans were surprisingly well-behaved. They didn't shove other attendees or try to grope her or have anything to say but positive things. A lot of them were already drunk—at noon—but not unruly. Maybe British drunks were less offensive than American drunks. Or maybe the insanity didn't start until the sun went down. After a while, their new potential fans started insisting on posing for pictures with their billboard arms, and once those started hitting social media, Baroquen was sought out at the main gates by people who'd been planning to stay in the campgrounds until later. Like the flyer situation, they had only needed that initial seed of excitement to grow a forest of new admirers.

"We're going to have to leave now," Lily said, signing in black marker, since white wasn't an option. "We have to be on stage in an hour."

An hour? How had over two hours flown by so quickly? Roux glanced up from the arm she was writing on between a sea of colorful tattoos and smiled at the middle-aged rocker it belonged to. "You're my last one," she said. "I have to go perform now. You'll be there in the crowd cheering me on, right?"

"Wouldn't miss it. I'll bring all my blokes."

"Perfect. We really appreciate your support."

Someone grabbed Roux's wrist and tugged her backwards. She felt a moment of panic, thinking that she was being accosted by an overzealous concert-goer, before realizing it was just Lily trying to get her to move. Those who'd been waiting to be marked were none too happy to be left without *Baroquen* and five colorful autographs written on their person.

"We'll come hang out with you after the show," Iona promised, her eyes glazed with excitement.

Security had to step in so they could pass and make their way to the backstage area. Roux was surprised to find Steve waiting for her in the wings. "I thought you might miss your first performance and that would be a shame. Will you look at the size of that crowd?"

Roux peeked over the stage and went instantly light-headed. Their publicity stunt had worked a bit too well. The area was swamped with an ocean of eager faces. Many of them held their arms proudly in the air, showing off the messages they'd scored from the band.

"Max will be wanting pointers from you ladies," Steve said with a chuckle. He extended his arm toward her. "Where's my mark?"

"Seriously?"

"I'm your biggest fan. I want in on this."

She grinned up at him—loving him a little more every second—and uncapped the marker she was still carrying. It was running low on ink, but she was able to pen the band name and her signature boldly on his arm and even added the event time and place, even though he obviously already had that information. "Knock 'em dead, Roux, who I'm not allowed to kiss right now." He lifted his fist, knuckles pointed toward her and said, "So I'll have to fist bump you instead." She tried to hide her disappointment over not getting that kiss but tapped her knuckles against his. "Consider that the deep, passionate kiss I'm thinking of."

She giggled. It wasn't *quite* the same.

"One with lots of tongue," he added in a near whisper. "I'm talking tonsil involvement. And of course, I'm squeezing your ass."

"Of course," she said, laughing. She knocked her knuckles against his again.

"Easy there," he said. "You wouldn't want to get me too worked up in front of all these people."

Who, luckily, weren't paying them much attention.

"Look who I found wandering around the hotel looking lost," Raven said. She hadn't ridden to the grounds on the shuttle bus with them, but Roux was happy she showed up to offer her support.

Zach stepped out from behind Raven, and Steve crushed him in a huge bear hug. "About time you got here," Steve said.

"The limo I was expecting to pick me up from the airport never showed."

Steve snorted. "Those are reserved for real rock stars."

"Don't feel bad," Roux said, offering Zach a much more

subdued hug than Steve had given him. "We didn't get limo service either."

"I guess I'm in good company then. Better than being a limos-only snob like this *real* rock star."

Zach lifted his knuckles and tapped them against Roux's. Steve immediately grabbed him in a headlock. "Watch that tonsil kissing, mister. Only I get to grab her ass like that."

Roux burst out laughing at Raven's confused expression.

"Did you get a new tattoo?" Zach asked, eyeing the forearm smashed against his face.

Steve released his friend and showed him his arm. "These brilliant ladies went to the gates and wrote their band name and the time and place of their performance on the forearms of fans."

Roux rolled her eyes. "They weren't our fans. No one had ever heard of us."

Steve pointed to the crowd beyond the stage, which had grown even larger since she'd last checked. "I think that's about to change."

"Fucking hell," Raven said, pressing trembling fingers to her cheeks. "Look at them all."

"I'd rather not," Roux said, taking a deep breath. "I feel sick."

"You'll do fine." Steve squeezed her shoulder. "All that rehearsing will kick in as soon as you start to play. It's muscle memory. Like riding a bike."

He'd never once told her that all that rehearsing that Iona insisted upon was unnecessary. She supposed this was why.

"And time will fly by so fast, you'll scarcely remember any of it," Zach added. "Will you write your message on me too?" He held his arm out to her. "I want to be a part of this."

She felt kind of bad as she wrote *Baroquen 3 p.m. Second Stage* across Zach's arm. He was supposed to be in her shoes right now. The older festival flyers still had Twisted Element listed in the slot. She capped her marker and gave him a tight hug.

"I totally get why Steve thinks the world of you," she said.

His arms tightened around her. "Likewise."

"I'd better bother the rest of the band for their autographs so I don't rouse suspicion," Steve said. "People will wonder if I have a thing for the red one."

He tapped Iona on the shoulder. When he presented his forearm to her, she lit up with excitement and scrambled to locate her purple marker.

He's so great, Roux thought. *I want to show him off to the world.*

But she shouldn't. She had recently witnessed the power Exodus End's name had over people. She doubted that first concert attendee would have even allowed Iona to write on him if she hadn't mentioned that they were opening for Exodus End this summer. So why was it okay for Iona to name-drop, but not okay for Roux to proudly show that she was in love with Steve? It wasn't the same, Roux realized, as she watched Steve get his marks from Azura and Sage at the same time. Name-dropping about who they were opening for was not the same as name-dropping about who she slept with.

"So I'm supposed to get written on by all five of you?" Zach asked. He was watching Raven fix Lily's wig, which was inexplicably on backwards again.

"It's the cool thing to do," Roux said.

"I'm glad he found you," Zach said, still not looking at her. "He's like his old self again. A little less fun, I must admit, but a whole hell of a lot happier."

"He's still fun," Roux insisted.

Zach snorted and laughed. "Yeah, okay, by your standards, I'm sure he is."

"Holy fucking shit!" Steve yelled. "It's really you."

Apparently Steve had discovered Jack Tanner hanging out with Lily.

Before Roux could respond to Zach, his eyes widened and he said, "Is that who I think it is?"

"The Fallen's Jack Tanner?" Roux couldn't stop smiling at Steve, who was jerking Jack's arm out of its socket as he simultaneously shook his hand and pounded him on the shoulder. "Yep, that's him."

"Holy fucking shit!" Zach shouted as he dashed over to join the other three drummers.

Dare and Reagan had come to wish them luck while Roux had been distracted. They were in some serious discussion about guitar riffs with Azura and Sage. Iona and Max were also bonding, probably over how to make band members behave rather than over their vocals. Once again, the keyboardist was left on the sidelines.

"Why do you look depressed?" Raven said.

"A stupid reason." She fiddled with her bracelet, longing to join Steve just so she could squeeze the bullet he was still borrowing. Maybe it was time to ask for it back.

"Is it because you're excluding yourself again?"

"I'm not . . ." She was. It was a vice of her more introverted nature. Because she wasn't likely to force her company on anyone, she expected people to approach her and include her.

She didn't have time to dwell on that tendency because someone called curtain, and the five members of Baroquen flocked together like terrified sheep. One of her sisters grabbed her hand, and she took someone else's in her other hand, until they were all involved in a pretzel of hand holding.

"Let's make Mama proud," Azura said.

"Ramona!" they shouted in unison before separating to take their places onstage.

Don't trip, don't trip, don't trip, Roux repeated to herself, her gaze focused on her keyboard, which was set up on a platform on the far side of the stage. *Don't trip.*

She released a relieved breath when she made it to her spot without falling on her face. For a second she felt completely at home standing with her fingers poised over the keys and her microphone adjusted perfectly at mouth level. And then she looked out at the crowd and forgot how to breathe. There were thousands of them—all expecting to get their faces rocked off—and she couldn't remember what song they were supposed to play first.

That was when she noticed a set list taped to the platform. Now, if only her eyes would focus well enough for her to read it. Luckily, Iona wasn't the least bit intimidated. She stepped up to the microphone center stage and managed to get out, "Thank you all for—" before horrendous feedback screeched at the fans. There was a collective groan as most of them covered their ears.

Iona stepped away from the microphone, and the screeching died. Iona glanced at Azura and then stepped forward to try again. "We're Baroq—" A loud buzz grew in intensity until everyone was covering their ears again. A technician dashed onstage. Someone threw a shoe at him, but he dodged the projectile. He fiddled with something on Iona's shiny purple bass guitar. Roux could see the front of house sound crew out in the middle of the audience scrambling to try to fix the problem on their end.

The crowd grew restless. Some idiot threw a water bottle on the stage, and it hit hard near Sage's feet. The bottle's contents splashed all over her lower legs. She hopped backwards a second too late.

"Hey, knock it off!" Azura yelled angrily, crossing the stage to check on her friend. A stagehand crouched low and hurried to collect the bottle and mop up the potentially slippery situation with a towel.

Roux noticed Iona waving at her and mouthing words she wished she didn't understand: *Talk to them*. Oh fuck, she was going to puke. But she did have a working mic. One that hopefully wouldn't sound like a hard-braking train when she spoke into it.

"S-sorry to keep you waiting. Sometimes a mic and an instrument don't play nice together."

But someone should have caught that during sound check. A technician was already unwinding the cord of a new microphone, to switch it out. Roux decided to introduce her band members while they waited. Her voice was surprisingly steady as long as she didn't look at the crowd directly. Staring over their heads worked best. Imagining them all naked did nothing but nauseate her.

"Playing for you today is Azura on guitar." Azura played a long, loud note on her guitar and held her bright blue instrument up over her head as the note carried. "And Sage, also on guitar." Sage had to one-up Azura by playing several notes of one of her fastest guitar solos. "Back on drums is Lily." Who doubled down on a drum solo of her own. "On bass and lead vocals is Iona." Iona played several rumbling bass chords. "And I'm Roux, keyboard." She played a few measures of chopsticks as a joke.

Some of the crowd laughed, but she very clearly heard someone yell, "Get off the stage!"

"Not until we're finished making your ears ring," Iona said with a wry grin. Her mic didn't screech this time. Roux felt like cheering.

Iona continued speaking, every eye in the audience focused on her beautiful face displayed clearly on the big screen and every ear soothed by her hypnotic voice. "This afternoon we're going to play a mix of our new album and some familiar songs by the legends of rock who inspired us. We are Baroquen."

Bright lights flickered overhead, signaling the start of their first single, "Starlight." It was the song that the concertgoers at the gates had been playing while they'd waited to have their forearms tagged with the band's name, so some of the audience recognized it. Roux played the intro, her keyboard sounding seamless with the two wailing guitars, heavy drums, and throbbing bass. Iona's voice carried across the festival grounds like a siren's call. And to Roux's surprise, even more festivalgoers rushed toward their stage. Steve had been right about the rehearsing and muscle memory. Once they started, the music flowed from her with ease. She hit all her notes, sang all her backup lyrics, and even started to relax enough to dance around a little. Her string-playing sisters were really putting on a show at the front of the stage, and Lily was so into her drums that occasionally her arm would extend high enough into the air that she could be seen.

A circle pit formed near the stage, and to Roux's utter astonishment, she recognized several of the faces leading the ring of racing men and women waving their Baroquen-marked arms high in the air. Steve, Zach, and Logan worked the crowd into a frenzy from inside the pit. Security was having a hell of a time trying to keep order, but it didn't seem like the rock stars in the crowd minded the jostling. Roux prayed none of them got hurt. At least Jack hadn't joined in the chaos. What were those guys thinking? God, she loved them all for doing it.

They played Heart's "Barracuda" next, which had the crowd singing along, followed by two of Baroquen's heavier songs, "Final Stand" and "Cross the Line," before playing Rush's "YYZ," one of Roux's all-time favorite instrumental pieces. They slowed their frantic pace for their ballad "Fuck You, My Love," which Lily had written about Jack several years before. Roux sang more in that song than any other.

Fuck you, for breaking my heart. Fuck you, for tearing me apart. Fuck me and take away my pain. Fuck you, you drive me insane.

The crowd caught on to the "fuck you" part of the song quickly and were singing along at the top of their lungs, their cellphones lit up and swaying above their heads even though it was the middle of the afternoon and the effect wasn't as breathtaking as it would have been as thousands of glimmering lights at night.

Roux searched the crowd for Steve, knowing this was his favorite Baroquen song—apparently because she sang so much of it, not because one of his favorite words was repeated so often. She located him easily, as if her eyes were primed to focus only on him. He had one arm looped around Zach's neck, and a beer dangling from his hand, but he was staring at her as if he'd been blind his entire life and had just been gifted with vision. She put a little extra soul into her voice just for him, and he lifted his glass of beer toward her before nearly strangling Zach as he drew it to his mouth for a drink.

A flash went off near him, temporarily drawing her attention from the man she'd never grow tired of staring at, and her heart thudded as she recognized Tamara. Fucking hell. What was she doing in the crowd? And why was she taking pictures of Steve? He either didn't notice or didn't care, but Roux could only guess how Tamara would twist a picture of Steve and Zach so close together into something perverse. Roux supposed the two men were used to that kind of fabrication. The lies the tabloids spread didn't make them keep their distance from each other. Roux thought it was nice that a man was comfortable enough in his sexuality to be affectionate with a gay friend. And Zach never showed the least bit of sexual interest in Steve as far as she could tell, so that was refreshing as well. She hated that the public tried to twist their friendship into something it wasn't and never had been.

Tamara followed Steve's gaze to the stage, and maybe she recognized the obvious adoration for what it was, because she snapped several pictures of Roux before slinking off into the crowd.

Just as Zach had predicted, their performance ended before it had even settled into Roux's mind that it was happening. They performed Queen's "Bohemian Rhapsody" as their encore, which sent the audience into a rapturous round of karaoke, and then it was over.

Roux took her bows, holding Azura's hand at the end of her line of sisters. She'd never been prouder to be considered one of them. They were hugging each other and laughing and crying in a big huddle as they shuffled sideways off the stage. When they had almost reached the wings, Raven launched herself onto their ecstatic mass of joy and relief. She was crying so hard, she was gasping.

And when she showed them why, they waved at the rest of their sisters and Mama Ramona, who'd attended the show via the FaceTime app on Raven's phone.

"You were spectacular!" Mama said, clutching her hands together tightly in front of her chest. "I'm so proud of you all. So proud." She wiped at her tears. "I knew they would love you. My girls, all so special. So unique. So beautiful. So talented. So, so talented."

She'd been telling each of them that from the moment they entered her house, until every one of her girls believed it of themselves and of each other. The woman was a rare treasure, a born mother, a true mentor. Roux was so lucky to have been found and rescued by her patchwork family.

"We love you, Mama!" Iona shouted, waving just as Kyle peeled her away from the group to kiss her passionately right there in front of everyone. Iona went limp and then threw her arms around him to kiss him back with palpable hunger.

Her five sisters exchanged looks of shock—Iona and Kyle kept their relationship under very tight wraps—and then squealed excitedly before crushing the typically private couple in a group hug. The only thing that could possibly make the moment more special was if Steve were there to share it with Roux.

A shadow settled behind her shoulder, and she knew her wish had been granted. She turned and reached for him. He was so gorgeous, smiling at her with love and pride in his expression. But the sneering face of Tamara, who was standing directly behind him, shattered Roux's moment. She lifted her knuckles and fist bumped the love of her life, hoping he recognized how much it meant to her that he was there. Roux glanced pointedly to Steve's left, and he turned his head.

Surprisingly, it was Reagan who went off on Tamara. "I am fucking sick of you showing up and ruining everyone's good time."

Tamara grinned and waved her press pass as if it were God's key to the universe.

"Haven't you caused enough problems for this band?"

"Don't give her the satisfaction of knowing she bothers you," Steve said, but he didn't reach for Roux, and she knew he would have if Tamara hadn't been there. "She's a nonentity. Let her take her pictures and fabricate her lies."

"Is your own life so boring that you have to make up shit about other people?" Reagan asked.

"Don't talk to the ghost, Reagan," Steve said. "Maybe it will go away."

"You wish," Tamara said. "My life's mission is to make your life as miserable as you've made mine, Steve Aimes."

"No idea what you're talking about," he said.

"You know exactly what I'm fucking talking about. And how did you manage to snag the keyboardist of Baroquen as your 'assistant'?" She finger-quoted assistant. "Or is she fucking her way to the top?"

Roux was too stunned to respond. Steve looked puzzled. "My assistant?"

"That's who Toni said she was this morning at breakfast."

"Are you talking about Katie?" Steve said.

Azura and Raven burst out laughing. "She thinks you're Katie!" Azura yelled at Roux, slapping her hard on the back and drawing her out of her stunned silence. "Like you and that *dork* have anything in common."

Dork?

"That's rich," Raven said. "I can't wait to tell Katie that someone thinks she looks like you."

"She wishes," Roux said, rounding up a bit of attitude, but feeling like a transparent moron.

"I can't stand this woman," Steve said, pointing at Roux.

"I saw the way you were looking at her onstage," Tamara spat at him. "I'm not blind."

"Well, I must admit I think she's hot."

"Even I think she's hot," Zach blurted.

"But we do not get along," Steve said. "Not even a little."

God, Roux fucking hated this farce. If it had been any person on the planet except Tamara, she would have come clean right then, but she wouldn't give this woman the satisfaction of knowing she'd figured out their stupid sham so easily.

"We need to set up for the next band," a stagehand interrupted.

That was their cue to stop clogging up the wings.

"What now?" Azura asked, deliberately turning her back to Tamara and effectively ejecting her from the conversation. "Do we get an after-party?"

Tamara huffed and crossed her arms, but the attention she'd once had, had shifted to Azura and plans for better times. Roux avoided looking at Steve so Tamara couldn't read the heartache that was surely displayed in her eyes.

"We have a few hours before Sinners takes the main stage," Reagan said. "You have to watch them perform. They're amazing!"

Exodus End didn't play until the next night, but they all wanted to support the other headliner of their tour.

"I think someone is a bit partial because her husband plays guitar in Sinners," Max said.

"Guilty of being in love," Reagan said, "but I'm not partial. They really do rock. But you all definitely need to celebrate. You were awesome! Like, I wanted to be you awesome."

Azura laughed. "Right . . . You want to be us, when you get to be part of Exodus End."

Roux chanced a glance at Tamara and was relieved to note she had vanished. She turned her gaze on Steve, who was staring at the ground, his jaw flexing as he clenched his teeth. Roux hadn't been oblivious to Tamara's tirade about making Steve's life miserable in retaliation for whatever he'd done to her; there had been something between them that Roux didn't know about. He needed to come completely clean about his involvement with Tamara.

"There's this electrifying connection between you all," Reagan gushed on. "It's hard to describe and impossible to replicate."

"I'll trade you," Azura said, but Roux knew she was only teasing. For one thing, Azura wouldn't be able to survive without Sage by her side.

Reagan squeezed Azura's arm. "I wouldn't let you."

Roux wondered what it must be like to be an outsider in a band with a long history. Reagan must feel isolated, and not just because she was a woman in a male-dominated profession, but because she had no history with her band. It hadn't occurred to Roux until that moment that the insanely talented guitarist might be experiencing something besides utter jubilation as a temporary member of a band as famous and successful as Exodus End.

"I'm insanely jealous," Reagan added. "Baroquen is going to be huge. As much as I despise Sam, I have to admit he was right." She stuck her tongue out and gagged. "Never thought those words would cross my lips."

Another non-fan of Sam's. They were sure adding up. Did anyone like him?

"Uh," the stagehand interrupted again. "I really need you to clear the area."

"Sorry!" Reagan said, looping one arm through Azura's and the other through Sage's. "I was so busy fangirling, I forgot we were heading to a party."

"What party?" Azura asked.

"The first one we can crash," Reagan said.

Roux smiled, loving that her sisters had found a kindred guitar-chick spirit in Reagan Elliot.

"If she figured out who Roux is . . ."

Roux perked up her ears at Iona's use of her name.

". . . it's only a matter of time before she figures out who I am," Iona said to Kyle.

"I don't care anymore," Kyle said. "I'm tired of hiding. Besides, I'm no longer on the show, and it's been three seasons since you competed. Everyone has forgotten the both of us."

Roux followed them away from the stage, very conscious that Steve wasn't beside her. She wasn't even sure that he was behind them.

"Well, yeah," Iona said, "until the entire scandal is revealed."

"No one will be scandalized." Kyle turned to Roux. His blue eyes appeared strikingly bright in contrast to his jet-black hair. "Are you scandalized?"

"Completely." Roux grinned to let him know she was being sarcastic.

Iona scratched beneath her ear. "I guess we could use the outing of our relationship to divert attention from Roux."

"I honestly don't care if I'm found out," Roux said. "And I don't care if people think I had to screw some famous drummer to get my band its big break. It isn't true, so I don't care what they think!"

Iona wrapped an arm around her shoulders and spoke to her in a low voice. "I know you're upset by that reporter following you around today, but we threw her off your trail again. She won't keep bothering you. You'll get plenty of private time with the guy in question. Just be patient."

"You don't get it at all," Roux said. "I don't want private time. I want blatant PDA. I want to hold his hand and kiss him and not have to worry if someone might be watching."

Iona glanced around. "Shh. Someone will hear you."

"Good!"

"This could be bad for Steve too," Kyle said. "In today's climate, a lot of men in positions of power are getting into trouble for coercing women."

"He didn't coerce me. He never coerced me."

"But if the tabloids take that particular slant—"

"I'll deny it all."

"Just think about what you are doing before you do something rash, Roux," Iona advised. "Once you go public, you can't take it back."

Roux rubbed her forehead. Was she being rash because she was fed up? She wasn't sure. She didn't want to regret any part of her relationship with Steve. But at that moment, her only regret was having to hide how she felt about him. She stopped and turned, scanning the crowd behind her, hoping that he'd heard her stand up for them. She smiled when she saw that he'd stopped quite a ways back. He was tall, so easy to spot in a crowd. For some reason he didn't look too happy. Her smile faltered when she saw who he was scowling at. What the fuck was Sam Baily doing in England?

CHAPTER 27

"CHRIST ON A CRACKER," STEVE GRUMBLED under his breath. What was Sam Baily doing there? Their manager never followed them on European tours. It was too difficult for him to fuck up their lives if he was overseas and far from the security of his embezzled-funds-sponsored office.

"Have you seen Max?" Sam asked, as if he had a right to talk to anyone in the band.

Steve was ready to tell Sam to fuck himself with a rusty chainsaw, but he remembered just in time that Sam was clueless that they knew he'd been stealing from Exodus End for years. Not that Steve's animosity was anything new. Sam probably expected such insults.

"He was around here earlier," Steve said, clenching his hands into fists.

"I was right about Baroquen," Sam said with a level of smugness only the most pompous of assholes could achieve. "Would you go round them up and tell them that a tent has been erected in front of the main stage entrance for them to sign more forearm autographs? Brilliant idea. Absolutely brilliant."

"Do I look like a fucking errand boy?"

Sam smirked. "You look like a man who wouldn't want Katherine Roux Williams to get hurt because she's been sleeping with the likes of you."

Steve's heart skipped a beat. How could Sam know . . . Steve mentally slapped his own forehead. How could Sam *not* know? He probably knew her social security number by heart and what her blood pressure had read at her last checkup.

"You wouldn't hurt her just to piss me off," Steve said.

"I wouldn't?" Sam chuckled, and then a shrewd and uncompromising mask slid over his aging features. "Round them up. They have work to do. And if you see Max, tell him I'm looking for him."

Steve so wanted to punch the guy in the throat, but what if he made good on his threat to harm Roux? Steve would never forgive himself for not protecting her and her sisters from that piece of slime. Was there any way he could get the band away from him? He knew Baroquen had signed a contract, and knowing what Sam Baily's contracts were like from personal experience, he figured it had been signed in blood with provisions about brain donations or something equally horrifying should they break their agreement.

Sam hurried away, looking for someone else to annoy. He settled on some poor stagehand, who he berated for the feedback issues that had plagued the beginning of Baroquen's set. And then Tamara came running up to him and actually hugged him, smiling a greeting so friendly, Steve thought he might puke. Unable to endure two of his least favorite people within spitting distance, Steve started walking in the direction he'd last seen Baroquen.

"Why is he here?" Zach asked.

Steve had completely forgotten Zach was beside him. "Who the fuck knows? He's up to no good, that's for sure."

"I thought he might say something about me tagging along, but he didn't so much as look at me."

"I'm sure he has bigger fish to fry." Steve huffed out a cynical laugh. "And I've always been his whale shark."

"He does love to annoy you."

And he was so good at it.

Steve spotted Roux, who had separated from the group looking for a party to crash and was watching him approach while fiddling with the ghost of the bullet she used to wear around her wrist. Though he knew she missed it, she had yet to ask for it back, but he unfastened the chain around his wrist as he walked toward her. He had the feeling she was going to need more comfort than he could publicly offer her.

When he drew to a halt in front of her, she asked, "Were you just talking to Sam Baily?"

"His twin brother," Zach joked.

Steve secured the bracelet around her wrist, removing the

extender he'd added to make it fit his thicker arm. She looked like he'd slapped her.

"Why are you giving this back? You're not dumping me—"

"Of course not." He couldn't stop himself from taking her shoulders between his hands and staring into her eyes, but he showed a huge amount of self-control by not dragging her against his chest and holding her tight. "I thought you might need it to help you deal with the stress Sam's bound to bring with him."

"More stress? I don't have enough already?"

"He knows we're involved."

She blinked those long fake lashes. "What?"

It was killing him that he couldn't comfort her. He wanted to stroke the hair from her face and kiss her wrist and press her fingers against his cheek, but he couldn't do any of that with so many eyes watching them.

"You should be fine if you do what he says," he told her. But what would Sam do if they refused?

Roux swallowed, looking pale even with all the makeup on her face. "What does he want me to do?"

"Not you specifically. He's had some tent set up outside the main stage and wants your band to continue autographing forearms. You'll probably be there all night and have to miss Sinners' show."

"Oh." She dropped her gaze. "Well, Iona did promise some fans that we'd sign more after our set, but everyone will be devastated that we have to miss Sinners."

"I'm sure you'll be able to hear them from the signing tent."

"Maybe no one will show up for our autographs and we'll get to leave early."

She smiled, and he didn't know whether to tell her he hoped that too, or if he hoped that they were so insanely busy catering to all their new fans that they wouldn't even realize Sinners was performing.

"I'm guessing that's not going to happen," Zach said.

Roux stood on tiptoe and glanced over the crowd, most likely trying to see where her sisters had gone. Her bandmates' colorful wigs and costumes made them easy to spot in a crowd, especially for Steve, whose height served as an advantage over those less vertically gifted.

"There they are." Steve pointed.

To his surprise, Roux took his hand and tried to lead him in that direction. Wishing he could let her, but knowing it wasn't wise, he pulled his hand free of hers. She looked back at him in question.

"I told you Sam knows about us," he said quietly. "And he's probably validating Tamara's suspicions as we speak."

"Then there's not much sense in trying to hide our relationship anymore, is there?"

He smiled and took her hand, leading the way. She grabbed Zach's hand in her free one to keep them from getting separated in the crowd of musicians, stagehands, technicians, and backstage-pass-wielding fans milling about. Steve's mood lightened now that he had two of his favorite people within spitting distance. Roux and Zach were a marked improvement over Sam Baily and Tamara Brennan.

When they caught up with Roux's sisters, Roux released Zach's hand—but not Steve's—and tugged on Iona's sleeve.

"Sam Baily is here," Roux said.

Iona brightened. "He is?"

"Yeah. He's having a signing tent set up for us outside the main stage's entrance."

"I'm sure the event organizers love that," Lily said with a snort.

Steve forced himself not to stare at her chest. She was even bustier than Toni, and Toni was stacked. He did so enjoy the female anatomy. He squeezed Roux's hand in case she could read his wandering thoughts, wanting to assure her that *her* female anatomy was the absolute best.

"Ah, come on," Azura complained. "Don't we get to celebrate even a little?"

"We'll celebrate with the fans," Iona said. "It will be fun *and* productive."

She was so like Max, Steve couldn't help but chuckle aloud. Lord help them all.

"And lucrative."

Sam's voice coming from behind Steve made his neck tense.

"I've managed to round up a few cases of CDs for you to sell," Sam added.

"Awesome," Iona said.

Roux's hand had become very damp against Steve's palm. Or maybe he was the one sweating buckets.

"You okay?" he whispered near her ear.

Her gaze followed Iona and Sam, who were now walking in the direction of the main stage, already deeply immersed in conversation.

"I don't trust him," Roux said.

"Because you're a good judge of character," he said. "Iona—like Max—is a good judge of opportunity. It's going to be damn near impossible to convince your sister that her aspiration's new best friend is bad news."

She moved close to whisper into his ear. "Maybe if you told me why you're firing him, I'd have suitable ammunition to sway her opinion."

"He's being fired for too many reasons to count," he said, "but the one that finally pushed Max over the edge . . ."

Her eyes brightened with curiosity.

"I can't tell you yet. It's not that I don't trust you. I just can't."

"He won't tell me either," Zach said, reminding Steve once again that his favorite third wheel was still hanging around.

"How did he find out about us? And so quickly?" Roux asked. "We were so careful in public."

Only one possibility made sense to Steve. "Probably some member of our security team."

"Butch?"

Steve shook his head. "No way. He hates that guy almost as much as I do, and he would never break a confidence. Some of our team aren't paid directly by us but by the tour company, which Sam runs, so their loyalty is slightly off."

Roux released a breath and then turned to follow her sisters to the yet-to-be-seen signing tent.

"I'm not sure we could get out of our contract even if we wanted to," Roux said, apparently not quite ready to drop the subject of Sam. "So maybe it's a good thing that we don't know what he's done."

Steve wrapped an arm around her shoulders, overjoyed when she didn't resist. So they were really going public? Several heads turned in their direction as they passed, but no one seemed overly surprised that they were together. They must not realize the significance of the seemingly casual interaction, but Steve recognized it.

When they reached the tent, event organizers were still setting up tables, but a line of fans had already formed. Their excitement over meeting Baroquen became frenzied when they recognized Steve had accompanied the new band.

"You're going to have to leave," Sam told him.

"But the fans want to see him," Roux protested, her hand

tightening on his.

"Of course they do," Sam said. "But he will serve as a distraction, and that's not what we're going for here. You want all the attention and buzz on your band, not on him."

Roux glanced up at Steve, obviously torn between wanting to keep him close and telling him to get lost.

"I have a bunch of stuff I need to do anyway." Lie. Huge fucking lie. But he agreed with Sam, damn it all. He would end up drawing attention away from Baroquen, and that wouldn't be fair to them.

"I'll miss you," Roux said, and to his utter astonishment, she wrapped her arms around his neck and kissed him in front of a huge crowd of catcalling fans and amid a multitude of camera flashes. "I had to do that in case any of these ass-ogling women weren't sure you were with me," she said with a grin.

"Wouldn't matter one bit," he said. "My insanely hot ass has no interest in being ogled by anyone but you." He shrugged. "Well, by you and this one other hot chick I'm undeniably attracted to."

She slapped his shoulder. "Who?"

"A sweet redhead named Katie."

"Oh." She rubbed the spot where she'd slapped him. "I'll allow that one to ogle at will."

He kissed her goodbye, and it felt so great to claim her publicly that he had a hard time letting her go. He watched her until she was safely inside the tent, checking to make sure there were enough security guards to control the crowd. His heart twisted a little when she squeezed the bullet he'd just returned to her, but he held his ground until she was seated between Iona and Lily. He took a deep breath and turned away before clapping a hand on Zach's shoulder, intending to seek out the never-ending backstage party he had no interest in attending.

"Did you see Tamara's face when you and Roux kissed?" Zach said with a delighted laugh.

Actually, he hadn't realized Tamara was even there. "Nope. I was too busy enjoying myself."

"I think she's still in love with you, man."

"Obsessed with me, you mean?" He shivered, even though the day was warm.

Zach nodded. "You remember how crazy she got the last time she was around you. Do you still have a restraining order?"

"I think it expired." Steve shrugged. "I don't think it would be valid in Europe, anyway. I'm not afraid of her if that's what you think."

"I would be. There's no telling what she'll do to Roux if she's jealous."

To Roux? Steve hadn't considered that. In the past, Tamara had always siphoned all her crazy toward him, until she'd finally given up on him ever being interested in her. Or had she given up? Had she positioned herself next to the band again out of spite, or did she have another agenda in mind?

"Good thing I have you here as backup," Steve said, whacking Zach on the shoulder several times. He didn't want to waste oxygen on Tamara by giving her any more thought.

"Speaking of me being here, I've been meaning to ask: Where am I supposed to sleep? The hotel is booked, and it's not like my tour bus is here, so I can't crash there."

"And you're assuming Roux sleeps in my room, so I'm not willing to share."

Zach's eyes widened. "She doesn't?"

"Of course she does. So maybe you can have her bed since she's not using it."

"Isn't she rooming with one of her sisters?"

"Raven, I believe."

Zach clapped his hands. "Sweet. Raven's a blast. Hopefully, she won't mind bunking with a dude."

"If she says no, you could always camp with the festivalgoers. I'm sure no one would notice if an extra guy ended up in the orgy tent."

"They'd notice if you were there."

"Yeah, but I'm famous. You're just . . . *Zach*."

Zach punched him, but he was laughing. "You're such an egotistical shithead."

"Do you love me because I'm a shithead or despite it?"

"Neither. In truth, I only love you because you're famous."

Steve covered his heart with one hand. "Ow. Wounded. Wounded."

"And for the record, I'm famous enough for your ex-wife to publish bullshit stories about me in her tabloid this week."

"Is it about hooking up with me or Enrique this time? Either way, does it bother you that the world thinks you have bad taste in men?"

Zach laughed. "I could do worse," he said. "But according to this particular line of bullshit, you're finished with me for good."

"That's a relief. I kept wondering when we were going to break up so I could move on with my life."

Zach licked his lips, and though he was talking to Steve, he seemed to find everything around them far more interesting to look at. "The story said you kicked my band off your tour because you found out I was fooling around with an unnamed actor."

"It laid the blame on me? Are you kidding?"

"I have to warn you that our fans are pretty pissed about it. We don't have the millions that you do, but the ones we do have are very loyal. They started a flame war against Exodus End online, and Toby is trying to calm them down, but in case you run into one of the twenty people on the planet who care, I thought I should tell you that they blame you specifically."

"It was entirely Sam's decision to fire Twisted Element."

"I know that. And he's probably the one who decided this was a great slant on the truth. He does so love to make your life hell."

"Just when I think I can't hate that man any more than I already do." And now he had to worry about Sam hurting Roux to get to him. Sam had done exactly that to Zach with those tabloid stories that stopped just short of libel. Or Bianca had. He still wasn't sure which of them spearheaded the slur campaigns against him. Maybe they were in it together. Her sister Tamara sure seemed to know, and inexplicably like, Sam.

"I think I know how to get to the bottom of this," he said. He just wasn't sure he could manage a civil conversation with his ex-sister-in-law. She'd always rubbed him the wrong way. Mostly because she was always trying to rub on him.

"Bottom of what?"

"Discovering who's out to make my life hell. Is it Sam, Bianca, Tamara, or some combination of the three?"

"Your ego is blocking out the sun again," Zach said, squinting up at the sky. "I don't think they spend their days trying to figure out how to fuck you over specifically."

Steve didn't agree.

"It's not ego," he said with a snort. "Paranoia, maybe, but you've seen how many stories are dedicated to making me look worse than I already do. I'm just the drummer. No one cares about drummers." He threw up his hands.

"Hey, I'm just the drummer too, and I'm the most recognized member of my band."

"Because you hang out with me," Steve said. That wasn't his ego talking. It was a fact.

Zach sighed. "So what's your plan?"

"I have to get Tamara alone and convince her to talk." Bianca hadn't told him much of anything when he'd confronted her a few weeks ago. And Sam didn't know how to speak the truth.

"Should be easy. Take your pants off and she'll not only materialize, but do anything you want."

Steve's balls attempted to crawl up into his body as a shudder of revulsion rippled through him. "Maybe you should come with me."

"You're not afraid of being alone with her, are you?"

Steve had the urge to beat the smug smirk right off Zach's face. "Terrified," Steve admitted.

"Me too," Zach said. "But I'm sure she'll open up to you if you're alone with her."

That was exactly what he was afraid of. Steve blew out a deep breath.

"All right, I'll try. But how do I find her?"

"That's easy," Zach said. "She's been following us since we left Baroquen's signing tent."

Steve stopped walking and searched over his shoulder. He didn't see her at first, but her rapidly ducking behind a light post drew his attention. "Shit. You don't think she overheard us, do you?"

Zach shook his head. "It's too noisy, and she was several yards back." He patted Steve's shoulder and gave it a shove in her direction. "Go get her, stud. I hear pillow talk is most effective in these situations."

"Not even funny." Steve blew out another breath—wondering why a potential interaction had him feeling so uneasy—and then stood straight. He wasn't afraid of her. What could she possibly do to him that she hadn't already tried? "Wish me luck." He turned and walked rather stiffly toward the lamp post and the burgundy-haired reporter trying to hide behind it.

"Do you need to borrow a condom?" Zach called after him.

Steve extended a middle finger in his direction, praying that Tamara hadn't heard him. He didn't want her to get any ideas. He just wanted to know who his real enemy was, and she was more likely to tell him straight than was weasel-in-alligator-shoes Sam or more-bitter-than-week-old-espresso Bianca. As he walked toward

Tamara's lame hiding spot, he mentally coached himself. *Be cool. Don't yell at her. Be charming. Smile.* He tried to smile, but ended up scowling. *This isn't just for you. It's also to protect Roux and Zach and your bandmates, your friends and family. Enough is enough. Fuck, tabloids suck! I hate them.* He could feel his anger growing. He took a deep breath. *Be cool.*

When he reached the light post, Tamara looked up at him, wide-eyed, and slipped around the pole as if the opposite side provided more protection.

"I wasn't following you!" she shouted.

"Then you were following Zach."

"No, I was just going in the same direction you are."

Seeing as he'd been wandering aimlessly, that seemed unlikely. "I want to talk to you for a few minutes," he said. "In private."

She licked her lips. "If this is about last night . . ."

He had no idea what she was referring to. "What about it?"

Tamara bit her lip. "You were pretty drunk."

He supposed that had been obvious even before he'd passed out, and she'd seen him just before he'd returned to his room. "This isn't about last night," he said. Why would it be?

"It isn't?" She met his eyes. "Is it about your new girlfriend?"

Not directly, but . . . "Did Sam tell you her name?"

She lowered her gaze and nodded. "He wants me to write a story about the two of you."

Steve threw his hands in the air. "Of course he does. What other stories does he want you to write?"

"I just do what he tells me."

"But why?" He was shouting, he realized, but couldn't help himself. "Why do you do what he tells you?"

She glanced around as if worried someone would overhear. "I have to go." She darted around the fans surrounding a group of musicians making their way either to or from a stage. He started after her, but was rudely poked in the shoulder by an angry-looking man.

"I came all the way from Dublin to see Twisted Element, you gobshite! Where d'you get off sendin' 'em packin', ay?"

"Um . . ." He wasn't sure what a gobshite was, but he knew a pissed-off, drunk Irishman when he saw one. Luckily, Zach hurried over.

"You let her get away," Zach said to Steve.

"You still speakin' to this geebag, Zachary Mercier?" the disgruntled fan spat in Zach's direction. "Are you bleedin' daft?

Zach scowled at the Twisted Element defender. Maybe Zach knew what a geebag was. Steve had no clue, but he was pretty sure it was an insult.

"He came all the way from Dublin to see Twisted Element," Steve explained.

"Is that right?" Zach said, brightening at once and wrapping an arm around the fan's shoulders. The man immediately went soft, his hostility toward Steve apparently forgotten. "Let's go grab a drink with my friend here." Zach jerked a thumb in Steve's direction. "Unless you have something better to do."

"Something better to do than drink?" Zach's fan broke into obnoxious peals of laughter. "With you?" He doubled over and slapped his knee.

Steve thought the guy might pass out, either from lack of air or because he was extremely drunk.

"Nah, ain't got a thing pressin' at the moment."

Once Steve was surrounded by booze, old friends, and a crowd of drunks in full revelry, it was a bit too easy to fall into old habits. He stayed away from the fucking whiskey, though, and stuck to beer all night. By the time Sinners took the stage, he'd forgotten why he'd sworn off alcohol in the first place. It sure made it easier to pass the time when he had nothing better to do than party. Especially since he had no desire to engage in his favorite pastime—fucking—unless Roux showed up, but he hadn't seen her since he'd left her at the tent.

Zach's fanboy, who was still hanging with them, patted Steve on the chest as they headed for the main stage to watch Sinners. "You're not the wanker I thought you were."

"Uh . . . thanks?"

"I'll be spreading the word that it's that other band—the one with the chicks—that's responsible for getting Twisted canned."

Steve cringed. That would be worse than laying the blame on him. Exodus End could weather the upset, but he wasn't sure if Baroquen could.

"Actually, it's not their fault at all."

"It was the tour manager," Zach said. "He made the decision on his own. Didn't consult anyone."

"You should fire that feckin' idiot!"

"Hell yeah, we should," Steve said, lifting his near empty glass of beer and downing its contents. As was the norm, his empty glass was immediately replaced with a full one courtesy of the next dude who wanted to buy him a beer. The fans loved that he'd hung around with them all evening instead of hiding out with the rest of the bands in areas inaccessible to them. If Steve had had a show tonight, he would have kept his distance, but since he didn't have to perform until the next night, he was just a music fan—who everyone happened to know by name—like the rest of them. There were always a couple of Exodus End's security team around when he did this kind of thing, but they seldom had to intervene. These were his people, and he didn't get to be around them as one of them very often these days. He missed being a part of the group.

"Are you going to watch the show from the pit or backstage?" Zach asked, his own perpetually refilled beer in one hand.

"Do you think we can make it to the pit?" Steve said, eyeing the enormous crowd already assembled before the main stage. The fans that were in the pit in front of the stage had probably gotten there several hours before the show began, not halfway through the first song. Sinners looked like ants on a miniature stage from where he and Zach stood. Still, the pyrotechnics were awe-inspiring, and as usual, the band sounded amazing. They had a great front of house sound board operator who rivaled Exodus End's renowned Mad Dog. Their drummer, Eric Sticks, had married her, if Steve remembered correctly. His brain wasn't working so well this far into drink.

"I'll get you to the pit!" shouted a nearby fan who happened to be built like a linebacker.

Surprisingly, the man didn't barrel through the crowd like he was carrying a Steve Aimes football to the end zone. He merely tapped people on the shoulder and introduced Steve and Zach, which made the exuberant and friendly fans insist that they move in front of them after claiming a handshake or a hug or a slap on the back. Eventually the crowd was crammed together too tightly to offer them the space to move forward. They were close enough now that Steve could make out which miniature member of Sinners was which. Sed Lionheart had the crowd jumping up and down to the beat of their rock anthem "Twisted."

"Do you think they wrote this song about you?" Steve shouted at Zach as they jumped in unison with the people around them.

Zach laughed. "They don't even know who I am."

"You're being modest. Let's get closer."

They both knew there was only one way to get closer and that was by surfing over the crowd rather than moving forward through it.

Their linebacker-esque companion agreed to give Steve a boost up, and soon he was being passed hand over hand above the crowd. He hadn't crowd-surfed for ages and was truly having the time of his life. He caught sight of Zach moving over the crowd near him. The song ended, and he could hear Sed talking to the audience.

"It seems there's a surplus of drummers in the crowd tonight," he said.

A camera captured the moment Steve thrust his arm—topped by a devil-horns fist—into the air and displayed it on the huge screen. The crowd screamed in approval. Steve grinned when he noticed how many of the arms waving on the screen had *Baroquen* written across them—his arm included. They showed Zach onscreen next; he got an equally loud shout of approval from the crowd, and more matching Baroquen forearms waved when Zach thrust his fist into the air.

"What are you guys doing down in the pit?" Sed shouted into his microphone.

"Everybody's gone surfing, surfing U-effing-K." Trey sang into his mic as if it were a Beach Boys song.

"I wonder if we can keep those two surfing for the entire next song," Sed said. "What do you say, Download? Are you up to the challenge?"

The crowd screamed its answer, and Steve's body suddenly changed trajectory. Instead of being passed toward the stage, he was now being passed perpendicular to it.

"Yes!" he shouted, thrusting his devil horns into the air again.

Lights flickered from the stage, signaling the beginning of "Shattered," a crowd favorite. The music was electrifying. Steve and Zach high-fived each other when they passed near enough atop the crowd to touch. Even Brian Sinclair got into the spirit of their extended surf, tripling the length of his guitar solo. *His fingers must be on fucking fire*, Steve thought as the crowd around and beneath him screamed in excitement.

When the song ended, Steve was passed directly toward the barrier. Several security guards assisted him to his feet in front of the stage. Several yards away, Zach was also being pulled to safety.

"You two are completely insane," Sed said into the mic.

Steve lifted both arms in the air and yelled at the top of his lungs to prove him right. He was far drunker on adrenaline than on alcohol.

"Get up here." Sed extended a hand over the stage and helped boost him up. "What do you have to say for yourself?"

Steve snatched the mic from Sed's outstretched hand. The audience screamed and whistled, stomped and clapped. Many smartphones were out and recording the scene. He pointed at the crowd and shouted, "I can't wait to perform for you crazy awesome motherfuckers tomorrow night! I love each and every one of you."

They cheered so loud that Sed covered his ears with both hands.

"And I'm completely in love with my Red," he said. "Do you hear me in that tent, Roux Williams? I love you!"

Yeah, he never would have announced that to the world if he hadn't been drunk, but he'd never spoken truer words.

CHAPTER 28

WHILE STEVE HAD BEEN SURFING THE CROWD, Roux had been watching it all on the big screen from just outside the signing tent. The entire time she'd held her bullet tight in one hand, one part amused, ten parts terrified that he'd be injured. When she heard his very public love confession, her heart swelled, and she cupped her hands around her mouth to yell, "I love you too, babe!" There wasn't a chance that he heard her from that distance, but her sisters sure did.

She was soon crushed in one of their breath-stealing group hugs. Even Iona seemed okay with how the situation was turning out. Let the world think what they would—Roux was in love, and not only did she not care who knew she'd fallen for the overexuberant man jogging off the stage with his arm around his best friend's neck, she hoped everyone knew.

"You know the best part about this?" Iona asked.

"More publicity for the band." Azura rolled her eyes at their very predictable leader.

Iona rolled her eyes right back at her. "No. Roux and Steve beat that stupid tabloid to the punch. So now whatever ridiculous story they come up with won't hold water."

"I hope it's already been printed, so they look like fools," Sage said.

Roux was still flying high from Steve's exhibition. "Number of fucks I give about that tabloid?" She peered at their smiling faces through the circle she made with her fingers and thumb. "Zero."

"Back to work, ladies," Sam said, and for the first time that evening he didn't look pleased. "You have fans waiting to meet you."

There were exactly two people in front of the table, but they went inside and dutifully signed the couple's forearms.

"Are you the one Steve Aimes is in love with?" the woman asked as Roux signed her name in red.

Roux smiled. "Lucky me."

"You do know he's a notorious womanizer, right?"

Always someone whose goal was to burst bubbles and rain on parades.

"Not when he's with the right woman," Sage said in his defense before Roux could respond.

"And Roux is the right woman," Azura added, squeezing Roux's arm.

"All we can do is try to make it work, just like every other couple." Roux's smile never faltered.

"Yeah, good luck with that," the woman said. She blew on the ink on her arm as she marched away. The man with her released an annoyed huff at her back, but followed her out of the tent.

"You know what sucks most about talking to fans?" Iona said, leaning back in her chair and capping her marker. "That you have to be cordial even when they say stupid shit directly to your face."

"But ninety-nine percent of them would never be that rude," Roux pointed out.

The tent flap behind them burst open, and Steve appeared in the opening, looking completely untamed with his shoulder-length hair in disarray, his eyes wild, and his chest heaving.

"Roux," he said when his searching gaze found her.

She stood and stepped toward him, stunned when he fell to his knees at her feet and wrapped his arms around her waist, burying his face against her belly.

"Oh God, I'm so sorry," he said. "I didn't know what I was saying."

She smoothed his hair with both hands. "You didn't?"

"I'm drunk off my ass. I never would have done anything that goddamn stupid—"

"Shh," she said. "I liked it."

He lifted his head and gazed up at her. "You liked me making a complete fool of myself?"

"Loved it," she admitted, knowing she was grinning like a lunatic.

"Told you so," Zach said.

"In that case..." He rose to his feet and turned to go. "I'm going to do it again."

She laughed and caught his arm, swinging him around. "Once is plenty."

He pulled her into his arms. He was sweaty and smelled like beer and the hands of thousands of fans, but she snuggled closer.

"You're sure you aren't mad?"

"I'm sure."

"And your sisters?"

"Are insanely jealous of her and happy for her at the same time," Iona said.

"In that case," Steve said, scooping an arm under Roux's legs and sweeping her up into his arms, "we have some celebrating to do."

Roux expected Sam to refuse to let her leave, but he watched Steve carry her out of the tent with a contemplative look on his face. The crowd near the back of the main stage area cheered and catcalled as Steve carried her away from the festivities. He was more than a little unsteady on his feet from the alcohol he'd consumed or because she was heavier than he'd anticipated. So once the cheering quieted, she asked to be set down.

"I'm not putting you down until I can spread you out on my bed and show you how glad I am that you're mine," he said.

"You're going to carry me fifteen miles?"

"Fifteen miles?"

"Yeah. The hotel is fifteen miles that way." She pointed in the opposite direction. "I think. Or maybe it's that way." She pointed toward what appeared to be a mostly empty campground. Few people were wandering the grounds since the headliners were performing. "Or over there?"

"Guess I'd better call Butch," he said.

She laughed. "So you're going to make *him* carry us fifteen miles?"

"No, I'm going to make him pick us up in a vehicle."

"We could make our way to a shuttle."

"And where would that be?"

"We'd have to go back through there to get behind the main stage, and then..."

"I'm calling Butch."

He used his cellphone while continuing to hold her, but when he described their surroundings and Butch said he couldn't get him a ride for at least half an hour, Steve had to concede defeat and set her down.

"I should have thought this through a little better," he said.

"It's fine," Roux said. "Wildly romantic even." She fluttered her lashes at him. "The ambiance of a roaring crowd, the smell of the porta potties and cooking grease." She took a deep breath through her nose and wished she hadn't. "Did you hear me yell at you when you were on stage with Sinners?"

He cringed. "Did you tell me to shut the fuck up?"

She shook her head. "I yelled, *I love you too, babe*, as loud as I could. I just wanted you to know since everyone on the planet heard you but almost no one heard me."

"I hear you now," he said, finding a dry patch of dirt to sit on. He drew her onto his lap, wrapped his arms around her waist, and rested his chin on her shoulder. In the background, the concert had faded to a subdued, rhythmic thumping, with lyrics mumbled and guitars barely audible. "I'm glad I made a fool of myself tonight," he said, "but I am sorry I drank so much. I know you don't like me to drink."

"You're going to drink sometimes; it's okay. There's booze everywhere, part of the culture. I don't expect you to abstain. I just don't want you or anyone else to overdo it like you did last night."

"I know several alcoholics who manage to abstain in this environment, so there's no excuse. I'd give drinking up for you. All you have to do is demand I stop."

Because she knew how much it sucked to try to live beneath ultimatums, she refused to give him one. "It's your decision," she said. "Not mine."

"But it would be easier for me to give it up if you forced me to."

"Do you want to give it up?"

"I want you to be happy, to feel comfortable, to trust me."

She plucked at the fabric of her skirt. "I am, and I do."

"How can you after everything you've been through because of alcohol?"

She rubbed his arm. "Alcohol might have made a horrible situation worse, but it was the alcoholic who was at fault, not the substance he abused." It had taken her years to come to terms with that—and she still faltered at times—because it was a lot easier to blame an inanimate liquid than a loved one.

"When we get home, will you live with me?" he asked. "I don't care where, just . . . I don't think I'd survive a day without you, much less weeks."

She knew exactly what he meant. When they were apart, she couldn't get through ten seconds without thoughts of him circling her mind and an ache settling in her chest.

"We'll figure out a way to be together." She kissed his nose. "Let's just enjoy Europe without further complicating things. Now that we don't have to hide anything, I can make out with you in public if the mood strikes me."

The current song ended, and the crowd cheered loudly, almost as if they were cheering for Roux's fortunate change of circumstance.

Steve grinned in the near darkness. "Is it wrong of me to hope that the mood is striking you at this very moment?"

She shook her head and cupped his face between her palms, leaning in to kiss him. The taste of beer on his lips was too much for her, though, and she had to break away. "The mood will strike a lot more forcefully after you've showered and brushed your teeth. You reek of beer."

"Fair enough," he said.

When a golf cart pulled to a stop before them, Steve was vividly describing his crowd-surfing adventure. Roux doubted she'd enjoy it as much as he had. Having the hands of strangers all over her was not her idea of a good time. But she loved listening to him talk, and he was much more vocal when he'd been drinking.

"Did someone order a limo?" Butch asked.

Roux was surprised he'd come himself instead of sending some junior lackey to do Steve's bidding.

"Yeah," Steve said, "but I guess this piece of junk will suffice."

"Watch it, smartass, or I'll make sure there's only room for Roux to sit and make you take laps behind us."

Steve stuck his tongue at him like a spoiled child and set Roux on her feet before standing and brushing off the seat of his pants.

"Thanks for saving us, Butch," Roux said, squeezing his shoulder as she climbed into the back of the cart.

"The cape is part of my uniform," he said, winking at her.

Steve slid into the cart next to Roux. "And so is his clipboard of torturous hell."

"What clipboard? You pretty much had the whole evening to make an ass of yourself on your own," Butch said. "Tomorrow is booked solid, however."

"I figured as much."

"So I won't get to see much of you tomorrow?" She'd probably suffer severe withdrawal symptoms.

"I don't care if you hang out for our interviews, meet and greets, and whatever else management has in store for us, but it will be incredibly boring."

"Not if I get to stare at you."

Butch made a gagging noise, but he was grinning ear to ear as he directed the cart into a U-turn and drove back the way he'd come. In the distance, the main stage flashed and flickered.

"Maybe we should stay for the rest of Sinners' show," Roux said. She hadn't gotten to see much of it while stuck in that signing tent.

"It'll be over soon," Steve said. "You'll get to see them in London and Glasgow and wherever we go after that."

"Madrid," Butch said.

Wow. This was really her life, and nothing could take her happiness away.

CHAPTER 29

STEVE TRIED TO IGNORE the knocking on his hotel room door as he enjoyed his morning breakfast with the gorgeous woman sitting across from him. She was still slightly flushed from the hot shower they'd shared—or maybe the quickie that had necessitated the shower—and only a bastard from hell would ask him to leave her now.

"I remember why we don't allow women on the tour," Butch complained loudly from the hallway. "If it isn't you fucking up the schedule, it's Logan."

Steve exchanged a grin with Roux, who reached across the table and squeezed his hand. "As much as I hate to say it, you really should go."

"I won't be able to see you until late tonight."

"That's okay, I'll be able to see you. I plan on watching you from afar all day."

"Stalker."

He lifted her hand and kissed her wrist several times, then forced himself to rise. He drew her to her feet and pulled her close, his hand slipping beneath her robe to squeeze her delightful ass. He kissed her until Butch's knocking became a pounding that would likely injure his hand.

"If you don't come out in the next twenty seconds," Butch said, "I'm coming in!"

"He sounds desperate," Roux said, patting Steve's ass and giving him a little shove.

"I love you," he said, kissing her once more before forcing his feet toward the door.

"I love you too."

When she released a dreamy sigh, he grinned. He needed to put a ring on her finger so she had something to stare at when he wasn't around.

The second he opened the door, Butch grabbed him by the ear. "Ow!"

"Do you see this schedule?" Butch shoved a mint-green paper so close to Steve's face that he couldn't have read it if he tried.

"If you had that woman in your life, you wouldn't want to . . ." He pulled the clipboard away from his face so he could pretend to read the first item on their agenda. "Have tea with the queen? I didn't know she was a fan."

"Not funny," Butch said. "Get your ass downstairs before I lose track of Logan again. You'd better hope there's no traffic."

"I love it when you boss me around," Steve said, offering him an overtly sexual look, biting his lip suggestively.

"Knock it off. I'm not in the mood." But Butch's mustache twitched as he tried not to smile.

When Steve arrived in the lobby, the guys looked happy to see him, even Max, who normally bitched him out when he made them late.

"We heard you made quite an ass of yourself over a woman on Sinners' stage last night," Max said, punching him in the shoulder.

He shrugged but couldn't deny it. "Yeah, well, I was pretty drunk."

"Was she mad?" Logan asked. "You were supposed to keep her identity a secret, weren't you?"

"I think she was relieved, actually." Steve smiled, glad she wasn't angry at him. Not even for drinking. He'd assumed she'd try to change him to make him fit her ideal man, but she accepted him as he was. Loved him despite his faults. He would try to be a better person for her because she deserved the best, and he was acutely aware of his faults.

"Why are you all standing around grinning like a bunch of idiots?" Butch smacked Steve on the back with his clipboard. "Get in the car."

"Is Sam joining us?" Max asked. Usually he'd want Sam to be in attendance, but from the I-just-swallowed-bleach expression on his face, Steve could tell he'd rather not have to put up with their soon-to-be-fired manager.

"No. I think he's sleeping off his jet lag," Butch said.

Even more good news to brighten Steve's day. He could get used to this. The band still hadn't told Butch that they were getting rid of Sam after the tour; Butch didn't need the stress of trying to keep that gem of a secret under wraps for the next three months. Besides, where would he get his beloved schedules without Sam's publicity machine to back the band?

They didn't have to travel far for their radio station interviews. All the local stations, and a few not so local ones, were broadcasting live from the Download festival grounds. They were on TV a few times as well, then made their way to a lunch with fans who had paid a shit-ton of money for the opportunity. Steve remembered a time when they would do this sort of thing for free, and when Sam was out of their lives, he vowed they'd go back to their old ways of letting people win these special interactions in raffles rather than having them fork over a pile of cash. While waiting for everyone to be seated so they could make their entrance, he mentioned his concerns to Dare. He didn't get the response he'd been expecting.

"Some of the people who won those raffles would sell their prize for way more than these people paid. Then they'd be the ones profiting, not us, who are footing the bill."

Max must have been eavesdropping, because he leaned in to say, "And scalpers buy up these packages and sell them for a substantial profit as well."

"I'd rather raffle winners profit than scalpers," Logan said.

"I don't think anyone should profit," Steve said. "These are our guests. You don't charge guests."

"These are the kinds of things we'll have to figure out when we go it on our own," Max said.

"Do we have time to make all these decisions?" Dare asked.

That was the reason Sam had been hired in the first place; they hadn't wanted to make all those decisions. They'd wanted an expert to do that for them, and the label had insisted that they'd scored a coup by bringing in Sam Baily. But now that they'd been in this game for over a decade, they had developed opinions. What was surprising to Steve was that those opinions were more in line with each other's than he expected them to be.

Halfway through their VIP lunch, he got a text from Roux. He excused himself from the table so he could read it with relative privacy.

Hope you're having a great day. Every guy in the band Scurvy Gums got food poisoning, so we're filling in their slot at seven. I won't be able to see you backstage before your show, but I will watch you perform tonight. Can't wait to see you after.

He was sure she realized what a big deal it was to be asked to fill in for another band, so he didn't comment on that. *Wish I had time to come see you perform again tonight. You know I'm your biggest fan. We have tomorrow off. I'm not letting you out of my sight for a single second.*

Now he was the stalker.

London. Can't wait. Love you.

A fan was standing uncomfortably close and staring at him with camera in hand wanting a picture, so he sent Roux a quick thumbs-up and tucked his phone back into his pocket. He spent his entire afternoon interacting with fans—one of his favorite pastimes—so the time flew by. Zach showed up in the backstage area and kept the party going, but by the time Steve had to change clothes to get ready for their set, he was really missing Roux. He hadn't even heard from her about how their second show had gone. Had Sam kept them busy all day the way he had Exodus End? It seemed likely, and since Baroquen wasn't well-known, he was sure it took a lot of work to get events lined up for them. Exodus End had to turn people down now, but it hadn't always been that way.

Dressed and waiting in the wings with drumsticks twirling and excitement coursing through his veins, he jumped when a woman pressed up against his back and wrapped her arms around his waist. He was about to politely tell her to get lost when she whispered in his ear, "I got here as fast as I could. I didn't want you to think I'd forgotten about you."

He covered Roux's hands with his and pressed them more firmly into his belly. "It's not possible for anyone to forget about me."

She laughed and pressed her elbows into his sides, making him jump again. "Ego check, Aimes."

"Checked and fully functional."

He took her arm and pulled her around to face him. He wasn't sure why he was disappointed that she was in full costume. She was sexy as sin in her corset and petticoats. Her face was flawless in her heavy makeup with every freckle concealed, and the wig flattered her beauty, the vivid red strands within the black drawing out the green flecks in her hazel eyes. Her black lipstick made her complexion glow like porcelain, but still, he preferred her natural look. Not that he'd kick this rock star sex kitten out of his bed.

"How'd your show go?"

"Perfect. And fans remembered us. They still have our band name on their forearms. I bet they can't wait to have proper showers and wash it off." She laughed.

"Is that lipstick kissproof?" he asked, cupping her face.

"No." She rubbed it off on the back of her hand, leaving a wide black smudge. "I think you're safe now."

He didn't much care if he went on stage with black lips—he couldn't not kiss her. And he didn't particularly relish all the camera flashes going off around them as he claimed her lips. He wasn't ashamed. He just wished people would have a little respect for their privacy.

Someone called *places,* and he released her, wishing he had a few more minutes to let her know how much he'd missed her today.

"Love you," he whispered into her ear, and she surprised him by shouting in front of everyone.

"I'm completely in love with you, Steve! Do you hear me, Steve Aimes? I love you!"

He laughed and saluted her with his drumstick before hurrying out on stage and settling onto the stool behind his drum kit. For the first night since the tour started, because they were using the same stage every opening act, his kit didn't rise out of the stage. But he didn't need the grand entrance to feel like he was on top of the world. That wonderful woman waiting for him in the wings was all he needed to elevate his game.

He let the rhythm consume him, scarcely aware of the rest of the band and their typical theatrics. They followed the beat, not the other way around, and could always count on him to deliver the tempo with precision, enthusiasm, and every piece of his soul. His muscles strained with each downbeat, his breath heaved, and sweat began to flow down his neck, back and chest. Soon it was dripping off his elbows and made his hair so wet, it stuck to his face and throat. The only time he paused during the set was to chug water between songs before diving into the next rhythm. Each drum progression was unique and familiar and fun. Steve lived for this shit. He didn't care about the cameras being on him, what Max was saying to the crowd, or that there even *was* a crowd. When he was playing, his ego took a back seat to his need to produce a perfect cadence.

For the next hour, music was his only love, his life, his entire reason for existing. He broke a stick during "Bite,"—not unusual since he hit the snare with uncompromising force the entire chorus—but it wasn't his usual tech, who handed him a fresh stick. It was Roux. When she smiled at him, he stumbled over the beat. That had never happened to him before. Not in the studio. Not during a jam session. And certainly not during a live show.

He found his rhythm easily again, muscle memory guiding him through the rest of the song as thoughts spun chaotically through his head. He didn't want to tell Roux she was a distraction during the show—even though she obviously was. He liked that she was there, was watching him closely enough to hand him a stick when he needed one, but if her presence resulted in his making mistakes, he'd have to ask her to keep her distance. Would she understand or be hurt? He chugged down another liter of water, wiped his face on a towel, and while Max was yammering on about who the hell knew what, he beckoned Roux over with a crooked finger.

She kept low as she creeped up behind his drum kit. He removed one of his earplugs so he could hear.

"Sorry I messed you up," she whispered. "I won't bother you again."

"You didn't bother me. I was just surprised. But maybe my tech should hand me new sticks."

She nodded and blotted his lower back with a towel. "And I can be your towel girl?"

He chuckled. "You have to stay out of sight, love. You're a total distraction."

She nodded, and he was glad there were none of the hurt feelings in her gaze that he'd expected. "But after the show?"

"You can water me, towel me, and stick me as much as you please."

She grinned. "I'd kiss you, but I can see you need to concentrate." She nodded in the direction beyond the front of his drum kit where the entire band and a good portion of the UK were all staring at him, waiting for him to begin the next song.

Roux scrambled out of sight. He shoved his earplug back into place, pounding out the intro to "Rebel in You" before Max could tease him about failing at his job. After three encores and a lengthy set of bows, Steve dashed off the stage, only one thing on his mind now that the show was over. He found his one thing surrounded by her sisters, all fangirling over Reagan.

"Oh my God, that cello piece is superb," Iona said. "I wonder if Cecelia would consider joining our band and adding in some cello."

Steve had no idea who Cecelia was—another sister, perhaps. He couldn't keep them all straight. He also couldn't keep his head on straight when Roux was near. He stepped up beside her and slipped his arm around her lower back. She started and then graced him with a beautiful smile before turning against his chest and pulling his head down for a lengthy kiss.

When she pulled away, she used her fingertips to trace paths through the sweat still wetting his throat. "Raven is going to kill me for getting Aimes sweat all over my costume."

"There's only one solution," he said, nibbling on her ear as he inhaled her scent. Performing always made him hornier than a triceratops. "Take it off."

"We have an after-party to attend. Mandatory. Your band invited us, if you were wondering."

And by his band, he was sure she meant Sam.

Typically the only thing he loved more than performing was celebrating at a wild party, consuming whatever mind-altering substance was readily available, and finding some interesting female to assuage his lust. But tonight he would much rather sneak away and celebrate in private with Roux. She was the only interesting female he cared to fuck, and he liked to keep his wits about himself when she was near. She made him think, made him laugh, made him feel more alive than any drug he'd tried—and he'd tried them all. He should probably consider marrying the woman. He smiled at the thought. Now there was an idea he never thought he'd sport again after the way Bianca had destroyed the beauty of love for him. And then Roux had happened. Not only had she rebuilt his desire to love and be loved, but had advanced those needs until he knew he couldn't live without them—without her—in his life.

"How long do we have to stay?" he asked. "I want you bare from head to toe. I haven't seen you out of your costume since this morning."

"Are you complaining about how hot I look in this corset?" She tried to give him a stern look, but her mouth twisted into a smile.

"I know for a fact that you look even hotter out of it." He kissed her nose. "And I miss your freckles when you're wearing all this makeup."

"And I suppose you prefer pink lips over black."

His thoughts immediately turned south. "I'm sure the lips I'm thinking of tasting are always pink, but yeah, I prefer your mouth pink too."

She leaned close and whispered into his ear. "Are you sure you don't want to see what my black mouth looks like circling your cock?"

He groaned and pulled her against his bare chest. "Now that you mention it . . ."

"You're getting her all sweaty," Raven complained loudly.

"I'm just getting started," he assured her.

"What, you can't keep your hands off her for a couple of hours?"

"Hell no." Now that their secret was out in the open, he hadn't just let off the brakes, he'd removed them entirely.

"The helicopter is landing!" Reagan shouted, and hugged the nearest person, who happened to be Max.

"Helicopter?" Steve glanced around and found Sam beaming with pride.

"Only the best for my stars," he said.

"Who authorized this expense?" Max asked, patting Reagan, who was shaking with excitement.

"Don't worry about that. You're going to make a grand entrance at the castle after-party."

"What castle?" Max asked.

"The one you rented for the night. I'd say ladies first, but we all know who the guests really want to see. The helicopter will come back and get the pretty ones after they drop off our meal tickets." Sam had the nerve to laugh at his own joke.

"Are you daft?" Max asked him. "You keep reminding us that our record sales are down, and then you rent a castle and a helicopter for an after-party? What is wrong with you?"

"Keeping up appearances," Sam said. "Now hurry. Time is money, and you're wasting time. Be sure to schmooze your asses off. Your fifty ultra-VIP guests' tickets more than paid for the helicopter, the hall rental, and the open bar."

"Un-fucking-believable," Steve grumbled, his previous good mood turning sour in an instant. He scarcely felt the swift kiss he offered Roux before he left her and climbed aboard the helicopter with his bandmates. The only one who was remotely excited about their flight was Reagan.

"Can we reevaluate when we'll fire that dumbass?" Steve said, speaking loudly to be heard over the helicopter blades. "I know we decided to wait until after the tour, but if he keeps pulling this sort of extravagant bullshit, we need to ax him immediately."

"He said it's paid for," Max said.

"I wonder what he charged our so-called ultra-VIP guests," Dare said, likely doing the math in his head.

"If it's ten bucks, it's more than we're worth," Logan said with a laugh. He leaned toward the window and pointed down at a race circuit as they passed overhead. "They have motorcycle races down there. Speed bikes, not dirt, so more up Steve's alley than mine." He slapped Steve's knee. "Hey, maybe we should rent the track and some bikes and have a race."

Steve was too pissed to be slightly tempted by thoughts of racing a bike around the track. He refused to even admit that it sounded fun. Beyond the racetrack were fields of tents—the campsites of festivalgoers.

"So what are we going to do about Sam?" he asked, still talking loudly.

"I'll talk to him," Max yelled. "Try to reel him in a bit."

"How about I reel him in completely by firing him? Tonight. I'm tired of his bullshit."

"The lawyers advise against it," Dare said.

Steve scowled. "What lawyers?"

"You don't think we should forge ahead without legal advice, do you?" Max said.

Steve hadn't thought about seeking legal counsel. He just wanted Sam to be gone. He turned to Logan. "Did you know about the lawyers?"

Logan shook his head.

Steve glanced from Dare to Max and back again. "So you two took it upon yourselves to hire lawyers without consulting me and Lo?"

"Oh, look at it!" Reagan squealed, pointing out the window at a large gray stone castle.

It was more of a rectangle than the sweeping spires Steve envisioned when he thought of castles, but impressive nonetheless. Had they really needed to rent a helicopter to fly such a short distance? How far had they flown? A mile or two? They could have easily walked that distance. Maybe not through the crowds that were making their way to the campgrounds between the racetrack and Donington Hall, but he didn't need all the extravagance to feel like a rock star.

Steve's stomach dropped as the helicopter descended rapidly toward a wide-open field near the castle. He hadn't realized it before, but there were a lot of open fields around the place. It reminded him of his family home—sans the castle, racetrack, and thousands of tents.

"It's my usual team of lawyers," Dare said, drawing Steve's attention back to the conversation. "I've also involved my accountant and my financial advisor."

"And his psychic and palm reader," Logan added.

Dare ignored the lame taunt. He had never been easy to bait, unless the cheap shots involved his younger brother. "We aren't talking about just firing Baily. We're going to destroy him legally and financially. He'll never work in the entertainment industry again when we're through with him. So be patient, okay? These things take time, and the less suspicious Sam is, the less he'll try to cover his tracks, the more mistakes he'll make, and the better our case."

Steve did like the sound of destroying Sam legally and financially and knew they were doing the industry a favor by taking him down. Steve wasn't sure how much longer he could be patient, however. Max had been keeping him on a tight rein for years, so now that he'd been given a bit of slack—of hope—he was chomping at the bit to run with this.

"Are you going after his fucking tabloid too?" Reagan asked, her face tightening into scowl. So she had been paying attention and not just gawking at the pretty castle. "You know how many people have been hurt by that stupid paper."

The tabloid had hurt Reagan more than anyone, though it had tried to cut Steve and the rest of the band down as well. As a veteran of having shit spewed about him, Steve hadn't been bothered by the most recent stories at all. He didn't care what strangers thought of him.

"It will be dealt with," Dare said, rubbing his sister-in-law's lower back. "We're working on a libel case, but we're not sure it will fly. Tabloids are very good at leading the reader to believe their lies without actually stating them as facts. Unfortunately, that falls under freedom of speech laws."

"Freedom of nastiness, you mean?" Reagan's scowl didn't lessen.

"You're going after Bianca's tabloid?" Steve asked. Not that he minded. He just never thought of the dumb tabloid as a huge issue. Not in the same league as Sam's alleged embezzling, in any case.

The helicopter touched down lightly, but Steve was far from ready for this important conversation to be over. It wasn't often that the five of them got to be entirely alone together where they didn't have to worry about being overheard. Steve jerked his head toward the pilot, but the man was too busy with his control panels to pay them any mind. He hoped those headphones the pilot wore had blocked their conversation from potentially spying ears.

"It's not her tabloid at all anymore, though she did manage to keep her job," Dare said. "Tradespar West bought the *American Inquirer* out about six months ago, just days after Bianca filed for bankruptcy. Her bankruptcy case was then withdrawn. My lawyer is still digging for the connection between the events, but I have a feeling the specifics are known only by Sam and Bianca."

Bankruptcy? After all the money he'd handed her in the divorce? And the only connection he knew of between Sam and Bianca was Exodus End—specifically Steve himself. "So when was I going to be informed about all of this?" Steve asked.

"We didn't want to bother you," Dare said with a grin. "You've been happy for the past few days. I was enjoying the new Steve, who isn't pissed off all the time."

Steve hadn't been pissed off *all* the time. Just most of the time. But he silently thanked Dare for giving him a few days to be ignorantly, blissfully happy.

The loud chop of the helicopter blades began to wind down, so they didn't have to talk quite as loud.

"Dare gets a report from his team every Friday," Max said. "It's not like we've been sitting on this information for long."

"Long enough for him to tell you," Steve pointed out.

"Yeah, well, I pester him."

Dare chuckled. "He does."

The door opened. Two members of Exodus End's security team helped them disembark and rushed them toward the building. Steve instinctually ducked as he passed beneath the slowly turning helicopter blades and followed his group toward the castle. He wasn't sure what he'd been expecting, but the place was decorated in fine elegance. He felt like he should be wearing a tuxedo and congratulating a bride and groom. The party of congregated guests applauded as the band entered a dining hall. Fine china, crystal glassware, silver utensils, and impeccable white linens decorated round tables. Flowers perfumed the air, and tapered candles offered an atmospheric glow to their surroundings. Steve and each of his bandmates were seated at separate tables with five eager strangers, so there was no way to continue discussing their future. Getting rid of Sam was top priority, but he wondered if they all envisioned the same goals once they were free to do what they pleased. Steve tried smiling and being friendly with the ultra-VIPs, but his thoughts kept returning to the situation with Sam.

When Baroquen entered the room about a half hour later, Roux was separated from her bandmates and seated at her very own table of strangers too. He knew she had her bullet clenched tightly in her fist as her troubled gaze met his across the room. If it weren't for Sam and his ridiculous events, the two of them could be enjoying some alone time in his hotel room right now.

God, he hated Sam. And soon he'd be rid of him for good.

BY THE TIME STEVE AND ROUX CRAWLED into bed after their VIP dinner, it was almost dawn. Their meal had consisted of ten courses, one for each table. Luckily, they'd been served tapas-style fare with a minimum of twenty minutes per table, so his stomach hadn't exploded from overindulgence, but he was uncomfortably full. For each course, the rock stars had switched tables so that every small group of ultra-VIPs got to interact with each of them. Once he'd let his anger toward Sam go—a little—he'd enjoyed interacting with the wealthiest of their fans. They were good people. He felt an instant connection with rock music fans no matter where in the world he happened to be. At least here in the UK, they spoke *mostly* the same language.

Unable to consider doing anything remotely energetic after such a long night, he spooned against Roux's back and let weariness pull him toward sleep. Today was a travel day, so at least Butch wouldn't be banging on the door in two hours to get him into the gym, but the band's taskmaster *would* be there in four, demanding that he get his ass on the plane so they could make their way to London for tomorrow night's show.

"Have you ever been too tired to sleep?" Roux murmured.

Apparently not, because the next thing he knew, Zach was standing over his bed, shaking him awake. Fuck. He'd forgotten he'd given Zach a key. What kind of ass used it to barge into a man's room and wake him up at—Steve glanced at the clock—noon. *Noon!*

"Babe?" He shook Roux gently, but she mumbled something that sounded a lot like *fuck off* before pulling the covers over her head.

"Why didn't anyone wake me?" Steve asked, shifting his feet

over the edge of the bed, putting his elbows on his thighs, and leaning forward to rub his face with both hands. It was times like these that he wished he hadn't given up cocaine. When running on a few hours of sleep, it sure beat coffee. "Weren't we supposed to be in the air at eleven?"

"The jet is making two flights today. It should be back soon to pick up the rest of us. Max said to let you sleep."

Steve snorted. "Since when does Max have my best interests at heart?"

"He's in a really good mood," Zach said, nibbling on a fingertip. "It's almost frightening."

"I figured Max would take the fact that I was right about Sam and he was wrong less graciously than he has."

Roux sat up. "Right about Sam how?"

Steve really should tell her their plans. He trusted her not tell anyone, but what if she was brought to trial, and had to testify under oath? If something like that led to Sam getting off on a technicality due to some contract provision, he'd never forgive himself.

"He's a douche," Steve said.

"We all get to ride on the jet today." Zach beamed at Roux. "Even you and me."

She didn't look overly thrilled by the news. "I think I've been in the air more over the past three days than I've been on the ground," she said, wrapping the sheet around her as she climbed to her feet and stumbled toward the bathroom.

Steve turned to Zach. "Do you realize what glorious sight I missed just now because you're here?"

Zach shrugged. "Eh, you've seen her naked before. Guess who texted me this morning?"

Steve cringed. "Please don't say Enrique."

"Enrique!"

"What did he want?"

"He says he misses me and knows a place where we can be alone together for a couple of days."

"Alone so that no one will know he's seeing you." Steve filled in a blank.

"I don't care if anyone knows," Zach said.

"Yes, you do."

Zach sighed and flopped down on the bed beside Steve. "I haven't texted him back with an answer yet," he said. "But I want to."

So there was hope. Zach just needed some support, and he'd be able to make the right decision, which Steve sincerely believed was telling Enrique to fuck off. Zach deserved a hell of a lot more consideration than that prick had ever shown him.

"Hey, Roux?" Steve called.

"Can't a woman pee in peace?"

Zach grinned. "Someone is cranky this morning."

"She prefers to be awoken slowly and gently, with kisses on her lips and then deeper kisses on her other lips." He wondered if they'd have time to reenact her preferred awakening before they had to leave.

Zach crinkled his nose. "*Eww.*"

"Mmm, pussy. I go at it all morning like . . ." He showed off some of his more impressive tongue skills just to make Zach gag. Steve then smashed Zach flat with one arm while making all sorts of juicy sounds with his mouth next to Zach's ear. "You like that don't you, sweet pussy?"

"Oh God, please make it stop." Zach squirmed wildly, trying to escape Steve's crude torture.

Roux cleared her throat. "What exactly is going on out here?"

"He's showing me how he eats you out," Zach said.

Her horrified expression made both Steve and Zach burst out laughing.

She shook her head. "And you two wonder why people get the wrong idea about your relationship."

"Nah," Steve said. "We get it. We just don't care."

"If you're worried, don't be," Zach said. "He loves pussy almost as much as it grosses me out."

"Well, pardon my genitals," Roux said. "You should probably leave now, because they're about to be exposed."

Steve made a fist of victory. "Aw, yeah."

"Gross," Zach said, scrambling off the bed. "I'll see you all on the plane."

"Don't text him," Steve said, knowing Zach would know what he meant. Steve would have to keep a close eye on Zach if he wanted him to stay strong when faced with Enrique's million-dollar smile—or dick—or whatever it was about the actor that Zach liked.

"I won't."

Steve didn't believe him, but he didn't stop him from leaving. Zach was a grown man, and Steve no longer felt like babysitting. Not when Roux was looking at him like she wanted him for breakfast.

"Are you hungry?" he asked as soon as Zach had left the room. "Craving anything special?"

Her gaze flicked down to his crotch. "Sausage."

"I don't think that's a vegetarian option."

"I'll make an exception." She dropped her sheet and crawled up onto the bed with him.

"Say, I always wondered: Do vegans swallow? Cum is definitely an animal product."

She paused with her mouth inches from his already hard cock and looked up at him. He hoped he hadn't made her reconsider her morning meal choice by cracking jokes.

"That's the main reason I'm not vegan," she said. "Milk and eggs are good and all, but cum? Can't live without it."

"God, I love you."

She didn't return his sentiment. Her mouth was already full.

"I WANT TO SEE EVERYTHING," Roux said, craning her neck to locate landmarks from the jet's window. "Buckingham Palace, Big Ben, the Tower of London, all the museums."

Steve yawned exaggeratedly, but he was only teasing. He'd take her anywhere she'd like to go.

"How far is Stonehenge from here?"

"No idea."

She turned, the excitement in her eyes melting him.

"You've never been there?"

He shook his head, ready for any adventure as long as she was beside him.

"We're not doing that lame stuff today," Raven said. "We're going shopping!"

Roux lifted an eyebrow. "With what money?"

"The plastic kind." Raven made a fist and pulled her elbow back toward her ribs. "Ka-ching!"

"We're in *London*. You can go shopping anywhere," Roux pointed out. "You don't even have to put on pants or leave the house to shop."

"It's not the same," Raven said.

"We decided on shopping while you *involved* twats were with your men," Azura said, nudging Iona, who was so involved in her discussion with Kyle that she merely swatted at Azura. "You were outvoted three to zero since we don't accept absentee ballots. And your men aren't invited."

Roux squeezed Steve's hand as if she expected him to try to escape. As much as he wanted to spend the day with her, he knew it was important for her to have girls-only time with her sisters.

"We'll go shopping," Lily said, "but only if our men can come."

Jack's eyes met Steve's and, with teeth clenched, he shook his head, a sure sign that he wanted rescuing. Steve would do whatever it took to rescue one of his drummer idols from shopping.

"We don't want to shop," Steve said. "We'd rather pub crawl."

"I'm up for that," Azura said.

"No changing your vote!" Sage poked her. "We decided on shopping."

"The women will shop, the men will pub crawl," Iona said, no room for argument in her tone.

It was too bad she was already involved with Kyle Schultz; she was perfect for Max. Though maybe they were too much alike to get along. Max would probably argue with her constantly, which might take away from his time arguing with Steve and that would take all the joy out of Max's life.

"Are there pubs in the shopping district?" Roux asked.

"Probably," Steve said.

"So we can split up for the afternoon—women shop, men drink." She stuck out her tongue and made a face of disgust. "Then meet up for dinner and go from there."

He drew her hand up to press against his cheek and kissed her wrist.

"That's our Roux." Raven rolled her eyes. "Always compromising."

"What's wrong with compromising?"

"Nothing," Steve said. "As long as you get something for yourself." He knew she really wanted to go the sightseeing, touristy route today.

"I get to spend time with my sisters, and later with you, and don't have to go to any pubs. All win."

He kissed her wrist again, grateful that he'd fallen in love with a positive person. He was having a hard time remembering why he'd fallen for his first wife. She'd been so different from Roux. Always negative and bullheaded. Never satisfied. It was Bianca's way or no way. She never even attempted to compromise. He'd been miserable. Even more miserable than he'd realized at the time.

"Do you want to get married?" Steve asked Roux.

She smiled gently. "Maybe someday."

"To me, I mean?"

Her smile widened, crinkling her nose and the corners of her eyes. "Maybe someday."

It wasn't a no. He could work with that.

When they landed, a shuttle waited for them. Steve tipped the driver well for making suggestions that would fit their plans and for dropping them off on London's West End instead of taking them to the hotel. Steve called Logan, who'd arrived on the first jet, and asked if he wanted to join them. He told him to round up as many guys—Max, Dare, the guys of Sinners and their opening band, Riott Actt—as he could find, and even remembered to invite the ladies to shop if they wanted to tag along.

They chose the closest restaurant for their regrouping and made a dinner reservation for thirty as they weren't sure how many people would be joining them. When it was time to part, he drew Roux against him and kissed her as if he wouldn't see her for months rather than a handful of hours. He pressed a credit card into her hand.

"Buy yourself something nice," he said.

Her eyes widened, and she tried to give the piece of plastic back. "No!"

"It will make me happy."

"I'm not using your credit card."

"It has your name on it."

"It does not."

She held it up to her face and discovered that he wasn't lying. He'd planned for her to have it for emergencies and had been carrying it around for over a week looking for the right time to give it to her. This time seemed right. And he didn't want her to use it just for emergencies. He wanted her to spoil herself as much as he wanted to spoil her.

"What the hell, Steve? Did you steal my Social Security number and apply for credit in my name? How did you get this?"

"It's my account," he said. "I had your name added as an authorized user. I wanted you to have it for emergencies."

"Shopping is not an emergency."

"Yeah, it is!" Raven said, nudging Roux with her elbow. "Take it."

"I will not."

Steve tried to think of a way to trigger Roux's natural tendency to compromise.

"I don't like to shop," he said. "I thought maybe you could get me some new clothes or . . ." He shrugged. "Some sexy underwear or something."

She looked down at the credit card again, obviously weighing her options. If he could get her to accept it, maybe eventually she'd start using it on herself.

"And socks," he said. "I could use some socks."

"Steve," she said, pressing her hand to his chest and looking up at him. "I know what you're doing."

He opened his eyes wide, feigning innocence. "I'm serious. When does a famous rock star have time to buy socks?" He threw his hands out wide.

She pursed her lips and shook her head.

"Please," he said, wriggling his toes in his shoes. "Help a guy's feet out here."

"Fine." She tucked the card into her purse.

He forced himself not to crow over his small victory.

"I'll buy you socks," she added.

"And if you find something nice for yourself, you should—"

She covered his lips with her fingertips. "I'm not buying anything for myself on your credit card."

"I'll work on her," Raven promised. Steve was glad he had at least one of her sisters on his side. "She doesn't know how lucky she is."

"I do." Roux stretched up on tiptoe and replaced her fingers with a soft peck from her lips. "I just don't need material things to remind me."

"Come on, lover boy," Zach said, patting Steve on the back. "Beer beckons."

For the first time in his life, Steve thought holding a woman's purse while she tried on clothes sounded better than drinking beer with his friends. He resisted the urge to grab his crotch just to make sure his balls were still where they belonged.

"Love you," he whispered to Roux, letting her go only when Raven forcibly pulled her away.

"Love you, sweetie," Roux called, walking backwards and waving at him. He wasn't the least bit embarrassed that her loud confession and horrendous pet name turned the heads of several bystanders.

Once she turned around, he kept watching her as her sisters drew her close.

"He gave her his fucking credit card," Raven said.

He didn't hear their responses—they were now too far away—but he smiled to himself and followed Zach into the nearest pub.

THEY WERE ON THEIR THIRD PUB, and Steve, who was answering Roux's text asking what size socks he wore, was on his fifth beer. Suddenly their cozy group of four guys became a rowdy crowd of twenty as all the members of Exodus End, Sinners, and Riott Actt—plus a few crew members and significant others—entered the bar. A few minutes later, a familiar burgundy-haired pest slunk into the bar, her eyes watchful.

"What is *she* doing here?" Reagan—who much preferred hanging out with the guys to shopping—asked Steve. "Is it illegal to throat chop bitches in London?"

"Technically, she's doing her job," Steve said, turning his back on Tamara, who, as usual, was watching him more closely than anyone. "But feel free to throat chop at will and hope for legal immunity."

"If she so much as looks at me cross-eyed, I'm throat chopping." Reagan jerked down her hand in a wannabe karate strike. "And why the fuck is she smiling like that?"

"Will you just ignore her?" Trey said, wrapping an arm around his wife's lower back. "She isn't bothering you."

Some of the tension eased from Reagan's rigid spine, and she released a heavy breath. "I hope Toni's article does more good than harm."

Article? Steve vaguely remembered Toni interviewing Reagan on the jet as they crossed the Atlantic several days ago. Steve wondered how the world would handle Reagan's polygamy, especially since it was the woman with multiple husbands and not the other way around.

"Her words will make the world love us as much as Ethan does," Trey said.

Reagan laughed. "I don't think that's possible. Where is Ethan, anyway?"

Trey nodded toward the big dark-haired man in the corner, who for once wasn't wearing his neon orange shirt announcing him as a member of Exodus End's security team. Ethan still looked like a guy no one should mess with, however, and he was watching his husband and wife closely as he sipped on a beer. Though it was true that the marriage between the three of them wasn't legal, it was obviously binding. And a bit weird in Steve's opinion, but hey, other people's love affairs were none of his business. If they were even half as happy together as he was with Roux, he wished them the best.

"He looks lonely," Reagan said. "Maybe we should go keep him company."

"You read my mind." To Steve, Trey said, "Will you excuse us?" before guiding Reagan to the corner of the room. She kissed Ethan's jaw, and the naturally tan man turned white, his eyes darting to the spot behind Steve where he'd last seen Tamara. Steve set his beer down and decided now would be a great time to confront her, since she'd slunk off the last time he'd attempted it. And maybe if he distracted her, she wouldn't notice the obvious chemistry between Reagan and her two husbands. Without another second's hesitation, he stalked in Tamara's direction.

Someone grabbed Steve's arm, drawing him to an abrupt halt. "What are you going to do?" Zach asked.

"Ask her why she's here." And also why she was always watching him, because it was creepy as hell.

"Do you need backup?"

"Nope."

Zach let Steve's arm slip from his grip and took a seat at a nearby table—undoubtedly so he could provide backup should Steve change his mind.

Tamara watched Steve's approach, and the smug smile she had plastered on her face rivaled the one Sam Baily typically sported.

"Why do you have to be such a pain in the ass?" Steve said, sitting across from her without waiting for an invitation. "Nothing's going to happen here that will be remotely interesting to your readers."

"I just came to unwind." Her smug grin widened.

"What are you smiling about?"

"Oh, nothing." But she kept right on smiling.

"Are you going to leave?"

"Are you asking me to leave?"

"Yes."

She shook her head. "I want to watch it all go down."

"Watch what go down?"

"Oh, nothing."

Steve was about to call Reagan over to deliver that throat chop she'd promised but decided instead to try making Tamara as uncomfortable as she was currently making him. Maybe he'd get some answers, or maybe she'd leave. He'd be satisfied with either outcome.

"How do you know Sam Baily?" he asked, leaning his elbows on the table.

That wiped the smug look off her face. "None of your business."

"So the lives of all my friends are everyone's business, but your life is nobody's? That doesn't seem fair, does it?"

"I know him through my sister." She shrugged. "Not that interesting, is it?"

"And how does Bianca know him? Why did he save her from bankruptcy?"

She crossed her arms and turned her face toward the wall beside her. "Why don't you ask her?"

"She doesn't answer my questions unless it's 'would you like some more money?' and I bet you can guess her answer to that one."

Tamara straightened, her eyes narrowing. "Don't you dare say anything bad about her. You ruined her in that divorce."

"I *ruined* her?" Steve laughed. "If anything, I protected her. I was stupid, I see that now. I was still in love with her at the time, but I've finally let all that go. I met someone who loves me for me, not for what I can do for her."

The smug smile returned to Tamara's face. "I can't wait to watch her dump you."

Steve frowned. "And why would she do that?"

"You'll see."

"What do you know that I don't know?"

"I'm not going to spoil the surprise." She pointed toward the door. "I think you might want to check on your friend, though."

Steve turned in time to see Zach dash out of the pub, and Steve was pretty sure he was crying. Oh fuck.

CHAPTER 30

ROUX LIFTED AN ADORABLE DESIGNER PURSE and checked the price tag. *Fifteen hundred pounds!* Surely the decimal place was off. She did some quick mental math on the exchange rate—two thousand bucks. Who the hell would spend two thousand bucks on a purse? That was a mortgage payment on a nice house. She set the purse down carefully, afraid that if she scuffed it, she'd be forced to buy it.

"You could get that for yourself," Raven said.

"And make payments on it for two years? No thanks."

"Put it on Steve's card. You know you want it. It's so cute."

Actually, no, she didn't want the reminder that she was broke. It was bad enough that she couldn't afford to buy him those socks he'd requested.

Maybe she could afford to add the bag's adorable matching coin purse to her collection. She squinted at the tag, hoping to make the price smaller. *Eighty pounds?* For a fucking coin purse? Perhaps she should start collecting thimbles instead.

Iona, who was trying on hats as if she'd been invited to a royal wedding, reached into her purse and pulled out her phone. "Google alert," she announced. She had dozens of them set up so that she'd know what anyone was saying about the band or its members on the Internet. She'd been getting a lot of them over the past couple days as people who'd attended the Download Festival had been posting about them. There had been a few slurs, but most of the attention had been positive.

"Will you stop obsessing?" Azura tried to take her phone from her hand. "We're supposed to be having fun as sisters today, not as bandmates."

Iona's eyes widened, and she glanced at Roux. Azura peeked at Iona's phone over her shoulder. Her face also registered shock before she looked at Roux. Iona clutched her phone to her chest and took a deep breath before stuffing the device back into her purse.

"You're right," Iona said. "Play today, work tomorrow."

"It was about me, wasn't it?" Roux said, digging through her purse for her own phone. All she had to do was search for her name on Google and she'd get the same results that the alert had shown Iona.

Iona grabbed Roux by the shoulders and crammed a hat on her head. "This hat is perfect for you." She forced Roux in front of the mirror and took her purse—the phone still inside—and handed it to Azura, who grabbed the nearest evening gown and made a beeline for the dressing room. Sage dashed after Azura while Iona, Raven, and Lily made a human wall around Roux to keep her in front of the mirror. The silly red hat with the feather shaped like a question mark was tugged from her head and replaced with a wide-brimmed black-checkered fedora. Roux knew her sisters well enough to know they were hiding something from her.

"I'm going to find out sooner or later," she said, removing the hat and passing it Iona. "What did it say?"

"It's not important," Iona said, but she drew Roux into a tight hug and squeezed her as if one of her favorite shelter dogs had been adopted by a dog-fighting ring.

"Was it about me and Steve? We were expecting our relationship to go public."

Iona crammed another hat on Roux's head. Was she fighting tears?

"How bad can it be?" Roux said.

"That motherfucker!" Azura bellowed from inside the dressing room. "I'm going to rip his entrails out through his ball sac and strangle him with them."

Roux's stomach dropped. "That bad, huh?" She pushed Lily aside and marched toward the dressing room, not slowed at all by Raven, who had her arms around Roux's waist and was trying to dig her feet into the carpet.

"The pictures are probably old," Iona said, chasing after her. "From before he met you."

Roux was trying not to jump to conclusions, but it sounded like what had her sisters so upset on her behalf was more about Steve than her. Roux checked under dressing room doors until she found the pairs of feet that belonged to Azura and Sage. She tried the knob, but the door was locked.

"Open this door and give me my damn phone!" Roux demanded, pounding on the door with her palm.

"That gown looks lovely on you," Sage said to Azura, as if Azura's outburst had never happened and Roux wasn't now trying to rip the door off its hinges.

"Roux," Iona said in her most calming alpha-bitch voice. "Let's go back to the hotel and we'll discuss this in private."

"Are you worried that I'll make a scene?" Roux spat, dropping to the floor and lying flat on her belly, squirming under the dressing room door. She got stuck when her butt—always too round, in her opinion—caught on the bottom of the door. "Oh, I'm about to make a fucking scene. Give me my damn phone!" She reached out and caught Azura around the ankle, trying to pull her down to her level. Her shoulder protested at the angle of her arm, but Roux refused to let a little pain stop her from getting her phone and finding out what had everyone so freaked out.

"Sage," Lily said calmly. "Unlock the door before she hurts herself."

The door latch clicked, and the bottom of the door scraped across Roux's back, forcing her to lie flat until she'd been freed. Lily helped her stand, and even though Roux didn't know exactly what all the drama was about, she could feel tears building inside her. Instead of directing her out of the store, Lily eased her into the dressing room. Raven and Iona squeezed in behind them and shuffled close so they could shut the door. Six grown women in a dressing room stall didn't offer much breathing room.

"Iona," Lily said, "tell her what to expect before we show her."

"I . . ." Iona sucked in a breath. "I don't want to."

"Steve," Azura blurted. "He's with some other chick. They're both naked and . . . and doing stuff."

Oh, was that all? Did they think she'd freak out over pictures of Steve's past lovers?

"I know he's been with other women," Roux said, taking deep breaths to calm her frayed nerves. "He is Steve Aimes, notorious womanizer."

"You're okay with him screwing around on you?" Azura blurted.

"Not cool, Roux," Iona said. "You deserve better."

"He wouldn't screw around on me. I mean I know that before we . . . got together . . . that he used to be with other women. A lot of other women, but now?"

"This was two days ago, dummy," Azura said. "Are you still okay with it?"

Roux's knees buckled, but Raven caught her to keep her from sinking to the floor.

"Not possible," she said. "I was with him almost all day. He couldn't have . . ." But how long would it take for Steve to find a woman willing to fuck him? Ten minutes? Ten seconds? "Let me see."

"Maybe now isn't the best time," Lily said, massaging Roux's shoulders in what she probably thought was a soothing manner, but which scraped Roux's already raw nerves until she wanted to climb out of her own skin.

"Let me see!" Roux demanded.

Once she saw, she wished she hadn't.

The room in the background was very familiar. She'd slept in it the night before, after all. The man sprawled naked across the bed was also very familiar. She happened to know his body as well as her own. The woman with his cock down her throat wasn't Roux, however. Roux couldn't see dick-sucking bitch's face clearly, because the majority of her image had been cropped out of the picture and the camera angle was terrible. The next picture—yes, there was more than one—showed the woman rubbing Steve's cock against her gaping pussy.

"Oh my God," Raven gasped.

The next showed the woman with her tit in Steve's mouth.

"He is going to pay," Azura growled. "No one treats one of my sisters like this. I hope he fucking enjoyed that repulsive dick of his while it was still attached to his body."

Azura squirmed her way through their tight huddle and forced the door open. Iona caught her before she could escape.

"Roux decides how we proceed," Iona said. "Not you."

Roux decides . . .

The next picture showed the woman straddling Steve's hips—their bodies undoubtedly joined. She was holding her breasts as she fucked him. The tattoo on the woman's forearm caught Roux's attention. She didn't have to see her face to know who it was.

"It's . . . it's T-T-Tamara," she said, her tight throat strangling her.

"What?" Iona spat.

"The journalist?" Raven asked, her voice squeaking. "Steve's sister-in-law? The woman he supposedly hates? *That* Tamara?"

Roux nodded and handed the phone to the nearest hand, unable to force herself to look at another image. "I recognize her tattoo."

"Maybe she photoshopped herself on him," Sage said quietly.

Roux tried to cling to that possibility, but how would Tamara have pictures of him naked in that particular room in order to doctor dirty pictures in the first place?

"I need to talk to him," Roux said, shoving everyone out of her way and stumbling out of the hot and stuffy dressing room. She rushed forward, running toward the exit. They hadn't made it too far from the bar where she'd left him behind. There was no sense in her wondering what had happened when she could ask the son of a bitch herself. Her sisters caught up with her quickly, some trying to stop her, others offering support. She was so blinded by fury and hurt that she wasn't even sure what was being said to her, who was holding her hand, who squeezed her shoulder, patted her back. Roux burst through the front door of the bar and several patrons glanced up from their drinks in surprise. A quick look around told her that Steve was no longer there.

"Can I help you?" the bartender asked.

"There were four men in here earlier," she said. "Long-haired. Tattooed. Did you see where they went?"

"Sorry, luv. I just started my shift."

"They couldn't have gotten far," Lily said. "I'll call Jack and ask where they are now."

"No," Roux said. "I don't want Steve forewarned." She figured he'd be more likely to tell her the truth if he didn't have time to fabricate lies.

"Maybe we should spread out a little," Azura said. "The first one to find him gets to kick him in the nuts."

Iona crossed her arms over her chest, her jaw set in a harsh line. "I want to hear what he has to say for himself."

"He'll still be able to talk," Azura said. "He'll just be doing it as a soprano."

Sage and Azura headed across the street to check the pubs there. Iona and Lily went back the way they came, and Roux headed farther up the street with Raven trying to keep up.

"This doesn't make any sense," Raven said. "Why would he do *that* with her? He hates her."

Supposedly. It sure didn't look like he hated Tamara when they were alone together. Roux squeezed her eyes shut, trying to erase the vile images from her mind, but it was no use. If anything, the pictures of him with that odious bitch became even more vivid when Roux's eyes were closed.

Roux entered the next bar. The guys weren't there, but the bartender remembered them. They were headed in the right direction. Unless they'd chosen a chaotic path. Maybe she should have allowed Lily to contact Jack. This hunt could be a huge waste of time. The next bar was also Steve-free, but he'd been in that one too.

"They must be chugging their drinks," Raven said, scurrying behind Roux as she marched toward the next bar.

Roux's anger wasn't cooling. The longer she looked for him, the more enraged she became.

They must be getting close; there was a hell of a loud party going on in a bar up the street.

"What am I going to say to him?" Roux asked Raven, struck suddenly with overwhelming emotion. She couldn't allow herself cry in front of him. Cheating assholes weren't worth a single tear.

"I wouldn't say anything," Raven said. "Let him talk himself into the deep hole he belongs in. He knows what he did. He just didn't think you'd find out."

Roux stopped walking a couple of doors down from the pub and squeezed her bullet in her hand. She took a deep breath to calm her nerves and another to steel them.

"Why would she post those pictures online?" Roux said, her anger cooling long enough to allow her more logical side a moment to ponder.

"Bragging rights," Raven said.

Roux's eyes narrowed. "That does sound like her."

"And she probably wants you guys to break up."

"I hate to give her what she wants," Roux said, her heart twisting. She loved Steve; that hadn't changed. But could she forgive him for this? If it had been any other woman in the world, maybe. But Tamara? Argh! How could he?

Raven squeezed her hand. "Are you ready? I've got your back. But if you want to call our sisters and wait for them, we can hang here on the sidewalk until they get here."

Extra backup would be nice, but Roux was already losing her nerve. She'd never been able to hold on to rage for long.

"Show me the pictures again," she said, waving a hand toward Raven's purse. She wasn't sure where hers had gone. Hopefully one of her sisters had it.

Raven took a step back. "What?"

"Show me!"

"I don't think—"

"I'm not all that pissed off anymore, and if I go in there now—"

"You're going to cave the second he melts you with those eyes of his. Okay, I get it."

Raven unlocked her phone's screen and after locating the pictures, made gagging noises and handed the phone to Roux. Roux tried looking at the images objectively. Now that the shock had worn off a bit, maybe she'd see something in the pictures that she could use against him. Honestly, she was looking for something to excuse him, but it was all there clear as day. He had fucked Tamara, and later that very same night, he'd fucked Roux. There weren't enough condoms in the world to block that cross contamination.

Roux growled, her anger fully restored, and rushed into the open door of the bar. She scanned the room for Steve, and though she saw dozens of familiar faces, she couldn't locate the one she was looking for.

"Hey!" Logan shouted. "Glad you joined us." He shoved a glass of amber liquid into her hand. "You look like you could use a drink."

Agreeing for the first time in her life, she chugged the liquor, the alcohol burning down her throat like fire.

"Where's Steve?" Raven asked, yelling over the noise. She took the empty glass from Roux's trembling fingers and set it on a nearby table.

"He was here a few minutes ago." Logan glanced around. "Maybe he's in the bathroom."

Raven stood on tiptoe and searched the pub. "I'll go check." She rushed off in the direction of the clearly marked restroom.

"You want another drink?" Logan asked.

Not understanding what had gotten into her, Roux nodded. She'd liked the taste of that last drink, and she really liked the dizziness that had rushed to her head, and even enjoyed the heat that flushed her skin. She was on her third whiskey when Raven returned.

"He's not in the bathroom," Raven said. She stared pointedly at the nearly empty glass in Roux's hand. "Are you drinking?"

"So?"

"I thought . . ." Raven tried to take the drink out of her hand, but Roux swallowed it down to protect it from thievery. "Roux, you don't drink."

"I can drink if I want to drink!" She shoved Raven out of her way and headed for the bar. What she needed was more drinks, not fewer.

"I didn't say you *couldn't* drink," Raven said when she caught up to Roux. "I said you *don't* drink."

"Yeah, well, people change." Roux's face was numb, and her tongue felt strangely thick, but it didn't get in the way of her swallowing another whiskey. Why had she sworn off alcohol? This stuff was great. She ordered another.

"Take it easy," Raven said, trying to take the glass from Roux's hand. "How many have you had?"

"Not enough."

"You're not used to drinking."

"So?"

"So you don't know your limit."

"Don't . . ." What was the word she was looking for? "Don't . . . tell . . ."

"Don't tell you what to do? Is that what you're too drunk to say?"

Roux nodded, the sudden motion making her head swim. She pressed her hand to her face and tried to wipe the numbness away, but she couldn't feel anything—inside or out—and that was a blessing.

Someone entered the pub, and she perked up, hoping it was Steve—she so wanted to see him even if she couldn't remember why—but it was just Lily and right behind her, Iona. A flash of burgundy in the corner near the door drew Roux's attention. Her breath caught. Tamara was here. Tamara was smirking at her. Tamara had touched him. Had *fucked* him.

An uncontrollable rage filled Roux's entire body. She rose to her feet, both fists raised, and shouldered her way through the crowd. She was going to fucking kill that whore.

CHAPTER 31

STEVE CLIMBED OUT of the cab at Heathrow Airport and searched for directional signs or signs of his idiot friend. He couldn't believe Zach was running back to Enrique. At least he'd been thoughtful enough to let Steve know where he was going so he could stop him. All he'd messaged was *I'm going back to LA. Enrique needs me.* But that was enough to allow Steve to give chase. He knew it was stupid to interfere in someone else's love life, but now that he had Roux, now that he knew how perfect a relationship could be when it was based on mutual respect and trust and compromise, he was happy to pass on endless words of advice whether Zach wanted to hear them or not. He was scanning the departure board for flights to Los Angeles when he got a text from Logan.

Don't look now, but she's at it again.

Steve didn't have time to decipher cryptic messages. He had to butt into Zach's business before the fool did something he'd regret.

There were four flights to Los Angeles in the next two hours. Steve would have to buy a ticket to one of them and hunt Zach down terminal by terminal. The process would be greatly complicated if Zach's flight wasn't nonstop. Or if he happened to be flying out of a different airport. Or if he had a connecting flight in some bizarre country that had flights out of an obscure terminal. But Steve would worry about those possibilities if or when he'd exhausted his options here. He'd been texting Zach for hints to his whereabouts, but so far, he hadn't answered. He probably knew that Steve would try to stop him.

He checked his phone as another message landed in his inbox—also not from Zach. Max? Max never texted him unless it was to give him the time and place for a band meeting.

Max's message had Steve scratching his head. *Dude, that is foul. Why would you risk what you have with Roux for that?* The text was punctuated with a green-faced vomiting emoji.

What kind of hallucinogenic drugs were his bandmates doing?

No idea what you're talking about. He'd just finished sending the same message to both Logan and Max when a third message—this one from Dare—arrived.

Your girlfriend is drinking.

Drinking? Roux? Surely Dare was mistaken. That or he didn't know which member of Baroquen was Steve's girlfriend.

Also from Dare: *Where are you? I think you have a major bomb to diffuse here.*

From Max: *Her, really? To each his own, but her? Foul.*

A picture from Logan downloaded. It showed Steve naked with some chick—who was too round to be Roux—riding him, her hands clutching her breasts and her head tilted back. Red hair, but not the coppery shade of Roux's. Burgundy—a color as fake as that picture had to be.

"What the fuck?" he said aloud, scanning his memory for the incident so conveniently caught in a photo. Scratch that—caught in *several* photos. Photos that arrived on his phone one after another. Steve had been with many, many women over the years, but he remembered each encounter, and he had no recollection of this one, or of that woman. Photoshopped? Had to be. But how? He squinted at the first picture, studying it closely.

Wait. Was that the bed he'd slept in last night in Donington? He flicked through the pictures, looking at the background. That was Donington. So they had to be phony. He hadn't slept with any women in Donington except Roux, and that woman sucking his cock there . . . Damn, she must be good at deep throat; she wasn't even straining, and they always strained when his impressive cock was involved.

He shook himself. *Focus, Steve.*

The woman sucking his cock was not Roux. And that was not Roux's tit in his mouth or her ass in his hand or . . . The tattoo on the woman's forearm looked familiar—dagger through a skull tattoo. Where had he seen it before? Burgundy hair . . .

A sour taste caught in the back of his throat. *Think, Steve, think.*

But his mind didn't want to grasp the reality of who it was. Every piece of him fought the realization for as long as possible.

A cold sweat trickled down his spine.

"Holy shit!" *Tamara*. No wonder Max had been calling foul. Tamara. He'd fucked Tamara.

But he hadn't. He couldn't have. He'd have ripped his own dick off and flushed it down the toilet if it had been engulfed by any of her odious holes. His skin began to crawl as he recalled he was a missing hour or two of his life, when he'd been dreaming that Roux had been trying to molest him while he'd been mostly unconscious. But that had been a dream. It had to have been a dream. The contrary was unthinkable.

Had Roux seen the pictures? She must have. What must she be thinking? He tried calling her, but she didn't answer. He sent her a text.

Please tell me you didn't see those pictures.

No response. He growled in frustration and slammed his phone on the ground. The screen shattered on impact.

"Shit!" Why had he done that? It was his only way of communicating with anyone.

He scooped up the ruined device and tried powering it on, but it didn't respond, no matter how many times he jabbed the fucking button.

"Shit, shit, shit!"

People were staring at him. He was used to being stared at. One did not look as good as he did without people staring on occasion, but they weren't looking at him with admiration or typical sexual interest. They were looking at him like he was crazy. At least there was one familiar person in that sea of judgmental faces.

"Zach!"

Steve waved, but Zach turned tail and ran. Should he go after him or return to Roux? How had his life gone from perfect to fucked up in the span of only a few minutes? He wasn't sure who he'd rather strangle at that moment, Tamara or Enrique. Hell, he had two hands. Why not choke them both?

CHAPTER 32

ROUX HAD NEVER HIT ANYONE out of spite before, so she was surprised by how much her knuckles hurt when they crashed into Tamara's smug mouth. Teeth, she thought blankly as her arm drew back and smashed against a rather hard cheekbone and then a jaw. She wasn't even sure what she was doing. She just wanted to hurt someone. Hurt someone like she was hurting. And the cause of all her pain was right there. Why not hurt her?

"You fucking bitch!" Roux screamed while Tamara covered her head with both arms and tried to crawl under the table. "Fight back, you cunt. Don't just take it. Fight back!"

What? No. Roux didn't want that. Someone else was using her mouth. Someone else was reaching under the table and yanking Tamara out of her hiding spot by her hair.

"You think it's okay to fuck another woman's man?" Roux spat—literally—in Tamara's no-longer-smug face.

Roux took another swing at her, but someone grabbed her wrist before it could connect.

"I saw him first!" Tamara shouted, showing a bit more bravado now that Roux was restrained. She backed into the nearest wall when Roux managed to wrestle free. Roux's hands had minds of their own as they circled Tamara's throat and squeezed.

Roux was breathing like a wild animal, blood thrumming in her ears, adrenaline surging through her body. She wanted the bitch to die. Not just hurt, but actually die. And she was more than prepared to do the honors.

"Roux!" Iona said sharply, trying to remove her hands from Tamara's throat.

It was like Roux was watching this from a distance. Surely she wasn't pummeling the hell out of another human being. She wasn't snarling like a caged beast and cursing a trail of obscenities with each blow. It couldn't have really taken three grown men to finally subdue her. Even when she found herself pinned facedown on the floor and unable to move, she was still completely out of control, thrashing and screaming as if she'd escaped a padded room but been recaptured to be sent back to her sad, solitary confinement. She'd completely lost it. Just like her father. Exactly like him. If there hadn't been someone to stop her, Roux was certain she would have killed Tamara. Not just hurt her. Killed her.

Just like her father had killed.

Like her father.

All the fight went out of her, and she began to sob. Even then it took the man with his knee in her back several minutes to trust her enough to free her.

Lily was the one who got to her first and pulled her into a tight embrace, stroking her hair and murmuring in a soothing tone.

"I'm sorry," Roux said through her tears. "I'm so sorry. Oh God, did I hurt her?"

"Not any more than she deserved," Raven said.

"I could have killed her."

"Nah," Iona said. "We wouldn't have let it go that far."

"I'm pressing charges," Tamara said, dabbing at the blood on her lip with a napkin.

"I wanted to hurt her," Roux said, completely inconsolable. "I wanted to destroy her."

"Get in line," Raven said. "If she thinks you hit hard"—Raven cracked her knuckles—"she doesn't realize you're the sweet one."

But Roux couldn't claim that title any longer. She'd never felt such uncontrollable rage. Yes, the woman was half responsible for destroying every wonderful thing between her and Steve, but that was no excuse. What had set her off like that?

"Well, now you know for sure that you should never drink." Iona crouched down beside Roux and rubbed the center of her back.

"I think she should drink more often," Azura said, a smartass grin on her face. "I know a few bitches I'd like her to beat the fuck out of."

Tears brimmed in Roux's eyes, and she shook her head. The

mere thought of hurting someone made her physically ill, where ten minutes ago she'd have told the bitches to form a line and let the ass kickings begin. Had it really been the alcohol, or was something inside her broken? Had her entire life, her entire belief system of never harming another living creature, been a huge sham? Had she just been fooling everyone, including herself? She really was her father's daughter.

"I think I need to throw up," she said, grabbing Raven's arm to pull herself to her feet.

"I'll help her," Lily said. Raven, who'd already taken her usual spot at Roux's side, exchanged a long searching look with Lily and then stepped aside.

Roux started toward the bathroom, leaning heavily on Lily, but realized she wasn't going to make it and began shoving her way through the crowd with one hand over her mouth. Thankfully, the women's bathroom was deserted. Lily held her hair back as she purged the poison from her stomach and then wet a paper towel for Roux's forehead. Roux's hands were shaking so badly, she dropped it several times before Lily sat on the surprisingly clean floor beside her and urged Roux to rest her head on her lap, gently pressing the cool towel to Roux's skin. Roux took deep breaths to calm herself, but she couldn't stanch the sudden flow of tears.

"I'm just like him," she whispered, her gaze unfocused. She rubbed her sore knuckles with her opposite hand.

Lily wiped at her tears with the paper towel and stroked her hair. She was a pretty good substitute for Mama in a bind. "Just like who, sweetheart?"

A fleeting image of his enraged faced as he pointed that gun at her chest and pulled the trigger flickered through her memory, and a wave of terror washed over her. "My father."

"No, love. You're much stronger than he is."

But not less terrible.

"Do you know why I play drums?" Lily asked, her hand still hypnotically petting Roux's hair.

"You have perfect rhythm."

A slight smile graced Lily's lips. "I like to hit things. Hard and repeatedly. When Mama first took me in, I'd hit anything I could get my hands on, including her."

"Because your mother used to hit you?" The sisters knew each other's past horrors and what had brought them to Mama. There were no secrets between them, but Roux hadn't realized Lily had been a hitter.

"Yes. That's how I learned to deal with my anger, and back then I was always angry. But instead of making me stop, Mama gave me an outlet. Something I could hit as hard as I wanted and as often as I wanted until eventually the anger lessened. The urge to hit never went away, though."

"So my urge to kill Tamara when I'm drunk will forever haunt me?"

Lily laughed softly and hugged Roux's head against her belly.

"Jack wants me to have a baby," Lily said.

Roux gasped and wrapped her arms around Lily's waist. "Oh, Lily, that would be wonderful."

"I refused." Her eyes flicked upward, and she swallowed hard.

Roux sat up and knelt on the floor, taking Lily's hands in hers. She could tell her eldest sister needed someone to confide in.

"What if I get mad at my child and I start hitting and I can't stop? What if I'm just like my mother?"

Roux squeezed Lily's hands tightly and shook them. "You're not like her, Lily. You're nothing like her."

Lily's eyes were brimming with tears when she cupped Roux's cheek in her hand and held her gaze as she said, "And you're nothing like your father."

Roux pressed her eyelids shut, which released a few tears to trace hot paths down her cheeks, and she nodded.

"But you really shouldn't drink," Lily added. "It doesn't suit you."

Roux released a short laugh, more an exhalation of relief than humor. "I won't."

They hugged it out until there was a knock at the door. "Are you two okay in there?" Iona asked.

"Be out in a minute," Lily called. She helped Roux to her feet and to the sink, where Roux washed her face and rinsed out her mouth and avoided looking at herself in the mirror.

"Are you going to try to give Jack that baby he wants?" Roux asked as she dried her hands.

"I'm sure I'll cave eventually." Lily chuckled. "You know I can't deny that man anything."

"Auntie Roux." Roux tested the name for the first time. "It has a nice ring to it."

When she opened the door, her four other sisters were standing there with anxious expressions. Again she was reminded how lucky she was to have these women in her life.

"Are you ready to go back to the hotel?" Raven asked, wrapping an arm around her shoulders and pulling her close.

"Shouldn't I wait for the police?" She hadn't forgotten Tamara's threat.

"Dare convinced her not to press charges," Iona said.

"Dare did?"

Sage sighed loudly. "Such a nice guy. And gorgeous too."

"Nope," Iona said, looping her arm through Sage's to direct her toward the door. "It's bad enough that Roux hooked up with one of them. We are *not* going down that road twice."

Hooked up? And past tense? Roux felt like she might throw up again. She wasn't quite ready to give up on Steve. She at least wanted to hear his side of the story before she ended their relationship.

"Your purse," Raven said, and she handed Roux's bag to her.

Roux didn't hesitate to dig through it for her phone. She had a missed call from Steve, but he hadn't left a voicemail.

He had texted her one very infuriating message, however: *Please tell me you didn't see those pictures.*

Not a denial. Or even an apology.

"That motherfucker," Roux muttered under her breath. She stomped out of the tavern behind her sisters.

Chapter 33

By the time Steve returned to the bar, almost everyone had left. Logan, Max, and Dare were still there, and for some reason they were talking to Tamara. She'd looked better. She had a split lip and a darkening bruise on one cheek. When she smiled at him, he had the sudden urge to add a matching bruise to her other cheek, but he ignored her instead.

"Where's Roux?" Steve asked his bandmates. "Was she here? What happened?"

"She was pissed," Max said. "She beat up your girlfriend." He pointed at Tamara. "And then she left."

"My girlfriend?"

Behind Tamara, Logan was shaking his head and miming, apparently to keep Steve from denying the outlandish claim. What the fuck was going on?

"I have to take a wicked piss," Logan said, now gesturing with a craning neck and pointing his eyes toward the bathroom.

Dudes didn't typically go to the bathroom in a congregation the way that women did when they needed a private word, but this was an emergency. He nodded at Logan, who walked away.

"I'm gonna grab a drink," Steve said as soon as Logan was in the bathroom. And he sure needed one, but he made a detour to the toilet on his way to the bar.

"What the fuck is going on?" Steve asked Logan, glad they were alone.

"That chick is completely delusional," Logan said, pointing toward the door.

"Yeah. So why are you talking to her and why does Max think she's my girlfriend? Roux is my girlfriend." Maybe.

"He doesn't think that, *Tamara* thinks that. She thinks you're here to protect her from that crazy woman who tried to take you away from her. Roux has a vicious right hook, by the way."

Steve couldn't believe what he was hearing. "Roux did that to her face?"

"Sorry you missed it. Awesome catfight."

"Roux is the gentlest person I ever met. She would never . . ." Steve rubbed his face with one hand. He'd done that to her. Made her act out of character and hurt someone.

"You have to tell me why you fucked Tamara in the first place. You can't possibly be that desperate. Did you freak out over commitment and self-sabotage, or . . ." Logan peered at Steve through squinted eyes, as if he were the most challenging puzzle ever construed.

"God, no. I don't remember fucking her."

"You don't remember?"

"I got really drunk that first night in Donington, and I saw her on the way to my room, but then I blacked out, and the next thing I remember, Roux is there trying to wake me up." The only thing that could explain his lapse was that Tamara had shown up at his room and he'd been so wasted that he'd done those things with her. Steve swallowed the bile climbing his throat. Every time he thought about what he must have done, he felt sick.

"That psycho probably roofied you."

"What?" Drugged him? She *had* taken a swig off his bottle of whiskey. Had she slipped something into it when he'd been distracted by hating her presence? "Does that work on guys?"

Logan snorted. "If you don't care that his dick can't get hard."

His dick hadn't been hard. That would explain how she could suck it without straining herself.

"So she drugged me, entered my room uninvited, molested me while I was unconscious, and then posted the pictures online. Is she that fucking stupid?"

"I think that's been established, but *ew*. I'm really sorry, dude. That's truly fucking horrific."

He had to tell Roux what happened. Or what he thought had happened. How could he be sure, though? Maybe he'd been so drunk that he'd invited Tamara up to his room for a good time. But even though he couldn't remember hours from that night, that possibility didn't *feel* right to him.

"Can they detect rope in the system, like in a blood test or in the urine?" He was very familiar with drug testing, but not with Rohypnol. It was one of the few drugs he'd never tried, and he sure as hell would never slip it to some unsuspecting female. "How long does it stay in the body?" It had been almost three days; maybe too much time had passed. He did have a rock star liver and kidneys, after all. He cleared drugs and alcohol from his system like a professional.

"How the fuck would I know? Do I look like the kind of guy who'd know anything about date-rape drugs?"

"You're the one who thought of it, so it must be the only way you can get laid." Steve was teasing, but he got a punch in the chest for his taunt. "Maybe Butch knows." Because if Steve had Rohypnol in his system, he could prove that Tamara had staged those photos. Or at least have enough evidence to convince Roux that he hadn't cheated on her. She'd have to forgive him then.

"If Butch doesn't know, he'll find out; he's that awesome. Now, can you leave? I really do need to take a wicked piss."

Steve frowned. They were in a one-person bathroom, not one with multiple urinals and stalls. What must the regular patrons be thinking about the two of them holed up together in there? More fodder for the rumor mill.

Steve went to the bar to order a drink. He wondered if the bartender knew anything about date-rape drugs but figured the man would think the worst of him if he started asking suspicious questions. He collected his drink and returned to the table, not sure how best to handle Tamara. Maybe she'd spill her secrets if he played along. He would not, however, touch her under any circumstance. He chose Logan's vacated seat so that he sat across from her rather than beside her.

"Does your face hurt?" he asked. *It's killing me*, he added silently, sipping at his Irish whiskey. He'd likely never touch Jack again. He stared into his glass, wondering what Roux had been drinking to set her off on a rampage. Or maybe her attempts to rearrange Tamara's face hadn't had anything to do with alcohol. It wasn't the first time a pair of women had come to blows over him, but it was the first time he hadn't found the idea entertaining. Had Tamara hit Roux in return?

He shifted, trying to get comfortable in an uncomfortable situation. Why was he sitting there sipping whiskey when he should be looking for Roux? No mystery there. He was afraid how much it would hurt his heart when she rightfully told him to go fuck himself.

He shifted again.

If he could prove that he'd been drugged and hadn't wanted to cheat on her, would Roux believe him? Would it matter if she did? He rubbed at his mouth with the back of his hand. Had he really allowed Tamara's tit to touch his lips? He rubbed his tongue against his upper teeth as if to scrape off an unsavory flavor. Had he licked her? Even accidentally. God! Did women have these odd thoughts after they'd been violated, as if what had happened was somehow their fault? And rather than blame their violator, did they imagine that if they'd done something different they could have avoided being molested?

He knew those feelings were bullshit, but there they were. How had she gotten into his room? He had to have let her in; no one but Roux and Zach had a spare key. Unless Tamara had convinced the front desk to give her one. Or maybe she'd gotten her hands on a housekeeper's key. She was sneaky enough to do it, but he doubted he'd ever discover the details. Surely she wasn't dumb enough to tell him.

"It hurts a little," Tamara said, touching the cut on her lip with the tip of her tongue, bringing Steve's attention back to the table. "I know I should press charges, but Dare's right. We'd be tied up in international courts for ages. Not worth it to me. Knowing that you're finished with her is enough punishment for her."

Steve choked on his drink, and Max whacked him heartily on the back.

"It's a good thing we pulled that crazy woman off your girlfriend here." Max's fingers dug into Steve's back. A warning? Or . . .

"Yeah, good thing," Tamara said. "Her father was a murderer, you know. No telling how far she would have gone."

"How do you know about her father?" Steve asked, pushing his hands under the table and clutching his thighs. Tamara's tongue was uncharacteristically loose. If he kept his cool, she might let something slip.

Tamara smiled. "It's my job to dig up dirt on celebrities."

He hoped the heartless wench didn't print a story about Roux's past. Roux didn't need the ghosts that haunted her to become public knowledge.

"Though she's not much of a celebrity," Tamara said. "Not like you guys."

Max leveled one of his million-dollar smiles at her. She blinked as if hypnotized.

"I'm sure Baroquen has a lot of secrets," Max said. "Do you think that's why they wear costumes?"

Steve punched Max's knee, but his gaze never strayed from Tamara's.

"Oh, for sure. Why do you think Sam is so interested in them? All of them have horrible stories in their pasts."

Steve stopped breathing. Sam was interested because they were talented and extremely marketable and . . . perfect little tragedies to exploit in his tabloid.

"That tabloid of his is gaining readership rapidly," Dare said. "Must be exciting to have your byline on every page."

"Not every page." She grinned. "Bianca writes some of the articles."

"About stuff anyone can find on the web," Dare said, and he actually reached across the table to stroke a line down the center of her hand. "But you're out in the trenches, getting the real juicy stories. I hope Sam is paying you well."

Tamara peeked at Steve and then at Dare's finger before drawing her hand away and tucking it under the table. What? Was she afraid Steve wouldn't like Dare to touch his *girlfriend*?

Logan flopped down in the seat next to Tamara. "What did I miss?" he asked.

He received three sharp, cautionary looks from his bandmates. They were working their collective charm on this woman, and hopefully they'd learn more before she realized she was being played.

"Dare making a move on Steve's woman," Max said, winking at Tamara, who flushed.

"He's always been a sucker for saving a woman in peril," Steve commented, hoping Tamara thought he was referring to her fight earlier and not to the fact that he was moments away from losing his cool and pulling a Roux on her.

Steve was ready to play a card now, though he probably wouldn't be as slick as the two sharks that had been baiting her before he'd arrived. "The other night was a pretty special evening between us." He couldn't bring himself to look at her. "Why would you post those pictures online?"

"I didn't."

Flabbergasted, he looked up. She had to be lying. Had to be.

But her expression read innocent.

"Who . . ." He breathed out the word.

"I sent them to Bianca. She said I'd never get you no matter how hard I tried. Guess she was wrong."

A toe brushed his ankle and pushed up his pant leg to trail up his shin. He scooted his chair back.

"Bianca posted them?" He massaged one eyebrow; his head hurt. "Why in the fuck would she do that?" He didn't expect an answer.

"So Sam can't blackmail her anymore."

Steve looked from Dare to Max to Logan. They looked as clueless as he felt.

"Sam is blackmailing her?"

Tamara shrugged. "Why else would she take his money?"

"Because her tabloid is going bankrupt," Dare said.

"She wanted it to go bankrupt. Tax write-off."

"So she isn't broke?" Steve asked.

Tamara laughed. "After all the money she got from you in the divorce? She's set for life."

"How is Sam blackmailing her?" Max asked.

And just how many people could one man screw over at one time? Sam had to have an infinite number of dicks in those Armani trousers of his.

"He has proof that Steve never cheated on her, and his infidelity was the whole reason she won such a huge settlement. He said you could file a mistrial or something and get all your money back plus interest. I don't know all the details, but she was really freaked out."

"Actually, lots of people know he didn't cheat on her," Logan said. "Steve let her win."

Steve couldn't deny it. He'd been called an idiot more times than he cared to admit for giving her the lion's share of his fortune. Bianca fearing that he would take all her money made him want to laugh. Why hadn't she asked him about it? How had she fallen for Sam's trickery? Probably for the same reason Max had fallen for it all these years: Sam was better at playing a role than any award-winning actor.

"But those pictures were taken recently," Dare said. "How does that stop Sam from proving Steve didn't cheat all those years ago?"

"Once a cheater always a cheater?" She shrugged. "I haven't talked to her since she posted them. Maybe she thought that defense would work retroactively. Or maybe she wanted to hurt you or even me for proving her wrong and finally getting the man she stole from me. Or maybe she wanted my boyfriend to see them, which is fine, because I don't need him anymore." She grinned at Steve. "Whatever her reason, things are definitely working out in my favor."

Yep. Totally delusional.

"Oh, I almost forgot," Logan said, reaching across the table to flick Steve on the shoulder. "That thing you wanted Butch to look up for you?" He bit his bottom lip, raised his eyebrows, and lifted his chin. "Seventy-two hours. I googled it."

Steve did some quick mental math and figured it had been sixty hours, maybe more, since Ms. Delusional had slipped him the drug. He'd better find a clinic or hospital that could take a blood and urine sample before it worked its way completely out of his system. He hoped he hadn't missed the chance to strengthen his evidence. Short of getting a confession directly from the perpetrator, he had no proof that she'd taken advantage of him, and while that wasn't the kind of thing he wanted the public to hear, he definitely wanted Roux to know that he would never intentionally hurt her. Especially not by messing around with the whack-job attempting to play footsie with him under the table.

"I've got to go get a blood test," Steve said, staring directly at Tamara for the first time since he'd arrived.

She giggled. "I guess your red-headed angel wasn't as clean as you thought she was."

Steve took a deep breath to calm himself. "If anyone gave me a disease, it would be you," he said, unable to stop himself. "But that's not why I need a blood test. I need to see if I still have Rohypnol in my system."

The blood drained from Tamara's face. She might as well have tattooed a confession across her forehead.

"Rohypnol?" Max asked. "What's that?"

"Rope. Roofies," Logan said. "I'm sure you've heard of roofies before."

"The date-rape drug?" Max lifted a brow at Steve. "Why would you take that?"

"I didn't. Tamara slipped it to me so she could stage those pictures," Steve said. He didn't have the patience for being sneaky about this. He might as well lay it all on the table while there were witnesses.

"You don't have any proof," she said, standing up.

"Hence the blood test." Or urine test. He wasn't sure which he needed, but neither did she, obviously.

She backed several steps away from the table. "Anyone could have slipped it to you."

"Only one person touched my bottle that night besides me, and that would be you."

"I'm not that desperate!"

Logan sniggered and then burst out laughing. Steve was surprised when Dare and Max joined him. "She has to roofie men to get laid!" Logan announced to the entire room.

"Aw, I'll shag the nutter if she's on the pull," a man at the bar said, lifting his glass.

Tamara darted out of the bar, and the laughter around the table died at once.

"Did she really roofie you?" Max asked.

"Almost certain she did."

"That is fucked up. Are you going to report this?"

"I just want Roux to know I didn't betray her." And he needed her to know as soon as possible. The fear of her breaking it off with him made him hesitate to contact her, but he didn't want her to anguish over the situation with Tamara for another moment. "Can I borrow someone's phone? Mine's smashed."

Logan offered his, but he didn't have Roux's number. No one had it in their contacts besides him, and he couldn't remember it off the top of his head.

"Shit."

"Maybe Butch has her number," Logan suggested.

He didn't, but he did have Iona's. And Iona would likely answer Max's call. It didn't take much to convince Max to call Iona. He put her on speaker and set the phone on the table.

"If you're calling for your *friend*," Iona said, "tell him to go suck a leper's dick."

Max grinned at Steve. He was obviously enjoying this.

"I just wanted to make sure you all made it back to the hotel safely," Max said.

"Yes, we're fine."

"Is Roux still upset?" Max asked.

"Of course she's fucking upset. Her boyfriend cheated on her with a tabloid reporter and was forced to resort to drinking and violence. Why wouldn't she be upset?"

Steve clutched at his thighs so he wouldn't blurt out some defense.

"You sound upset as well."

"No one fucks with one of my sisters. You'd better tell Aimes to watch his back."

"I have good evidence that those pictures were staged," Max said. "Steve is not a cheater."

"Everyone knows he's a cheater. It was all over the news during his divorce. He didn't deny it. Not even once."

"If you knew Steve at all, you'd realize he doesn't tolerate stress well."

What the hell was Max talking about? Steve handled stress just fine. When he was stressed he just needed a bit of alcohol or some drugs, or to disappear from the spotlight for a while, or . . . So maybe he didn't tolerate stress well. But that wasn't why he hadn't bothered to set the public record straight during his divorce. The truth hadn't been worth the . . . stress. Steve rubbed a hand over his face. Apparently Max knew him a lot better than he'd realized. But he wasn't going to make the same mistake with Roux. Getting her to understand the truth was worth any level of stress he'd be forced to tolerate.

"So rather than drag the divorce out into an even messier spectacle," Max continued, "he let her vent her rage and just signed the papers."

"Sounds like something Roux would do," she said. "Can you believe she wants to hear his side of this? Like there is anything he can do or say to make this better."

Steve blew out a quiet breath of relief. Roux was willing to hear him out. He prayed she believed him.

"I'm telling you, he was set up," Max said. He gave Steve a pointed look. "I just hope he can find a way to prove it. The clock is ticking. He'd better find an open clinic before it's too late."

Steve slid his chair back, and he and Logan stood simultaneously.

"A clinic? He better not have given Roux any of that skank's STIs."

Max waved Steve off, letting him know he'd try to get Iona to understand the situation. Steve had to hurry. The clock really was ticking.

HOURS LATER, STEVE STOOD at Roux's hotel room door, his hand raised to knock. Butch had already scored him a new cellphone and had his data transferred to it—there were so many perks to this rock star gig—but Roux hadn't answered his calls and voicemails or replied to his texts. Hope had started to wither, but he had no plans to give up yet. He wished Zach was there to offer support, but he was halfway to Los Angeles by now. Logan had helped Steve secure the drug tests he needed, but it would be days before the results were in. He'd also discovered that a hair sample could be sent off and the drug—along with any he'd purposely taken—would be detectable for months after ingestion. The clinician had carefully recorded details of the incident in case he decided to take the case to the police. Apparently spiking a drink could lead to years of jail time, but he wasn't sure he wanted his business made public. He felt like a fool for falling into Tamara's trap, and though there was photographic evidence of the crime, he didn't remember the violation clearly. It felt like it had happened to someone else. But if Roux hated him now and dumped him, he'd probably file charges against Tamara out of spite.

He took a deep breath and knocked on the door. It was close to midnight. She might be asleep. Maybe he should have called her room first. Maybe . . .

The door eased open, and he was leveled by a blue-eyed glare. Raven crossed her arms over her chest. "You have some nerve showing up here after all this time."

"I had important issues to take care of before I could explain what happened." And he'd been more than a little nervous. He knew he wouldn't handle Roux's anger or her disgust well. His heart was already thudding in his chest. This kind of confrontation should be easier for a rock star, shouldn't it? It wasn't.

"Explain what?" Raven's eyes narrowed. "How getting your rocks off is more important to you than my sister's love? Fuck you." She tried to close the door, but Steve lifted his arm to block it. Now that he was here, there was no way he was backing down without seeing her.

"Roux," he called into the room. "I know you're hurt and you probably hate me, but—" Raven kicked him in the shin. "Ow!"

"Go away or I'm calling the cops," Raven threatened.

"I don't care."

"Or maybe I should call Iona."

That woman was far more frightening than cops.

"Roux, I didn't sleep with her on purpose."

"But you did sleep with her," Raven said.

"You found me afterwards," he called to Roux, hoping she could hear him. "Remember how out of it I was that night, how sick? And all I did was have some whiskey."

"A lot of whiskey," Raven said. "Being drunk does not excuse your behavior."

He hadn't wanted to announce the depth of the situation to the entire corridor, but seeing as Raven was blocking the door, he didn't know what choice he had.

"I know that, but I wasn't drunk. I was drugged."

"That doesn't make it any better!" Raven shoved him.

"Tamara drugged me. She slipped something into my bottle."

Raven cocked her head. "What do you mean?"

He lowered his voice to a whisper. "She put rope or ketamine or GHB or something in my whiskey and then molested me when I was unconscious."

"Are you sure?" Raven said, some of the tension going out of her.

"That's where I've been for the past few hours, at the hospital getting tested so I'd have proof. But it takes a while for the results to come back, and . . . I couldn't wait until then to tell her the truth. Roux? Please say something."

Raven searched his eyes for a long moment and then sighed. "She isn't here."

"What? Why didn't you tell me that in the first place?"

"Because I think she's an idiot for running back to you, for not wanting to believe the worst about you even though the entire world has seen proof of your cheating."

"Running back to me? I haven't seen her. She hasn't answered her phone. I've been trying to reach her for hours." His heart began to thud out of control. Maybe something had happened to her. He wouldn't put it past Tamara to hurt her. Although Roux had effectively kicked her ass earlier that day, he wasn't sure she'd even try to defend herself if she wasn't drunk.

"Yeah, I know you're obsessed. I have her dumb phone, and it's been ringing and binging nonstop." Raven shoved the phone into his chest. He took it from her hand, rubbing his thumb over the familiar puppy-picture case. "I thought I could get her to stay here if I took it away from her, but she left anyway."

"Do you know where she is?"

"Maybe you should check your hotel room, dumbass."

"My room . . ."

Steve turned and sprinted down the corridor and to the stairs, not wanting to waste time waiting for an elevator. Security stayed out of his way as he fumbled with his keycard and threw the door open. A single lamp glowed beside the bed, and he didn't see her at first. A huge sigh of relief escaped him when he spotted her curled up on the end of a loveseat, her eyes closed and her head resting on her arm.

She believed in him. He'd never had another person demonstrate that level of trust in him. Of course, she could be there to tell him off to his face, but she was there.

He crossed the room and squatted in front of her. He watched her sleep for a moment, knowing the peaceful expression of slumber would soon be replaced with fury or agony or any number of unpleasant emotions. He couldn't resist touching her for long, however. He slipped a lock of hair from her smooth cheek, tucking it behind her ear. She murmured something unintelligible, and her eyes blinked open.

"Steve," she said, sitting up straight.

"Hey, sleepyhead."

Her eyes were puffy. She'd been crying, and the thought of her suffering over this tore at his heart. He hadn't been there to hold her and assure her that everything was going to be okay.

"How could you?" she shouted. "How could you? With *her*?"

"I couldn't," he said.

"You did!"

"I didn't."

"Don't play me for a fool, Steven Aimes."

He tried to take her hands in his, but she slapped them away.

"I'm not playing you, baby. Will you listen to what really happened?"

She crossed her arms over her chest and nodded, but she didn't look at him as he tried to figure out where to begin.

He set her phone on her lap. "I've been trying to call you since I got my phone replaced. I broke my old one when I saw those pictures of Tamara online."

"That doesn't erase them from the Internet, you know," she snapped.

"Wouldn't it be nice if I could erase them?"

"And they weren't pictures only of Tamara. That was you there with her."

"Roux . . ." He shifted to his knees, as squatting was starting make his legs cramp, and knelt at her feet. "Those pictures were taken at Donington that night you found me naked in my puked-on bed."

"I figured that much out, and I know you were really drunk that night, but still . . ." She blinked back tears. "Are you going to screw around on me every time you get drunk?"

"Of course not. I'm not a cheater. I'll never screw around on you."

"You already have."

"I wasn't drunk," he said.

Her eyes narrowed.

"I was a little drunk," he admitted. "Maybe a lot drunk, but I don't pass out cold like that after drinking. I sure don't throw up, black out, and lose hours of time. She drugged me, Roux. With a date-rape drug. I'm sure of it. I had samples taken to try to prove it, but she all but admitted it in front of my bandmates earlier tonight."

"She drugged you?"

Apparently Max hadn't convinced Iona to spread the word of Steve's innocence.

"She fucking *drugged* you?" Roux bellowed.

Steve leaned away from the fury radiating off the sweetest woman he'd ever known.

"I believe so."

"And then did those, those *things* to you while you were unconscious?"

Steve nodded. His stomach churned with queasiness. He couldn't remember much about Tamara's actions, but that feeling of nausea persisted every time he thought about what she'd done.

"I should have killed that bitch when I had the chance." Roux sprang from the sofa and began to pace. "Can you have her arrested? Deported? Hanged?"

"I only care about not losing you," he said, shifting from the floor to sit on the sofa that was still warm with Roux's body heat. "I don't care about her being punished."

"I care. She raped you."

"She tried," he said. "But she couldn't get my dick hard." That was the one thing about that night that he remembered clearly. He tried smiling, but that sick feeling returned to the pit of his belly.

Roux stopped midpace and whirled to face him. "This must be

terrible for you," she said, moving to stand in front of him. She lifted a hand toward his head, but hesitated. "Is it okay for me to touch you?"

"Why wouldn't that be okay?"

"One of my sisters was raped, and she couldn't stand for anyone to touch her for a long time after. If you want me to keep my distance, I understand."

"I want you touch me," he said. "I need to know that this hasn't destroyed what we have."

"Of course it hasn't."

She slipped her fingers into his hair and pressed his face against her belly, curling around him protectively. His arms slipped around her waist, and he hugged her close. Why was he trembling so hard? He couldn't stop.

"I'm here," she whispered, stroking his hair. "You don't have to go through this alone. I will always be here for you. Always."

Her vow triggered silent tears to steal from beneath his clenched eyelids and slide down his face.

CHAPTER 34

Roux held Steve against her belly for a long time. She wasn't sure how he felt about losing himself to emotion, so when he finally loosened his grip and lifted his face, she smiled and didn't comment on the wetness he'd left behind on her shirt.

"Do you think I should press charges against her?" he asked, his fingers lacing through hers. He brought her scraped knuckles to his lips and kissed them gently.

"Absolutely."

"Then I'm sure she'll retaliate by having you arrested for physical assault."

Roux shrugged. She didn't much care if she got in trouble for knocking the snot out of the woman who drugged her man and took pictures of herself violating him while he was unconscious. "I have countless witnesses that will say she started it."

"Did she start it?"

"I was too mad at the time to remember who threw the first punch, but my sisters said she did." Then again, her sisters would say anything to protect her. She wasn't sure their testimony would hold up in court.

"Dare told me you'd been drinking."

She ducked her chin. "Seemed like a good idea at the time. I was so hurt, so *angry*."

"I'm sorry about all of it."

"You have nothing to be sorry about. The one who will be sorry is Tamara."

"She didn't act alone," Steve said. "She told us that Bianca is the one who actually posted the pictures online."

Roux supposed crazy ran in the family.

"She'll probably include them in a story in her tabloid, so be prepared," he said.

"Why has Bianca made it her life's mission to hurt you?"

"I have no idea." He released a breath. "Well, I did spend a lot of time away from home, and back then the band really stuck to the no-women-on-tour rule."

"That might explain why she cheated on you." Roux made a face. "No, fuck that. There is no excuse for her screwing around on you. Stop making excuses for her. She doesn't deserve the slightest bit of consideration from you."

"But I—"

She pressed her finger to his lips. "I'm not listening to you take any blame for what happened with Bianca or with Tamara, so knock it off. You hear me?"

"Yes, ma'am. You aren't going to hit me, are you? I heard you have a mean right hook."

Grinning, she lightly tapped his jaw with her fist, and he threw himself backward onto the sofa as if she had superstrength. He grabbed her wrist to tug her down onto his lap.

"I have an idea," she said, hugging her arms around his to draw his arms close to her belly.

He used the tip of his nose to brush her hair aside so he could nibble a sensitive spot just beneath her ear.

"I have an idea too," he murmured, and a shiver of delight raced down her spine.

She was certain his idea was far more X-rated than hers, but she was starting to come up with a few ideas of that caliber as well.

"I'm not sure if you'll like mine."

"I've liked every idea you've ever had," he said. "I'm sure this will be no different."

"I want to be open about our relationship," she said. She turned her head to look at him. "I mean really open. Embarrassingly open."

"In what way?"

"You know those celebrity couples that post pictures on Instagram showing how nauseatingly perfect their love for each other is?"

He grinned and rolled his eyes.

"I want to do that."

"Why on earth would you want everyone in our business?"

"For one thing, it will drive your ex-wife insane."

He laughed.

"And I want the entire world to know you're mine, that I love you, that I will stand by you through anything."

"Isn't it enough that I know that?"

"It's more than enough," she said, turning on his lap and straddling his hips. She kissed him lovingly, her heart so full she could scarcely breathe. "But maybe I want to brag a little."

It wasn't her true reason for thinking this was a good idea, but his proud smile delighted her.

"I scored a rock star," she added, kissing him again, allowing her lips to linger on his.

"So did I," he said against her mouth.

Her? A rock star? Yeah, right. But she couldn't help teasing him. "And you don't want everyone on the planet to know what a prize you've scored?"

"I do want everyone to know. It's been hard keeping this secret."

"So let's beat them at their own game. You know that tabloid of your ex-wife's is going to shape our relationship to their liking—especially our secrecy about it. You also know that first impressions are vitally important. If people start with thinking of what we have in a negative light, it will stain our relationship forever."

"So we have to do this before the potentially shitty article comes out."

"*Potentially* shitty? We both know it's going to happen, and it's going to be incomparably shitty."

He nodded slightly. "What about the pictures that Bianca posted of me with Tamara? Everyone thinks I've cheated on you already."

"We're going to be very open about that too."

"About me cheating on you?"

"About what she did to you. It wasn't cheating. Don't ever think of it that way."

He shifted her off his lap and stood, pacing to the far corner of the room.

She shouldn't have pushed him so soon about the part of her plan that would expose the sexual assault. He was still rightfully disturbed about the incident. He might always be distressed over it. But she didn't want him to blame himself. She wanted Tamara to be forced to take all the blame, and if millions of people knew what a fucked-up cunt she was, Roux was certain Tamara would be the one blamed. What Roux wasn't certain of was if people would try to make Steve feel weak because it had happened to him.

"I don't want everyone to know that I fell for her ploy. It's embarrassing," he said quietly.

Roux crossed the room and pressed a hand against his back. "More embarrassing than *voluntarily* fucking that woman? Because that's what everyone thinks happened." Everyone but her and a few others who were close to him.

He shuddered beneath her palm. "She doesn't look bad," he said. "Outwardly, she's someone I might have once . . ." He shook his head. "Nope, I can't even say that. Something about her has always given me the willies."

"She's a sexual predator, Steve."

"I thought she was just hyperaggressive, but you might be right. You *are* right. I've always given her the benefit of the doubt because she's female."

"Which is bullshit," Roux said. "If a man gave a woman that much unwanted attention, he'd have been called out on it a long time ago."

"I did have a restraining order against her for a while. She was always grabbing at me. The order made her keep her distance, so I thought she'd gotten over wanting me, but . . ."

"She has a pathological obsession with you." Roux could understand that to a degree—Steve was completely obsession-worthy. But Tamara had taken her preoccupation much too far.

"I feel like I should have been able to stop what she did to me. I was stupid."

"You're blaming yourself again."

He licked his lips. "I can't help it. Not yet anyway. I'm sorry for what you went through today. I know you were incredibly upset if you were drinking."

"I always wondered if I'd be like my dad if I drank. Alcohol definitely unleashed a violent side of me." She reached for the bracelet on her arm, but not the bullet that she usually found comforting. She instead fiddled with the diamond and ruby bracelet that Steve had given her, watching it sparkle in the low light of the bedside lamp.

Steve took her hands in his. "You're not like your father."

"You sound like Lily." She smiled. "Waiting for you here alone gave me a lot of time to think, and the truth is, I *do* share some qualities with him," she said. "But instead of being frightened by that idea, the knowledge gives me strength to make different choices than he made. I won't ever drink again. That's all there is to it."

"But what if I need you to take down my enemies again, slugger?"

He tried to maintain a serious expression, but she could see the corner of his mouth twitch as he fought a smile.

"I'll just have to use my wits instead of my fists." There were three of Steve's enemies she planned to help take down with a few of her wits: Tamara, Bianca, and Sam Baily.

"That sounds more like the woman I fell in love with."

She slid her body against his, wrapping her arms around his neck to hold him as close as possible. When his hands began to wander down her back and over her ass, she smiled. He really did seem to be okay with her touch, but she vowed to be considerate of his feelings if physical closeness made him uncomfortable. The sexual chemistry between them had been explosive from the start, but wasn't the most important part of their togetherness. She could wait until he was ready, just as he had waited until she was ready in the beginning.

She decided she wouldn't have to wait long when he pulled at her clothes until she was naked. She allowed him to touch her as much as he wanted, delighted in it, actually, but kept her hands to herself. After a few minutes of stroking her skin and kissing her neck, he pulled away, frowning.

"I thought you forgave me for the Tamara thing," he said.

"I told you there's nothing to forgive."

"Then why won't you touch me?"

"I figured you wouldn't want to be touched. Not so soon after..."

He took her hand and slid it over the hard ridge in the front of his pants. "Does that feel like I don't want you to touch me?"

"That feels like it wants to be free," she said, unfastening his pants and pushing them and his underwear down to his knees. She couldn't help but watch him for signs of distress as she stroked the hard, smooth length of him with one hand. Was he really okay? She wanted him to be okay, she just didn't want to push him. She relaxed her guard after a moment, hoping he didn't realize that she was still wary of his receptibility. Was he thinking of Tamara? Of all the ways she'd touched him when he'd been unconscious? Roux couldn't seem to stop those thoughts from swarming through her mind, and it must be a thousand times harder for him.

He pressed gently on her shoulder, and she knew what that signal meant. He helped her sweep his T-shirt off over his head so that she could kiss his chest and belly as she slowly lowered her body. Tamara had sucked his cock, which had definitely been entirely soft—Roux had closely examined every photo by that point, which had made it incredibly easy to believe him. She knew what her man looked like when he was turned on. He didn't lie prone and just take it. And he was never soft by the time he was naked.

Would he be thinking about Tamara's mouth on him when Roux reached her destination? God, why was *she* thinking about it so much?

Because she was pissed at that woman for violating him. She would do her best to scrub those memories from both their minds. Dropping to her knees, she squeezed his ass in both hands and looked up at him, her mouth wide open inches from the tip of his cock.

"Now there's a picture I'd like to have," he said, appearing equal parts delicious and naughty.

She stuck her hand into his dangling pocket and pulled out his phone. She handed it to him, loving the look of surprise on his face as he accepted it.

"You don't mind?"

She shook her head.

He fumbled with the phone. She wanted him to be comfortable with this too. Not just the touching but having photographic mementos of their time together. She heard the shutter sound effect of a picture being taken. He groaned as he examined the shot he'd captured.

"That's sexy as fuck."

She extended her tongue and gently licked his cockhead. He sucked in a breath and took another picture.

"But not as sexy as that."

She wrapped her lips around his tip, and he snapped a third shot.

"Every time I think you can't top your sexiness, you prove me wrong."

Encouraged by his compliments, she opened her mouth wide and eased him as deep as she could without gagging. She circled the base of his cock with one hand so as not to leave an inch of him neglected.

"I'm going to film this."

And she treated it like a performance because she trusted him not to let the video be seen by anyone but him. She wished the rest of the world deserved her infallible trust. Because even with photographs posted all over the Internet, she hadn't really believed he'd betray her. Maybe that made her a fool, but she didn't care. Being a fool for Steve Aimes wasn't so bad.

"Oh God, that feels good," he said, and she upped her performance, loving how she could make his legs tremble.

A moment later the phone dropped on the floor as his hands shifted to her hair, clenching her scalp as his hips began to move. She felt around for the phone with one hand, still sucking the head of his cock gently and rubbing her lips over the rim as she rocked her head forward and back. She held the phone near her chest, pointing the camera upward to give him a view he'd never seen before.

He pulled back unexpectedly, his cock popping free of her mouth. A sick feeling settled in her belly. He must be dwelling on Tamara violating him. She lifted her gaze, her heart breaking over his suffering, but he was grinning crookedly.

"Come to bed with me now," he said, shifting his hands to her upper arms and helping her to her feet. "Or I won't last."

He never seemed to get that she liked it when his excitement got the better of him and he completely lost himself to the pleasure she could give him. She pressed him down on his back, and he scooted across the mattress. He took the phone from her hand and aimed the lens toward his cock, which was glistening with her saliva and standing at rigid attention.

"I want to film it going in you."

She wouldn't mind watching that herself. Normally, if she wanted to watch him enter her, she had to attempt contortionism.

"How's the lighting?" she asked as she crawled up onto the bed with him.

He fumbled with the phone, and a light switched on. He aimed it at his crotch. She bit her lips, torn between finding the action incredibly hot and a bit silly. She straddled him and reached for his cock, careful to keep her arm out of his shot as much as possible, and rubbed his cockhead through the juices between her legs. Fuck, she was swollen and wet. Her pussy was more than ready for its theatrical debut.

"Oh yeah," he said, "rub it all up in there." When she did as he directed, he sucked a breath through his teeth. "That looks so beautiful. Now put it in just a little."

She slipped him into her opening and moved her hands aside, hovering over him with just his cockhead inside her.

"Your cum is trickling down my dick. I've never seen you this wet."

"I want it all over you," she said.

He drew two fingers down his shaft, collecting her fluids. He rubbed her juices into a small spot just under his navel and then grinned at her. "This might take a while."

"I'd say I'll wait, but I can't." His slight penetration was already driving her insane with need.

"I can speed this up a little." He slid his thumb over her clit, massaging rapidly. He quickly drove her over the edge. Her thighs quaked as her pussy clenched repeatedly around his tip. She tossed her head back, moaning in bliss. She sank her hips down, taking him deep, and the tease in him vanished as he groaned. The phone dropped from his grip—she was blocking his shot anyway—and she leaned forward to pick it up. She switched from video mode to camera with the flick of her finger and lifted her hips. His head tilted back, mouth dropping open and eyes reduced to narrow slits as he kept his gaze on her. He was the sexiest damned thing she'd ever seen. She snapped a picture and then dropped the phone, far more interested in the feel of him than his looks as she moved her hips to slowly rebuild her pleasure.

She knew that if she gave him control of their joining that they'd both find orgasm quickly, but she relished this slow build, the time spent enjoying each other's bodies. Yet eventually impatience got the better of him, and he gripped her hips, encouraging her to ride faster, and when she didn't comply, he rocked up into her. She caught his hands and leaned forward to pin them to the mattress on either side of his shoulders.

"You always say you want to take your time at this." She nibbled on his lip and then soothed the rough treatment with her tongue.

"The longer I'm inside you, the more I feel you with my heart."

She kissed him tenderly, and released one hand so she could stroke the day's growth of stubble on his jaw. "You mean that?"

He nodded. "You wouldn't want me to cry during sex, would you?"

"If it's because you're overcome with deep, loving feelings for me, then I'd be okay with it."

"Roux, oh, Roux," he said with exaggerated passion. "I love your sweet, tight pussy so much it makes me weep."

She poked him in the ribs. "For that, I'm taking this even slower."

"Such cruelty." But he was grinning, and he stopped trying to speed her motions, giving himself to her completely.

Her legs and hips were starting to fatigue when the urge to find release overpowered her need to have him inside her for as long as possible. As her tempo changed, Steve met her strokes to drive himself deep. She opened her eyes and held his gaze, teetering on the brink of orgasm, waiting for him to find his peak. She worried that he might be doing the same as his forehead crinkled with intense concentration. She churned her hips, not willing to give him the victory. He clung to the sheets and tightened every muscle in his sweat-slick body. She reached behind her and gently cradled his balls in one hand. He gasped, and his back arched. Still fighting release, he let go of the tangled bedspread with one hand and shifted his fingers to her clit. She sucked a breath in through her nose, massaging his balls with her palm, extending her fingers toward his ass. She was willing to play dirty to win the battle. The instant her fingertip slid against his hole, he went off like a cannon, crying out in triumph over his ultimate defeat. The hard, pulsing twitches of his cock inside her sent her tumbling over the edge to join him in rapture.

Body completely spent, she dropped down onto his chest, trying to catch her breath while aftershocks of pleasure continued to ripple through her pussy.

"I win," she whispered. Her first victory in their "who came first" tournament. He was still the champion, though.

"You win," he said, turning his head to kiss her temple. "You win."

By a second, if that, but the specifics of her rare victory didn't wipe the smile off her lips. And their subsequent rematch—when she lost by three points—only spread that smile wider.

EARLY THE NEXT MORNING, ROUX SAT ACROSS the table from Steve, enjoying her room service breakfast of fruit and toast and replaying the footage Steve had captured on his phone the night before.

"Not bad for my film debut," she said with a grin.

He was scarfing down eggs like a starving man. "Hottest fucking thing ever," he said, his mouth full. He chugged down half a glass of orange juice before reaching for a bowl of steel-cut oats.

"What's the rush?" she asked.

Steve pointed at the clock. It was just before seven. "Butch will be here in a few minutes."

Roux eyed his gorgeous naked chest appreciatively. Breakfast had arrived just when he'd stepped out of the shower, and he had yet to put on anything but a towel. "Are you going to your interview like that?"

"He'll wait for me to put on clothes. He won't wait for me to finish eating."

"I thought this rock star gig involved a lot more pampering and a lot less work," she said, nibbling on a strawberry.

"Not while on tour. At least not for us." He tried a sip of his coffee before setting it down with a wince. "The coffee in England is always vile. When will I learn?"

"You should have ordered tea. Best I've ever tasted."

A knock sounded on the door. "Time!" Butch yelled from the corridor.

"I have two more minutes," Steve yelled back. He grabbed his toast to munch on as he hurried to an open suitcase.

Roux watched, wondering if she'd died and this was her heaven when he dropped his towel and gave her a glorious view of his naked ass. Toast caught between his teeth, her rock star put on his underwear, then pants—one leg at a time, as the saying went.

The video that had been playing on his phone ended, and the picture she'd taken of his face when he'd been inside her the night before appeared on the screen. It was the sexiest image she'd ever seen in her life. And perfect for her campaign against the Brennan sisters. *Eat your heart out, Tamara.*

"Can I post this online?" she asked, rising from her chair and approaching Steve. She caught his toast midair when the shirt he was pulling on knocked it from his mouth.

When his face came into view, he looked incredulous. "Our sex video?"

"No. That's for you to watch when you miss me."

"Which is whenever you're not near—including while you're in the bathroom."

So sweet. She kissed him and then stuck the piece of toast back in his mouth. "This picture of you."

He snorted when he saw it. "Me with my sex face on? Why would you post that?"

"It's sexy."

"Is this that perfect-couple bragging thing you were talking about last night?"

She nodded.

"You have my permission to post any picture of me you want."

"This is going to be fun," she said. "I should have taken a picture of your naked ass a few minutes ago. The world would thank me."

"Any picture not showing my naked ass or junk," he amended his previous permissions. "Now, give me my phone, I have to go."

"Send me that photo," she said.

"You're so obsessed with me."

She rolled her eyes—even though he was right—and pulled him close for a kiss.

"Will you stop fucking? You're making us late!" Butch called out in the corridor. But his voice sounded like it was coming from a few doors down.

"Reagan or Logan?" Steve asked.

"My money's on the newly wed."

He grabbed his shoes and socks and kissed her one last time before hurrying toward the door. "Last man in the car has to rub Butch's feet."

She laughed and said, "I love you."

"Love you."

When he closed the door behind him, she went back to the table and began plotting out her revenge against Tamara and her sister. She figured the only thing that would bother them more than being publicly called out on their heinous bullshit was knowing that Steve was in love and happy. Roux hoped her plan worked out the way she intended and didn't come back to bite her in the ass. But no one messed with the man she loved and got away with it.

CHAPTER 35

AS THEY ALWAYS DID WHEN THE BAND WAS ON TOUR, the weeks had flown by. Steve hadn't thought he could be any happier than he'd been a month ago, but each day was a little more spectacular than the last. It had all started with that picture Roux had posted online. He'd been a little embarrassed at first to be depicted at his most vulnerable, but women—and more than a few gay men—had gone wild, declaring exploded ovaries and drool-induced dehydration. He'd gotten a kick out of it. He was accustomed to sexually charged attention and was glad that Roux trusted he would never take advantage of all the lust that had been stirred up by his sex face. A few days later she'd posted pictures of the two of them as lovebird tourists in Madrid and embarrassed the hell out of him by revealing his tradition of offering her three gifts at every opportunity. Like his sex-face picture, the recognition of his generous and sappy nature had sent the romantic hearts of tens of thousands rooting for their continued love. It turned out that the *American Inquirer* hit newsstands the very next day, too soon after they'd gone public to stop the distribution. Highlighting their story with front page headlines, the paper had published a derogatory and obviously false account about his relationship with Roux. The rag hinted she was hiding her identity because her band was a joke. Everyone already knew better on both counts. Roux had won over the public in their favor, having slanted her initial hesitance in revealing her identity in a more favorable light: she shouldn't have mixed business with pleasure, but who could resist bragging about Steve?

Scrambling to save face—though the libel lawsuits had already been set into motion by Dare's oddly gleeful attorneys—the paper had published a retraction about the first story and in the same issue had included the pictures of Tamara and Steve together. He wasn't so great after all, was the inference. He'd cheated on Roux, who obviously loved him with all her heart. What kind of selfish man-whore asshole was he? He'd cheated on his first wife as well—proof provided in the signed divorce papers citing infidelity as the cause. Surely this would turn the public's opinion on the rock star couple who posted adorable selfies and threw their intense passion and love for each other out for all the world to see.

But brilliant Roux was one step ahead of them again. Days before, she'd posted a video of Steve talking about his experience with being roofied. She hadn't asked him to reveal who'd drugged him, but his lab results had come back positive, and in the video he'd encouraged anyone who suspected they'd been drugged and sexually violated to at least get tested. That way they'd have proof if they wanted to try getting a conviction.

Roux hadn't even had to put two and two together for people. Just hours after she'd posted the video on their already widely read page, a side-by-side picture meme had been generated by a follower. It showed Steve's much loved sex-face picture on one side—labeled "man enjoying some good pussy"—contrasted with one of the slack-faced unconscious pictures of him with Tamara—"man forced to take bad pussy." The meme quickly went viral. Accusations against Tamara exploded on other sites. Their followers were adamant that Steve press charges of molestation, drink spiking, and even rape against her. He still hadn't decided if he'd go forward with a criminal case or not. Yet such a bold action might encourage women who'd experienced similar situations. If he could speak out, then so could they.

So by the time the second article about Steve "cheating" with Tamara hit the newsstands, people already knew the truth. A follower spread the idea of buying copies of the paper and burning them as worthless, but Roux was quick to point out that it was far better if not a single copy of that garbage was sold. Stores were surprised when people who initially purchased the paper returned it for a refund.

Steve had no idea how Roux had known that going public would not only destroy Tamara but also cause Bianca's stupid tabloid to fold. She'd even managed to make him out to be a hero with just a few well-timed pictures and videos. The woman was brilliant.

He stepped up behind her at the table in their hotel room—she never even bothered to store her luggage in Raven's room anymore—and kissed the top of her head. She was posting a picture on their page of the two of them riding in a horse-drawn carriage around the immense Schonbrunn Palace in Vienna. They were laughing because the horse had chosen to take a shit while they were posing.

She looked up, and when their eyes met, his heart melted.

"Are you plotting to have horses outlawed for ruining our selfie?"

"Nope," she said. "I've got no beef with horses."

"You never have a beef with anyone, Ms. Vegetarian."

She giggled. "That was totally a dad joke."

He perked up and slid a hand down to cover her belly. "Does that mean you're pregnant?"

"No."

"Do you want to be?"

She covered his hand with hers and pressed it more firmly into her stomach. "Maybe someday."

"With my baby?"

"Maybe someday," she said again with a dreamy smile. She turned back to her screen and corrected a typo in the picture's description before posting it.

"I still have a tofu with your ex-wife," she said.

"A tofu?"

"Since I can't have a beef with her."

He laughed. "Now *that* was a dad joke."

"We should let people know that you never cheated on Bianca. She cheated, not you. That divorce? Her idea."

"It's in the past, baby. Let it go."

Roux shook her head. "I'm taking her down. She doesn't deserve any consideration from you. And then when she's curled up in the fetal position crying with her disgusting sister, I'm going after Sam."

Steve cringed. "Max and Dare will not be happy if anything we do messes up their legal battles."

"I can wait."

"Remind me never to do you wrong, baby."

"It's not doing me wrong that you have to worry about. It's

doing someone I love wrong that I can never forgive."

"Your sisters are all divine goddesses!" he declared. "And your mother should be sainted."

She nodded sharply. "Agreed."

He slid his hand into his pocket, the three small boxes inside impossible to ignore. He'd meant to wait until they were taking a romantic boat ride through Venice—their next stop on the tour—but he'd never been a patient man. He knelt before her, removing the three boxes from his pocket and setting them in a row across her bare thigh. The pink one said *maybe* on top, the white one said *no*, and the red *yes*. She drew in a sharp breath, and her gaze darted up to meet his.

"Steve?"

"I'm sure someone will say it's too soon for this. I just hope it isn't you." He took her hand in his. His heart was thudding so hard, he felt light-headed. Where was his rock star cool when he needed it? "The only thing that could possibly top having you at my side is being able to call you my beloved wife while you're there."

Her eyes widened. "Steve?"

"You are everything I've waited for my entire life—with uncharacteristic patience, I might add—and everything I want for the rest of my years. Roux—"

Her eyes widened further. "Steve?"

He kissed her knuckles, offering her strength when he probably should have saved what little remained for himself.

"Roux," he tried again, "will you make me even happier than you've already made me and marry me?"

She reached for the red box so quickly that the other two boxes tumbled from her leg. She dropped out of the chair and tossed herself against his chest, smashing his lips into his teeth as she kissed him breathless.

"Yes?" Even though she'd snatched up the *yes* box, he had to hear her say it.

"I picked the red one, didn't I? Yes, I'll marry you, Steve. A million times yes."

"I picked the red one too." But he was referring to his favorite member of Baroquen, not a box. Smiling, he took the ring box from her trembling hand. When he opened it, she gasped at the two-carat diamond sparkling at her from within. She held her left hand out and allowed him to slip the ring onto her third finger.

"It's huge, Steve," she said, holding the perfect princess cut diamond to catch the light. "How will I ever be able to play my keyboard with all this weight on my finger?"

"Then be glad you weren't indecisive," he said. He retrieved the pink *maybe* box from beneath the table and showed her the three-carat ring inside. The entire band was also covered with diamonds. In the box was a sad-faced puppy dog picture on a tiny card that read, "Please."

"I knew I'd made the right choice," she said. "That ring is a tad excessive."

She picked up the white *no* box and opened it. There was a cheap plastic ring in that one. The card read "You lose. Try again."

She laughed and hugged him again, staring at her hand and the new diamond over his shoulder. "I'm so glad I won."

"Nuh-uh," he said. "I'm the winner."

"Me. I win."

"Not having it, Roux. I won fair and square."

"We'll just have to call this one a tie."

He took her elbows in his hands—knowing damn well he was the real winner, but not wanting to argue—and urged her to her feet. Kissing her, he slowly walked her backward to the bed. He predicted a winning streak in his near future. He was going to make her come first this morning even if it meant tying a knot in his dick.

A knock at the door made him groan aloud. He'd checked the schedule; he had two hours before they had to be on the plane to Venice.

"Go away, Butch!" he called before lowering his voice to say to Roux, "I'm about to get busy with my fiancée."

That did have a nice ring to it.

"Butch no here," a very familiar voice said. "Housekeeping! You need towels? You need lotion and tissues?"

"Isn't that Zach?" Roux asked, giving Steve a little shove.

She knew how worried Steve had been about him. He hadn't heard much from Zach since he'd dashed off at the airport. Steve had even tried searching on the Internet for any leakage of Enrique's private getaway with a mysterious lover. He hadn't found a single clue as to Zach's whereabouts. If he hadn't gotten a text a week ago that said *Knock it off, I'm fine*, Steve would have filed a missing person's report by now.

He kissed Roux once more—offering her the promise of later in a heated glance—before rushing to open the door.

"You have some seriously bad timing, man," Steve said, noting that his friend looked thin and tired, not like he'd been enjoying a relaxing beach vacation with his lover.

"If I waited until you weren't having sex or about to have sex, I'd never—"

His words were cut off by Steve jerking him into a tight hug and pounding him on the back.

"I've missed you."

Zach hugged and pounded on him in return. "I'm not sure how. You've been having way too much fun without your third wheel. It's been great to see you so happy."

Steve pulled away to squint at him. "How could you know . . ."

"Instagram," they said in unison.

"Brilliant move, by the way," Zach said. "I hear a certain tabloid is going down fast. Just don't tell me that perfect couple stuff is all staged. I don't think my broken heart could take it."

"It's real," Steve assured him. He backed into the room. Zach followed him inside and the door shut behind him. "So you haven't been enjoying a romantic two weeks with Enriq—"

Zach lifted a hand. "Don't say his name."

"Sorry."

"Hey, Zach," Roux said, her voice soft and full of concern. "We've been worried."

"I needed some time to work things out. Been putting miles on my new motorcycle on the backroads."

"That sounds nice."

She squeezed his arm, and he grabbed her wrist to hold her hand up in the air. Her new engagement ring caught the morning sunlight streaming in through the window.

"What the fuck is this?"

Roux beamed. "Steve just asked me to marry him."

Zach crinkled up half his face as if he'd tasted something extremely bitter. "And you said yes?"

She laughed and nodded. "Of course I said yes."

"I told you that you had bad timing," Steve said. "We haven't even consummated the engagement yet."

He slipped an arm around Roux's back, resting his hand on her hip.

"Fuck, I'm sorry. I should have stayed away—"

"No," Roux said. She took Zach firmly by one arm and shoved him into a chair at the dining table. "You look like you haven't eaten since I last saw you. There's some fruit there to get you started," she said. "I'll order you a hot breakfast."

Steve wasn't sure why her fussing over his friend made him love her even more. While she was on the phone ordering enough food to make up for two weeks of starvation, Steve sank into the chair across from Zach.

"Are you okay? Why did he dump you?" Steve was careful not to use Enrique's name.

Zach was helping himself to the half-eaten slice of ham on Steve's plate. "Why do you automatically think he dumped me?"

"Because you're obsessed with him."

"While I was on my way to meet him in the prearranged secret location, I realized I want what you have with Roux, and I'm never going to get that with Enrique. So I stood him up, and then I was ultra-lame and broke up with him via text message."

Which was probably a good thing, because if Zach had seen Enrique in person, he likely would have faltered.

"What about you," Zach said, "are *you* okay? That date-rape stuff with Tam—"

Steve lifted a hand. "Don't say its name."

"Sorry I wasn't here for you when you needed me." He glanced over at Roux, who was grinning ear to ear and texting a flurry of messages—most likely to her sisters about her new ring. "I left you in good hands, though. Congratulations, by the way. So will you rent your house to me now?"

Steve chuckled. "If she doesn't want to live there, but don't make her feel sorry for you so she'll let you have it. I love that place and hope she does too."

"Hey, Roux?" Zach called to her. "You don't want to live in California, do you?"

"Yeah, I do. Especially in the winter," she said.

"Steve's house is really small," Zach added.

"I like cozy. Keeps us close."

"Knock it off," Steve warned Zach. He would love to build their lives together in his little shack by the sea.

"I also love wide-open spaces," she said, and Steve cringed, thinking she'd want a big ol' mansion in Malibu like Bianca had. "I hope we can stay on the family farm in the fall at harvest time. We'll need a relaxing, quiet place to stay after all the summer tours."

He loved that she wanted to spend months on the farm and winters in California, but what about seeing her family?

Oh.

"And there's no place like New York in the spring," Steve said, catching on to where she was going with this. They could make their lives together in all the places that were important to them, and once they decided to start a family, they could settle somewhere more permanent. He didn't care where, as long as they were together.

"I couldn't agree more," she said, smiling at him with utter devotion.

A loud knock sounded, and Roux turned toward the door. "Fastest room service ever," she said, hurrying to answer.

"You will not post another picture on the Internet for the rest of the tour," Sam said. He jabbed a finger into Roux's chest, and Steve was on his feet in an instant.

"Hey, hey, hey," Steve said, rushing forward and shifting Roux behind him. He blocked Sam's entry into the room by taking up as much space in the doorframe as possible "You touch her again, and I'll break your fingers."

Sam didn't touch her again, but he did continue to yell.

"If I see one more cutesy picture of you with this character"—he pointed at Steve—"posted anywhere, I'm sending Baroquen back to New York and canceling your appearances."

"You can't do that!" Roux squeezed into the doorframe next to Steve, but he threw out an arm to stop her from entering the hall. There were sharks in those waters.

"I can do whatever I want." Sam crossed his arms and his chin jutted forward. "I *own* your band. Without me, you're nothing."

"You're so wrong," Steve said, surprised he wasn't angrier. The man he loathed above all others was threatening the woman he loved, and some strange sense of calm had washed over him. "Without us, *you're* nothing."

"What? I made you." He jabbed a pointed finger in Steve's direction but wisely did not touch him. "And her. And even him." He nodded toward Roux and Zach.

"No, you promoted me, and her, and not so much him, but you didn't *make* anything. We're the ones who make the music. You just help us find people who like what we make. And I can't speak for Baroquen or Twisted Element, but I can speak for Exodus End. We don't need you anymore. You're fired."

Oh yeah, the guys were going to kill him later for that one, but he didn't give a fuck at that moment, and the astonished look on Sam Baily's face was worth any browbeating Max would throw Steve's way later.

"You can't fire me."

"I just did."

"Well, I'll . . . I'll cancel all the promotional events I've arranged." Sam's face had turned a delightful shade of red.

"Which would be welcome," Steve said. "You have us running ragged all the time. Besides . . ." Steve shrugged. "If we want to reschedule any of those events, I'm sure a simple phone call to the organizer will fix everything to our satisfaction."

Sam puffed out his chest. "A, I control the money. B, I control the band. Therefore, C, I control you."

Steve laughed. "We're working on A. Remember that audit Max ordered? Well, don't imagine that we've been silent about it because we were happy with what our very thorough accountant found."

Sam's face went from red to white.

"As for B, you might think you control the band, but if it weren't for Max's insistence that you were worth the headache, you'd have been out on your ass years ago. He'll be pissed that he didn't get to tell you himself, but he no longer thinks you're worth the headache. He wants you gone as much as I do. The only thing keeping you here is that it's taking Dare's lawyers a bit longer than planned to file all the lawsuits and criminal charges against you."

Sam took a step backward. "What?"

"And with your tabloid publishing pictures of my sexual assault, well . . ." Steve shrugged. "I guess we have a civil case as well, don't we? It was very traumatizing for me—the victim—to see those pictures in print."

Sam's mouth opened and shut several times, but for once in his hot-winded existence, he couldn't seem to find a single word to utter.

"As for C," Steve said, "you never controlled me. Max kept me under control as best he could, but if I didn't love and respect the hell out of him and our music, I'd have hit the road years ago. This band isn't about you. Baroquen isn't about you either. So go fuck yourself, Sam. We'll survive without you."

"God, why won't you quit?" Sam threw both hands in the air. "I've tried everything I can to make you leave, and you just keep coming back for more."

So Steve hadn't been imagining things—Sam did have it out for him. "Why would I leave? I belong with the band. You're the one who's leaving."

"You've just ruined your girlfriend's career," Sam said. "I'll make sure she and her sisters never get a leg up in this business—"

"Are you threatening us?" Iona said from behind him.

Sam spun around. "Iona!" he said, his sharkiest smile splitting his face. "What are you doing here?"

"I came to congratulate my little sister on her engagement."

"We all did," Raven said from the group of congregated women.

Actually, the crowd spreading down the hall in either direction was more mixed than Steve had first noticed.

When had his bandmates arrived? How much had they overheard? How pissed were they that Steve had taken it upon himself to confront Sam openly and without a lawyer present? He cautiously met Max's eyes, and Max did look angry, but he was sending his most ball-withering glare in Sam's direction, not Steve's. Dare looked resigned that yes, this had happened and now they'd have to work with what they had. Logan grinned and made a victory fist, which Reagan tapped playfully with her own.

"Oh," Sam said, "is she engaged?" His voice was uncharacteristically squeaky. "Congratulations! Did you post that on Instagram too?"

"Not yet," Roux said. "But if you think people were defensive of us before, try messing with us after they hear how Steve proposed."

Sam rolled his eyes. "It's very sweet, I'm sure."

"You didn't answer my question," Iona interrupted. "Are you threatening us?"

"Don't forget who owns your contract," Sam said.

Dare crossed his arms and smiled crookedly. "That would be me."

"Huh?" Sam blinked.

Actually, they were all blinking at Dare. How had he managed to gain ownership of Baroquen's contract?

"Your business partners were quite interested in quietly selling their shares in your sinking ship. I got a very good deal." Dare's smile broadened. "On all of them."

"Even if you bought every share available, I still own the majority," Sam said, but his usual bluster had diminished to a mere breeze.

"True," Dare said, "but once all of our various lawsuits are officially filed—"

"And won," Max said with complete confidence.

"And won," Dare said agreeably, "you'll have to liquidate your assets, and who in their right mind would invest in an entertainment conglomerate reeking of scandal?"

"No one," Logan said.

Max elbowed him and nodded at Dare.

Logan's eyes widened. "Dare?"

"Keep up, Logan," Max said.

"But why would he . . ." Logan shook his head.

"So all the entertainers who have contracts under this greedy motherfucker aren't left footing his legal bills and losing everything," Steve said, wishing Dare stood closer to him so he could hug him. "If you need additional finances, I've got some money burning a hole in my bank account." Steve nodded, meaning every word.

"I might take you up on that," Dare said. "It's a lot of power for one man to hold."

"And responsibility," Max said. "I'm in too."

"You guys aren't leaving me out of this," Logan said.

"I don't have much, but I'll risk everything I have," Reagan said. "Down to the shirt off my back."

"If you're really interested in buying," Sam said, "we could come up with a fair deal for my shares."

Steve laughed. "Are you trying to bargain with us? Why would we do that? In case you haven't been paying attention, we hold all the cards here."

"It will put you in charge more quickly," Sam said, "and I'll quietly go away. You'll never hear from me or my girlfriend again."

Steve pressed his eyebrows together. "Girlfriend?" What woman would date the sleazeball?

"Tamara. My girlfriend."

"Tamara!"

Sam snorted. "With all your digging around my business, you didn't come across that little gem?"

"Did you know she staged those pictures of us together?" Steve asked. Because what boyfriend would put up with that kind of behavior?

Sam laughed and started backing away from Steve's open door with renewed confidence. "You guys don't have shit on me," Sam said. "I should have known this was a ploy to make me nervous or, I don't know, but—"

"You stole from us," Max said, his hand wrapping into the

fabric of Sam's lapel. "Twenty-seven point eight million dollars. We have all the shit on you we'll ever need. As for the libelous bull in Bianca's tabloid? She's going down too. And your sex-offending girlfriend? Steve is going to press charges against her as soon as possible."

"I am?" Steve asked. He was still reeling over the knowledge that his two least favorite people in the world were a couple. Had that been why Bianca had been so smug when he'd met with her all those weeks ago? Because the man watching Tamara flirt with Steve wasn't Pyre—as he'd suspected—but Sam? What the fuck? How had they gotten together? Why? When? He had so many questions. Like why did Sam find it humorous that his girlfriend had drugged and molested a man he loathed? Unless he'd put her up to it. Steve wouldn't put that past him. Maybe he even gave her the key to Steve's room so she could stage those disgusting pictures. Hell, he might have been holding the fucking camera. And maybe Bianca had posted those pictures online to get Sam and Tamara to break up, not to hurt Steve. But what did it matter? The three of them were all going down in flames, and their disastrous crash was so fun to watch.

"Yes, you are pressing charges," Roux said quietly, her hand warm against Steve's lower back.

"Yeah," Steve said, standing straighter. He should press charges. He probably had the evidence he needed. He definitely had the support to get through the ordeal. "I guess you and your girlfriend can enjoy conjugal visits while you're both in jail."

Sam snorted, but he was craftily working his way from the center of the group toward open space farther down the hallway. "White collar criminals don't go to jail."

"So you admit you're a criminal," Reagan said. "I heard him. Did you all hear him?"

There was a general murmur of consensus.

"That's not admissible in court," Sam said. "God, musicians are morons. I don't know how I put up with you types for all these years."

"Guess you don't have to put up with us anymore," Max said. "As Steve said, you're fired. We'll see you in court."

"If you can find me," Sam said. He broke free of the crowd and hurried down the hallway. Butch stepped in front of him, looking angrier than Steve had ever seen him.

"Going somewhere?" Butch asked.

Two additional security guards stepped in to flank Butch. One of them—Reagan's husband Ethan—looked particularly lethal with his biceps bulging above his crossed arms.

"You can't legally detain me," Sam said, stepping backward.

"I wasn't planning on this being legal," Butch said.

"Allow me," Ethan said. "I still remember how to give Miranda rights."

"We aren't in the US," Butch reminded him.

Ethan grinned. "True. Guess he doesn't have any rights, then."

He dropped Sam to the floor so quickly that a collective gasp filled the hall.

"You have the right to keep your lying, conniving mouth shut," Ethan said, placing a knee in Sam's back and whipping out a pair of handcuffs. They were lined with velvet and were obviously of the novelty variety, but that didn't stop Ethan from clicking one bracelet closed over Sam's wrist or from them being effective restraints. "You have the right to pay an attorney a lot of money to try to defend your sorry, undeserving ass."

Steve liked this guy. He needed to hang out with him more often.

"If you can't afford an attorney, you're shit out of luck, asshole. No public defender is going to work very hard to help a swine like you."

"You can't do this," Sam said. "You have no authority to—"

Ethan slammed a fist into the floor inches from Sam's face. "I suggest you exercise that first right before you say something that makes me really mad."

"He got fired from the force for beating the crap out of some perpetrator," Reagan said helpfully.

"And that perpetrator didn't make my wife's life a living hell," Ethan said, "so just imagine how much crap I could beat out of you."

"Buckets of crap," Logan said.

"Now, I'm not sure how we get you extradited back to the States, but someone at the US embassy will know." Ethan stood and yanked Sam to his feet. "Are you going to ask your girlfriend to join us peacefully, or should I pretend she resisted my citizen's arrest as well?"

"You can't threaten us. Who do you think you are?"

"If this was an action movie, I'd come up with a sweet one-liner right now," Ethan said with a smirk. He settled for shoving Sam toward the elevator.

"Justice," Reagan said, following the security team down the hall. "That's what you should have said, babe. You're justice."

"Your worst nightmare," Max called out his suggestion.

"Your wettest dream!" Azura shouted, and then she lowered her voice to add, "Actually, he should say that to me. *Rawr*!"

"He's married to my brother," Dare pointed out.

"And to your sister-in-law," Logan said.

"That has to be a total mindfuck," Max said with a laugh.

Dare grinned. "Not really. If Trey's happy . . ."

". . . I'm happy," half the group said in unison.

"Did you really buy out all of Sam's partners?" Steve asked Dare.

Dare's grin changed from sentimental to devious. "Nah. That was a total bluff. I knew it would make that weasel squirm, though."

"I think we should consider doing it for real," Steve said. "I thought maybe we'd get around to starting our own label, but if we can buy out our previous label, and all the contracts it currently holds, we could do great things for some truly talented people. As much as I despise Sam, he does have excellent taste in music."

"Let's give it some thought," Max said. "We can have a meeting about it in a few days."

Steve silently vowed not to push his opinions on Max in this situation. He'd learned from their experiences with Sam that if Max thought he was being pressured, he dug in his heels and didn't give an inch, whether his stubbornness ultimately hurt him or not.

"I can't believe Tamara is with that guy," Roux said. "He must be twenty years older than she is."

"More like thirty," Max said. "But if you ask me, they're well suited."

"Not sure how my research team missed that piece of the puzzle," Dare said, scratching his temple. "Guess we need to do some more digging."

"Some people are good at hiding relationships," Iona said.

She must be speaking of herself and Kyle, because Steve and Roux sucked at it.

"If no one else is going to say it," Roux said, "I will. *Ewwwww*. Just ew." She visibly shuddered.

"I hope to God they didn't procreate," Raven said.

"Well, it's been great seeing you all," Steve said. He loved these people, but enough was enough. He turned and slowly backed Roux into the room. Zach was behind him watching the excitement in the hall, but with a quick turn, Steve had his third-and-normally-welcome wheel moved out into the corridor. "I have some celebrating to do."

"We should go down to the bar," Logan said. "You've been wanting to fire that guy for years. You must be flying high right now."

"I am," Steve said, "but that's not what I want to celebrate."

Roux waved her engagement ring at their friends. Her sisters squealed and rushed forward as if they'd just remembered why they'd showed up outside his and Roux's hotel room door in the first place. They twittered excitedly, asking so many questions and offering so many repeated words of congratulations and advice that he could couldn't make heads or tails out of what any of them were saying. He and Roux found themselves squished together in the center of a rather painful group hug, accompanied by happy tears and contagious excitement. When all the guys formed an outer ring to their tight huddle, Steve had to brace himself to prevent Roux from being completely squashed, but she was laughing so hard, he doubted she minded their enthusiasm.

"Is this what we call a blended family?" he asked close to her ear.

"Yours, mine, and ours," she said breathlessly.

The bright smile on her face added to the sparkle in those remarkable green-gold eyes and made his heart overflow with all the love he had to give.

"Ours," he repeated. He liked the sound of that.

When he kissed her, everything around them, including the enthusiastic catcalls of their friends, faded into the background until there was nothing in his world but his sweet Red.

Author's Note

Who knew Steve was so dreamy? The man took even me by surprise. I miss him and Roux already—they're a perfect match. What was not perfect was how absolutely stuck I got while writing this book. I'm known for writing steam, and creative kink, and this couple just wasn't having it. I finally get them into bed—I've never written a book where the couple *waits* to have sex—and they're on a private island—the perfect place for one or the other of them to reveal their dirties kinks—and I discover their sexual relationship is all about emotion. *Emotion?* Really? I tried to fight them on it, but somehow it works for them. So once I let go of trying to come up with some wild, inventive sexcapades for Steve and Roux, the book finally started to flow again. I guess all my rock stars don't have a sensual twist. This drummer—the epitome of the sex, drugs, and rock 'n' roll lifestyle—had an unusual romantic streak instead. How's that for a twist?

In the next book, I'm faced with the near impossible task of finding a woman good enough for Dare Mills. If you've been with me from the start—clear back in the Sinners series—we first met Dare over a million words ago. You'd think I'd know him by now and be chomping at the bit to finally get him to his happily ever after, but I'm so attached to the mysterious introvert, I fear I won't do him justice. I guess we'll find out soon. Dare's ready for his turn. I'm glad he's a patient man. It's been a long time coming. The next book in the Exodus End series is tentatively titled *Ovation*. I hope you're as patient as Dare while you wait for me to write it. I'll do my best to not get stuck this time! *Speak to me, Dare! What turns you on?*

If you're wondering, I do have plans to write a series about Baroquen, but I need to finish up Exodus End, Sinners, and Sole Regret first. The last thing my poor brain needs is another set of characters to keep straight, but those women all have stories that need to be told, and I can't help but want to tell them.

I always seem to thank the same people at the back of each

book, but that's because I have a fabulous team. Why mess up perfection with change? Thanks to Beth Hill, editor extraordinaire, Cyndi McGowen, beta reader and book-signing sidekick extraordinaire, Charity Hendry, designer extraordinaire, and Sean Davis, sounding-board you-guessed-it-extraordinaire. I'd also like to thank my human family for being so easy to love and my furry family (Shortie, Sissy, Aggie, Jace, and Buddy) for making me feel like the center of the universe—I fill the food bowls. And I especially want to thank my fans, dream-maker extraordinaires. You make everything possible.

About the Author

Combining her love for romantic fiction and rock 'n roll, Olivia Cunning writes erotic romance centered around rock musicians. Raised on hard rock music from the cradle, she attended her first Styx concert at age six and fell instantly in love with live music. She's been known to travel over a thousand miles just to see a favorite band in concert. As a teen, she discovered her second love, romantic fiction—first, voraciously reading steamy romance novels and then penning her own. Growing up as the daughter of a career soldier, she's lived all over the United States and overseas. She currently lives in Illinois. To learn more about Olivia and her books, please visit www.oliviacunning.com.

AVAILABLE NOW
IN THE EXODUS END WORLD TOUR SERIES

INSIDER
EXODUS END WORLD TOUR #1

Toni wants to be an insider. Logan just wants inside her.

She's finally ready to rock...
Toni Nichols set aside her dreams to raise her little sister, but now she's reaching for the stars as the creator of a revolutionary interactive biography about Exodus End. She's on tour with the rock band to immerse herself in their world, but how will she ever gain the trust of four veteran superstars who've been burned by the media before? Nobody said this was going to be easy. Then again, good things can come in hard packages.

He's always ready to roll...
Adrenaline junkie Logan Schmidt lives for the rush of playing his bass guitar before thousands of screaming fans. When he's not performing onstage or in the bedroom, he's looking for his next thrill in extreme sports. So why does a sweet, innocent journalist get his heart pumping and capture his full attention? Is Toni the real deal or just digging up dirt on his band? Logan's eager to rock Toni's world and roll her in the sack, but when she starts to get too close to his heart, she takes her insider look to a place he may never be willing to go.

Available Now
in the Exodus End World Tour Series

OUTSIDER
EXODUS END WORLD TOUR #2

Reagan Elliot should be living her dream...

She's touring with Exodus End as their new rhythm guitarist and gaining more notoriety and fame than she ever imagined possible.

She's earned the devoted love of not only one, but two spectacular men. Her committed threesome with sexy guitarist Trey Mills and her hunky bodyguard Ethan Conner is stable, loving, deep, and satisfying for all involved.

But sometimes the world sees things differently and is determined to destroy what it doesn't understand.

Can Reagan's relationship with Trey and Ethan survive the cruel backlash of the media, her family, and a bigoted public? Or will the talented musician lose everything she holds dear in the face of her own burgeoning doubts?

DISCOVER A WHOLE NEW WORLD OF ROCK STARS

One night is never enough with the members of Sole Regret

Gabe—rock's most inventive drummer. He's all about pleasing his lady with kinky devices of his own design.

Adam—the tortured lead guitarist. He's a recovering addict trying to do things right onstage and in bed.

Jacob—the mysteriously tender vocalist. He's got his eyes and hands on the one woman who's completely off limits.

Owen—the sweet and kinky bassist. He'll try anything once, and most things as many times as she wants.

Kellen—the broken-hearted rhythm guitarist. He's been celibate for years, but he's about to come undone by being tied.

Made in United States
North Haven, CT
21 May 2024